Romancing the South

Finding Love in the Carolinas

A Two-Book Collection Featuring
Somewhere a Rainbow and
Smoky Mountain Sunrise

Yvonne Lehman
with
Lori Marett
Eva Marie Everson

An Imprint of Iron Stream Media
Birmingham, Alabama

Romancing the South

Iron Stream Fiction
An imprint of Iron Stream Media
100 Missionary Ridge
Birmingham, AL 35242
IronStreamMedia.com

The first editions of *Somewhere a Rainbow* and *Smoky Mountain Sunrise* were revised and updated for this collection.

Cover design by Hannah Linder Designs

ISBN: 978-1-64526-340-1 (paperback)
ISBN: 978-1-64526-341-8 (e-book)

1 2 3 4 5—26 25 24 23 22

To the Writers
Younger and Older
Beginners and Seasoned

We celebrate you!

Lori Marett and Eva Marie Everson
in memory of
Yvonne Lehman

Acknowledgments and Memories from Lori Marett

At this writing, Valentine's Day 2022 is just around the corner. My most recent and most cherished memory regarding this holiday was last year when my mother, Yvonne Lehman, had a lobe of one of her lungs removed. The surgery went well, and she had been told she could go home in a few days. Then her lung collapsed. The doctors decided to keep her for another week, which did not sit well with my mother. She didn't see the issue. Wouldn't her lung reinflate at some point? Couldn't it reinflate while at home?

Those of you who knew Mom, know that she was a determined woman. She had rebounded quickly after her stroke in September 2020, even being released from physical therapy early. However, during follow-up checkups with her doctors, she was told they found two spots on her lungs, one of them an immediate concern. She had cancer. But she approached this news just as she had when she was diagnosed with breast cancer twenty years earlier. She would beat it. The doctors advised her to have the lobe of her lung removed that contained the spot. So, she did. But the outcome was not what she had anticipated. Just the previous year, my mother had run a 5K race at the age of 84, not only finishing but coming in second place for her age division. Now, a year later, she was in a hospital bed, tethered to tubes and monitors, with the doctors refusing to let her go home. On one of those nights during that extended stay, I experienced one of the most special memories with Mom that I will cherish forever.

There was a shift change taking place where the day nurses were getting ready to hand Mom over to the night nurses, with the next round being around 3:00 in the morning. Mom and I decided we would get some sleep between that initial night shift visit and the 3:00 check, so I turned the lights out and curled up in a chair. I got as comfortable as I could and was beginning to drift off when my mother broke the silence.

"Why don't you write a Valentine story. I'll include it in the collection."

I knew my mother was referring to her most recent project, a collection of Valentine novellas she was writing with several other authors.

"Can you do that?" I asked. "I thought you had all the stories you needed?"

"I can do whatever I want. Would you like to write a Valentine story or not?"

I thought for a moment, "If I do, I want to write a Valentine story where the protagonist *doesn't* find love."

My mother was quick to respond. "This is romance, Lori. A Valentine collection. You have to have the main characters fall in love in the end."

"Well, if I write a story for your collection, I don't want the main character to find love. Do you know how many people hate Valentine's Day because they are not in love? Because they don't have anyone? I want to write a Valentine story where the main character doesn't have someone to love. I want the main character to come to love herself. She will come to realize she doesn't *need* a Valentine."

"You can't do that," my mother said sharply.

"I can do whatever I want."

And there it is. I am my mother's daughter.

So much for sleep. My mother and I brainstormed my Valentine story despite the fact it was a departure from the status quo. She listened to me as I told her *why* and *how* I would ignore the rules of the standard romance novel. We batted ideas back and forth until the 3:00 nurses came in and left. Then, as my mother began drifting off, she said one final thing before falling asleep, "You need to write it. It's a good story."

I would have written that Valentine story if Mom had lived. But she didn't. Her unexpected death changed a lot of my plans. So, for right now, I will honor her with this project, the retelling of two of my mother's romance novels, *Smoky Mountain Sunrise* and *Somewhere a Rainbow*, a project that would not have been possible without the foresight and hard work of Eva Marie Everson.

I knew of and had spoken with Eva Marie for decades but had not had the honor of working with her until she approached me a few weeks after my mother's death, suggesting we honor Mom by resurrecting some of her earlier novels. Because of Eva Marie's reputation and professionalism, and because she knew my mother well, I felt with her guidance, we could edit and update these novels with the utmost honesty and integrity. This would never, ever, have been possible without her vision, grit, and determination (and mad editing skills). Eva is not only a peer and colleague of my mother's but she's also someone Mom greatly respected. Eva "understood" my mother, her ways, her quirks, and her talents. And it was an extreme pleasure to work with Eva on this collection that means so much to me. Thank you, Eva Marie, for helping me honor the spirit and faith of my mother. This has truly been a blessing to work with you on this.

I'd also like to thank the amazing team at Iron Stream Media for allowing this work to happen. May this be as great a blessing to you as it has been to Eva Marie and me.

Finally, thank you, Mom. Because of you, I know Jesus. Because of you, I have my strong work ethic. And because of you, I have become a writer. May I glorify God through my own words and may I continue to live out your legacy. And yes, I'll get around to writing that Valentine story one day. It may break some rules, but it will reflect your life, a story of love and triumph when things don't go as planned.

***Smoky Mountain Sunrise* (originally published 1984)**

I admit I'd not read *Smoky Mountain Sunrise* until Eva Marie approached with this project. This book was written by my mother in the early 1980s while I was in college. The only reading I did back then was required, not recreational. So, I was excited to jump into the story, immediately recognizing the setting for this novel—a boys' camp located in the Blue Ridge Mountains, not far from our home, where my mother had worked as a secretary.

While the backdrop was familiar, I knew the characters were fictional. Yet, they contained the very essence and spirit of my mother.

These four main characters—Ramona "Rae" Martin, Olivia "Livi" Doudet, André "Andy" Doudet, and Lucas Grant—were striving to achieve their dreams. They had goals and ambitions, whether relational, occupational, or living out God's calling. These characters were an extension of my mother. They dared to dream. And they dared to do!

When this novel was published in 1984, my mother had already directed the eighth annual Blue Ridge Mountains Christian Writers' Conference, soon approaching its Year of Jubilee. My mother was happily married and a mother of four. She was working and writing, successful at both. But the most poignant memory I have of my mother was in the late 1970s, around the time I decided to go to college, when she decided to attend college as well. Because of all her activities and responsibilities, she could only afford to take one or two classes each semester and summer. My mother wrote *Smoky Mountain Sunrise* while slowly obtaining her college degree. In 1986, two years after the publication of this novel, she earned her bachelor's degree in English Literature from the University of North Carolina at Asheville. My mother, the overachiever, then went on to receive her master's degree in English from Western Carolina University in Cullowhee, North Carolina, in 1991. This achievement was so inspiring, my father (sixteen years her senior, who had dropped out of school and lied about his age to join the Marine Corps to fight in World War II), went back to get his GED. I have a wonderful picture of my parents holding their degrees on that celebratory day!

As you can tell, *Smoky Mountain Sunrise*, is more than a nostalgic trip for me. Her characters capture her essence. So, in the spirit of my mother, and these wonderful characters she has created, may we carry on Yvonne Lehman's legacy.

I can hear her now. "Dare to dream, sugar! But then, dare to *do*!"

Somewhere a Rainbow (originally published 1999)

In 1993, I got a call from the sheriff's department in St. Petersburg, Florida, where I lived at the time. My then husband had been arrested and they asked me if I'd like to come get my car before they impounded it. I honestly can't remember who I called to help me get the car; the only thing I remember is that I was going to have to take my two-month-old daughter with me. Once arriving at the mall where my car was parked, I was informed by the deputies that my husband had been arrested for forgery. There were multiple charges and each one a felony. They told me he would be in jail for a long time. I thanked them for letting me pick up my car and the rest is a blur. That is, until the following day when my father and brother-in-law drove in from North Carolina to help me. They rented a truck to pack up what we could in a few short hours before we made the ten-hour drive back to my parents' home. Within twenty-four hours, I had become a single mother of a two-month-old daughter, I had no income since I was on maternity leave at my job, and I had no way to pay my bills. I would lose the home that I owned. And I had no time to say goodbye to my friends. My life had literally changed overnight.

Somewhere a Rainbow was written during the five-year span that I and my daughter Emily lived with my parents. It was a dark time for me but a period in my life where I felt an incredibly strong connection with God. In this story, I was the inspiration for the protagonist, Brooke Hadden, a single parent trying to rebuild her life with her five-year-old son. While some of the circumstances are different (such as how Brooke became a single parent and the fact she didn't live with her parents), her struggles were very real and authentic. But there are happy moments too. Like Brooke, I found romance and am still married to the man I met during this transitional time in my life. Rodney and I have three wonderful daughters and two exceptional grandchildren. So, there is a happy ending to both stories!

But I could not have found this happy ending without prayer, which is such an integral theme to *Somewhere a Rainbow*. Without a continual conversation with God, sometimes a crying out, I would not be where I am today. I weathered this difficult time in my life through my prayers and the prayers of others. This is a central theme to this novel. There is one special prayer in this story, however, that is especially sentimental and personal to me. It takes place when another single parent and her children bring a spaghetti meal to Brooke and her five-year-old son, Ben, who offers to say the blessing for it.

"Mmm. God bless Mommy and my doggie and the buh-sketti." Ben then takes his hands, spreads them and adds, "That's all."

On the surface, this prayer is very simplistic. But it is exactly how my five-year-old daughter, Emily, would pray. With childlike innocence. With certainty and brevity.

My grandson, Emily's five-year-old son, continues the legacy. While not brief with his thoughts (he has been known to go on and on and I think he will be a writer one day!), once he's said all he needs to say to God, he concludes with "that's all" or the occasional "the end."

Somewhere a Rainbow was a sweet reminder to me of how important prayer is. No matter what we're experiencing in life, we should feel comfortable approaching God with childlike innocence, with certainty and brevity. We don't need to be eloquent. We simply need to go to our Father, spread our hands, and say, "that's all."

Book 1

Somewhere a Rainbow

One

Brooke Haddon drove her Nissan Altima along Highway 278 toward the resort island of Hilton Head and recognized the depression settling over her like a gray sky over the ocean. She tried to concentrate on her son's enthusiasm, to be as excited as her five-year-old. But all that Ben found so fascinating only mimicked the same feelings she'd had seven years before. She'd been a blushing bride of twenty then, with a model's face and figure, and as innocent and trusting as a child. Now she felt ancient—not so much in years as in experience.

She'd spent her honeymoon in blissful *naïveté* on this island off the coast of South Carolina. Then, after a little more than six months of wedded bliss, her figure ballooned with pregnancy and the marriage took a downhill turn. Her new husband, politician Barrett Haddon, seemingly had everything going for him *except* a happy marriage. Now Barrett was dead, Brooke was a single parent, and the only thing between her and homelessness—or dependence upon her parents—was the honeymoon cottage owned by Barrett's parents and recently deeded to her dreams.

A year ago—had it only been a year?—when she'd sat in the back of a limo, driven from Barrett's highly publicized funeral, she'd known that the following day the body of his lover would be laid to rest on the other side of town. She'd cried and grieved over a failed marriage, a son without a father, an auto accident that took two lives, and for truth that would have to be told someday.

"Go slow, Mom," Ben pleaded from the back seat, his dark eyes so like those of his father's. "I want to see the gators."

Brooke forced a smile as she told her son, again, that alligators were found in lagoons and not along the main roads. She also emphasized the danger of getting close. Then she pointed out and said, "See the trees,

Ben? Those are called live oaks. And that stuff hanging down? That's called Spanish moss. And see those really tall ones? Those are palms. And see—"

"But can we go see the gators tonight?" Obviously, Ben was having none of her lesson on the trees of Hilton Head.

"No," she said, "we can't go alligator hunting tonight. I have to get to the Realtor's office and pick up the key before dark."

She pushed the call button on her steering wheel and, when prompted, commanded the phone to dial the number for Jessica Lawler. Within a moment the woman, whose voice was now familiar, answered.

"Hi, Jessica," Brooke said. "I just wanted you to know that I'm getting closer. According to my GPS, I'll be there in about ten minutes."

"Sounds good," the Realtor said. "I'm waiting right here for you."

"Thank you. See you then," she said, ending the call.

Just as the GPS had predicted, about ten minutes later, Brooke pulled into the parking lot of the real estate office. As she turned off the car, her stomach knotted. She had no idea what she may be getting into coming back to Hilton Head. She only knew she'd had few other choices.

Ben was unbuckled and ready to hop out by the time Brooke stepped out and put her hand on the back-door handle. The poor child had been exceptionally patient on the two-day trip from Indiana. Brooke had stopped only to get food and a few hours' sleep at a hotel the night before. "Come on, buddy," she said, reaching for Ben's hand.

"Mrs. Haddon?" the Realtor asked from an inner office when they stepped through the door.

Brooke nodded as a woman dressed casually in slacks and a cotton blouse stepped into the front room. "Jessica Lawler? I'm so sorry we're running a little late." Brooke tucked a strand of blond hair that had escaped her ponytail behind her ear.

"Not a problem," the Realtor assured her, giving a gentle push to fashionable glasses that covered friendly blue eyes set in a pleasant face. "Gave me an opportunity to catch up on some picky things I always put off and rarely get—" Her words stopped in mid-sentence as she saw

Ben's smiling face and outstretched hand, which she leaned over and shook.

"My name's Ben," he said, and Brooke knew that between his brown eyes fringed with dark lashes and his mop of curly black hair, her son had charmed the Realtor. By the time he'd reached age two, Ben had started mimicking his father this way, realizing it attracted and pleased other people. Brooke was all too aware that she had a big job ahead, instilling in Ben the kind of inner qualities that had been neglected while his father was alive.

"Would you like to have a seat?" Jessica asked, gesturing toward the chairs.

Brooke grimaced, touching the back of her jeans. "I've been sitting in a car for two days. If you don't mind, I'll just stand."

Jessica picked up a set of keys from the desk, holding them as if reluctant to let them go. Her smile quickly turned to concern. "The electricity and water are on, like you requested." She paused. "As I told your in-laws, last year we had a few storms come through that did a little damage. That, plus time . . . I'm afraid the cottage is going to need some work."

Stabbing concern hit Brooke in the pit of her stomach. Yes, her in-laws had informed her that the cottage needed repairs. But since Barrett had died, they'd simply not felt up to taking care of things outside of their range of vision. Brooke had been unsure if deeding the property over to her had been a gesture of goodwill toward their daughter-in-law or one of good riddance. "But it is habitable?" she asked Jessica.

"Well, yes," Jessica agreed, glancing away as if she couldn't quite meet Brooke's eyes.

"I'm sure we'll be fine," Brooke said, holding out her hand for the keys.

Jessica reluctantly laid the keys in Brooke's palm. Then she picked up an invoice. "Here's what you owe for yard work."

Brooke gulped, looking at the bill. Would the bills never stop? All she'd done for the past year was try and settle his accounts. Barrett had made good money and had left a substantial insurance policy, but he'd also run up significant bills so he could portray the image of a successful politician. She'd had to sell their home, which she took a significant loss on. She'd traded the sporty Cadillac for the more-sensible Altima. After she'd paid off the funeral and their credit card debt, she'd put aside the rest for her and Ben to live on until she could begin to make a living. Thank goodness she had Ben's Social Security check coming in every month.

With nervous fingers, she opened her purse and took out her wallet. "I assume you accept bank cards?"

Jessica took the card and ran it through a reader, punched in a few numbers, then handed the debit card back to Brooke.

"Thank you," Brooke said. "For everything."

~ ~ ~

Jake Randolph pulled his cell phone from the back pocket of his jeans and answered with a swipe of his thumb. "Hello," he said.

"Jake," the caller quipped. "It's Jessica."

"Yes, ma'am. What's up?"

"I thought you'd want to know. Mrs. Haddon just picked up the keys to the cottage at 26 Seabreeze Lane."

"Okay."

"I told her the cottage needed some work."

Jake straightened. "Yes, ma'am."

"But I didn't tell her just how many repairs it needed. Jake, she has a little boy and, quite frankly, I think she may have bitten off more than she can chew. Honestly, she doesn't look a day over twenty-five."

"I'm more than happy to drive over and see if I can help her," Jake said as he turned his truck into his sister, Gracie's, driveway.

"Well, good," Jessica said with a sigh. "Because she's really going to need your help."

Two

"This is Seabreeze Lane," Brooke said to her son as she read the street sign, turned the corner, and slowed the car. Seven years ago, the cottages had looked pretty much the way they did now, but she'd had eyes only for Barrett, not the cottages. "Help me find number twenty-six."

"I think it's this one," Ben said, seeing a little white terrier running toward the road as if preparing to chase the slow-moving vehicle. "Can we keep the dog?"

Brooke glanced at the dog, now wagging its tail and barking a friendly hello. "It's cute, but I think it belongs to someone." She didn't want to squelch his exuberance by adding that she was concerned enough about feeding the two of them—she certainly couldn't take on another mouth. "Anyway, the house sits farther back from the road than these."

"I like that one," Ben said. "This one's okay too."

Brooke felt a pang of guilt, knowing Ben was trying to encourage her. He'd done that ever since he'd caught her crying to her mother about the events of the past year. She had no job skills and a checking account that depended on a monthly check from the government. But she forced a blessing-thought that at least they had the promise of a roof over their heads and then reminded herself that at the very least she had Ben's Social Security check.

"Here we are," Brooke said as they passed #24.

"Oh, neat, Mom," Ben exclaimed when Brooke turned down a short winding drive and pulled up beside a cottage that appeared smaller than she remembered. Ben was out of his seat belt and opening the car door before she pushed the ignition button.

Definitely neat . . . if she didn't mind a picket fence with half the slats missing. And if she didn't mind several notable shingles missing from the left corner of the house. And if she didn't mind a gutter sticking out precariously from the eaves, or boards in need of replacing and those that didn't need replacing needing paint.

When she'd come here seven years ago, this had been a honeymoon cottage. Now it felt like a last resort.

Ben ran up on the porch and plopped down in a swing hanging from a rusty chain hooked to the ceiling before she could do more than call, "Be careful." She breathed a sigh of relief when he began to glide without the swing collapsing and bringing the roof with it.

"Listen," Ben admonished.

Brooke smiled and nodded. "Has a real nice squeak," she said.

The Realtor had reminded her more than once that the cottage needed repairs. Nevertheless, unprepared, she reached for the screen door, yelped, and jumped back when it came loose at the top, swinging back and forth as though it might topple any minute. "Don't get close," she warned Ben, who only laughed.

Brooke shoved the key into the front door lock and looked up to note that two of the three panes of glass near the top each bore a single crack. After opening the door, she entered precariously, allowing her eyes to adjust to the dimly lit room that smelled like old books, before looking for the light switch.

Ben was beside her now, pulling on her hand. "Come on, Mom. Let's go in."

"Slowly," Brooke cautioned as she flipped on the light.

She took a step. "Well, the sound of the floor matches the squeak of the swing," she said with false brightness. Ben laughed as he found a particular spot that creaked, and he began to rock back and forth on it. "Old boards," she told him.

Brooke pushed aside the drapes at the front window, then sneezed as the dust danced around her nose. A memory washed over her. She'd stood in that very spot watching and waiting for Barrett to return from buying a few groceries for them. She'd felt so overcome with joy and love when he drove their car back up the driveway. So lucky, so blessed. How had it gone so wrong? A thought threatened to answer, and she felt the drape tear in her grasp. She let go. The fading evening light revealed a lining thin and worn. "I'll take these down tomorrow," she told Ben as if he needed to know the details. "And we'll wipe down these shutters and make do with that. What do you say?"

Ben shrugged. "Fine by me."

Her honeymoon cottage—now falling apart as her marriage had done. At least this physical structure could be fixed. What about her broken life? How could that be fixed, especially in a house that was a constant reminder of pain, heartache, and failure?

No. No, no. She wouldn't go there. She would make this place a home for her and Ben. There were enough DIY videos on Pinterest and YouTube. She could do this, and she wouldn't need anyone's help. She tried the lamp switches but saw no light. She found light bulbs in the pantry and then replaced the old ones in the bedrooms. "At least it's . . . furnished," she said, eyeing the furniture that had been old enough seven years before. "We'll call it 'Early Haddon.'"

Ben opened the refrigerator door to expose empty shelves. "Mom, I'm hungry," he said.

"We'll have to go to the store," Brooke told him. She pulled her phone from her back pocket and opened her Note App. "Let's see . . . we need food, light bulbs, and cleaning supplies." She placed her hand on Ben's head. "We'll leave the kitchen light on, but we've got to be real careful about leaving on too many lights, okay?"

They went back onto the porch and Brooke locked the door, then followed her son to the car. She had made sure Ben was buckled up in his car seat, then walked around to the driver's side as a dark blue truck drove up. The driver leaned out the open window, his muscular arm across the door. "Evening, ma'am."

"Evening."

"Jake Randolph," he said and hesitated. When Brooke didn't introduce herself, he continued. "Jessica Lawler gave me a call." He paused and when Brooke didn't respond, he added, "I'm a carpenter.

She said I might want to offer my services." He looked toward the house and whistled. "Looks like you could use some help." He smiled briefly. "My prices are the most reasonable you'll find around and I do very good work."

Before Barrett, Brooke might have been swayed by that approach, and reasonably priced certainly appealed to her. The man seemed pleasant enough as far as she could make out in the dusk, but she'd learned the hard way that appearances could be deceiving. "I'm in a hurry," she said. "I need to get to the store. But I'll be glad to take your card."

"Sure thing," he said, then looked down at the seat before looking back with a grimace. "Sorry. I left my folder back at the house."

She'd always warned Ben about talking to strangers. She certainly wasn't setting a very good example. "Well, thanks anyway," she said, opening her car door wider. "I plan to get estimates from local carpenters."

She jumped in and shut her door before he could say anything more and quickly started the engine. Looking in the rearview mirror as she drove away, she saw the man watching her. Then he moved back from his window, started his truck, and drove away in the opposite direction.

Frankly, it seemed strange that Jessica would call "the most reasonably priced carpenter in the area" without telling her. Then again, maybe this was the way people did things here on the island. She looked out the windshield and frowned at more than her thoughts. Dark clouds were blowing in, quickly changing the gray sky to black.

"Let's not dawdle," she encouraged Ben as she parked at the supermarket. The chilling wind picked up as she and Ben hurried inside, hand-in-hand.

After buying only the immediate necessities: light bulbs, toilet tissue, cleaning supplies, milk, cereal, PB&J, and bread, she made a quick stop at a fast-food restaurant to pick up their supper.

Brooke glanced at the sky, rolling with dark clouds. Palm trees on both sides of the road swayed. She remembered only sunny days and cloudless skies from her honeymoon. Maybe this was the same cloud that had followed her for the last several years. Immediately she reprimanded herself for that attitude. Those years had yielded Ben, after all. The most wonderful blessing one could have. She smiled, remembering her mom's saying: "Good comes from the worst of things."

Full darkness had fallen over the island. The wind howled by the time they arrived back at the cottage. After they ate in the kitchen, Brooke walked around the cottage replacing reachable light bulbs. When she returned, her son's head rested against his arm, bent on the table. For the past two nights he'd been up past his bedtime. She would let him stay up a little longer, so he wouldn't be awake before dawn. She needed her own rest too.

"Hey, Ben," she said. "Want to hold a chair for Mom while I change the light bulbs in the bedrooms?"

"Sure," he said with little enthusiasm.

With that done, she went out to the car and removed the few boxes she'd brought with them. Boxes filled with sheets and towels, Ben's toys and books, and her own mementos. She made the beds while Ben sorted through his box of books for a special bedtime story, then walked into the bathroom and frowned.

The tub was disgusting. Not filthy. Just disgusting.

Ben came up behind her and extended the book he wanted read to him. "Do I have to take a bath?" he asked.

"No," she said. "Not tonight. In the morning I'll clean the tub and then you'll take a bath."

Ben groaned. "Fine," he said with all the drama of a Broadway actor, which brought an unexpected giggle from deep within Brooke.

Brooke pulled her phone from her purse and made a quick call to her parents in Indiana to let them know they'd arrived, had found the cottage and the grocery store, and that she was about to read a goodnight story to Ben. After a final "I love you both," Brooke read to Ben, who fell asleep before she hit page five. She slipped out of his bed, then went to the kitchen and washed away the surface grime from the kitchen countertops and appliances. She'd deep clean one room at a time, she decided.

Beginning tomorrow.

Three

Brooke woke in the middle of the night to a storm that seemed more inside the house than out. She rushed into the living room, switched on the lamp, and opened the front door. Beyond the broken screen door and front porch, the trees blew at an unnatural angle against the dark of the sky. She'd heard about the sudden storms that could sweep across the South Carolina low country, but she'd never witnessed one. What additional damage might it be doing to her cottage? Their home?

"Mommy? What's wrong?"

Brooke turned to see Ben behind her, blinking his sleepy eyes. "Oh, it's just rain," she told him. She closed the front door and walked over to where her son stood, then picked him up in her arms. His warmth penetrated her. "Do you know what your dad told me once?"

Ben shook his head.

"He told me that around here, in the South, they call it 'coming up a bad cloud.'"

"Will it hurt us?"

"No," she assured him, now walking out of the room. "Nothing can hurt us because we're together, right?"

He nodded, then laid his head on her shoulder.

"Let's walk around the rest of the cottage and make sure everything is okay," she said.

After a quick inspection, she saw that everything appeared dry, but for the first time she noticed a dark spot on the kitchen ceiling. She wasn't sure if this was something old or new and in a cottage the age of this one, the answer could go either way. She sighed helplessly. "Let's go back to bed."

Brooke took Ben back to bed with her and the two of them snuggled beneath the covers. She should pray. But she couldn't ask for anything. Once upon a time, she'd had everything, and it had only brought misery. *I'll count my blessings,* Brooke reminded herself, forcing her mind away from disturbing thoughts. *Thank You, Lord, that I have my son. Help me to be able to make a secure home for him here in this last-resort kind of place. I'm trying, but I'm scared.*

Brooke was out of bed before the soft morning light drifted through another cracked window, exposing another torn curtain, a dusty floor, and walls in need of fresh paint. Then she turned her attention to the grimy night table beside the four-poster bed where a precious little boy lay breathing easily through parted lips. A sheet twisted tightly around him except for one arm that was flung out on her side of the bed.

Blessing, blessing, she reminded herself and smiled at her precious boy. God had let her keep the most important part of her life. She must learn how to be grateful. With that determination, she headed for the kitchen and ate a bowl of cereal while looking out upon the small back yard, filled with fresh puddles, surrounded by a broken picket fence. Who was it who said it's better to live in a corner of an attic rather than in a mansion with a cranky woman?

Oh, yes. The Bible.

Ben came into the kitchen as she ran a sink full of sudsy hot water. "It's not coming up a bad cloud anymore," he said, looking disappointed. Then he brightened. "But there is still a squeaky place in the floor. It sounds funny to jump on it."

Brooke laughed. Leave it to her son to find something positive. "How about you *not* jump on it," she said, "until we know if it's just an old board or an old board that needs replacing." She pointed to the table. "You need to eat breakfast. We have a lot of things to do today." She poured his cereal and milk into a bowl, one of the few dishes she'd found in the cupboard.

Just then bells rang out. The clear notes resounded and vibrated as if waking up the landscape and sending a musical message across the morning sky and created a similar effect deep within her soul.

"What's that sound?" Ben asked, his spoon poised above his bowl.

"Church bells," Brooke said contemplatively, realizing that she hadn't heard church bells since she and Barrett had been here. It had a nice sound, as if reminding her that God is alive and well. At the same time, she felt slightly guilty. She'd resolve to get Ben in church even though so many things in her own life remained *un*resolved. The guilt increased when he asked excitedly, "Can we go and see the bells?"

No way could they go to church. "Not today," she said, and seeing his downcast countenance, she added, "But we can read a Bible story." Then she remembered the Bible was still packed away somewhere.

"Okay," he said. He took a big bite of cereal. Then with milk running down his chin, he jumped out of his chair and ran from the room.

In an instant, he returned with one of his favorite books that her parents had given him for Christmas. "*This* Bible story," he said.

"Perfect," Brooke said. "Noah and the Flood." She'd read it a million times to him, and he knew it by heart, but it seemed to fit after the previous night. They hadn't drowned, and perhaps the church bells were a reminder that there was a rainbow somewhere. "You eat and I'll read," she said.

She read, "And Noah took the animals into the ark. The birds, the butterflies, the rabbits, the dogs, the cats—"

"It didn't say alligators," he said, peering up at her.

"Well . . . no," Brooke agreed, realizing what she knew about which animals were in the ark could probably be balanced on the head of a pin. "But alligators are like whales and fish," she said quickly. "They live in water, so maybe God figured they didn't have to be put in the ark."

"Oh, okay," he said, and Brooke realized how much this child trusted her. She must teach him the right way. That was a huge responsibility, considering how much she had to learn herself.

Ben picked up his bowl and drank the milk. "Can we go to the lagoon and see the gators?"

Gracious, her son. There was so much to do, not that she'd ever get it all done. "Not today, Ben," she said. She heard the weariness in her voice and saw the disappointment in his eyes. First the church bells and again the alligators. How long would it be before she stopped saying that she didn't have time to do anything that was important to Ben? And what could she get done, after all? She couldn't call around for estimates on repairs until the next day. And the grime wasn't going to kill them.

"How about we go to the beach," she said.

"Yeah," he shrieked and ran to her, throwing his arms around her, almost knocking the chair over.

Brooke laughed. This little boy didn't need a clean cottage nearly as much as he needed a mother to spend time with him. She hugged him, then admonished, "Get your clothes on. What you wore yesterday will be fine."

"Can I go barefoot?" he called as he struck out across the kitchen.

"Put your sneakers on. We'll walk. It's not far."

The few blocks to the beach turned out to be a little farther than Brooke remembered; however, the crisp breeze and warm sunlight felt wonderful on her skin.

"God created such a beautiful world, didn't He, Ben?" she commented as the ocean came into view.

"Yeah," he agreed. "I can't even see the end of it."

"Hey, you're right," she said, looking toward the horizon. In Indiana, the view where the sky met the earth was stopped by city buildings, community houses, or a forest of trees against the sky. "It looks like you can see forever."

"I never saw white sand before." He scooped up handfuls and let it sift through his fingers. Then he stood still, his eyes wide, listening.

She heard it too—puppies.

"Oh, Mom, c'mon!" Ben pulled on her hand, leading her down the beach toward a small crowd of people.

Going closer, Brooke saw a young couple in folding chairs behind a cardboard box. Ben rushed up to join other children while adults looked on with smiling faces.

"Can I have a puppy?" Ben asked loudly, and it seemed to Brooke that everyone looked at her for the answer, as expectant as Ben.

Then she saw the sign on the box: "Free Puppies." She walked closer and peered into the box. That was a mistake; the puppies were nothing short of adorable. "What kind are they?" she asked.

"The mother is a miniature Japanese Spitz," said the young man in the folding chair as he held his hand about six inches off the ground. "We're not sure about the daddy," he said with a grimace.

The young woman spoke up. "The female is our dog. The male *could be* our neighbor's dog that got out of its fence." She took a breath. "Or a black mutt that wandered into our back yard a while back. So . . ." She shrugged.

Brooke could see that the puppies were a perfect blend of colors. Ben picked up one that was coal black with a spot of white on the back of his neck and a streak of white beneath his mouth and down along his chest. "Oh," he exclaimed, spying another. "I want to see that one."

Brooke leaned closer and saw a coal black ball of fur curled up in the corner. It was so fuzzy she couldn't even tell where its face was. Apparently, the young man couldn't either. When he picked it up, its bushy little tail faced the group. He turned it around and set it on the ground.

The onlookers, including Brooke, gasped at the adorable puppy face surrounded with a thick mane of hair, reminding her of a lion or, she realized more accurately, a werewolf.

The puppy shook itself, lifted its tail and its head, and waddled across the sand as if it owned the world. Its tail was longer than its legs, which were so short, its tummy scraped across little piles of sand, making a groove. Everyone laughed, so intrigued by his cuteness, they didn't make a move until the puppy began to scoot closer to the ocean.

"I'll get it," Ben said and began to run.

The puppy ran faster but Ben caught it at the ocean's edge and swept it up into his arms. He brought the squirming puppy back to the group but wouldn't let go. "I saved its life, Mom. Just like Noah."

While he was pleading, "Can I keep it? Please?" Brooke had visions of countless shots, and visits to the vet, and puppy food, and the cost of neutering.

"How big will he get?" she asked.

"Mitzi weighs twelve pounds," the young man said. "So, I'd say this one shouldn't get over . . . say fourteen, fifteen pounds."

It wouldn't eat much at that weight. Ben had no father with him, no friends, and was without his grandparents who had doted on him. This puppy could be a friend to Ben and maybe free her up to do her chores. He'd become glued to her since Barrett died, as if afraid something might happen to her.

Looking at Ben and the puppy, she doubted she could pry them apart with a crowbar. "Okay," she said with a sigh. Why hadn't she taken him to church to see the bells . . . or to the lagoon to see the alligators?

His little face simply glowed with delight, and he nuzzled the puppy's fur with his chin. Then his big brown eyes rolled up to hers. "Can I have two like Noah?"

Brooke shook her head. "That's where I draw the line." The onlookers laughed. "Come on, young man," she admonished.

They headed on down the beach, Ben hugging the little critter. He looked up. "Thanks, Mom. I really knew I couldn't have more than one." He rubbed his cheek against the top of the puppy's head. "I love this one. I really love him."

Brooke touched his shoulder. Finances were tight, yes, but if a puppy made her son happy, then a puppy he would have.

Four

Early Monday morning, Brooke and Ben played for a while in the back yard with the puppy until Brooke stood and stretched. "You two play for a while," she said needlessly, remembering that Ben and the dog had been content with each other for most of Sunday, while she worked on getting the bathroom into decent condition. Now, she was ready to tackle the rest of the cottage again.

"Pardon me," she heard and turned with a start toward the voice. A man came striding across the yard in her direction. "I knocked but nobody answered," he explained. "The car was out front, so I thought you might be back here. Again, I'm Jake Randolph."

The carpenter. What did he want? "I'm . . ." She hesitated, not wanting to be impolite, yet not wanting to be too familiar. "I'm Mrs. Haddon."

"Yes, ma'am," he said in that same friendly drawl from Saturday night. Definitely a Southerner. "As I said the other day, my friend Jessica Lawler said you'd moved in and might have some things that needed fixing around the cottage."

The Realtor. Well, all right then. She nodded briefly for him to continue.

"I'm here to offer my services. I have a contracting company. General repairs, building, things like that."

"Thanks for stopping by," Brooke said, a tad relieved. For one, he certainly looked the part, being bronzed by the sun and with sun-bleached golden highlights through his brown hair. And he appeared to be in great physical condition. Muscular . . . like a man who swung a hammer for a living. But if he were good at his trade, would he be running around begging for work? She thought not. "I appreciate your coming by," she said, although she thought it a little odd. "But I plan to ask around, maybe get some estimates and then make my decision. If you want to leave a card—"

"I do have one this time," he said then laughed lightly, as if embarrassed that he hadn't on Saturday night. "However," he continued with a wry smile as he moved his hand to the back pocket of his jeans. "I do better than offer a card. To prove my worth, I always make at least one small repair free of charge."

Brooke's eyes locked with his warm brown ones for an instant before she quickly lowered her gaze to the card he offered. That instant was long enough to see a flush begin on his bronzed face as if he knew what she was thinking.

She stared at the card. Puppies might be free, but not a carpenter's services.

"How did you manage during that storm Saturday night?" he asked, and she looked up. "I noticed you've got some roofing missing."

"We . . . managed." She almost mentioned the spot on the kitchen ceiling but decided against it. He'd want to come inside, perhaps, and she wasn't ready for that until she'd had a chance to talk with Jessica Lawler.

"I'm glad to hear it," he said, then walked over to Ben, who was offering the puppy a stick, then pulling it away when the puppy tried to bite it. "Hi, buddy. I'm Jake." He stooped down.

"I'm not Buddy. I'm Ben." They laughed, but Brooke's motherly protective instincts surfaced seeing Ben welcome Jake as if they were long-time friends—even letting him pet his puppy.

"Look at that purple tongue. Looks like you've got a little Chow here."

"Yeah, I saved his life," Ben said.

Jake, on eye-level with Ben, remarked, "Well, son, according to an old Chinese proverb, that means you're responsible for him all his life."

Ben's eyes were big and round, basking in the man's attention. "He was going to drown in the ocean."

"That's a slight exaggeration, Ben," Brooke admonished, wondering if he got that from his politician father too.

The man grinned. "Have you named him?"

Ben nodded, his dark eyes gazing trustingly into the eyes of the stranger. "Taz," he said.

That was the first Brooke had heard of that. Ben had simply been calling him "Puppy." She hadn't known it was a Chow either, but now that Jake mentioned it, she'd heard or read that Chows have purple tongues.

"Taz," the man mused and glanced up quickly at Brooke. "Like the cartoon character? The Tasmanian Devil?"

"Yeah," Ben said. "He's neat."

The cartoon character might look neat with those rather innocent eyes, his tongue hanging out, and that cute laugh, but inside he was an out-of-control, wild, crazy thing. This man kneeling in front of her son looked rather neat too, with that quick smile over perfect white teeth in a ruggedly handsome tanned face with laugh lines at his mouth and eyes. But who could trust what might be lurking inside that exterior?

She studied the card for a moment. RANDOLPH CONSTRUCTION. It looked authentic. Jake's name followed by his address and phone number under the title. Again, she was tempted to ask him to look at a few things around the house, but she'd trusted better-looking men than this—her late husband, to name one—and where did that get her? No, she simply could not take a person at face value.

"Thank you for stopping by, Mr. Randolph," she said abruptly. She couldn't stand here all day. "I'll get back to you if I need your services."

Jake immediately rose from his kneeling position. "I understand," he said, color coming to his face. "I shouldn't have barged in. I should have explained—"

"No," she said, uncertain about the whole situation. "I just don't like people I don't know coming to my door, making offers."

Ben came over, holding the puppy beneath its arms, exposing its belly, the only spot that wasn't covered with thick black hair. "Yeah," he said. "One time this man said he was going to give us a million dollars' worth of groceries. Do you remember that, Mom?"

"A thousand, Ben," Brooke corrected.

"Well, lots of groceries. A whole room full and Mom asked why, and he said he wanted to come in and vacuum the carpets." Ben snorted and shook his head, his eyes wide. "Mom said no."

"I see," Jake said. "And your mom was right. You should never let strangers in the house, and I should never have approached you this way." His brown eyes looked truly repentant as he glanced from Ben to Brooke. "When Jessica called and said a woman and her son moved in, she also explained that there were some repairs the cottage needed. That it hadn't been lived in for quite a while."

Had she also told him that she had no husband? That there was no man around? "Thank you again, Mr. Randolph," Brooke said, trying not to be fooled by this now-contrite, apologetic, seemingly trustworthy, helpful man. How many of those were in the world anyway? "I'll let Jessica know if I need your services."

∽ ∽ ∽

Jake was smart enough to know when he'd been dismissed. "All right, then." He shook his head. "I probably should have had Jessica contact you before I came out. Sorry I bothered you." He pointed to the card in her hand. "But, if you need someone to help you, contact Jessica."

"Thank you," she said again.

"Goodbye, Ben," Jake said with a wave to the young boy. "Bye, Taz. Goodbye—" Jake hesitated, realizing she hadn't given her first name. And Jessica had only said the Haddons were moving in. He nodded and added, "Mrs. Haddon."

"Goodbye," she said. The word sounded final. He knew, without a doubt, there was no way this woman was going to call. How had it gone wrong? It never had before. Maybe his showing up Saturday night, then appearing today. Or was it that she was more distrusting than anyone else he'd ever approached? Or perhaps there was no Mr. Haddon, and she was being particularly cautious.

Whatever, she obviously wasn't accustomed to having someone come by and offer to help. Now how was he going to get himself out of this? He spread his hands and stepped away. "I'll try and approach this in a different manner next time," he said with a smile.

She didn't return his smile, and her dismissing gaze plainly said, "Don't bother." He'd better get out while he could. He felt certain that if he showed up here again, she'd call the police. He didn't need that. An accusation, founded or not, could prove to be disastrous in his situation. Even something as simple as a call to the Better Business Bureau could reach his parole officer and land him right back in state prison.

Five

Brooke went about the process of cleaning and throwing away as she tried to dismiss the incident with the man claiming to be a carpenter or own a contracting business or whatever. The next-door neighbors on the left, a young couple, left before eight o'clock, apparently going off to work. An older couple, on the right, came over just to introduce themselves as Mary and Frank Lee and give advice about trash pickup. Brooke asked about some of the minor wear and tear on getting the house fixed, and they mentioned a couple of construction companies that might be able to help, but there was no mention of a Jake Randolph or Randolph Construction.

"Less expensive if you can get somebody that knows a little about carpentry," Frank informed her.

Brooke nodded. Would that be Jake Randolph?

She didn't know whether to be proud of herself for having sent Jake packing, or ashamed that she'd turned away well-needed *free* assistance.

But no. She could not chance endangering herself or Ben.

At least the adrenaline was flowing and that spurred her on with the cleaning. Working in such humidity, she'd become hot and sweaty. Ben suggested popsicles, but she said it was too close to suppertime. Just as she poked her head in the refrigerator, basking in the coolness that touched her face and trying to decide what to do for supper, a knock sounded on the door.

She straightened immediately, slammed the door shut, and stiffened. *Oh, surely not that man again.* "Ben?" she called.

"I'm out here," he said, his voice coming from right outside the back screen door, where he often played when she wanted him to stay nearby.

"Just stay where you are," she said and guardedly walked through the kitchen, the small foyer between the other rooms in the center of the cottage, and through the living room. If the person at the door was Jake, she would slam the front door and lock it, then run and get Ben and lock the back door. If he tried to open the front screen door, it would probably surprise him as it had her, by hanging solely on its lower hinge.

Guardedly, she approached the door. A sigh of relief escaped her, and she cautioned her erratic heartbeat to calm down when she saw a pretty woman with short auburn curls, friendly brown eyes, and a light sprinkling of freckles across her nose, holding a box. Three stair-step boys stood with her, each holding something in his hands. A late model SUV was parked in the driveway.

"Hi, I'm Gracie," the woman said after she saw Brooke approach. "I'm from a church down the way. Hope you haven't had supper."

"No," Brooke said, half laughing with relief. "Watch out for the screen. It might fall on you."

They stepped aside while Brooke opened the door slightly, then put her hands near the top to open it wider. "I should just take this thing off," she apologized.

"If you have children like mine, you should," Gracie agreed. "These kids nearly broke me with buying new screens. They don't know how to push on the wooden part. Finally, I decided to quit fussin' and live with holey screens. Of course, we do get quite a few flies."

Brooke had no idea how much of this was exaggeration, but both women laughed as Gracie and the three boys paraded through the house to the kitchen. Brooke called Ben inside.

The woman introduced herself again. "I'm Gracie Harris. This is Alex and he's ten, Collin, eight, and Aiden, five."

"I'm five," Ben piped up. Brooke introduced herself and Ben. She'd have to question Gracie about school. But for now, Gracie had set the box on the table and was taking off a towel. "Spaghetti."

"Wow," Ben said, along with Gracie's children who seemed about as hungry as she felt.

"Okay if we eat with you?" Gracie asked.

Brooke laughed. "Shouldn't that be my question, since it's your food?"

"Nope, it's your food. We cooked it for you."

All her children beamed as if they'd played a huge part in it—and enjoyed themselves.

"This is so thoughtful," Brooke said, feeling slightly embarrassed that all the dishes, pots, and pans were out on her counter tops. But at least the kitchen table was clean. "Are you a neighbor?"

Only the slightest pause ensued as Gracie continued taking the dishes out of the box. "Got a microwave?" she asked.

"That I do have," Brooke replied. "And it's in top working order." She put the dish of sauce in it and punched the buttons.

"Who is my neighbor?" Gracie asked, tilting her head and sort of looking toward the ceiling. Brooke recognized the phrase as something in the Bible. Maybe it was Jesus who asked, "Who is your neighbor?" and the answer was that we all should be neighbors, Good Samaritans, brothers and sisters in Christ.

Brooke nodded, seeing the gleam in Gracie's eyes, and she felt as if her spirit were communicating with this woman. Maybe she could accept friendship from her. "Okay," Brooke conceded, "we're neighbors. Now, do you live on this street?"

"No," Gracie said and avoided Brooke's eyes. "You forgot about the napkins, kids. Who wants to place them?"

"I will," Collin offered immediately, as Alex stuck out his hand, then withdrew it in deference to his brother. These children really wanted to be a part of this. How wonderful if she could teach this attitude to Ben. He and Aiden were near the back door with the puppy, already totally accepting of one another.

Gracie's next glance at Brooke, who was watching her closely, held a note of concern, but she smiled. "We'll get to particulars later, okay?" She turned toward the boys. "Okay, wash your hands."

Brooke was glad to see that Ben put Taz in his box and ran along behind the other children to the bathroom. If he hated anything, it was to wash his hands. Gracie reached into the box and brought out a plate of brownies. Wow! The woman had even brought dessert.

The microwave beeped. "Soup's on," Gracie called.

"I thought we were having spaghetti," quipped Alex, coming into the kitchen. He and his mom exchanged an affectionate gaze before Gracie reached over and mussed his hair.

"Okay, who wants to say the blessing?" Gracie asked after the other children gathered round.

"Me. Me. Me," came the replies in unison from Gracie's children, followed by Ben's weaker "me" that sounded like a question.

"Maybe we should let Ben say it," Gracie said, "since it's his house."

They all looked at him. He thrust out his hands, like he and Brooke were accustomed to doing together. They all held hands. Brooke wondered what he'd say. He hadn't prayed before in front of anyone but her and her parents. She watched him through her lashes.

"Mmm. God bless Mommy and my doggie and the buh-sketti." He moved his hands out of the others and spread them. "That's all."

"Amen," Brooke and Gracie said, then smiled while the children giggled until Gracie cast them a warning glance.

Everyone dug in. Brooke thought the food delicious, and the others wasted no time eating. The conversation was about children, school, the area, but nothing personal, which pleased Brooke. She was curious about Gracie, but didn't ask, so she wouldn't have to reciprocate by revealing her own personal stuff. She didn't know if she wanted to do that just yet.

After they finished, Gracie said, "I'll do the dishes tonight, kids. Your turn tomorrow night."

"You always say that when we eat off paper plates," Alex said with clear affection for his mother.

"You've got to get up early in the morning to be quicker than me," Gracie said pointedly to her son. She turned to Brooke. "Where's your trash can?"

"There and there and there and there," Brooke replied, pointing at plastic grocery bags placed around the kitchen.

Gracie made eye contact with her boys. "You guys know what to do."

They each took their plates and put them into the trash. "We don't throw away our silverware," Gracie joked about the plastic forks. She filled the sink with sudsy water and put the forks in. "If you want the leftovers, you can put them in something, and I'll wash out my dishes. Now, you kids run outside."

Brooke brewed a pot of coffee in an old percolator she'd found while cleaning while they worked together with clean-up. "I had to Google how to make it like this," Brooke said. "But all the comments say it's way better than a K-cup."

Gracie smiled at her. "My mother still swears by hers so I'm going to have to agree with Google."

The children's laughter filtered from outside to the kitchen. "Your children are so well-behaved."

"Thank the Lord," Gracie replied, then sighed. "I'm a single parent," Gracie explained. "My husband walked out on us while I was pregnant with Aiden. It's been difficult, this being a single mother, and I couldn't have done it without my family. They remind me that God can work in and change even the worst situations."

Brooke nodded. She didn't know how that might be for her. She didn't have the *faith* it would, only the *hope* it would. The phrase, "You of little faith," crossed her mind, and she knew it applied to herself. "I need to hear things like that," she admitted. "Did God send you to me?" she asked with a smile.

Gracie gazed at Brooke for a long moment. "God . . ." she said, then added soberly, "and Jake."

Six

Brooke felt like the breath had been knocked out of her. What was going on here? "You know Jake?" She sat in a kitchen chair.

Gracie dried her hands and sat opposite her. "I've known Jake all my life. After my husband left, I had a rough time. But it's easier now since Jake moved in with me."

Brooke regretted that her intake of breath was audible. Her immediate emotion was that this divorced woman and a man lived together, apparently with children in the house.

Stop being so judgmental. This woman was being a good neighbor regardless of her personal situation. She was obviously an excellent mother with children who adored her. She gave every indication that she was a Christian. Besides, who was she to judge being in the aftermath of a failed marriage. Perhaps her sins were not of overt commission but omission. Was that any more excusable?

Then, making Brooke's thoughts even worse, Gracie said quietly, "I'm Jake's sister."

Brooke wasn't sure whether to laugh or be upset. "Did he send you here?"

"Oh, no. He wouldn't send me out to repair any damage he's done." Gracie laughed, realizing what she'd said. "He does his own repairs; he's in that business," she teased. Her expression grew serious. "But after he told me he hadn't approached you in a businesslike manner, I just didn't want you to have the wrong impression of him. And he's not begging for work, believe me."

"He was very nice," Brooke admitted. "I'm the problem. Right now, my trust-quotient with men is at an all-time low."

Gracie snorted. "Tell me about it," she said, understanding. "When a man walks out on a wife and three kids, you never even want to look at one again." She grinned as the tiniest gleam appeared in her eyes. "Well, almost never."

Brooke couldn't help but smile. She really liked Gracie. "I understand that. My husband stepped out on me during our marriage. He died a year ago, which felt like being abandoned in a whole new way. But all that's no excuse to treat your brother so rudely."

"He understands. And he really would replace some of your roof shingles free of charge." She lifted her hand. "Oh, I know what you're thinking—nothing's free, right? But that's not the case here. And if you want, we'll come with him."

"That's really not necessary. I mean, yes, you can come with him. Of course you can."

"Great." Gracie said, smiling broadly. "If you don't mind, we will. It's good for the kids to make new friends." She looked toward the back yard. "They love that puppy."

Brooke told her how they'd acquired their newest family member. "I just couldn't refuse Ben."

Gracie laughed. "They know how to work us, but I'm not taking on an animal. They'll all be in school in a few months, and I'm looking forward to a little peace and quiet. Oh, speaking of school," she said, "Ben and Aiden might be going to school together since they're the same age. There are no children Aiden's age who live nearby. They're either older or younger or their families come here only for vacations. Looks like he and Ben have really taken to each other."

"It's helpful to me for them to play together," Brooke assured her. "I don't want to impose, but you're welcome to come over and bring the children any time."

"Great! I'll stop by in a few days and let you know when Jake can do the job."

"Okay, but supper's on me," Brooke insisted. "That is, if you don't mind sandwiches."

"A staple at our house," Gracie said.

"Any preferences?"

"Yeah," Gracie said. "We'll eat anything that doesn't bite us first." She laughed at her own joke, then screwed up her face. "Except the boys can't stand the salad type—you know, egg salad, chicken salad. They like the solid kind, like bologna or ham. Peanut butter's fine too."

"I can handle that," Brooke said confidently.

⁂

Although Ben was anxious to see his new friends again, Brooke was glad to have the next few days to herself, Ben, and Taz. She took Taz to the vet for his preliminary visit and then went to the store to find just the right collar—a bright red strip with shiny rhinestones. When they got home and she fastened the beautiful new collar, it promptly sank into the mane of thick fur around the dog's neck, completely hidden.

She made a dent in her deep cleaning, bought new sheets and curtains for her bedroom. Each night she fell into an exhausted sleep.

Early Friday morning, Gracie stopped by to say Jake could start on the roof that evening and to confirm that supper was still on. Brooke and Ben went to the store to buy more peanut butter, jelly, bread, lunch meat, lettuce, tomato, cucumbers, potato chips, and a bag of chocolate chip cookies along with a bag of oatmeal raisin.

Brooke wondered about seeing Jake again, wondering if she should be apologetic or what. He and his sister seemed so good and helpful, but outward appearances could be deceiving.

Gracie drove up in her SUV and parked in the driveway a little after five. The blue truck pulled in behind her. While greeting Gracie and the children, Jake pulled equipment from the back of the truck.

Brooke carefully held the screen while Gracie and her brood filed in and Jake headed toward the corner of the house with a ladder. She needn't have worried about what to say. He looked her way, nodded once, and commented, "Looks like that screen could use a little fixin' too," then continued on. Before she had time to think about any conversation with him, Gracie and the children crowded in around her. Brooke already had the lettuce leaves separated, the tomatoes sliced, lunch meat on a plate in the refrigerator, and the paper plates and napkins on the table.

"Okay, give me your clean hands," Gracie instructed her boys, and they all held hands. Brooke and Ben completed the circle, and Gracie gave thanks for new friends and the food.

After she finished, Brooke asked, "Would your brother like to join us?"

"He wouldn't know how to sit down and eat. That guy's on the run all the time. I'll take him something."

Feeling embarrassed, Brooke insisted, "He's welcome."

"He'd rather eat while he works."

"It's really my . . ." She looked around at the children, each fixing their own sandwiches expertly and reminded herself she'd have to teach Ben to be more independent as she fixed his sandwich for him. "It's my attitude, isn't it?" she added finally.

"No. You were perfectly right. He simply hadn't thought about how his cheap and free offers might look to you."

"I want to at least invite him in," Brooke said. She handed Ben his sandwich, then headed for the front door.

She was so intent upon doing the right thing that she completely forgot the front screen, pushed on it, and nearly fell on her face, squealing as she tried to balance her feet and the door at the same time. She mumbled reprimands to herself, chagrined at her inability to even make a simple request of a man she had insulted, while at the same time telling herself she was right because he had been a stranger.

Just as she neared the corner, a head stuck out from over the roof. Brooke jumped back. She caught herself on the swing. It squeaked then moved back, taking her with it. She almost lost her balance again.

Jake politely stared at the ground beneath him, but she felt sure that a grin played around his lips. She straightened herself, then realized she was again at a loss for words. She still wasn't sure about him. He remained silent as she struggled for something to say.

Finding her voice, she spoke in what she hoped was a congenial tone, but it sounded irritated to her. "Would you like to come in for a sandwich? Some sandwiches? Um, something to eat?"

"Thanks," he said. "But I want to try and finish this before dark. Would you ask Gracie to wrap me up a sandwich for later?"

"Sure," Brooke said. Something about this man unnerved her. She wasn't sure if that *something* was with him or with her. And she knew it was because she had lost her trust in many things, particularly people, after having been duped by an unfaithful husband.

She turned, hearing a movement behind her. Gracie held out a paper plate laden with food. "Here you go," she said.

Brooke took it and immediately knew that was a mistake. She was going to try and hand this up to the roof, while he would try and reach down for it. She'd surely drop it, or he would topple on his head. "You want to come down?" she asked.

"Just lay it on the swing," he said. "I'll get it."

Seven

Jake didn't want to chance falling, but he did chance leaning over the roof and taking a look at Brooke Haddon when she'd held up the plate. She was a natural beauty without even trying, he could easily tell, although she didn't seem to wear a trace of makeup and her blond hair was pulled back in a ponytail.

Previously, her expressive gray-green eyes, fringed with long, dark lashes, had held a touch of wariness. When she'd looked up at him on the roof however, he'd sensed a trace of warmth, matching her hesitant smile, as if she might decide to give him the benefit of the doubt concerning his character. He felt a sudden emptiness in the pit of his stomach and told himself he'd better go down and devour the sandwiches and keep his mind off both his character and the pretty woman.

While he ate, alone, he pondered what Gracie had told him. Brooke Haddon was a widow whose husband had died a year ago. Having a single sister and being actively involved with the singles at church, he could understand the caution of a mother without her husband around. That would explain her wariness when he approached her about repairs.

She was even sorry if she'd treated him unkindly, Gracie had said, and she'd decided that he could look at the roof of the house. Replace some of the shingles that had become damaged over time. Jake had breathed a sigh of relief at that. He didn't relish any kind of confrontation or explanation with his parole officer, who wasn't interested in excuses, just adherence to the letter of the law.

Brooke, he thought, with a sense of pleasure. A beautiful name that reminded him of a gently rolling stream in a green pasture. Or a melody. *I wonder, where did you come from and where are you going, gentle Brooke?*

Jake poked the last bite of sandwich in his mouth and placed the paper plate on the swing. What was he doing? He could not afford the luxury of thinking about a woman as if he were some young man looking for a companionable mate. He was thirty-five years old, with a past that had its consequences. And one thing he certainly knew was how temptations worked on a man.

He had no excuse for thinking about Brooke Haddon, or any woman, in a way that hinted at a personal relationship. So, with that, he climbed back onto the roof. How many times did he have to keep giving his personal life to the Lord? He answered that immediately. *As many times as needed.* Fighting back his frustration, he pounded nails into the wood with renewed vigor.

After finishing the replacement of the front shingles, he stood and walked the roof to check the back of the house. When he reached it, he spotted Gracie, Brooke, and the boys out there. The two women sat in kitchen chairs under a tree, watching the children give bits of bread crust to the puppy.

Jake regretted having to break up that jovial group but felt impelled to yell down, "Hey, kids. Don't feed that bread to the puppy. He'll get a tummy ache."

"What do we feed him?" Alex yelled back, squinting toward the evening sun.

"Puppy food."

"Mom?" Ben stood and faced Brooke. "Do we got puppy food?"

"We do," she said. "But I think Taz has had enough food for the night."

"Throw a stick," Gracie said. "Teach the dog to fetch."

The dog wasn't as excited about a stick as he was about the bread. If Jake's sister weren't sitting there with his little nephews, Brooke would inform the man, who apparently thought he had a right to tell her how to raise her dog, that she'd had dogs when she was a child. Every dog she'd ever known ate table scraps. They didn't go to the vet either, except to get a rabies shot. And they all lived to a ripe old age. Jake should be paying attention to the roof, not little boys playing with a dog.

As if anticipating Brooke's now-somber mood, Gracie explained, "Jake has a friend who runs an obedience school for dogs. He's learned a few things from him."

Brooke looked toward Jake as he walked over the ridge of the roof toward the front. "If he's finished, I need to thank him and see what I owe."

Gracie stood. "We need to go too. We'll wear out our welcome."

"No way," Brooke said. "You're welcome anytime. And I mean that. But I do have to get this house in shape."

Gracie smiled. "I'll have you guys over to my place soon. That is, if I can make a pathway through the clutter."

Brooke laughed. "Couldn't be any worse than mine."

"Three boys?" Gracie commented with raised eyebrow, then turned toward the boys. "Okay, you guys. Time to go. Scoot your booties."

Gracie paid no attention as they protested, asking if they could stay a little longer, if Ben could go home with them, if they could have a dog or at least a cat, that they were the only kids in the world without a pet. Finally, Gracie began to count, "One . . . two . . . three . . ."

Off they went, running around the side of the house, with Ben and the puppy on their heels.

"You amaze me, Gracie," Brooke said. "I've never seen anyone control their children as easily as you do."

"It hasn't always been that way," she confided. "My husband couldn't discipline himself, and the boys were wild. After Jake came to live with us, he began disciplining them in a teaching way, and it makes life better for all of us. I was indulging them too because their dad left. Jake said I was doing them no favors by letting them get by with things. They'd turn out to be as irresponsible as my ex. I realized he was right. Now they know that if we're going to have fun, we're going to be responsible first. Works better for all of us."

"I think I could learn a lot from you," Brooke said sincerely.

"The most important thing," Gracie said, "is teaching them about God and Jesus. I don't know how people do it without that kind of reference. What do they use as a guideline?"

Brooke nodded. "That's something we neglected 'til I moved back in with my parents. I want to get Ben into Sunday school. That's been neglected for a long time now."

"No time like the present," Gracie said, reminding Brooke of something she'd entirely forgotten. "Sunday is Easter, you know."

Eight

When her phone's alarm woke her that Sunday morning, Brooke popped up and stared into the darkness. In an attempt to shut off the offending sound, she only succeeded in knocking the phone off the table. It hit the floor with a dull thud that left her grateful she'd opted for the screen protector.

If she hadn't had to nearly stand on her head and roll out of bed to end the ringtone, she'd pull the sheet back over her head at least until daylight. But leave it to her trusty watchdog to begin barking and her son to come into the room asking, "Is it time to go, Mom?"

"Can you see to turn on the lamp?" she asked.

He did, causing her to close her eyes tightly, then open them slowly. Finally, she stared accusingly at her phone. Five-thirty a.m. Had she promised only Gracie, she would call and say they couldn't make it. But Ben had been looking forward to this. And if she was going to teach her son that Easter was more than bunnies, baskets, eggs, and new clothes, then there was no time like the present to begin. With a groan, she swung her legs over the bed and smiled faintly at her precious boy who said, "I've never gone to a sunrise in my life, Mom. I'm real 'cited."

Pushing back her hair from her face, a faint smile was all Brooke could manage. Yes, Ben was excited about going to church on the beach. And she felt reasonably sure it wouldn't hurt her either—if she could stay awake for it.

~ ~ ~

When Brooke pulled into the church parking lot, Jake stood near the entrance, illuminated by her car's headlights. She wondered if he were the assigned parking attendant for the morning. Surely he wasn't waiting just for her. She stopped and powered down the window.

"There are plenty of spaces back there," he said, pointing. "You'll see Gracie's SUV."

"Thanks," she said. She spotted the vehicle. Gracie and the boys got out and reached them by the time Brooke and Ben had exited the Altima. She was glad Gracie had told her to wear a sweater. The early morning air was chilly, although Ben and the boys didn't seem to notice.

When Jake joined them, Brooke figured Gracie must have stationed him at the parking lot entrance. Gracie and Jake both turned on the flashlights in their phones, as did many others. They made their way from the parking lot, around the church, past two rows of homes, then to the beach.

While holding Ben's hand, Brooke saw people walking from all directions, walking toward the great rustic wooden cross, stark and black against a deep gray background where, under an overcast sky, the horizon could not yet be distinguished from the ocean.

Ushers were stationed along the beach to hand out programs. The people kept coming. The people kept coming, their voices subdued as they stepped onto the beach. A hush settled over the crowd as, one by one, the lights clicked off. Everyone stood together on uneven, soft sand. The only sound was that of the power of an ocean that could hardly be seen in the darkness. People, like dark silhouettes, stood beneath the cross, which left Brooke to wonder . . .

How many had seen Jesus die on the cross that day in Jerusalem? His mother? A few disciples? Several curious onlookers? Roman soldiers? Had their hopes died when Jesus took His last breath on that cross? Did Jesus know today that's how she felt? Like her feet were not on solid ground? That the light that shines on her life's path is as unnatural and single-beamed as that from her phone's flashlight? And why were all these other people here? Curiosity seekers? Worshipers? More importantly, why was she here? To teach a religious holiday to Ben? Or—

The crowd's intake of breath seemed to catch in her own throat. Even Ben, knowing something spectacular was occurring, looked up at her and pointed ahead. Brooke nodded. Yes, she saw it. A golden arc of light appeared far off in the distance and seemed to rise from the ocean, as if God were separating the heavens from the water.

One voice began, then others joined in. Never had Brooke seen or heard anything so spectacular. Human voices raised in praise to the Lord as He painted a masterpiece across the sky before their very eyes. They sang while the great golden sphere dispelled the darkness and began turning the sky pink, gold, and blue. The rays glinted against the cross and cast a golden glow on the faces of those emerging from the darkness into the light.

The words of an Easter hymn rang out, stronger and stronger as light illuminated the programs. Brooke could now see the lyrics. But more important, she could *feel* them. *Alleluia! Alleluia!*

When the group, most with their hands lifted, sang with assurance about Jesus being a risen Savior, Brooke looked up as the sun made a pathway from just over the horizon, so far away the distance was unimaginable. And yet, it was right there for her to see. The rays reached across miles and miles of mighty ocean waves to make a golden, glistening pathway from the sun to the shore.

Brooke's throat was too closed to sing, but the words were like a balm to her soul as they sang of a Savior who was the hope of all who seek Him and the help of all who find Him.

Later, during the sermon, the preacher spoke about living by faith.

Could she do that? She believed in Jesus. She'd believed since she was a girl. But how much faith did she have? Could she *live* by faith? Or had she been stumbling around in the dark?

Later, as they made their way back to the church, she glanced at Gracie, who smiled through her tears. Brooke realized she'd shed her own tears. A glance at Jake revealed a swipe of his hand across his cheek.

"Stay for breakfast," Gracie entreated when they reached the church.

"Yeah," Ben pleaded.

Brooke had thought they'd go home after the sunrise service, but now she didn't want to lose this wonderful feeling of peace and assurance that she hadn't felt in so many years. She wanted to be with this group of believers—and with God.

Breakfast in the fellowship hall turned out to be a feast of colored eggs, sausage and egg casserole, ham croissants, Danishes and other pastries, yogurt, juice, and coffee. For so long, Brooke had wondered how it would feel to go to a singles' class after having been married. And she didn't want to answer questions about her marriage. Or her husband's death. But on this day, nothing was said about why a person was single. There were so many visitors there wasn't time for more than introductions and each person telling where they were from, if they lived on Hilton Head or were visiting.

Jessica Lawler came over to speak to Brooke, introduce her husband, and ask how things were going. Brooke was able to mean it when she thanked Jessica for sending Jake Randolph her way. "That's our Jake," Jessica said. "He's a godsend."

Brooke had asked Gracie if God had sent her that evening with her pot of spaghetti. She'd said it rather jokingly, but now she wondered if it were true. Her vision of walking into a sanctuary in a strange place had been unfounded. By the time of the worship service, she'd been introduced to so many people and had smiled so much that she felt like she belonged. Sitting on the pew next to Gracie with Ben on the other side of her helped too. Jake sat at the other end of the pew next to Gracie's oldest, Alex.

When they first sat, Brooke was aware of the long double rows of pews, the color of light oak, separated by a wide strip of royal blue carpet reaching to the steps of the raised dais, on which stood a wide lectern with white Easter lilies all across the front. Great exposed wooden beams, like dark oak, slanted high, crossed in the center, forming a cathedral ceiling. Recessed lights shone from between each beam. Behind the dais, partitioned off by a low wooden railing, sat gold velvet chairs. Above the choir loft was a round, stained-glass window of multicolored Christian symbols such as the lamb, the dove, and the cross.

But Brooke forgot about the lovely interior as soon as the choir members in white robes filed in and began to sing "Christ the Lord is Risen Today." Once again, Brooke could feel the words when the congregation sang; she joined in.

"We're going to my parents' house for traditional Easter dinner," Gracie said. "Come eat with us."

When Brooke began to shake her head, Gracie tempted, "Ham, melt-in-your-mouth sweet potatoes with marshmallows on top, little green peas—"

"No, really, we need to get home."

After a long look, Gracie nodded and smiled. "I understand. I'll call you soon," she said, and squeezed Brooke's arm affectionately.

Brooke had the feeling that Gracie really did know how she felt. Maybe once upon a time Gracie too had come to a crossroad with wanting to trust God. Wanting to trust others, wondering how things were going to work out and if she should accept gracious offers. Wondering if such kindness was out of kindness or pity.

On Monday, for the first time in a long time, Brooke began the day with a prayer. Then, before breakfast, she read a Bible verse to Ben, and they prayed together. Afterward, she had him help clear the table and make his bed before he went out to play with Taz. She went inside and started a load of clothes.

During the week, she tackled the house with renewed vigor, feeling more at peace with herself, her situation, the friendship developing with Gracie, Ben's friendship with a boy his own age, and even her changing feelings about Jake Randolph. She hadn't felt like contacting him yet about other repairs, but when Friday's forecast said to expect rain on the weekend, she called Gracie and asked if she thought Jake could check on her roof once more.

Right after she hung up the phone, she heard a knock on the door, and her immediate thought was that Jake Randolph had ESP and had decided to come and see what she needed. However, when she answered the door, there stood Ben's new Sunday school teacher, whom Brooke had met but whose name she didn't remember.

"Hi," said the petite brunette, about her own age, dressed in a pretty summer dress. "I'm Carleigh," she said. "Ben was in my class Sunday."

"Come in," Brooke said, after warning her about the precariously hanging screen door. She was grateful that airing out the place had eliminated the musty smell. The living room had been thoroughly dusted and mopped. She'd taken the curtains down, wiped down the slats of the plantation shutters until they nearly gleamed.

"I don't have *everything* fixed up yet," she apologized, "but I'm getting there."

"At least you have furniture," Carleigh replied, "which is more than I can say. I'm also a single mom and live with my parents. That's about to change, though." She sat in the easy chair. "Is Ben here?"

Ben and Taz chose that moment to enter the room.

"Uh-uh," Brooke chastened, just as Ben got that knowing look on his face and said, "Taz, go home." The dog ran.

Brooke grinned as she sat on the couch. "The dog knows he's going to get a cookie. Well, a dog biscuit, but we call it a cookie."

Soon, Ben returned, and when Carleigh said, "Hello, Ben," he stuck out his hand. Before Brooke could ask if his hands were clean, Carleigh shook it. *Oh, well,* Brooke remembered. *She has a child too.*

"I have a little something for you, Ben," Carleigh said and held out a small white bag.

"Oh, neat. Look, Mom," he said. Ben pulled out a book and handed it to Brooke.

"Oops," she said, as a gold bookmark decorated with a big red apple fell out. She returned it to the book and read the title. "*Apples from God,*" she said. "How nice."

"Thank yoooou!" Ben said to Carleigh, and then began to pull red apples from the bag.

"He can read above his level already and he just loves books," Brooke said and then laughed lightly. "And apples."

Carleigh smiled. "We give a bag of apples and a copy of that book to all the children in the area who visit our class."

"Can I go out and read it in the swing?" Ben asked and Brooke nodded.

Carleigh gave a rundown of activities for children in the church, saying that Ben fit right in on Sunday and had listened eagerly.

Brooke nodded. She knew Ben was an outgoing boy. And it was certainly her responsibility to channel his energy in the right direction. "He has a friend there already," Brooke noted. "Aiden Harris."

"Yes," Carleigh said. "I saw you sitting in the sanctuary with Jake and Gracie."

Had Carleigh thought she was sitting with Jake? "Gracie's been a lifesaver to me."

Carleigh nodded. "She's a wonderful example to all us single moms," she said with feeling, then stood. "Speaking of being a mom, I need to get home. My mom keeps Sara all day and cooks supper for me, so I'd better scoot."

Brooke thanked her for the visit and the gift to Ben.

They stepped out onto the front porch where Ben sat on the swing, pumping his little legs and holding the book open. The swing groaned in protest. Just as Brooke was about to open her mouth to tell him to be careful, Carleigh said, "Hope to see you Sunday, Ben." Then, to Brooke, "See you then too."

As soon as Carleigh pulled away, Ben called out, "And the apple fell out of the tree on the boy's head, and it had a worm in it," as if he were reading from his new book.

"What? The boy's head had a worm in it?" Brooke shrieked, and Ben laughed. Brooke sat carefully on the swing with its still-rusty chain and grabbed the book. "Why, you little kidder," she said playfully. "You just said that to get me to read it to you, didn't you?"

"Yup," he replied, his big, dark eyes shining, melting her heart.

The way things were going, she might just bring this child up the right way after all.

Nine

Jake came on Saturday, although the forecast said showers. Beneath the graying sky, he hammered away at one of the broken slats in the fence. Brooke didn't like the idea of leaving someone at her house while she went away, but she had an afternoon appointment to take Taz to get his rabies shot. After she and Ben ate, she thought perhaps Jake had made a special effort to work for her on Saturday, so she made him a sandwich and took it out to the swing.

She walked out into the yard until she stood directly behind him trying to decide what to say. She didn't want to give the impression that just because she was a friend of Gracie's, she expected Jake to be her friend. However, she could at least treat him like she would any other ordinary human being—or the dog.

"Um, excuse me," she called, "we have to take Taz to the vet. There's a sandwich on the swing if you want it."

He lifted his hand in a kind of salute. "Thank you, ma'am," he said. "'preciate that."

The first drop of rain plopped on her arm and she brushed it away. She held out her hand and said, "It's starting to rain. You might be gone when we get back, so . . . if you will, just leave an invoice . . . and for the roofing shingles."

"I can do that," he said, his smile broad, reminding her of what a ruggedly handsome man he was. Shaking away that image and annoyed with herself for her thoughts, she quickly turned and hurried Ben and Taz into the back seat of the car. The last thing she needed was to be thinking of a man. But she reminded herself, as if she needed to be defended, her thoughts about him were mainly spiritual.

Jake shook his head as Brooke Haddon and her son drove away. She certainly knew how to keep her distance. He could accept that. He could even understand it. Once a person's life had been turned upside down, having that innocent kind of trust that once was a part of you didn't come easy.

At the same time, part of him wished he could be that happy-go-lucky kind of guy he used to be and let a girl know he was interested in her. In his college days he could do that, and those few times he'd been rejected, he shrugged it off. After all, there were plenty of others eager to accept his advances.

He wasn't like that anymore. His approach to life wasn't the same as in his younger days. He'd learned the hard way that you couldn't always take a person at face value or at their word. Maybe after today, Brooke Haddon would realize he was not a scam artist or a lecher—just a hard-working man doing his job, and yes, hoping to favorably impress her.

He hadn't met a woman in years who sparked this kind of interest in him. Maybe it had started because she didn't trust him, and he wanted to correct that impression. Maybe it was because of her physical attractiveness that a seeing man couldn't deny. But a lot of it had to do with watching her trying to get back into the mainstream of life after a devastating personal experience and beginning those efforts at a church service.

He knew how hard it was to face people when inside you felt like a tidal wave had come along and swept away everything in life that you'd thought was important. He would never forget the day two average-looking men in business suits got out of a car in front of his shop when he opened it up.

"Jake Randolph?" one asked.

"Yes, what can I do for you?" Jake asked with a smile. He had a lot to smile about that morning. He was working on the biggest job he'd had since he and Martin Gage bought the company from Jake's dad after his heart attack. Their construction business was booming, Jake was saving money, he and Meagan had spent a night to remember the night before. They had also talked about marriage. Kids. So what was there not to smile about?

"A Martin Gage work with you?" one man asked.

"We're partners," Jake said. "Come on in. Martin should be here any minute now."

Jake led them to the office, offered them chairs, made a pot of coffee while they asked the usual questions prospective clients might ask. When the coffee was done, they refused a cup. When Martin came in and was introduced, they flashed badges, read them their rights, and said they were under arrest.

"Arrest?" Jake stammered, looking from the men to Martin, whose face had turned nearly every shade of red. "For what?"

"For refusing to pay income taxes for the past two years," one of the men explained.

"What are you *talking* about?" He looked at Martin, who blanched. "What are they talking about?"

"Jake," Martin said. "I'm sorry . . . I—"

Jake took a step back and held up his hands. "Wait a minute. Wait. A. Minute." He shook his head. "You're *sorry*?"

"I should have told you. I should have—"

"Okay," Jake said, trying to catch his breath. "Is there a bill? An invoice or something? Just give it to me. I'll pay it right now. How much? How much are we talking about here?"

"I'm sorry, Mr. Randolph," the man said bluntly. "It doesn't work that way. Your company owes a significant amount of back taxes. We gave you plenty of warnings and more than enough time. So, now . . . we're going to have to go for a ride downtown."

During that *ride*, whenever Jake looked at Martin, his partner turned his head and looked the other way. Jake had to clench his jaw to keep from exploding. To keep from pounding the man. How could Martin have done this to him? To the business? Martin of all people. The man who had worked for Jake's dad for many years. After a beam fell on Martin's leg, Jake's father brought him in as office assistant while he recuperated. After his leg healed, Martin knew his leg would never be the same and—realizing he was getting a little age on him—asked to stay on as assistant bookkeeper. He'd always been a good worker, so Jake's dad had no problem with that.

And Jake had no problem with Martin's interest in gambling. After all, Jake wasn't exactly lily-white, so who was he to spout off about it? None of his business what Martin did with his own money. But after Jake's dad decided to sell the business, Martin's big win during a trip to Vegas enabled him to come in as a partner.

That suited Jake. He liked Martin. He'd been a good employee for Randolph Construction on both outside and inside jobs. Never in a million years did he suspect Martin would be guilty of this kind of "inside job." After all, who would suspect that a man would steal from his own company or not pay income tax on his own business? Unless—the thought hit hard—he'd had a lot of gambling losses.

Jake expected this would all be over in a short while. His one phone call was to his dad's attorney. After Jake posted his own bail, he was free to go until he was to appear for trial.

He drove straight to Meagan's. The moment he said, "I've been arrested for income tax evasion," her mouth dropped open, and she looked like someone turned her to stone.

"I didn't do it, Meagan. It's Martin. He ran the office. He kept the books. And now, he's gambled away his part of the profits and didn't pay the taxes. That's why he's been saying things like wanting to get back down to Vegas where the big bucks are. But I didn't suspect he'd do something like this."

"You're part owner, Jake," she said, as if he thought her a fool for believing he hadn't known what was happening. "And you told me about all that money you've been saving." She threw up her hands. "Oh, Jake! How could you?"

That was the second shock of the day, and only the beginning of the personal earthquake that hit on the day of the trial. Martin had plea-bargained, pled guilty, was put on probation, and was out walking the streets.

Against the advice of the attorney, Jake refused to plead guilty to something he didn't do. Surely the jury would understand that he had principles, morals. After all, Martin had said he was guilty. But the jury adhered to what the law had to say. Jake was a partner. Ignorance was no excuse. Jake was found guilty.

"Six months in state prison," the judge sentenced, and at the pound of the gavel, Jake felt like he'd fallen through a crack in the ground and the earth had swallowed him up.

A flash of lightning brought Jake to the realization he was no longer in that hole. He was on probation and kneeling in front of Brooke Haddon's cottage with a hammer in his hand and raindrops falling on his head—a perfect lightning rod. He gathered his tools then went to sit on the covered front porch. There he ate his sandwich then did one more little chore before packing up his tools for the day.

By the time Brooke and Ben returned, the rain had stopped. Ben ran around the house toward the back yard with Taz racing beside him. As she walked toward the house, Brooke glanced at where Jake had been working on the fence, but he wasn't there. She studied the repaired fence for a few moments, noting that Jake did good work. The new wood needed to be painted, but then, so did the whole cottage.

When she reached the porch, she saw a folded paper plate underneath the screen. Couldn't he have taken it out back to the trash can? She carefully opened the screen door, then looked up, startled. It stayed in place. It was fixed. He'd put on a new hinge. She must remember to thank him . . . in addition to paying him.

She reached down and picked up the paper plate. It was folded, and he'd written what looked like an invoice, which did not include the cost of labor for the roof.

Was that man trying to get her attention? Well, maybe she didn't know how to make repairs herself, and maybe she had to be careful about her spending, but she didn't have to accept charity. No matter how charming Jake might be, she didn't want to feel indebted to any man.

She tossed the paper plate on top of the refrigerator and tried to forget it. She would go about her business and deal with that when her mind was clearer. In the meantime, she would wait and see if Jake Randolph tried to press her with coming around to do the other repairs—like replacing the cracked glass panes, and the peeling outside paint and, well, maybe he could look at that front porch swing.

He didn't, and she told herself she was glad. Gracie didn't even mention him when she called mid-week and encouraged Brooke to take advantage of the church's Mother's Day Out program. Brooke said she'd take a look and get Ben's reaction.

"Cool!" he said when he saw the fenced-in children's playground, complete with sand, tunnels, slides, monkey bars, swings, and about anything a little child's active heart could desire.

"Can I stay, Mom?"

Aiden's eyes also pleaded with her.

"Okay," she said, seeing there were plenty of volunteers to watch them, some of whom she had seen or met on Sunday. And Gracie's boys would be there with him.

Brooke and Gracie spent the morning shopping. Brooke was grateful Gracie knew where to get all the bargains, not only on groceries but on cleaning supplies and household items, including a sale on indoor paint and painting supplies. "I've decided that, room by room, I'm going to give each room a fresh coat," Brooke said. Then she grinned. "Wanna help?"

"Do you think you can manage to wait until after school begins?"

"If it means you'll help, I will," she said.

"Then consider it a yes."

When they returned, Gracie showed Brooke the prayer garden—a lovely spot between two buildings, surrounded by lush foliage, tall palmettos, and live oaks. She walked down the steps and onto the bricks. She could see how this place was conducive to prayer, as if she had stepped away from life for a moment into a private place to reverently commune with God.

Ten

For the first time in years, Brooke felt as eager as Ben to return to church.

Only a few people attended the singles' class, and they spent a brief time getting to know each other and introducing those who hadn't met. But most of the class was spent on Bible study since the group met twice a week to interact and talk about personal needs. Brooke liked the class members, the teacher, and the warm, friendly feeling she got from everyone. Jake's friendly manner, she noted, was the same with everyone. So, she reasoned, perhaps it *wasn't* just her he was nice to.

Even the sermon that morning seemed designed just for her. The pastor read from Romans 8:39 and talked about how nothing could separate a person from the love of God. "Death can't, life can't, the angels can't, and the demons can't," he said.

A feeling of hope and joy touched Brooke's heart when he read that our fears for today, our worries about tomorrow, and even the powers of hell could not keep God's love away. She was overcome by both elation and guilt. Even though her faith wasn't strong, God hadn't abandoned her. She and Ben had their needs met, and they had each other. He even brought friends to their door, and the church was filled with caring Christians and people who understood what it's like to be broken and need help beyond what she could provide.

The song leader stood and asked them to sing "Leaning on the Everlasting Arms."

While the people sang, Brooke became vaguely aware of Ben and Aiden rocking back and forth in time with the music.

She had an odd memory then. One of her and Barrett. Of how they'd walked arm in arm. He'd been happy with her until she got pregnant. Then he thought she no longer looked good beside him. Their son was a burden to him that he hadn't been ready for.

Oh, how she'd prayed during those six years of marriage. But the relationship had gone steadily downhill. The prayers weren't answered. She glanced toward the high beams. If there was really a caring God, where was He during that time?

She quickly looked down again. She mustn't do that. She'd always known there was a God. It was just that she hadn't called upon Him until her marriage had deteriorated beyond repair. And Barrett hadn't seemed to consider God very much. Now, Brooke was reminded that God had given her parents who took her in. He'd kept that little cottage tucked away on this resort island for a roof over their heads. He'd given her a wonderful son. Ben had new playmates, and she had a friend she could confide in.

Her glance inadvertently wandered over to her left, and she glimpsed Jake Randolph, whose voice and face were lifted in praise. Despite her aversion to receiving his charity, she could even be grateful that God had sent her a much-needed handyman.

"Come eat lunch with us," Gracie said after the service ended and they were all in the parking lot. "We're having every boy's favorite."

"Pizza!" Alex shouted, and the others followed with, "Yea! Yea!"

Gracie took a deep breath and blew out through her lips as she shook her head of auburn curls and glanced at Brooke with chagrin. "No. Not pizza. We're having every boy's *second* favorite meal, cooked on the grill." She looked at Alex. "Got a clue?"

"Yeah. Barbecue chicken."

He grinned mischievously while his mother said, "You know better."

He nodded. "Grilled bread! And water to drink."

"That's exactly what you deserve," said a male voice. Jake had walked up and rested his hands on Alex's shoulders. Alex looked up at Jake with utmost admiration as he added, "How about grilled hot dogs and homemade potato salad?"

Alex nodded. "I can live with that," he said, and Jake winked at him in approval.

Brooke wondered if being asked to Gracie's home was going to be an every-Sunday kind of thing. And, if so, would she be expected to reciprocate. Adding two mouths—hers and Ben's—to five was one thing. But adding five mouths to their two was another thing entirely. She'd never been the greatest in the kitchen and she'd not ever had to cook for more than three without the aid of her mother.

Just then, Aiden interrupted with a plea to his mother. "Can Ben bring his puppy?"

"Yeah, yeah," the other boys chimed in, and Ben tugged on the skirt of her dress. "Oh, Mom. You should've seen how 'cited Taz was when they were at our house. He was jumping all over creation. Can we go?"

They all laughed at his childish prattle, and how *'cited* he was over the prospect of playing with his new friends. Brooke recognized the expression of doing something "all over creation" as one her mom had inadvertently passed down to her. Now Ben said it. Like mother, like child.

Just as she started to refuse, Jake spoke. "I could keep an eye on these guys for a while and give you two a chance to do whatever needs to be done in the kitchen." He tousled Collin's hair.

"Okay, thanks," Brooke said to Gracie, avoiding looking at Jake. "But Taz?"

"Oh, go get him," Gracie encouraged. "Alex can go with you and give directions to our house. It's only a couple of miles from you and easy to find. You might want to bring a bathing suit too. We have a pool."

"Bring a little dog food with you," Jake said.

For an instant, Brooke wondered if he were testing her to see if she had allowed Ben to feed Taz bread again. On second thought, he probably was just thinking of the puppy—as if she didn't have sense enough to know his feeding time.

Collin and Aiden wanted to go back to Brooke's too, and Brooke assured Gracie that would be fine. It might take four boys to hold onto a dog so *'cited* he jumped "all over creation."

Brooke exchanged her dress for jeans but didn't bother with a bathing suit because she had no intention of running around half-dressed in front of Jake. Ben changed into play clothes. He moaned that he didn't have bathing trunks.

"I have two," Aiden said. "You can wear one of mine."

Alex shrugged. "Or you can swim in your clothes if you want to."

Just in case, Brooke picked up an extra set of play clothes for Ben.

The boys set Taz on the floorboard of the back seat, but before she could pull out of the driveway, the puppy had somehow managed to get into the front passenger seat with Alex. Despite puppy licks, Alex was able to give simple and concise directions. After she'd driven about two miles, he pointed and said, "There it is."

Brooke recognized the low country-style house as one that had appealed to her years before. She'd seen many of those, typical of the southern spacious houses ideal for large families. Steps leading to the front door separated the expansive porch that stretched the entire width of the house. The light brown banister and shutters complemented the cream-colored house, which was topped by a gray roof. The yard held an assortment of magnolias, live oaks, and palms while a hedge of blooming azaleas—red, coral, and white—adorned the front of the house on both sides of the front porch steps. An immaculate green lawn lay like a lush carpet. Brooke found herself duly impressed.

"They'll be out back," Alex said after Brooke parked on the white sand-and-shell driveway at the side of the house facing a high, light brown wooden fence. The boys ran yelling toward the back yard by the time Brooke got the box and puppy food out of the car.

Brooke walked through the gate—left open by the boys—closed it behind her, fastened the latch, and walked around the corner of the house when she heard Gracie calling for the boys to come inside and change clothes.

"Leave the puppy out here," Brooke said, glad she'd brought his box. Ben put the puppy down, and it started to run along behind him but couldn't make it up the step. She set the box down, placed the puppy food beside the steps, scooped the puppy up, and put him in the box. His whimpering and scrambling to get out indicated absolute displeasure.

Brooke glanced around at the back yard, understanding why the front of the house seemed to belie the fact that three active boys lived here. The yard was perfect as a children's playground and looked like a safe haven. The rectangular pool and surrounding concrete took up almost the entire left side of the yard. At the far end stood a swing set on white sand and enclosed by timbers. It appeared to be any child's dream with its three swings, a long slide, and a climbing rope beside a ladder leading to a small, enclosed landing. Several flowering azalea bushes lent spectacular color, and a yellow jessamine trailed up one corner and along the top of the wooden fence.

Scattered along the pool side, the patio chairs and two chaises looked particularly inviting. Behind those on the right sat a long picnic table with attached benches. Nearer the open narrow porch, on a cobbled area, sat a large grill with a domed lid.

Smiling at the perfect picture, Brooke started out of her reverie, hearing Gracie yell, "Don't get in the pool yet," at the same time the screen door was flung open, and four boys dashed across the porch, racing to the swing set. Alex got there first but let the other three boys take the swings.

"Look, Mom," Ben called. "I'm swinging up to heaven."

"I see." She smiled. It hadn't been too long ago that he'd learned how to push himself with his body and feet. He watched his new friend Aiden and tried to go as high as the other five-year-old.

"I know you're out there somewhere, Brooke," Gracie called from a window. "Come in and make yourself useful."

Just as she turned ready to step up onto the porch, Jake opened the screen door and stepped out. He greeted her with a nice smile and immediately turned his attention to the dog.

"Okay to let Taz out?"

"Sure," she said, then clamped her lips shut to keep from telling him not to let Taz fall into the pool. After closing the screen, one backward glance revealed Jake standing with his hands on his hips, chuckling, while the little puppy waddled as fast as he could toward the exuberant boys.

∽ ∽ ∽

Jake asked himself what he'd expected of Brooke. Had he thought she'd turn cartwheels just because he repaired her roof and fence and fixed her screen? He needed to keep everything in perspective and just hope that a word or glance from her would indicate she could accept him—if nothing else—as a friend.

Gracie had told him that Brooke had had an unpleasant experience with an unfaithful husband before he died in a car accident. He'd like to talk to her, let her know he understood the difficulties of starting over. He'd like to be her friend, and the more he saw of her, he knew he'd like to be more than a friend. Not that he could allow himself to go there quite yet. He was a man on parole. A woman in his life, even one who'd caught his attention the way Brooke had, a woman with such grace and style, was something he had to think clearly about before leaping.

Unlike many of the single women Gracie and he knew, Gracie had come to terms with her single status. She had confided in her brother on more than one occasion that she wasn't expecting God to bring a man into her life to make it meaningful.

So, then why couldn't he be as accepting?

He turned the hot dogs with the grilling fork, feeling as if a skewer had done such to his heart. Common sense told him to be realistic. And he had been since Meagan rejected him. But he hadn't expected someone like Brooke to come on the scene and disturb his carefully controlled emotional life just by being distantly near. He had to face facts. This could get him nothing but heartache. He wasn't a teenager; he was a grown man. A man with a past. If Brooke Haddon distrusted men in general, imagine what she would feel if he told her he was on probation. That had proved to be disastrous with Meagan.

So, how in the world could he ever say to a woman like Brooke, "Hey, by the way, I've spent time in a state prison"?

∽ ∽ ∽

The day was gorgeous, sporting a mild temperature, complete with a clear blue sky and a soft gentle breeze.

Brooke was grateful that despite there being two mothers without husbands and four little boys without daddies, there was a good-natured man around to tell them to wash their hands and then to give thanks to God for the food.

They all held hands as Jake bowed his head and prayed. "Thank You, Lord, for the blessings of this day and those who have come to share this food with us. Thank You for the food, and may it nourish our bodies. Guide us, Lord, that we may use our lives in service to You. In Jesus' name we pray, amen."

After lunch and clean-up, Brooke and Gracie, seated in the rocking chairs on the porch, held glasses of lemonade and watched. Jake showed the boys how to coax Taz to sit and lie down, then reward him.

So that's why he wanted me to bring puppy food. Okay. So he hadn't been concerned she still allowed Ben to feed bread to Taz. All along, he'd been planning to teach the boys more about training a dog.

"Sit, Taz," he said again, and when Taz obeyed, he received a nibble.

"Well, would you look at that?" she mumbled to herself. Slowly, Jake Randolph was making a good impression on her.

Then again, once upon a time, Barrett had made a good impression too. So good, she had married him. He'd gone to church many Sundays, shook hands, and kissed babies—but not for the love of Jesus. Everything he'd done had been for votes. No, she was not going to be fooled by any seemingly caring man again.

∽ ∽ ∽

When Jake returned to the yard in his bathing trunks and with a towel slung over his shoulders, Gracie and the boys were nowhere in sight.

Brooke still sat in the rocker on the porch looking toward the far corner of the yard as if she didn't see him.

It wasn't easy figuring out how to relate to her. He'd come to understand a little of how women like Gracie and some of the other single moms felt. He'd heard enough stories of men being abusive or unfaithful. He didn't know Brooke's situation fully, only that her husband had died a year ago and that he had been unfaithful, which explained her wariness. But as far as he was concerned, any man who could be unfaithful to a woman like Brooke didn't deserve her in the first place.

He wanted more than anything, to walk over, sit next to her, and have a simple conversation. But he could practically see the wall she'd built around her where men were concerned and knew it best that he didn't. So instead, "Taz," he called. "Come."

The dog came running and stood in front of him, his tail shaking wildly. Jake gave him a piece of food, then tossed his towel onto a chair, stepped to the side of the pool, and jumped in.

Just because Brooke wasn't interested in a man didn't mean she couldn't appreciate Jake's bronzed, athletic body as he smoothly swam several laps across the pool while the boys changed. The combination of his work and swimming apparently kept him in terrific shape. She needed to do something about her own body. Not that she was out of shape, but she knew the importance of aerobics and toning.

Soon, ahead of Gracie, the boys came running out, Ben in a pair of Aiden's trunks. They jumped, screaming, into the pool—except Ben.

Brooke jumped up, ready to run toward him as he teetered on the edge of the pool while the boys encouraged him to jump, but he was frozen, scared to jump and scared to move away.

The boys yelled for him to jump in. Jake immediately realized the dilemma and told the boys to be quiet. "Come down the steps," Jake encouraged. "I'll hold your hand. I won't let you go."

Jake had Gracie's boys swim away from him and Ben while he gave some basic instructions, and before long Ben was holding onto the side, kicking his feet, sticking his head under. Soon Jake had him bobbing and was giving him instructions on how to float.

"My boys are fish," Gracie said, "thanks to Jake."

"I'm afraid Ben's a rock," Brooke retorted. "The weather in Indiana is quite different than here on this mild-climate island. He never swam much and then only in shallow water. He loves water and had a great time in a plastic pool. But he's not comfortable in deep water."

"It's only three feet at this end," Gracie said. "He'll be fine."

Before long, Ben was a regular little trooper in the shallow end. When he got past the three-feet level, he'd do what Jake instructed and float or hold his breath and swim toward the side or shallow end. The other boys swam across alone or jumped onto Jake's shoulder from where they dove off, headfirst.

Ben wouldn't. "I'll do it next time," he promised.

Brooke was impressed. "Your brother's very good with children," she said. "And dogs."

Gracie nodded. "I was about ready to throw up my hands and quit before Jake moved in with us. I try to keep the boys from disturbing him too much. But most of the time, he's just like a dad to those boys. We'd be in a pickle without him."

They both gazed out at the man being so patient with the little boys and seeming to love every minute of it. Brooke and Gracie laughed as Taz kept going to the edge of the pool, but the minute water splashed on his face, he'd run away.

Brooke's glance returned to Jake. "I take it he's not married," she commented.

"No, he's single," Gracie said. "By the way, I teach water aerobics here three mornings a week from ten to eleven. There's usually about eight or ten of us. Come join us. Give you a chance to meet some new people."

That sounded wonderful to Brooke, but she also knew a change of subject when she heard one. "You're a mind reader. I was thinking about getting into some kind of regular exercise routine. Maybe after school starts and I get the inside painted?"

"Um, how long would you say the walls of that cottage have needed a fresh coat of paint?" Gracie asked with a sly grin and a tilt of her head.

Brooke laughed. "I get your point. And I know with a boy and dog around it's never going to be fingerprint-free."

Gracie wagged her finger. "All work and no play, you know."

"Okay," Brooke conceded. "Maybe you win. How much do you charge for lessons?"

"Fifty dollars a month. And you can come once a week or three times a week. A couple of the single moms bring their kids. I know they'd love it if you brought Ben and Taz."

"I just might," Brooke replied, knowing it would be good for both her and Ben. She could manage the cost. "Oh, speaking of money," she said. "I need to talk to Jake about his invoice. He didn't charge me for the labor." She spoke somewhat apologetically, knowing she was talking to Gracie about her own brother. "I know he does *something* for free and I'd understand if the hanging of the screen door was it. But not all that work on the roof."

"I know what you're thinking, Brooke," Gracie said. "You think there are ulterior motives and Jake's going to make a move on you. But it's not just you. Jake does this on every job he takes. Believe me, Brooke, this isn't personal."

Okay . . . so, Jake wasn't *personally* interested in her. But a man like him should be interested in someone. He was handsome, had a business, was in his mid-thirties, had a great personality, was a Christian, a father-figure to little boys, a good dog-trainer, and a skilled carpenter. So then, why was this seemingly extraordinary man living with his sister, not married, and not with some special woman on this fine Sunday afternoon?

Eleven

Mid-morning on Monday, Jake's phone went off, indicating that someone had texted him. He finished nailing the last beam in place on the house he and his crew were building, then pulled the phone from the back pocket of his jeans. Gracie had sent a simple message: CALL ME.

He called his sister, who answered on the first ring. "Hey."

"What's up, sis?"

"Brooke just called wanting to know if you can call her at your earliest convenience."

Jake wiped a trickle of sweat that threatened to drop from his brow and into his eye. "Did she say why?" he asked around a smile. Yesterday, although he glimpsed her speculative gaze upon occasion, she hadn't seemed offended by him. Maybe today she'd even smile, but no matter what, she'd have to wait. Unless an emergency call came in, he never left his crew to finish up without him for the day. They all had families, and Jake wanted them to be able to get home in time to eat supper with them.

"No," Gracie answered, drawing out the word.

"Do me a favor, please. Call her back and let her know I'll get back with her as soon as I'm done here. Couple of hours or so."

At quitting time, Jake and his crew cleaned up around the property, put their equipment into their trucks, then headed for the shop.

Jake washed up while the crew dropped off their equipment. He changed shirts and ran a comb through his hair, then called Gracie to say he would drive by Brooke's before he headed home. "Don't wait supper for me."

"I'll save you something," she told him.

A keen sense of anticipation swept over Jake as he drove along the road headed for Brooke's. He had powered the windows down. A breeze cooled his face and blew his hair and tickled a memory of Brooke Haddon's cool gaze the morning he'd stopped by when she'd treated him like a potential hazard. Then he remembered how the color of her eyes had changed to gray-green when she'd looked up at him with his head hanging over the roof. The expression then had been possible repentance, thanks to the fact he had a sister who'd come to his rescue. Then she'd looked down, and he'd noticed her eyelashes, long without the aid of makeup.

Jake! he warned himself. *You can't do this.*

He could not form an interest in any woman until his probation ended, until he'd fulfilled the sentence of the court. Only then would he legally have paid his debt to society.

So why was he?

He shook his head as if to clear it. Of course, he knew why. He was a thirty-five-year-old single man, with parents he could see any time, working with a crew of spirited guys, involved in the church and particularly with singles, and living in a house where he had access to a sister and three lively boys. His life was full.

But he was lonely.

His parents had each other. His crew had their own lives. Gracie and the boys were his sister and his nephews, not his wife and his own children. And he knew perfectly well, there's nothing in the world he could do to change this situation. He was going to Brooke's cottage on business and only business. He was a man with a past. A man with a secret. God had blessed him beyond measure, and he needed to be content with where he was and with what he had.

Lonely or not.

He needn't have worried. Brooke met him on the porch, holding onto the screen door he had repaired. Serene gray eyes erased his friendly smile and turned his expression to frustration.

He glanced at the corner. Had it fallen in or something? The screen door appeared intact, but her lips formed a firm line.

"Mr. Randolph," she began, holding his paper-plate invoice. "I didn't want to say anything yesterday in front of everybody, but this is ridiculous."

He relented, realizing he'd goofed again. "You're right," he agreed. "I should not have written an invoice on a paper plate. That was totally unprofessional." He sighed, mentally kicking himself in the seat of his jeans with his heavy work boots. How could he have thought that was acceptable? He'd never done such a thing before. The reason was, she'd been so concerned about getting estimates, he'd felt upbeat that his price would beat anybody's around. He wanted to impress her with that. And he wouldn't care if she didn't pay the fee.

It dawned on him then that the reason she had called was not out of any kind of appreciation or to ask him to do further work but to complain about his lack of professionalism. That suddenly nagging fear welled up in him. If any complaint, no matter how minor, got back to the Better Business Bureau, he was sunk. That could be all it would take—one dissatisfied customer.

Jake spoke seriously. "Hey, look. I'm sorry. Believe me, I would send a legitimate receipt upon payment. I've got some invoices in my truck and I can draw up a proper one if you like." He turned back toward his truck.

"Mr. Randolph," she called, causing him to stop and look back at her over his shoulder. "I'm not referring to the paper plate. I wouldn't care if you wrote it on the side of the house. I'm referring to the amount."

His brows drew together. "You're complaining about the price?"

They stared at each other, both silent, as if he were speaking Chinese and she could only understand Portuguese.

Finally, Jake broke the confusing silence. He gestured with his hands. "Throw away the invoice . . . um . . . the paper plate." He grimaced at his own words. How could a businessman have been so unprofessional as to write an invoice on a paper plate? What was wrong with him? Why did he keep making a complete fool of himself? Particularly in front of the one woman he'd met in years that he'd like to favorably impress.

Brooke let the screen door slam behind her, and she held out the plate to him. "Even if you meant this as a nice gesture, it's totally unacceptable."

He didn't attempt to stop her ranting. Strangely, he was concentrated on how the late evening sun glinted in her steely gray eyes. How the color of indignation tinged the cheeks of her fair, flawless skin. How her soft lips moved as she spoke. And there was the tiniest little dimple at one corner of her mouth that showed up when she spouted her displeasure.

"Maybe I've given the impression that I'm destitute and can't pay my bills," she said, bringing him back to the present. "Well, that's not the situation. Money is a little tighter than it was when Barrett was alive, but I assure you I can pay my bills."

So that was it. It was all he could do to keep from laughing out loud. She thought he pitied her. Not so. He'd done many jobs for those who couldn't pay up front, and they'd worked out a payment plan. One single mom needed a gate built across the entry to her back porch so her toddler would have a safe place to play outside without falling down the steps or wandering off. The job hadn't cost much by his standards, but with her limited income, they'd worked out a plan and she'd paid a few dollars a month for over a year.

"It wasn't charity, Mrs. Haddon."

"Just what would you call it then?" Her eyes dared him to have a satisfactory answer.

He understood her now in plain English. He knew she suspected he was trying to impress her for some personal reason, and she was trying to convey that such attempts would be useless.

"I've given the wrong impression from the moment we met," he said, glancing toward the graying sky as if seeking help from beyond. He looked back at her then, his face serious. "It's my water-basin theory," he said. "If you have a few minutes, I'd like to explain it to you." He felt her skepticism as she stared.

"Water basin?" she queried, looking at him as if they'd reverted to speaking in foreign languages.

This kind of problem had never occurred before. He'd always done his work, added a free job, explained why he did it, and it had been accepted and appreciated. So then why was this going so wrong? Maybe he should just write out a new invoice or charge her for the labor and let it go. But that thought hit hard in his chest. He wanted this woman to believe in him, trust him, maybe even like him. Maybe he'd wanted that too much since that morning when he'd walked into her back yard and thought there was something unidentifiably intriguing about her. Perhaps it was the mystery of her situation. Perhaps it was her instant wariness of him. Or because, watching her, the little boy, and a dog, he felt that deep-seated loneliness, or longing for such a life—a cottage, a woman, a little boy, and a dog.

Why was she fighting this man? She knew he worked in the construction business. His sister, whom she felt instant camaraderie with, vouched for him. His work on the corner came as its own excellent recommendation. He had not shown any indication of improper behavior.

So, why couldn't she just take him at face value, accept his charitable gesture, regard him as the brother of a woman who offered friendship, and just let it go? Instead, she had to make an issue of that and everything else, apparently. She hadn't refused Gracie's food, nor had she questioned it. But a gift from a man was a different thing. She could reciprocate Gracie's hospitality, but Jake's was something else entirely.

But what he nor Gracie understood was how hard she had worked to get where she now was. She had moved back in with her parents. She had settled all of Barrett's debts, and then finally returned to Hilton Head where she wanted to be independent. She wanted the last act of charity (if she could call it that) to have been the deeding over of the cottage to her from her in-laws. Now she wanted to pull her own weight. Take care of her son. And she would. She had Ben's Social Security check to get by on until he went to school in the fall. She had to remain frugal—at least until she went back to work—but there were so many others who needed work done for free more than she. After all, her parents had reminded her more than once that they were still there for her. And if there were a great financial need for Ben, the Haddons would come through. She just didn't want to have to resort to calling them.

But was that any reason to be rude to a man offering nothing more than his help and kindness? This was no big deal. All she had to do was tell him in a calm way that she would pay the cost of labor. Period.

"I need to check on Ben," she said instead. "He's out back."

"I'll walk around," Jake said, beginning to move as he spoke.

Brooke hurried through the house and reached the back door by the time Jake stepped around the corner. Ben and Taz were playing tug of war with a sock.

"Hey, Ben. Looks like you and Taz have a battle going there," he said to her son.

"Yeah. And I think I'm about to pull his teeth out."

Jake laughed. "I don't know about that. He'd probably let go before he hurt himself. But if you let him pull on cloth like that, he'll think it's all right to chew on cloth in the house. He wouldn't know the difference between chewing on a sock or chewing on clothes and furniture."

"He likes it," Ben said, looking at the dog pulling as hard as he could on the sock, his back legs having trouble keeping his balance as he pulled back. Then Ben let go and Taz began to chew on the sock. Ben looked up at Jake with soulful eyes. "He liked that bread you told us not to feed him too. But boy, did he get sick. Didn't he, Mom?"

Jake glanced at Brooke.

"Mom was up all night cleaning Taz, and the kitchen, and herself, and—"

"Ben," Brooke said, looking away from Jake's knowing glance and small grin. "I think he gets the point. Taz had quite a time of it. From now on, it's dog food. *Only.*"

"An occasional snack's all right," Jake said, "but a steady diet of people food just doesn't sit well with a puppy. Hey, you want to learn to play ball with him?"

Ben's eyes got big. "Yeah."

"Okay, but first your mom wants to talk business with me." He turned questioning eyes toward Brooke.

She spread her hands. She understood what he'd said about a dog chewing up things in the house, and she'd known of dogs doing that.

She couldn't keep Taz outside until they had some kind of enclosure, and she didn't want to chain him up. She shrugged. It might be good to teach the dog a few tricks. Give Ben a purpose other than pulling on one end of a sock. She relented. "If you want to show him, go ahead."

While Ben rushed inside to get a rubber ball and puppy food, Jake knelt and gently pinched Taz's nose to make him let go of the sock, which Jake then threw onto the porch.

After Ben came out, Brooke sat on the top step, her elbows on her jeaned legs and her chin resting in the palms of her hands, watching the two do what a father and son might do.

Jake explained to Ben, "The main reward should not be the food, but love. So when he does what you tell him, say, 'Good boy.'" Jake showed Ben how to toss the ball a short way, command the puppy to fetch, then say, "Give it to me," or "Bring it here," or something like that. "Don't throw it a long way until he learns. And don't give him a treat unless he does what you say. Okay?"

"Okay," Ben said, and after watching Jake perform the exercise, he was ready to try.

"Very good," Jake said and mussed Ben's dark curls. Ben looked up at him admiringly.

What a lesson, Brooke thought, remembering all the nice things Barrett had given her when all she'd wanted was love. And little Ben responded with glowing eyes when Jake mussed his hair. Yes, that was what the world needed—love. Pure and simple. Puppy dogs, little boys, and grown women too. She wondered who loved this interesting man who took time to play with a little boy and his dog.

"You practice," Jake said. "When the puppy tires of it, just stop and let him play the way he wants to. As long as he's not destructive."

While Ben and Taz tirelessly played, Jake and Brooke watched and laughed. Sometimes Taz would ignore the ball and Ben would forget and give him a piece of food anyway. "Oops, I forgot," he'd say, and Jake would reply, "That's okay. Try again."

Try again seemed to lodge in Brooke's brain. Maybe that's what she should do with Jake. Not be angry with him simply because he was a man or for what Barrett had done to her.

Brooke could readily see that a dog would be a better pet if he were disciplined, just as children and parents had a better lifestyle with order and discipline. Watching Jake with Ben served to remind Brooke that a little boy needed guidance from a dad. She would make sure Ben's needs were met, but just as her own life would have been lacking without her father, she was aware that Ben's was lacking without a father to spend time with him. Could Jake be a good male influence for Ben, as Gracie said he was for her boys?

"Keep on until he gets tired of it," Jake repeated. "Right now, I need to talk with your mom."

Twelve

Jake walked over to the step and stood at the side, reaching up to hold onto the banister. "Mrs. Haddon. If it would make you feel better to pay for that corner, then I'll take the money. But I would appreciate you hearing me out on that."

"The water-basin thing?" she asked, trying not to appear too skeptical.

"Exactly," he said, appearing quite serious as he walked in front of her to sit beside her on the top step. Jake folded his hands and rested his forearms on his thighs, looking out toward Ben and Taz, but Brooke thought he was looking beyond the boy and dog—even beyond the sky turning to gold and pink.

"There was a time when I lost everything and had no money. I decided to give one hundred percent to my work and offer a free service of some kind so the customers would ask why and then I could witness to them, telling them that the reason is because I'm a follower of Jesus Christ who admonishes us to do good to others, to be charitable. If the person is interested, I witness further. If they're not interested, then I've at least attempted to plant a seed, and they will remember that free gift. Jesus gave freely to us—the gift of eternal life is ours if we just receive it. Just accept it."

What a wonderful attitude, Brooke thought. And yet, she'd treated him poorly, to say the least. But then, she hadn't known him. And some people knew how to put a spin on anything and make themselves look good. She mustn't be judgmental, but she could look at a person's fruit to evaluate his character.

Stealing a look at Jake, she saw what appeared to be a sincere man, a true Christian who was serious about his commitment to the Lord.

His attitude was commendable. "What about . . . the water basin?" she asked.

He nodded and smiled, the glorious sunset reflecting a spark of gold in his warm brown eyes. "That's what gave me the idea," he said. "Our preacher talked about it one Sunday morning during the worship service. He read the Scripture where Jesus took a wash basin and towel and washed the disciples' feet. Jesus then told His disciples to do the same."

Brooke's head turned toward him. "You belong to a foot-washing group?"

He grinned. "No, but that might be good for a lot of us to do, literally. The example was for us to serve each other. Jesus taught that we should do good to others. We should serve them."

"That's commendable," Brooke said while a thought pressed in on her mind. If she were going to be interested in a man ever again, she'd want it to be someone like Jake. Feeling the blush in her cheeks, she looked down at the toes of her scuffed tennis shoes. "Do others give you such a hard time about it, as I did?"

He laughed. "No, but I don't generally barge in the way I did with you. Most of my customers know my company's reputation and come to me. Jessica lets me know about some clients, and she recommends me to some people before I approach them. She felt your situation was an emergency because you hadn't been here in quite a while and the house really hadn't been kept up."

"I'm just not trusting enough," Brooke admitted.

"I understand that," Jake said. "I have the same trouble at times. Gracie and other singles we work with find it difficult after they've lost trust in someone or something."

"It's not always fair to the other person," Brooke said.

He smiled. "I don't think you were unfair to me. Sometimes the people we trust most disappoint us. It's a fact of life that we need to be aware of and yet try to not let it get in the way of interaction, of friendship."

She nodded, knowing she mustn't let the past control her life. She wanted interaction and friendship. But not yet.

"Well," she said suddenly, looking away from his questioning eyes that seemed to say that he thought she had an answer, when in truth, she knew she certainly did not. "Now that I've accepted your explanation, I'll run in and get my money."

She returned with cash. "Keep the change," she said with a smile.

He didn't argue. Rather he simply said, "Thank you," and stuck the money in his pocket. "When you're ready, I can paint the house if you'd like."

"Yes, I want that," she said, plopping down beside him again. "But for now, I have a lot of other fixing up to do around here."

He nodded. "I know there are several roof shingles to be nailed down," he commented.

"That's for sure," she agreed. "And I have a kitchen ceiling with brown splotches all over it, two leaky faucets, cracked windowpanes, and a pitiful picket fence." She paused and shook her head. "That's for starters."

"Obviously, no one has lived in it for a while," he commented.

"Before last year, my in-laws had seasonal renters. But then you guys had those storms that hit, and Jessica called my mother-in-law to tell her that things needed to be repaired before they rented again. That all happened about the same time as Barrett's death and well, my in-laws weren't in the right frame of mind to oversee anything. Even from a distance." She released a sigh. "All in all, it doesn't look like too much in the way of real damage, but there are a lot of minor repairs to be done, and the whole house—inside and out—needs painting. I'm planning to paint the inside after Ben starts school, but the outside? *Way* outside of my pay grade." She laughed lightly. "Do you do that?"

"I do a little bit of everything," he said. "My crew and I work a five-day week, and I moonlight on Saturdays. Right now, we're working on a million-dollar house on the beach. But we also have small jobs like replacing a set of steps. It might be twenty steps leading to an upper deck or it might be two steps on a porch." He smiled. "I'm the owner, but I'm also my own secretary-treasurer, accountant, handyman, and part of the clean-up crew."

"Wow. That makes you a *Jake*-of-all-trades," Brooke said.

He laughed, then turned serious. "I can't do everything. I have men on the crew who are much better than me at certain aspects of building. Tim's the best roofer you could find. Marcia can't always hammer a nail in straight, but she can paint a room without leaving a streak or an air bubble. But that's part of owning a business, employing workers with different skills. I'll tell you this, Brooke. I give it my best. I don't scrimp anywhere. I don't get by with cheap materials. I don't put my stamp of approval on a project until I think God would approve. My crew and I have a prayer each morning before we start working. That keeps us where we ought to be."

Maybe she should have a prayer right now, to keep her mind where it ought to be, because she found herself warming to, not just a man, but to a rather good-looking one. And she had no business whatsoever letting a man come into her life and into the life of her boy and his dog and sit there talking like they're close friends.

Forcing herself to look away from the interesting way the light formed a golden gleam in his warm brown eyes, she spoke quickly. "I think I should probably start with nailing down those shingles and repairing the windows."

Jake nodded. "I don't like the idea that the front door lock isn't secure. Let's put that at the top of the list."

"I appreciate that."

"Then I'll be glad to work up an estimate."

"I would appreciate that too," Brooke said.

They sat for a moment in silence, then Jake stood. "If it's all right with you, I'll go ahead and measure the broken windowpanes and stop by tomorrow evening after work and bring you an estimate on those and the roof."

Brooke nodded.

"Good night, then," he said and called goodbye to Ben.

"This is a good trick, huh, Jake?" Ben asked.

Brooke knew Ben was playing with a Tonka truck, filling it with sand, dumping it, making mounds that Taz pawed through, and then beginning again, but it only now dawned upon her what Ben was doing. He was hiding dog food in the mounds, and Taz was finding and eating it.

"It's a good trick if you realize that's his supper. He mustn't have too much food either. The bag tells you how much he should get," Jake told him. "Tell you what, if your mom agrees, when I stop by tomorrow, I'll help you teach Taz how to heel, so you can take him for walks without him taking you for walks."

"Neat," Ben said. "That's okay. Right, Mom?"

"Well, we don't want to take up too much of Mr. Randolph's time."

"I *did* offer." Jake said, glancing at her with a broad smile.

Brooke returned the smile, then quickly brought her attention to Ben. "Time to come in and get cleaned up, Ben. I'll start supper."

Jake said goodbye again and disappeared around the house. Brooke suddenly realized she wasn't apprehensive about him anymore.

Only about herself.

~ ~ ~

On the drive home, Jake denounced himself for the mistakes he'd made with Brooke Haddon. No wonder she thought he had ulterior motives. Would an electrician or a telephone repairman sit down beside her on the step? Would a plumber? He thought not.

Then why in Sam Hill had he done it? He'd never done that with any of his other female customers. He'd always kept a professional distance. But with her, he was going overboard, and sometimes going overboard indicated you just might sink. What had happened to his good sense?

Maybe Gracie could tell him.

After he ate the supper Gracie had kept in the fridge and then microwaved for him, Jake sat on the top step of the back porch while Gracie sat in a rocking chair, and the boys played on the swing set. He told his sister he'd seen Brooke Haddon and Ben that evening.

"I'm behaving as if she's my friend, Gracie. I know you two hit it off right away, and it's not that way between me and Mrs. Haddon." He snorted. "See. She hasn't even asked me to call her by her first name. This is a business proposition, and I'm behaving like it's something personal."

"Maybe it's because you want it to be, Jake," she said. "I mean, Brooke has some emotional problems to deal with, but otherwise, she's a strong woman. She has looks, guts, maternal instinct, and faith in God."

Jake agreed. Brooke had sun-streaked, golden blond hair and eyes that changed with the color of her clothes, or the grass, or the sky. She had full lips with a little dimple at one corner of her mouth when she smiled. She had a musical laugh and an angelic expression on her face when she looked at her son. He couldn't deny it when Gracie added, "And Jake, you're a man who hasn't met a woman who appealed to you since Meagan."

Jake gave a short laugh. "I wouldn't go that far," he said. "A lot of women appeal to me, but I've known I can't get involved. I can't even tell them the truth about myself. I know we talked about this before. When I told the truth to Meagan, she turned and ran the other way, so to speak. She didn't trust me anymore."

He picked up a stick and poked at the dirt in front of the step. "Brooke mistrusted me from the first time I pulled up in that truck and offered my services."

"That's because her emotions are in a turmoil, Jake. It's only been a year since her husband's death, and the memory is still part of her life, just as Leo's will always be a part of ours. That's inescapable. Brooke shared her husband's dream. Then when she got pregnant, he wanted her to choose. She chose the unborn baby. She was no longer his dream girl. They drifted apart. His goal was ambition and power. Hers was family life and her son. Then Brooke's husband was unfaithful. Now he's dead. I think it's easier for me to be judgmental about my husband than for her. It's not considered proper to condemn a dead man."

Jake turned and gazed at his sister. "I didn't know all that."

"Of course not," Gracie replied. "We women who've been trampled by a man have to put on a front of having it all together, as if we don't need a man."

Jake thought he knew his sister. But it seemed he learned new things about her every day. She was a strong woman, in many ways stronger than him, although she was younger. She'd grown in many ways since she and Leo had separated. Her faith in herself had been restored. Her faith in God had grown. And yet she was admitting she would like to have a man in her life, not just an older brother. Of course she would. He'd just accepted her lifestyle and his . . . until now.

"She's doing a great job with Ben," he said.

"It's not easy, Jake. I'd be lost without you."

"You'd make it."

"Not as well without you," she said softly. "So, she's going to let you make repairs."

He grinned. "Seems that way."

"You like her, Jake. Don't deny it."

"Very much," he admitted. "But you know I'm in no position to even think about going beyond friendship with a woman."

"Jake," she said, surprised, "you told me the business was going well, and besides buying that property, you're saving and—"

"I'm not talking financially, Gracie. Living here has enabled me to save almost all my profits."

"Ha," she exclaimed. "Your living here has been a lifesaver for me and the boys, Jake. In more ways than financially."

He laughed lightly. "Don't you think we've complimented each other enough for one day?"

Her shoulder lifted in a light shrug. "Well, I probably don't tell you enough how much I appreciate you."

"Mutual admiration society," he said, then grinned and stared into the distance. His brow furrowed.

"What is it, Jake?"

He sighed heavily. "You know I can't consider anything beyond friendship, Gracie."

"Of course you can, Jake. Someday the right woman will understand—"

"Meagan didn't," he interrupted.

"Meagan wasn't the right woman."

"I know that now," Jake said, "but at the time I thought she was. After all we'd meant to each other, it seems she didn't even know me." *But she did know me*, Jake corrected himself silently. *She knew, and she still didn't believe me.*

"Brooke is not Meagan," Gracie reminded him. "She has a lot more maturity and character than your former fiancée."

"But a lot less trust," he said. "Meagan trusted me at the beginning. Brooke's mistrust was immediate."

"You said it went well tonight."

"Yes. But I should have checked out the repairs she wanted done, assessed the needs, and suggested some of my crew or the volunteers from the church. Instead, I offered myself several nights after work and Saturday, for as long as needed. I play with her boy. I train her dog. I sit beside her on the back step without invitation. I sit on the church pew with her." He sighed and shook his head like he'd committed the crime of the century.

"You said you're going back every night after work?"

"Yep. I committed myself."

"And she didn't tell you not to come."

He glanced around, then turned back to stare at the holes he'd made in the dirt. "Maybe I did wrong there too. I told her about my water-basin theory, my spiritual reasons for doing some work without charging for it. Maybe I was playing on her sympathy. It's a little hard to refuse a person when he says he's doing it for the Lord."

"Oh, quit doubting yourself, Jake. I know your intentions are genuine. She will learn that. And I don't think she'd ask you to come back if she didn't believe in you, no matter what you told her."

Both were silent for a while, watching the boys enjoy life without a care in the world except which one could swing the highest. After a long moment, he asked the question that pressed hard on his mind.

"What do you think Brooke will think of me when she learns the truth? Honestly, I wish she didn't have to know. And yet, I want her to know. What do I do?"

Usually, she would advise him on almost any subject. But this time was different.

"I can't answer that, Jake. It's a decision only you can make."

He knew that. To blurt out the truth about his past would imply to Brooke that he thought there was, or could be, something personal between them. Wouldn't that be the height of presumption on his part? Shouldn't he first try to discover if there could be a personal relationship?

Knowing Gracie couldn't begin to answer his question, he muttered, "When is the right time to tell another person about your past? How much do you tell? When does withholding information become lying?"

Gracie smiled at him. "Stop overthinking this, brother. If that time comes, you'll know it. Besides, you're *friends,* right?"

Thirteen

When Jake came to start on the agreed-upon repairs for the cottage, he brought Gracie's boys. Brooke and Ben went out to greet them and the boys immediately ran around back with Ben to play with Taz.

"Thought you might want this," Jake said, lifting a wire cage out of the truck bed. Brooke eyed the cage skeptically.

"It's a crate for Taz," he explained, realizing she wasn't pleased.

"You mean . . . lock him up?"

"A dog doesn't look at it that way," Jake explained. "It's a home for a dog. A place where it can feel protected. You just need to teach him to go home. Get some puppy food, and I'll show you."

Brooke went through the house to get the puppy food and took a handful out to Jake. He had placed the crate on the ground and began to demonstrate how to teach the puppy.

"Go home," he said and tossed a piece of dog food into the crate. Taz ran in, chomped on the piece of food while looking at them with his soulful, black eyes in that werewolf face, then ran out. Jake repeated the exercise a couple more times, then addressed Ben. "Do that a few times during the day and at night when it's bedtime. He'll soon learn to *go home* whenever you say the words."

Brooke tried to ignore the thoughts that came into her mind. How many times Barrett had said, "Don't run . . . don't yell so loud . . . don't track dirt in the house . . . no, you can't play in the rain . . . no, I can't play with you right now." All his disciplinary words had been harsh instead of loving.

How different. This man was taking time to teach a little boy how to train a dog. How gratifying to watch a man interact with a child instead of just making demands. Not that she should compare

Barrett to Jake or vice versa. Besides, Barrett hadn't been abusive, just preoccupied with being a politician. But was it any less important being a carpenter?

Her next thought startled her. Jesus had been a carpenter! Had He done work for people without pay to show His generosity? Had He been helpful like Jake? Had He stopped to speak to little children before tackling His work?

An overwhelming urge to be kind to Jake swept over her. She could think of no reason whatsoever not to accept him as a friend, or at least as a friend of her son.

"Jake," she said and saw the light of surprise in his eyes before it quickly disappeared. An incredible look of pleasure settled on his face. Was that because she had called him by his first name? Perhaps. He obviously tried to have people like him and accept him as a Christian witness. Did she not want the same? Hadn't she spent many years feeling that she was not completely accepted by Barrett or his family, and didn't she wonder about his friends?

She smiled. "Thanks for the crate and for teaching Taz to sit and lie down," she said. "He's doing that for me *and* Ben. Watch." Brooke reached into the bag for a few pieces of dog food. "Taz, sit," she commanded, holding the piece of food at his nose, and moving it slightly over the puppy's head so he'd sit back.

They burst out laughing. Taz sat all right—right into his water bowl. And he stayed there.

Brooke gave him the dog food, patted him on the head, said, "Good boy," then turned an impish glance at Jake. She shrugged a shoulder. "Well, so now he has his own private bathtub."

∽ ∽ ∽

The ice was broken. Or at least it had begun to thaw from around Brooke's heart. The cottage was becoming transformed from a broken-down, neglected honeymoon cottage to a renovated, restored home for her and Ben.

On weekday evenings after work, Jake came and finished nailing down the roof shingles, cleaned out the gutters, tightened them against the house, and applied a coat of primer to the repaired corner.

On Saturday, he arrived early to scrape, patch, and paint the outside of the house, getting it and the front and back porches into shape. Gracie came by to help Brooke put up new shelves in Ben's room. The walls had not needed to be repainted. Brooke had simply given them a basic washing.

Taz really loved the newspapers spotted with paint and tried to chew them up. "Ben, tell Taz to go to his crate," she said.

"Taz, go home," Ben commanded and Taz promptly scrambled out.

Brooke turned to Gracie, saying proudly, "It's beginning to look like a boy's room."

Gracie shook her head, her brow making a furrow above her nose. "Not yet," she said. "You need to toss a shoe under the bed to join the dust bunnies, make sure the bed's not made, open the bureau drawers, scatter toys all over the floor, sprinkle dirt—preferably wet—in several places, scribble a little crayon on the wall, and *then* you'll have yourself the ideal boy's room."

By the time Gracie finished, Brooke was laughing. What a joy her new friend was. She mentally thanked God for Gracie's friendship. How rejuvenating to be reminded that she and her son didn't have to be perfect and that she didn't have to expect such behavior from Ben. A house to live in was much more important than a house to look at.

Gracie took her boys and Ben along with Taz to their house so Brooke could finish up Ben's room uninterrupted. She hung the blue valances, put the matching spread on the bed, topped it with two red-and-white pillow cushions, dragged the box of toys out of the closet, neatly stacked some toys along with books on the new shelves, and then mopped the hardwood floor. As soon as the floor dried, she dragged in his freshly vacuumed throw rug. Perfect! A wonderful room for a little boy to grow up in.

Around five o'clock, when Jake had finished replacing broken rails in the banister, Gracie returned bearing pizza.

At Brooke's insistence, they all came in to look at Ben's room and to exclaim over the new look before going out back to eat pizza. Brooke spread a blanket on the ground for the boys to sit on while they ate, trying to keep their pizza out of the range of Taz's mouth. Finally, Ben got puppy food and ordered Taz to go home, which he did.

Brooke, Gracie, and Jake sat in kitchen chairs on the back porch. When Jake went around the house to clean up from his repairs and put his tools in his truck, Gracie left with her boys, saying they all had to have baths and get to bed early since tomorrow was Sunday. Then, when Jake was about ready to leave, Brooke went out to say goodbye.

Ben stood looking up at Jake. "You wanna teach Taz some more tricks?" he asked.

Taz tugged on the bottom of Jake's jeans, as if he, too, didn't want Jake to go. Brooke realized then that she felt a little lonely each evening when he went home.

"He's been here all day, Ben," Brooke said with an apologetic look toward Jake.

"I don't mind, if you don't," Jake said.

She shook her head. "I don't."

Jake smiled broadly, as if he were in no hurry to go. He commanded Taz to sit, which he did, while looking up soulfully, waiting for his food. Jake simply patted him on the head and said, "Good boy."

Taz continued to sit, giving the impression he preferred food to a pat.

"If you have a leash, we can take him for a walk and teach him to heel," Jake told Ben, which sent the boy off like a flash.

"It might seem cruel to keep Taz on a leash," Jake said. "But it's best for him when you first begin to teach him. This is a smart dog. And he's strong-willed. Before long, he'll try to take over as the leader of the pack. If you tell him to sit and he wanders off, you've lost it. Keep him on a leash when training. He'll learn the commands and obey them after he's off the leash. Also, when you take him for a walk, keep him on the leash."

Brooke soon learned what he meant by a strong-willed puppy.

They took Taz for a walk along a nearby bicycle path that ran along through the trees. Jake was teaching her how to make him heel as they walked the dog. It wasn't too hard for Ben, since he was closer to the ground than Brooke, which meant he was closer to the dog's mouth with the food.

Jake did all right at keeping Taz at his left heel while reaching over, behind his left leg, with an occasional piece of dog food.

When Brooke tried it, she felt awkward holding the leash with her left hand while stooping down and reaching across herself with a bite of rewarding food.

More awkward than that was Ben's enthusiastic blurt of, "We look just like a family, don't we, Mom?"

Flustered, she looked away. When she did, she straightened from her cramped, sideways, leaning-over position. Her hand moved around in front of her, and Taz followed it, coming after the food. He came across the front of her legs, then ran around to the other side, wrapping the leash around her legs. Then he began to pull on the leash, tightening its hold on her.

"Oh, yes, we're like a family," Brooke spouted, trying to keep her balance. "The man and boy laugh at the woman who gets tied up by a dog." She struggled to get a piece of dog food in Taz's mouth so that he would stay still, hoping she could keep her balance. "Help me!"

Jake and Ben grinned at each other, but Jake came over, stood for an instant very close, his warm twinkling eyes looking into her irate ones for a long moment. He took the leash from her hand, then unwrapped her and gave the leash to Ben.

"Food," he said, and Brooke gladly slapped her handful of food into his outstretched hand.

"I can do it," Ben said confidently.

Jake gave her a sly glance. "Got all tied up in knots, huh?"

She gave him a warning look, then watched as Ben executed the command and reward quite well before sighing into her own thoughts. Yes, she was tied up in knots in more ways than one and for many reasons. Ben had said they looked like a family. Maybe someday she could put the past behind her and get her life straightened out enough to consider something like that. She wanted it to be right next time. When she thought about it or when it entered her mind unbidden, the ideal man began to look suspiciously like Jake Randolph.

Each evening during the following week, Jake painted the front porch and the shutters a deep gray. On Saturday he brought two crew members and a retired house painter from church who volunteered to help singles and by that evening the cottage looked like a new house.

After all the men except Jake left, Brooke and Ben stood with him, surveying their handiwork.

"Cool," Ben exclaimed.

"Oh, Jake, it is beautiful," Brooke said, looking at the soft, dove gray cottage with its darker trim and gleaming white banister. It didn't look like a broken-down cottage anymore. It had become a rejuvenated home for a mother and her son. "I think my next step will be to get shrubs and plant flowers below the banister to give it a more finished look," she added. "Do you have any suggestions?"

"We're clearing land around the church where a new conference center and housing is being built. There are some azaleas that we have to take out and have permission to give away. I can bring several of those," he offered.

"That would be perfect," she said. "And I'll get some pansies. We'll just have a riot of color." She could almost see the finished product. A background of blooming azaleas, or just the green leaves, bordered by splashes of yellow, maroon, purple, blue, and white. Yes, it was beginning to shape up and she was beginning to enjoy the present enough to look ahead with anticipation, instead of dwelling on the past.

Sunday at church proved that to her more strongly.

Since that first Sunday, Gracie and her boys always saved room in their pew for Brooke and Ben. Jake usually sat at the end of the pew, next to Alex. This Sunday, at the end of the worship service, the congregation took communion. The pastor related the meaning of the

Lord's Supper and reminded the listeners that Jesus died to take away the sins of the world.

Brooke felt that she was rededicating herself once again, making a new commitment to live closer to the Lord as she partook, but she had to tell Ben he couldn't. Her son was close to six years old. She must make as her first priority Ben's spiritual training. If she succeeded in every area but failed to clearly teach God's love for him and the salvation that was offered through Jesus, then she would fail as a parent.

With determination and a feeling of well-being, Brooke joined in with the others and was able to hear Jake's baritone voice as they sang the closing song. Moments later, she hummed as she leaned to pick up her Bible and purse from underneath the pew in front of her. She straightened up and turned toward Ben, but her glance met Jake's gaze. Their eyes held for a moment. He smiled in a way that had begun to affect her heart in unexpected ways.

How could anyone not respect him? Admire him? Want to be around him?

Brooke brushed at her cheek as if to erase the warmth she felt rising to her face. She knew where her thoughts were heading. How could she not respect and admire Jake, want to be around him, and want to love him. Love? Yes, love. That's where her thoughts had gone. But she erased them as quickly as they had come. She shook her head and lowered her gaze to Ben.

"You have all your papers?" she asked, reminding herself that other "ties that bind" had for a long time held a negative connotation in her life.

Despite her fears, however, was her heart binding with Jake's? And much as she might try to dismiss her feelings as Christian love, if she were honest, didn't they hold something else as well?

Fourteen

Jake had heard Gracie complain that during her last months of pregnancy, time had dragged interminably, almost stopped. That's what time seemed to be doing for him. He kept busy and looked forward to the evenings and Saturdays he could spend at Brooke's, and ever-present on his mind was that he had four months and three weeks to go until his probation was over. Then it was four months, two weeks. Four months, one week. Four months.

But the time dragged. Could he keep letting his feelings grow for Brooke without telling her the truth of his past? Shouldn't he find out if she thought there was a chance for them together? Suppose she said there was a chance and she suggested they go to Indiana so she could introduce him to her parents? This was certainly within the realm of reality. He'd barely thought the word *love* much less said it before Meagan insisted that he meet her father and mother.

Of course, then there had been no issues. He could come and go as he pleased. Now? Now he'd have to say, "Sorry. I wouldn't be allowed to go out of state just to meet someone's parents." Now what kind of relationship could be built on that kind of information?

There was no denying to Brooke's mind that Jake had become, to say the least, a friend. She was not indifferent to him and could not pretend so. But a man like him deserved a woman who was as openly committed to the Lord as he, and she wasn't sure she was there. Yet. She determined to follow through with her renewed dedication to God.

She also decided that Ben should memorize some basic verses from the Bible. The first and most important to her was John 3:16.

She had him repeat each phrase every morning, and by the end of the week, it should be a part of him. To her delight, he said it verbatim by Wednesday morning.

This was also the morning she decided it was time to get her body in shape. She wasn't overweight by any stretch of the word, but she knew her body wasn't toned the way it should be. She would give water aerobics a try. She, Ben, and Taz showed up at Gracie's before ten a.m.

Gracie and the boys were delighted to see them. As soon as the children gathered at the side of the pool, Ben asked, "Hey, you guys want to hear me say John 3:16?"

"I do," Aiden said, and they all stood quietly while Ben recited it.

"For God so loved the world, that he gave his only begotten Son, that whosoever believeth in him should not perish, but have everlasting life."

Alex tousled Ben's hair like Brooke had seen Jake do. "That's really good, Ben," he said. He looked over and grinned at his mother, who nodded her approval.

Other women began to arrive. Brooke met a middle-aged neighbor of Gracie's and her friend; a fourth-grade schoolteacher; two women who wanted to lose a few pounds they said, become more fit; a writer who said she needed the exercise since she sat at her computer from six a.m. until time for aerobics, pausing only for a quick breakfast; an older woman; and two single moms who shared an apartment. One worked the second shift as a nurse and the other worked as a waitress. The nurse brought her two daughters, ages six and four, and the other woman brought her daughter, age eight.

Alex drew a hopscotch outline on the concrete with sidewalk chalk, and the children began to play, except for the four-year-old girl who wanted to swing. Her six-year-old sister had to keep running over to push her little sister. All of the children had to be careful not to stumble over Taz who liked to pick up the pebble and take it away, which sent the children into a fit of giggles.

"It's so good to see children doing something other than sticking their noses into a cell phone or iPad," the older woman said. "And instead playing a game I used to play with my friends, sometimes all day long."

Brooke had to agree, even though there were times she handed her phone over to Ben just to keep him occupied. She told herself that some of the games were good for him. After all, when he went to school, he'd have to know how to navigate a computer. But her maternal instincts also had to work overtime to protect him . . . and at this stage of their lives, she didn't have that kind of extra time.

The women were ready to get into the pool by ten o'clock. Brooke was not surprised at Gracie's expertise. She called, "Straight-leg kick while moving the opposite arm toward the opposite leg." The worst thing about it was seeing that the children, mimicking their mothers, did the exercises with such ease. To Brooke's relief, they soon became bored with that and returned to their own games.

While exercising, the women talked about themselves between listening to Gracie give commands. The singles talked about their difficulties, the older woman about her age, and those who needed to lose a few pounds, about how this was so much better than running for miles, especially when the island's humidity picked up.

"Fanny kick while pushing the water toward yourself. Heel kick behind and touch the heel with the opposite hand, then heel kick in front," Gracie commanded. "Leap frog" was next, and Brooke could feel her body moving in ways she hadn't imagined. But she could also tell that wet exercise was much more pleasant than dry exercise.

They ran in the water, then checked their pulses. Brooke's heartbeat had definitely accelerated by the third round. The toning part was what she liked best, wrapping her arms around a noodle to keep herself afloat and working the leg and tummy muscles. After a cool-down of stretching and finally hugging themselves while taking deep breaths and exhaling, Brooke felt like every muscle in her body had been massaged—and it felt great.

After an hour, the women dried off. Some slipped on T-shirts over their suits, and some left in their suits with a towel slung around their shoulders.

"Stay awhile," Gracie said to Brooke as she was drying off.

After the others left, Gracie invited Brooke and Ben to lunch, which turned out to be peanut butter and banana sandwiches. Carrot sticks.

Juice for the children. Brooke and Gracie had lemonade with lunch and, after lunch, went out onto the porch with tall glasses of sweet iced tea.

"This is really a nice place, Gracie," Brooke complimented. She laughed.

Gracie nodded. "Thanks to my parents, I have it. Jake and I were raised here. My parents bought it years ago before the island was built up, so they got it for a real bargain. Then they built a new house in Bluffton and rented this out to me and Leo." She lifted her eyes and brows toward heaven. "That's my ex-husband. You wanna hear about a real skunk?"

Brooke grinned and nodded. She really did. She wanted to know how Gracie could be so warm, friendly, and well-adjusted with all her responsibilities.

"Well, it's like this," Gracie began. "Leo was raised on the golf course. When he was younger, he worked as a caddy for a famous golfer, so he was away on the circuit almost all the time." She groaned. "He *said* he wanted a big family, but he must have meant he wanted *me* to have a big family while he traveled." Gracie looked away from Brooke for a moment, then back again. "I had tried to understand. After all, he was our meal ticket. *A man's gotta work* and all that. But it started to seem that he was away when he . . . when he should have been home."

Gracie chewed on her bottom lip for a moment before adding, "So then one day, Leo *claimed* it wasn't fair to me and the boys to wait for him to come home. In all honesty, the boys love their father, but they don't really seem to know him. When Aiden was a baby, he cried every time Leo came near him because he didn't know his dad." Another sigh followed. "So, Leo became a golf instructor for a while, which he could have stayed with if he'd wanted to make a living and take care of a family. But, you know, he enjoyed hobnobbing with the pros and decided he wanted to be one of them.

"So, now he's on the golf circuit and making good money," Gracie said. "He pays alimony and child support. That eases his conscience, and the children think it's great that he's a golf pro and sends them presents." She threw up her hands. "That's his way. Make a big splash.

Be noticed. But everyday living with and caring for a family is not part of the picture."

Brooke could understand. "Barrett didn't want to be tied down either," she said. "We were happy . . . for three months.

"Ours was a whirlwind romance. I was in my second year of nurses' training when he returned from law school, ready to become part of a big law firm. When we ran into each other after a couple of years, he was—surprised—I guess you could say at how much I'd changed." She laughed lightly before adding, "What does it say about me that all it took was him calling me a *real beauty* before completely sweeping me off my feet?" She grimaced as she cut her eyes toward Gracie.

"What young woman, or older woman I guess, doesn't want to hear that?"

"Maybe so . . . but anyway, the next thing I knew he was taking me out of my ordinary life and dipping me headfirst into *his* life of grandeur." Brooke rubbed her forehead with her fingertips before continuing, "To the public, I lived a charmed life as the wife of Barrett Haddon—the handsome, young state senator. We went to the governor's mansion and attended political fund-raising dinners. And at every event, photographs were taken and used to publicize Barrett with his model-perfect wife who was never anything but dressed to the nines and made-up to look like she belonged on the cover of *Vogue* or *Elle*. Social media ate us up, posting and reposting. Seriously, Gracie, it was like—I don't know—to reach a certain level you *had* to have your picture taken with Barrett and me." Brooke shook her head in disdain.

"But our private life was entirely different." She took in a deep breath through her nose and released it slowly between pursed lips. "Barrett didn't want a child so soon in his career. Nor did he want a wife who refused to leave her son with a nanny and go on the campaign trail with him. At one point, I mentioned that I wanted to return to nurses' training, and he nearly busted a blood vessel." Tears stung her eyes and she brushed them away. "The more public acceptance Barrett received, the worse he became at home. He was verbally abusive, unfaithful, controlling, and"—Brooke caught her breath—"before I knew it, he had completely and utterly destroyed my self-esteem and he all but ignored his son. Our marriage was over a long time ago, but . . ." Again she looked at Gracie, this time more fully. "But, a year ago, when I walked away from Barrett's funeral, I knew his lover had just been buried on the other side of town. He was with her—or she with him—when they ran into a concrete median strip. The car flipped over, and the gasoline tank exploded. Tests proved their blood-alcohol content was above the legal limit."

Brooke turned her face away from Gracie's shocked expression. "Still, I cried, and I grieved, not just because the man I'd promised my life to was dead, but for six years of a failing marriage, for a son without a father . . . and for truth that will have to be told someday."

Gracie touched her hand lightly with her own. "Jake has helped me regain some of my self-esteem," she admitted. "But I don't know if I will ever shake the feeling of failure and guilt. God is healing me, but it's not easy losing a husband and knowing your children have lost a father." She raised her voice on the next words. "Even if he was a skunk."

"At least I have a roof over my head," Brooke said, realizing she was more blessed than many. "And Barrett's parents said to let them know if we need anything, but the way they looked at me at the funeral, I knew they blamed me for their son's death. If I had been the kind of wife I should have been, Barrett wouldn't have gone to another woman. He wouldn't have been drinking that night. They met me when I was young and fit and my hair and makeup were the most important thing. You know what I mean?"

Gracie chuckled. "I *may* be able to remember those days."

Brooke's smile lasted only a moment. "Thing is, that wasn't the real me at all. I'm really just a small-town girl with basic values." She sighed. "At least I used to be. The more I needed God in my life, the more I pulled away from Him."

"I know exactly what you mean. Not that the Lord causes them, but He sure can use our failures to get our attention. When you take a good long look at what's important in life, you discover it's not all those things the world can provide. Basically, the things God provides, like purpose and meaning and love, are the things that last."

Brooke nodded. "I was raised to know those things. But it was head knowledge only. I'm realizing how important family life is." She smiled more fully. "And friends. You have helped me so much, Gracie, just by being a friend. And Jake's attitude about serving others is admirable. I'd like to volunteer to do what I can to help. I know I haven't been to their nightly meetings yet, but maybe I could help with the single moms some way." She shrugged. "If nothing else, I can identify with them."

"Ah, perfect," Gracie exclaimed. "We can always use help there. As a matter of fact, Carleigh is moving into her own place and could use some help with freshening the place up and unpacking boxes."

"Ben's teacher?"

"That's the one."

"Oh, she's nice," Brooke said. "I'd love to do what I can to help."

"Great. Hers is one of the older homes on the island and, even though the owners *say* they had it cleaned, Carleigh says it still needs some work. Let's go tomorrow and see what we can do to help."

Brooke threw back her head and laughed.

"What's so funny, girl?" Gracie wanted to know.

"I was just thinking. In Indiana, I had my own housekeeper. Now, I get a kick out of thinking about going to Carleigh's and cleaning her house when mine is still under construction."

"If I waited until I had my own life straightened out before I helped another person, I'd never get anything done."

Brooke studied her for a moment, then asked seriously, "Is that what makes you so happy, Gracie? Helping others?"

"That's part of it. But it started when I decided I couldn't handle my own life and gave it to the Lord. I began to use His Word as my road map instead of making up my own. It works. And the more I try to give of myself without expecting anything in return, the blessings just come. Like with you, Brooke. I was just trying to be friendly and let you know that Jake wasn't some kind of ogre, and I'm ending up with a strong friendship between us." She looked over at Brooke. "You don't still think Jake's an ogre, do you?"

"Of course not," she said. "He's a good worker and a fine Christian." Brooke stood quickly, lest her face reveal what she felt in her heart. "Now, I'd better go and buy some sandwich makings if we're going 'foot washing' tomorrow."

~ ~ ~

When they arrived at Carleigh's the next day, Brooke reprimanded herself a dozen times. All went well at first, and Carleigh was so grateful for the visit, the lunch, and the offers to help. And then she began telling Gracie how great Jake was.

"Jake brought me those azaleas," she said, taking them out front to show them. "He even planted them."

Jake had told Brooke he was helping clear land at the church for a new center to be built and he'd offered to bring her some azaleas that the church didn't want. But he hadn't brought *her* bushes yet. Her body twitched with jealousy, which resulted in a mental kick in the pants. How could she possibly be envious of Carleigh—who was clearly smitten with Jake—when she didn't even want a man in her life?

Or did she?

Maybe it was just that Carleigh seemed to be harping on the same subject. Okay, so Jake had come by her place several evenings after work, and he had torn out the bottom of the cabinet beneath the sink where pipes had leaked and rotted out the wood. And he was going to replace the whole blessed thing. And he was going to do it free of charge.

Later, with her adrenaline flowing and trying to control her attitude, Brooke scrubbed the inside and outside of the kitchen cabinets that were in reasonable shape and would be fine for use if the shelves were covered with shelf paper. With Gracie being as much a workaholic as Jake, the kitchen took shape within a few hours while the boys and Carleigh's seven-year-old daughter played out back. The windows sparkled, the walls were stripped of old, peeling paper, and the ceiling was cleaned.

Gracie talked about patching the holes in the wall so someone could either paint or paper later on.

Carleigh tilted her head. "Jake does that kind of thing, doesn't he?"

"Yep," Gracie said. "But so do I."

Brooke got the strong impression that Carleigh would prefer Jake to do the job.

Well, what did she expect? Had she thought she was the only recipient of Jake's water-basin principle?

"What's wrong with me?" she asked her reflection as she washed up in the bathroom. "And where's *my* Christian spirit?" She was supposed to be feeling good about herself, not feeling like the fifth wheel on an old car.

Fifteen

Jake sat at his sister's kitchen table, wolfing down another late supper. "Does she ever mention me?" he asked, hoping his question sounded casual enough. "I mean my work or anything?"

"Who?"

Jake gave her a hard look. "Who were we talking about?"

Gracie wrinkled her brow, as if trying to think. "Brooke and Carleigh?"

"Exactly," he said, knowing his sister was playing games with him. "You were telling me about y'all's visit to Carleigh's."

"Oh, yes," she said. "She talked about you almost the whole time."

Jake continued chewing as he stared at Gracie. This wasn't funny. But that silly little grin on her face indicated that she thought it was.

"Okay," she said. "Carleigh did. She praised you for bringing the azaleas, planting them, repairing the cabinets—free of charge." Gracie lifted her brow. "Brooke didn't say a word."

Jake pushed his plate away and sighed. Now, how was he supposed to handle this? How could he keep Brooke from thinking he was interested in another woman, without letting her know he was interested in her? Could he act uninterested for three more months, then tell her it was all some kind of waiting game?

"I've sure got myself in a mess," he ground out.

Gracie gently rested her hand on his arm. "Just tell her how you feel, Jake," she said softly.

He didn't have to ask if she meant Carleigh or Brooke. Jake also knew he couldn't just tell her how he felt. He'd have to reveal his past first. But before doing that, he had to have some indication she could care about him in a personal way. He couldn't just blurt out, "Hey, look, I've sinned, and you need to know it. I spent time in prison where I got my life on track with God. Now I'm a practicing Christian, so accept me."

No, he knew it wasn't that easy. It hadn't been easy to admit to himself he'd been a deliberate sinner, even though his time in prison wasn't because of anything he'd done. It was harder admitting it to a woman he cared about. But it had to be done if he expected to have any kind of close relationship with Brooke.

First, however, he'd have to have some indication she was ready for a relationship. And if so, with him. And too, how could he expect a classy, beautiful woman like her to give him the time of day? She'd been nice to him lately, but was it because of himself, or because he was her repairman? Or because he was Gracie's brother? She didn't have anything against him, but did that mean she had anything for him?

Didn't he have to make sure she knew and trusted him? After all, they hadn't known each other very long. She was trying to get a handle on her life. Gracie had needed a couple of years after Leo left before she could shake her bitterness and turn it over to the Lord. Even then, she had to take baby steps before she learned to walk through life with joy and confidence. Now, Gracie was running with the kind of endurance the Good Book spoke about.

The best he could do for now was to simply let Brooke get to know him better. He'd taken her some nice azaleas and he planted them. He'd like to tell her that the reason he'd gone to Carleigh's on weekdays and Brooke's on Saturday was because he had more hours to spend with Brooke if he went on Saturday, but he couldn't blurt that out. So, he got on his hands and knees beside her in the flower beds.

He admitted he loved the way she dug her hands into the rich soil, not once mentioning the dirt getting under her fingernails. She just laughed and said, "My in-laws' gardener did all the planting and landscaping at our house in Indiana. Barrett would have never, ever allowed me this little bit of creative digging." She shrugged as if saying such a thing was common.

He wouldn't allow her? What *did* that mean?

"But I love doing this," she said, bringing his thoughts back. "You know what I mean? Getting my hands in the dirt. Getting down to, well, *earth*, I guess you'd call it."

Jake's heart thumped fast against his chest as he looked at her face so close to his. She had a little smudge of dirt on her cheek, which made her even more appealing. He warned himself that it was the dirt that put the joyful look on her face, not him.

So he discussed the plants. "The pansies like acidic soil," he said, pushing the dirt around them. "So do azaleas. They'll thrive well together." *As we could*, he added silently, hoping he hadn't blurted that out.

He liked the way she looked at him with appreciation after they stepped away from the beds, which had turned out better than he'd hoped. She gave him the same gratitude when he pruned off the dead and damaged leaf stalks from the trunks of the palms, which gave them a tidy, healthy look. He could easily have told her how much he enjoyed working on her household projects, asking her opinion, talking to Ben, training Taz. All that had begun to mean more to him than he could have imagined.

She was even receptive to his suggestion when he said, "You might want to consider putting a fence out back. Taz is getting mighty big, and he'll be shedding a lot of that long hair before long."

She gave him a wry glance. "He's already passed the twenty-pound mark by six pounds." Shaking her head, she added, "That was supposed to be our little miniature puppy. But you're right, I'm already finding fur everywhere. I'm definitely going to have to consider a fence."

It took another week and all day on Saturday for him to take care of the living room carpet, which they thought only needed a good shampooing. But when he'd looked under one corner of the carpet, he discovered a beautiful hardwood floor. He suggested getting rid of the carpet and refinishing the floor. "I can strip it down pretty easily, then stain it and add a coat or two of polyurethane. It'll look amazing."

And, wonder of wonders, Brooke agreed.

"I'm not the greatest cook in the world," Brooke said the afternoon he began work on the floor, "but I fixed enough supper for all of us if you'd like to join us."

As they ate, the conversation centered around the repairs, Ben, and Taz. Jake couldn't imagine that anyone would not love that little boy, with such winning ways, and even the werewolf-looking puppy who sat with big, black eyes looking soulfully from one to the other, hoping for people food, which Ben couldn't resist sneaking to him.

Yes, Jake decided. The time had come to find some answers for himself.

Gracie presented the opportunity when she suggested they all go to Harbour Town on Saturday, instead of working. Telling himself not to be apprehensive about it, Jake broached the subject with Brooke after he finished working on her floor Friday night.

He spoke as casually as he could. "Um, Gracie and me and the boys are going to Harbour Town tomorrow. Gracie wanted to do some shopping, and I plan to take the boys on a boat ride to watch the dolphins. Would you and Ben like to go along?"

Brooke chewed on her lower lip before saying, "We wouldn't want to impose."

He smiled. "I asked you," he said. "And Gracie is going to call you. So if you want, just save your answer until Gracie calls." He raised a hand in parting. "Night, Brooke. I'll run around and say goodbye to Ben before I go."

"Thanks for the invitation," she called after him as he hastened around the corner of the house.

Early Saturday, Gracie and her boys picked Brooke and Ben up in her van while Jake drove alone in his truck. While Gracie and Brooke sat in the front seats smiling, Gracie's sons filled Ben in on all they would see, telling him in high octaves that he would see the dolphins jump clear into, maybe right into, the boat. As they neared the harbor, Brooke turned in her seat as Ben's wide eyes took in all the yachts, sailboats, and fishing charters docked there.

Brooke was most fascinated by people sitting in rocking chairs, looking out across a sea of red geraniums and live oaks, while others walked a few feet below along the walkway between the shops where baskets laden with brilliant, red geraniums hung from the awnings, and the harbor.

"The most famous attraction here," Gracie said, after Jake and the boys had left on the boat, "is the candy-striped lighthouse. There's a great gift shop at the top. But let's start here and work our way around, okay?"

"Sounds good to me," Brooke said, looking around at the quaint area, patterned after a Mediterranean fishing village.

After about two hours of shopping and sightseeing, Gracie suggested that they sit in a couple of the rockers in front of the long row of shops where they could look out at the harbor and wait for Jake and the boys to return for lunch.

"Over there's the famous Liberty Oak tree," Gracie said, pointing. "Sometimes they have live entertainment beneath it." She leaned her head against the back of the rocker and closed her eyes. Then after a few moments of rocking, her eyes flew open and she said, "And, oh my goodness. They have the most spectacular sunsets here."

"This is so peaceful," Brooke said. "I could sit here and rock forever. Oh," she said, looking to her right, "he has the right idea."

Gracie opened her eyes and laughed, looking over at the sculpture of a man sitting on a timber, resting his feet on another timber, his elbows propped on his thighs. He had a sandwich in one hand and a book in another. "The sculpture is called *Out-to-Lunch,"* she told Brooke.

"Mmm. I don't think I've relaxed since I've been here," she said. "I needed this."

"Yep," Gracie agreed. "We should always take time for ourselves. You know what they used to say? Stop to smell the roses?" She looked over at Brooke and grinned. "Or the geraniums." Her smile faded and she grew serious. "You know, Brooke, I really value your friendship. A lot of the single moms think they can't relate to me because I'm not as stressed for money as they are," she admitted. "But we live on alimony and child support and rely on my brother for repairs and plumbing and roofing. I do the water aerobics to make a little money of my own and give myself a feeling of independence and contributing."

"It looks to me like you're contributing double as a parent."

"But the world doesn't always see it our way. Anyhow, I'm planning to take computer and accounting courses after Aiden starts school. When Jake moves out and all the boys are in school, the way Jake's business is booming, I can keep books for Jake and take his calls. And I can do all that at home."

"Jake is moving out?" Brooke asked.

Gracie shrugged. "I expect he will one of these days. He could have moved in with Mom and Dad—um, but I—uh, he moved in with me to help with the kids. Anyway, I mean he will want a place of his own one of these days. You know, marriage and children and all those good things?"

Brooke's heart fluttered at the thought, and it dawned on her how much and how quickly Jake Randolph had invaded her and Ben's lives. And his presence was no longer unwelcome. But was he this way with everyone? Or could he, perhaps, be more serious about Carleigh than he'd let on? "He's getting married?" she asked.

"Oh, no," Gracie said. "I mean, he doesn't have any definite plans."

"But is he dating someone?"

"Not at the moment."

"I would think a fine man like Jake would have married long ago."

Gracie shook her head. "Nope. He's never been married." She stood and gazed out over the water. "About time they returned, I think."

"Are they late?" Brooke said, feeling an instant of concern.

Gracie looked at her watch. "No. It'll be thirty more minutes or so. Let's go get something to drink."

So Gracie deliberately changed the subject from talking about Jake. As they walked past the shops, Gracie kept pointing out items of interest, but Brooke's mind stayed on Jake. Why had Gracie said he had a choice of moving in with his parents or her? And, come to think of it, where had he lived before? Had he lived with someone? Had he lost someone? And why did it seem that Gracie was so open and aboveboard about everything except Jake?

ᔕ ᔕ ᔕ

The boat trip turned out to be a success. Especially for Ben. Just as he'd been promised, he saw dolphins "jump sky-high" and he thought they might even jump into the boat, but they didn't. And he loved his new T-shirt because it had a dolphin on it. He insisted on putting it on right then, tag and all. He intended, he said, to sleep in it that night.

"Jake knows all about alligators," Ben reported. "He said sometime, if you let me, we can go see some."

"We'll see," Brooke answered.

Jake, taking the hint, said they needed to find some lunch for those boys.

"I have an idea," Gracie said. "Why don't we buy some sandwiches and go out for a picnic on the property?"

Brooke had no idea what the property was, but there seemed to be a challenge in Gracie's eyes as she and her brother gave each other a long look before he grinned and said, "Great idea."

As it turned out, the picnic spot was a couple of acres of oceanfront property in a section of fine homes in Sea Pines. Beneath a couple of live oaks dripping with Spanish moss sat a picnic table like the one in Gracie's back yard. The beautifully landscaped land, with its spectacular view of the ocean, boasted its own private walkway leading to the beach.

Brooke knew that three adults with four rowdy boys didn't come to places like this for an outing unless they had a friend who owned it or owned it themselves. "Whose is this?" she asked curiously, looking from Gracie to Jake, while the boys frolicked around the trees, searching for alligators.

Jake's grin said it all, while Gracie spread out the quilt she'd taken from his truck. "I've been buying it for several years," he said. "And as soon as we finish the house we're working on, I'll be close to having it paid off."

Well, then. Jake's business must be doing all right. "It's wonderful," Brooke said.

"Thanks," he answered. "I'm planning to build my own place here."

"I'll bet you've already got the plans," Brooke said and Jake looked at her with a grin. Now she could see why Gracie mentioned his moving out of her house. After it was paid for, he'd probably build. But no matter how beautiful, wouldn't he be lonely . . . alone?

Sixteen

The following Friday evening, Jake announced that he was going to take Gracie's boys out to the lagoon on Saturday to see alligators. With the warmer weather, the gators would be lying in the sun.

"Could Ben come along?" he asked.

Brooke grimaced. "He's wanted to do that since before we came here when an alligator was mentioned, but frankly, that frightens me. You see how active he is. And with four boys for you to watch . . ."

"Don't you know I wouldn't put that boy in danger?" Jake asked with a notable edge in his voice.

She took in a breath and held it as their gazes held. "I know," she said finally. "I'm just overly protective, I guess."

"That's not such a bad thing," he said in a softer tone. "But you can trust me."

She caught her breath for a moment. She had the feeling he was not just talking about with Ben.

She nodded. "I do trust you, Jake."

He smiled. "Good. Then if the gators don't eat us, how about me taking you out to dinner tomorrow evening?"

Strangely, his quip about the gators eating them didn't disturb her nearly as much as his asking her out to dinner.

"Well, I guess you do deserve a good dinner after eating my cooking all week."

"The food was fine," he said. "The company exceptional."

"Well, yeah," she said, trying to hide her unexpected elation, "Ben's a great dinner companion. I assume you're inviting him too?"

"Not this time," he said. "I've already talked to Gracie. He can stay over there. After all, the boys will need to do a lot of gator talk."

Brooke figured that his reason for asking her out without Ben could be to discuss church trips or activities. There were many for children, and she'd already learned that Jake never asked about an outing in front of Ben, instead asking her discreetly when her son wasn't right there. And, too, Gracie could have mentioned to Jake Brooke's intention of getting more involved with singles. Jake could have some possible ways that he wanted to discuss, since he was actively involved—like repairing her house . . . and Carleigh's.

So this wasn't necessarily personal. "Dressy or casual?" she asked, hoping her voice sounded the latter.

"What about Henri's? Anything goes there. From dressy to casual."

Henri's. She and Barrett had gone there on their honeymoon. They had dressed up.

"I'd like to go casual," she said, and Jake nodded.

~ ~ ~

This is casual? Jake asked himself when he came to pick Brooke up. She looked anything but casual, although she wore white capri pants and a sea-green silk blouse that turned her eyes the color of warm summertime. Long brown lashes fringed her eyes, and she'd blushed her lips with a coral tint. Tiny gold hoops gleamed at her ears. He'd seen her dressed stylishly with her hair down to her shoulders at church, but the rest of the week she'd worn jeans or shorts and had pulled her hair back into a ponytail. This evening was different. She'd dressed *for him*. She'd let her hair down for him. She was having dinner with him.

No. No way. There was not a blessed thing casual about their going out for dinner together. This was his first date in three years. For her, it was probably the first since before she married, more than seven years ago. Casual? No.

But was tonight the time for him to reveal his past? His silent prayer was for God's leading on what to say, how to say it, and when to say it. But for now, he wanted nothing to intrude upon this special time. Surely God wouldn't have brought this wonderful woman into his life without reason. Surely. No, God was not cruel.

But on the way to the restaurant, Jake kept the conversation casual by talking about Ben's day with the boys and the gators, which brought several wide smiles and a peal or two of laughter from Brooke.

"Have you been here before?" he asked as he pulled into Henri's parking lot.

She nodded. "Barrett and I came here on our honeymoon."

Jake put the truck in PARK and turned to look at her as she stared toward the building. "We can go somewhere else."

Brooke looked at him and shook her head. "No. The food here is wonderful. You've been before, right?"

"A few times."

Jake opened his door, then went around for Brooke, pleased that she'd waited for him to do so. When they entered and the maître d' greeted them, Jake asked for a table by the windows.

"That can be arranged," the maître d' said, then he led them to a section of two-top tables. On the opposite side of the windows, divided by a low brick wall and brick columns, were long planters filled with lush ferns and vines. Green shutters were pushed aside, revealing the main dining room. The walls, carpeting, and tablecloths were in a subdued maroon and green hue. Dim light glowed from the Tiffany chandeliers, and on each table a candle flickered in a silver goblet, surrounded by a frosted globe.

Jake gave the maître d' a grateful glance when he seated them at a table where they could look out the window into the courtyard.

"Oh, this is nice," Brooke exclaimed, looking out.

In the courtyard, groupings of small cast-iron tables, some for four, some for two, sectioned off by flowering purple and white azalea hedges, sat on fine white gravel. A cocoa palm, with its spiked branches making it as wide as it was tall, was draped with small white lights and flanked by tall palmettos.

"This really is lovely," Brooke said, and Jake smiled.

They ordered the same thing—combination seafood dinner of scallops, shrimp, and flounder. "I'll have mine fried," Brooke said.

Jake laughed as he placed his hand over his chest. "A girl after my heart." Then, to the server, he said, "Same here."

After they'd been served their drinks—they'd both ordered sweet tea—Jake asked if she liked living on the island. "So far, I mean," he added.

Brooke looked down at her glass and ran a finger around the rim, a small reflective smile on her lips.

"What?" Jake asked.

She looked up at him. "I was just thinking that, well, Barrett had never asked how I liked living . . . anywhere. Or being anywhere." She took a sip of her drink before adding, "He could be very romantic and sweet, but the focus of attention never left . . . him. I've tried to rationalize it, you know? The way he was raised—the only son with every opportunity, always expected to achieve."

"Was he . . . was he mean to you?"

"If you're asking if he beat me, no. He was just full of himself." She nodded briefly. "But thank you for asking. Yes, I'm enjoying living on the island, especially now that I'm beginning to understand the island. To use Ben's words, it's *really neat* how the island is shaped like a shoe. So now if someone tells me a store is located in the heel or the toes, I know what they mean."

"And the sole of the shoe," Jake said laughing, "is a twelve-mile beach."

Their conversation continued about the island—mostly about Jake's favorite places to go—and when their food came, shifted. Between bites, Brooke talked about her parents and Jake about his. When they finished eating, neither wanted dessert, so Jake suggested they have coffee in the courtyard and Brooke agreed. They sat at a small cast-iron table, surrounded by the array of azalea hedges. The hot coffee was the perfect balance to an evening with a slight chill in the air. A full silvery moon rose in the deep blue-gray sky, brushed gently by a whisk of cloud like a smudge of cotton candy.

The evening seemed so perfect. They got along well, and he felt there wasn't a pretentious bone in her body, which appealed to him. She smiled at him. Maybe this was a real date after all. He could tell she liked the restaurant, the food, and their walking out into the courtyard.

Brooke reached up and lightly touched a strand of moss hanging from the oaks.

"It's so graceful," she commented. "We don't have Spanish moss in Indiana. How do they get it to hang like that?"

"It isn't Spanish at all," Jake said. "And it has no roots. It's an air plant."

"Is it a parasite?"

"Nope," Jake said. "It just dangles freely, getting its nourishment from the rain and the sun. But the downside is, it attracts little red bugs called chiggers. Believe me, if they get under your skin, you're gonna itch."

Brooke jerked her hand down and grimaced with such drama, Jake laughed, then said, "Would you like to walk on the beach for a while?"

"That would be perfect."

They walked up the timber steps, along the concrete and oyster shell walkway, and onto the boardwalk leading to the beach, passing sea oats, low growing cocoa palms, and tall palmettos.

Jake took off his shoes and rolled up his jeans as best he could while Brooke took off her sandals, cuffed her capris, and spoke of the warm, white sand feeling so good on her feet and between her toes. Then she looked up at the full moon and commented on the beauty of its reflection casting a silver shadow on the blue water. The night was perfect. Just cool enough that he wondered if it might seem natural for him to put his arm around her shoulders or hold her hand.

But did he dare? Maybe he could tell her how he'd come to care for her in such a special way. Surely this night meant more than friendship to her, as it did to him. Maybe this was the time to tell her the truth about himself. But then—

"Barrett and I came here when we were on our honeymoon," she said, which dispelled Jake's thought of holding her hand or putting his arm around her shoulder or turning her to face him and taking her in his arms. But they continued to walk side by side. He stayed to where the tide had receded while she walked along the water's curving edge.

Just as he was thinking he should have taken her somewhere else, she turned her face toward his and spoke to the contrary. "But I'm glad we came here tonight, Jake. I never really appreciated the setting. I was so young and so blinded by love. I'm sure you know what that's like."

Jake looked down to where the sand took on an iridescence under the moonlight and chuckled. "To a degree," he replied. "But I sort of took all this for granted, having grown up here." He didn't elaborate further. He'd never been blindly in love, where everything faded into the background except the object of one's affection. He stole a glance at Brooke. Was he not a little too old, too mature, for such feelings? Obviously not.

Brooke shrugged. "I felt that way even in Indiana, without such perfect scenery as this. In one sense it was wonderful, being blindly in love. But I can't be like that anymore. In a way, it's a loss, but in another way, it's a gain."

How had they gotten on the topic of love? He wasn't sure, but the subject was here and something to be faced realistically. But they were talking about Barrett, were they not? "I suppose human love comes down to what Jesus taught when He said, 'Love your neighbor.' The very vivid lesson is that love is not just a feeling, but an action."

Brooke nodded. "I expected action to follow and believed that the same feelings could never die." She sighed. "There is such a sense of personal failure when marriage doesn't work out."

And then she opened up unexpectedly and told him about her life with Barrett, how she had failed to be the kind of public wife he wanted, and how he had failed to be the homebody she wanted. They weren't suited for each other, she said. They had looked at external appearances and liked what they saw. She had thought his dreams were what she wanted, but after having Ben, her priorities changed. Barrett and his goals were no longer first in her life.

"Maybe it would have been different," she said, "if I had kept God as the center of my life. But instead, I put Barrett there."

Jake waited a moment before saying, "I know exactly what you mean. My life hasn't always been exemplary. In my college days I experimented with just about everything that I shouldn't. I didn't want to be in love, so I played the field, so to speak. It wasn't until I was in my early thirties that I met Meagan when I was working on a summer house for her parents."

They stopped long enough to watch a small flock of birds dart along the water's edge, then run in the direction of the dunes. When they started walking again, Jake told her about having believed he was in love with Meagan. They both were going to church, and although he was a Christian, he did not resist the temptation to engage in a physically intimate relationship, justifying it by saying they were only human, they were consenting adults and they were planning to spend their lives together.

"But those were only excuses to gratify my own desires," he admitted. He paused, looking over at Brooke. "You don't want to hear this kind of thing," he said.

"I do, Jake," she said softly. "If you want to tell me."

He didn't want to tell her. But he knew it was the only honest thing to do if their relationship was to grow. She put a lot of stock in honesty. After a long sigh, he admitted the relationship was based primarily on the physical. Or maybe it was their concentration on the physical that kept them from getting to know each other fully. "After about two years, the relationship ended."

"You must have loved her very much," Brooke said.

"I suppose I did," he said. "I've learned there are many kinds of love and many degrees. But what I felt for her at the time was what I called love."

He heard the hesitancy in her voice when she looked over at him and asked, "How does that differ from what you call love now?"

Jake wasn't sure how to answer. He knew that so-called puppy love or a crush to a young person could be as real as mature love to an older person. "I suppose it involves all the feelings I had back then, which includes the physical, the selfish, the human aspects. But the kind of love that lasts is not just based on feelings, but on action as well. My actions in my younger days did not fill all the empty spots in my life.

Only since I've made God my first priority have I found the peace and purpose that had been missing in my life. I think that love of the right kind must involve the kind of commitment based on biblical principles."

Brooke nodded. "Many times, I felt Barrett did not have the kind of commitment to the Lord or to me that he should have had. But I never spoke to him about it. In fact, I tried to gain his approval by trying to be the socialite he wanted." She kicked lightly at the water that curled around her feet. "It didn't work. And I knew that God was missing from our lives, but I was as guilty as Barrett of omitting God. Maybe I was more guilty because I knew more about it, having been reared in a Christian home."

"Sometimes," Jake said reflectively, "the worst experiences in our lives are what bring us to our knees before God—where we should have been in the first place." He turned and she followed. "We'd best head back."

They walked back toward the boardwalk. No, this was not a time for taking her in his arms. They were quiet, walking together, as if they were one with the ocean, the sound of the water pounding against the shore, the moonlight shining on them both.

Taking her in his arms would not satisfy the longing within himself. It would only perpetuate it and perhaps turn his feelings into primarily physical ones. His feelings for Brooke were physical too, but he wanted more from her, wanted to give her more. He wanted their relationship to be deep and meaningful and lasting. Taking her in his arms would not convince her of that.

Was this the time to tell her more? Should he stop right now and say, "Brooke, there's more"? Perhaps his hesitancy was God's way of telling him to wait. Or perhaps it was his own cowardice. Either way, the opportune moment had passed.

When they reached the boardwalk, the talk turned to the wet sand clumped on their feet. He showed her where they could rinse the sand off. After she did, she slipped into her sandals while holding onto his arm for support; something he found warm and comfortable. But he did not take her in his arms for a moonlight kiss. He did not know the touch of her lips, the feel of her body against his, a warm breath against his cheek. He did not know and perhaps that increased his desire for it, intensified his feelings, made their relationship stronger.

He felt she had begun to trust him, just as he'd begun to distrust himself. If he took her in his arms and kissed her, he'd never want to let her go.

"Thank you," Jake said, after they were heading for Gracie's. "Thank you for making this such a special evening. I'm glad you had dinner with me."

"So am I," she said and glanced over to return his smile.

∽ ∽ ∽

They picked up Ben, who fell asleep on the way home. When they arrived at the cottage, Jake took him inside, laid him on his bed, and then slipped off his tennis shoes and socks. Back in the living room, Jake said what Brooke had already observed.

"I'm real fond of that little boy," he said. "He's fit right in with Gracie's boys."

Brooke nodded. "Gracie's boys take after their mama. They're easy to relate to." She paused and then added, "And their uncle."

"Thank you," he said. "And that little boy sleeping in there takes a lot after his mother. You're a good mother, Brooke."

Emotion welled up in her eyes. She couldn't think of a better compliment. Words like that meant so much more than if he'd said she was pretty or that he liked her hair. "Thank you, Jake," she said. "You couldn't have said anything nicer."

She could have added that his actions toward Ben in the short time they'd known him were more like a father's than Barrett's had ever been. Barrett had never abused Ben except by omitting the good times they might have had together.

"Well," Jake said after a moment, "thank you again for tonight."

"No, thank you, Jake," she said, then walked him to the door. She wondered if he would kiss her goodnight, but he didn't. He only turned to her and said, "Good night, Brooke."

Later, Brooke lay in bed staring toward the moonlit window, thinking about the evening. She remembered an adage her mother had quoted upon occasion: "One rose does not a summer make."

Brooke added her own interpretation. "One date does not a relationship make."

Just what had been Jake Randolph's intentions? Was he simply being a friend, wanting to ultimately dispel any traces of mistrust she might have of him? Had he suspected she might come to care for him in a special way and wanted to let her know he was still in love with a woman who had rejected him? Had he been trying to tell her she was a fine person, a good mother, and they could be friends? Or was he implying that her spirituality had not matured to the point he wanted in a woman he could be serious about? Maybe Carleigh was more the type of woman a dedicated Christian like Jake deserved?

She closed her eyes against the doubts. Of course she knew. Those years of never being good enough for Barrett had taken their toll. But what was it Jake had said? Something about our hardest times are those when we learn the most. What had she learned? The answer was as close as the question. She'd learned she could make a life for herself and her son without her husband—without a man. She did not have to depend upon a man for her happiness. Gracie was a wonderful example of that.

So, Lord, she prayed, *if Jake Randolph is not for me, I accept that. I can handle that because I have handled losing the love of a husband who meant the world to me. You know what is best for me. I will not struggle with this relationship, and I'm giving it over to You.*

Right before falling to sleep, Brooke realized another important thing. She had gone out on a date with a man, had a wonderful time, and had related well. That was something she'd thought she'd never be able to do. That was a major accomplishment. "Thank You, Lord," she breathed, as she drifted off into dreamland feeling certain that everything was resolved within her heart and mind. She could handle whatever the situation.

However, she chided herself the following morning when she remembered that her night had been filled with dreams of a couple's walk along the beach beneath a full moon with the sound of mighty ocean waves against the shore. In her dreams, the man put his arm around the woman and drew her close.

Seventeen

Jake didn't need more dinners to determine how he felt about Brooke. A dinner date couldn't possibly tell him more about her than he knew by seeing her in everyday life relating to her son, caring about a shedding dog simply because her son loved him, paying rapt attention to a pastor during church, singing praises to the Lord, relating to people like Gracie and her boys, and planning for her future with determination rather than wallowing in self-pity. He admired her, respected her, and with a feeling of both joy and trepidation, he admitted that he loved her. And he loved Ben, that big-eyed, mischievous, exaggerating, active little boy who was a part of Brooke.

With the way he felt about Brooke, he couldn't just put his feelings on hold for another two months, maybe not even two days. They were growing closer. Once Ben started school and Brooke started back to resume her studies as a nurse, it might be easy for them to drift apart. He couldn't chance her growing away from him.

He'd been talking to Brooke about putting up fencing since Taz was growing bigger every day and had already begun to run off around the neighborhood, refusing to come until the mood struck him. Without a fence, they'd soon have to chain him up when Ben played with him outside. Otherwise, they would have to keep him in the house.

"I can take you to Bluffton Saturday afternoon to look at fencing," he mentioned to Brooke. "While we're there, I'd like for us to stop in and see my parents."

His heart skipped a beat when she readily accepted the invitation. Maybe after meeting them, she'd see he was from good stock. She would believe him honorable and serious about her.

Surely, by now, she knew he was trustworthy. She'd had a failed marriage and an unfaithful husband. She understood how things could go so wrong without anyone intending for them to, how people could even be blind to it for a while, and the emotional toll it could take. Yes, Brooke was an understanding woman. It was time to tell her about his past.

For sure, he mustn't let her hear it from anyone else. He hated that he'd need to ask his parents not to mention the past, or at least not the past few years. Still, that call needed to be made before Brooke and he arrived. So he made it and he listened and he heard the inflection in his mother's voice when she asked, "Jake, if you're serious about this woman, don't you think it would be a good idea to bring everything out into the open?"

"I intend to, Mom," Jake assured her. "I just don't know how serious she is about me, and this is not the kind of thing I go around telling everyone."

"I understand," she said. "You have to do what you think is best. I just don't like having to be careful about what I say."

He laughed lightly. Gracie and their mother—two peas in a pod. They usually spoke their mind. He used to, but he had become more careful in the past few years. "Sorry to put you in this position, Mom. I really am."

"I know. And I'll talk to your dad for you. But, Jake, if you're interested in this woman, at some point, she'll need to know."

∽ ∽ ∽

That afternoon, Carolina's sun spread its warmth across a brilliant blue sky. As Jake and Brooke sped along the William Hilton Parkway heading toward Bluffton, Brooke powered down the window and tilted her face upward. She didn't care how mussed her hair became. The wind in her hair brought such a feeling of freedom.

Sitting beside Jake also felt good, and she doubted life could be more perfect. Maybe, just maybe, she had finally overcome her feelings of guilt, failure, loss, and the fear of raising Ben alone. She'd come to this island feeling washed up. But thanks to Gracie, her boys, and Jake, she had a new lease on life.

Particularly, she owed these feelings to Jake. She'd come to the island feeling she never wanted to be involved with a man again. But Jake had won her trust. He'd shown her what a Christian man should be like. He loved the Lord and tried to live for Him daily. *This* is what she'd hoped for all along with Barrett. But Barrett had been unable to give her that much of himself and he'd certainly not given that much of himself to God.

Jake had also given her a whole new set of emotions. She'd come here hurt, disappointed, afraid. Jake made her feel like she could conquer the world. Maybe even allow a man in her life again. The past had begun to fade. She'd come to know people whose situations were far worse than hers, and she could count her blessings.

"Penny for your thoughts," Jake said from across the seat.

Brooke smiled. "You were in them," she said.

Jake glanced over to return the smile, took his hand from the wheel, and held hers for a brief moment.

"I hope your parents won't feel like I'm imposing upon them," Brooke said.

"I called and told them I was bringing you. They're looking forward to meeting you," he said. "But just so you know, they're good, ordinary people."

Bluffton was just across the causeway on the mainland. Jake pointed out homes and a mall he and his dad and their crews had built. Brooke was impressed with both his work and the pride he took in it.

In no time at all, he turned off the main road and drove up a long, curved, tree-lined drive to a lovely, lowcountry home at the end of a cul-de-sac. The wraparound veranda-style front porch lent a gentle Southern flavor to the peaceful setting. As soon as they parked, Jake's parents walked out on the porch. The woman was unmistakably related to Gracie. Her auburn curls were shorter and sprinkled with gray, but Gracie and she were definitely mother and daughter. And the man could never deny Jake as his son. Same height, same look, although his hair was a tad darker and thinning.

While being introduced, Todd Randolph shook her hand, but Cora hugged her. "Come on in, hon," she said, then opened the door to an elegant home of cathedral ceilings, hardwood floors, and the warm scent of cookies baking in the oven. "I'm making Jake's favorite oatmeal raisin." She led the way to a large eat-in kitchen lined with country-white cabinets and gleaming marble counters.

"She always bakes me cookies," Jake said with a grin. "Made from scratch."

"And you've never been too old for them either," his mother said as she raised a plate stacked high with perfectly shaped cookies. Jake and Brooke reached at the same time, their hands bumping.

"Keep your mitts off my cookies," Jake teased, swatting her hand away.

"Jake!" Cora pretended to scold.

"Okay," he said, handing his cookie to Brooke. "You can have one."

"I will treasure this moment always," she said, playing along.

Todd and Cora each helped themselves to a cookie too. "Come outside," Cora said, "and see where we live most of the time. I've got a big pitcher of lemonade waiting on us."

When they stepped outside, Brooke understood why, even in the humid heat of summer they would spend time there. An inviting pool sparkled in the sunlight, surrounded by white concrete and a low white railing. Beyond that was a tennis court. The rest of the spacious lawn was like green velvet, dotted with oaks and tall palmettos, and farther back stood a huge magnolia tree.

"Have a seat," Todd Randolph said, gesturing to the chairs beneath the shade of an umbrella-covered patio table. The patio itself was flanked by azalea hedges that had lost their spring blossoms several weeks ago and now boasted summer's lush green leaves. Brooke took in the full view—after Jake helped her into her seat—to spot a lagoon.

"This is lovely," Brooke said.

"Thank you," Cora said. "Todd built it for us several years ago. I guess you know Gracie and Jake live in our old home place."

Brooke nodded. "It's a great house too."

For the next several minutes, Cora and Todd talked about having grown up on Hilton Head. Todd's dad had been an architect and had helped design many of the structures on the island. "My dad used to talk about the day they turned on the electricity on Hilton Head," Todd said.

"That was in 1951," Cora said, completing his thought. "Slightly before our time."

Todd nodded. "I wasn't even a spark in my daddy's eye."

"So, what made you decide to leave the island?" Brooke asked.

"We liked Hilton Head," Cora added. "But after Todd had his heart surgery, he sold the business to Jake—" She reached for the pitcher of lemonade and began pouring drinks into tumblers. "Here you go," she said, handing a filled glass to Brooke.

"Thank you," Brooke said. Had Cora been about to add something more?

"Anyway," Todd said, after what seemed to be a strained moment of silence, "we always talked about traveling after I retired, doing things together that we'd not done when we were raising the kids. I was always too busy. She was busy too, teaching those little kids in the second grade. I'd seen men younger than me end up gravely ill and then dying, so I decided that since I'd had surgery, it might be now or never to grab hold of the retirement idea. I could leave the business in good hands. And I did," he said, patting his son's shoulder with one hand and raising his glass in a salute with the other. "The best."

Brooke smiled, seeing the obvious love and pride in Todd's eyes when he looked at Jake. Then Cora said, "Well, tell us about you, Brooke."

What could she say? "I'm from Indiana. I started nursing school but then I met Barrett and we got married. Five years ago, I had a little boy. Then, a little over a year ago, my husband was killed in an auto accident. His parents deeded me their cottage on Hilton Head that Jake's been making repairs on. Let's see," she said, wondering what else to say. "I'm planning to resume my education after Ben starts school." She thought a moment. "Oh, and I have a dog."

They laughed as she and Jake talked about some of Taz's experiences, especially being a *miniature* who now weighed about twenty-five pounds.

"You two apparently play tennis," Brooke said, looking toward the court.

"Play?" Jake scoffed. "I don't think Gracie and I ever beat these two."

"Now, there was one time," Todd said playfully, and they all laughed. Then he looked at Brooke. "I guess you know the island's famous for its golf and tennis courts. The best women pros in the world come to play in the Family Circle Cup every year."

Brooke had known about the golf but hadn't realized that the island was so famous for tennis.

"We could have a game right now," Todd said, standing, ready to get the rackets and balls.

Brooke couldn't help but laugh at his enthusiasm and his challenge. "Maybe another time," she said and blushed to think she assumed there *would be* another time. "I haven't played tennis since I was in high school."

He sat again. "It's a date then."

Jake drained his glass of lemonade, then clapped his hands together. "Well, folks. We'd best get to Home Depot to look at fencing."

"I like them very much," Brooke said after she and Jake were on the road. She held up the zipper bag filled with cookies for Ben and her to enjoy later. "Especially your mom. And your dad—he's very proud of you, you know."

"I grew up knowing how to use a hammer and a saw nearly before I knew how to ride a bike. I worked for Dad every weekend, all summer, and through college when I could."

"What did you major in when you went to college?"

"Architecture and design—I thought I wanted to become an engineer." He shook his head. "But that wasn't for me. I'm an outdoor person. I love the manual work, so I went to Dad and told him I'd like to come to work for the company. Then, like he said, he retired and sold me the business."

His jaw flinched then and, again, Brooke felt there was more. With Cora, she'd thought it had to do with Todd's heart attack. But now . . . Was there something they'd not told her? Something between the purchase of the business and now? Then again maybe not. Jake's face beamed suddenly as he turned into Home Depot's parking lot.

"Ah," he said, "the best store on earth."

Brooke laughed. "Maybe."

~ ~ ~

Jake could tell his parents took to Brooke and liked her immediately. They didn't have to say it. He saw it in the way they talked to her and in how his dad found a way to ask her to come back again. He saw it in the way they both looked at him and grinned like he'd won the lottery right before he and Brooke left. Not to mention that his mom had given her as big a bag of cookies as she gave him.

But however much he wanted it, he didn't have to have his parents' approval. He was a grown man who wanted Brooke's approval. He was happy to have her sitting beside him in the truck as if they belonged together. It seemed natural when they walked down the long aisles of Home Depot and she started to turn in one direction and he in another that he reached for her hand.

"This way," he said. He kept holding her hand, and she didn't try to remove it. *I want her by my side, Lord,* he prayed silently, *always.* Surely God wouldn't have brought her into his life and given him this love for her if it wasn't right. He squeezed her hand and she squeezed back. Okay, then. Tonight, he would tell her. The time was right and, he believed, she would understand.

He was still holding her hand when it happened. He stopped so quickly, Brooke nearly slipped. She looked up at him as he stared at the couple in front of them. "Jake?" she asked. "What is it? What's wrong?"

But Jake didn't answer. He couldn't. He was standing face-to-face with Meagan.

Eighteen

Brooke felt Jake's hand tighten on hers again before he let go and stared straight ahead. She looked from him to the man and dark-eyed woman who stood straight ahead staring at them.

After what seemed an incredible eternity, Jake spoke, although Brooke could hardly make out what he said. Then the man mumbled a half-hearted hello while the woman stared as if seeing a ghost before they hurried away. A muscle in Jake's jaw tightened and his face flushed. After a moment, he shook his head. "I'm sorry. That caught me off guard. I—um—I know that couple, and it would have been pointless to try and introduce you."

"Don't worry about it," Brooke said, sorrier for the broken camaraderie that had vanished between her and Jake than that he had not introduced her. She glanced over her shoulder and saw, way up the aisle, that the woman, whose black hair shimmered under the fluorescent lighting, looked back at them, then turned away.

"Here's the fencing," Jake said as they rounded into another aisle.

"Maybe chain link would be best. I liked the effect of your parents' backyard, and since I have close neighbors, it might be best to have a fence I can see through."

"Sounds like a good idea," Jake agreed. "Ben and Taz would probably be happier with that too. If this is what you want, I can measure and see how much you need."

They walked back through the store toward the front, but Jake didn't take hold of her hand again. He hadn't been his pleasant, natural self since seeing the couple, although Brooke suspected this was more about the woman than the man. Brooke didn't know if she had a right to ask, but she and Jake were becoming closer, and she wanted to know.

"Who was the couple?" she asked after they'd returned to the truck and Jake had started it.

Jake sighed heavily before backing up and then traveling slowly toward the street. He pulled up to a traffic light, then turned left before answering. "That was Meagan," he said, which was no surprise to Brooke. After a pause he added, "The man was Oswald Jenkins. He used to work for Dad and me. There was a time when I asked him, as a friend, to watch out for her while I—I had to be away." Jake paused. "He did. They're married now."

When he didn't add anything else, Brooke said, "There seemed to be a lot of tension there in the store." Could it be that Jake was still in love with Meagan?

"You're right, there was tension," he said. "But not for the reasons you think. I have to talk to you about all this."

Brooke waited, but he didn't say anything more and his mood had most definitely changed. She could understand if Jake were still in love. But he had denied it. Or was he living with regrets, as she had done for so long about Barrett? She could certainly understand that.

"If you want to talk to me, Jake, I'm willing to listen," she offered.

"The sky is turning dark," he said, avoiding the topic at hand. "We're going to get rained on."

Brooke couldn't help but wonder at the ominousness of Jake's last lines. *The sky is turning dark . . . we're going to get rained on.* Was this a sign of something to come? Something between her and Jake?

Rain pelted the windshield in fat drops that slapped against the glass. Jake switched on the windshield wipers. His shoulders tensed and he leaned forward. "There is something I should tell you, Brooke," Jake said, keeping his attention on the cloudburst striking the truck and the road. "I haven't known when the time is right. But I need enough time to explain things to you because—because you've come to mean so much to me and I—"

"Maybe now isn't the best time when you need to concentrate on the road. Maybe later would be better," she said.

Jake nodded. "Yeah. Yeah. For now, let me get us safely home."

She'd hoped that Jake would talk with her after they got home, but Ben took center stage and, after only a few moments, Jake told her he would talk to her later. And that was that. Brooke got Ben and herself ready for bed and did her best to fall asleep. But long into the night, she thought about Jake's words and his mood after seeing Meagan. He indicated there was something he had to tell her and the way he said it, the whole thing sounded ominous. She felt she could take or accept whatever he might tell her. After all, Jake had already revealed that he'd had a physical relationship with Meagan, and she could live with that. If the Lord had forgiven him, then who was she not to do so?

Whatever it was, it couldn't be as bad as he made it seem. Whatever the situation, he'd probably magnified it in his mind since he was so intent upon making a good impression and being a Christian example. She could understand that too. She remembered well how she felt that all eyes were upon her at Barrett's funeral. Feeling as though everyone there—including his parents—were judging her, believing that had she been a better wife, Barrett would not have been where he'd been and with whom he'd been with on the night of the accident.

Then another thought struck her. Perhaps he had an incurable disease. Could that be a reason why, at his age, he wasn't married or seeing anyone? No, he was obviously healthy. And if he were dying, he wouldn't be taking her out and saying he cared for her, would he?

Brooke rolled over and punched the pillow, getting into her usual comfortable sleeping position on her stomach. She really shouldn't spend the night trying to figure out what she couldn't possibly know. She knew Jake. Or, at least, she *thought* she did.

Then again, she'd thought she'd known Barrett too.

Finally, she did what she should have done to start with—she prayed, asking God to give Jake the courage to tell her whatever he needed to say and her the grace to accept it in a Christlike manner.

Morning came too soon. She hadn't slept enough, and Ben complained of not feeling well. She felt his forehead with her lips—something her mother had always done—but he didn't seem to be running a fever. "You're cool as a cucumber," she told him with a smile. "Maybe you and I had the same sickness last night—the I-can't-sleep disease."

"I didn't sleep so good," Ben said.

"Well, maybe tonight we'll need to go to bed a little earlier than usual. We could both use a good night's sleep."

"I guess," Ben mumbled.

Brooke ruffled his hair and said, "All right then. We need to get ready for church."

Later, during Sunday school, Jake seemed to be his usual jovial self, talking, laughing, greeting, discussing, but Brooke had come to know him well enough to realize all that was colored with a touch of reserve. If she were a betting woman, she'd put all her money on Jake *acting* the part this morning rather than meaning it.

After church, Jake asked if she'd stick around a while so he could talk with her. "Gracie said she'd take Ben home with her and she'd save lunch for us."

"Okay," she said. "Sure." She gave Ben a kiss and told him to be good for Miss Gracie, then waited until he was safely strapped in to turn back to Jake. "I'm ready," she told him, her shoulders straight.

Jake led her out to the privacy of the sunken prayer garden where they walked down the steps to a bench beneath a live oak. Brooke stopped to touch what was likely one of the last remaining blossoms of a bygone spring and when the sound of the crowd dispersing from the church and parking lot faded, she turned to see that Jake had sat, leaning forward with his forearms on his thighs, his hands clasped, his head bent, and his eyes closed.

He straightened when she sat beside him, ready for whatever confession he wanted to make to her. She smiled encouragingly. Whatever he had to say, she could take it. She was ready. Or at least she thought she was until Jake turned and took her hand in his and said, "I've spent time in federal prison, Brooke. And I'm still on probation."

Her head jerked and she blinked. He had *what*? He was *what*? This made no sense to her. How could a man as good and kind—as *Christian*—be a—what would it be called—a felon? And in *federal* prison?

She opened her mouth to say something, but nothing came. *Breathe, Brooke. Breathe.* No. First Barrett. Now Jake. Would she ever learn? Would she *ever* pick a man without a plethora of issues?

She slipped her hand from his.

ꕥ ꕥ ꕥ

The instant he spoke, Jake knew he'd blurted the news too quickly. He should have led up to it with an explanation. The color drained from Brooke's face and her smile faded. For long moments—too long—she only stared at him. Her lips parted as if she wanted to say something, but then nothing but short bursts of air followed. This was Meagan all over again.

As if in slow motion, she pulled her hand out of his.

"Brooke," he said. "I *wasn't* guilty."

A tinge of color appeared in her cheeks. She shook her head, then stood, still staring at him.

He repeated, "Brooke. I wasn't *guilty*."

For a moment she swayed like a fragile tree in a storm, and he feared she would faint so he stood and reached for her, but she shrugged him away. Just then, his cell phone buzzed and, like Pavlov's dog, he pulled it out of his pocket. "Gracie . . ." he said. "It's a message from Gracie."

The words got Brooke's attention and she looked up at him. "What?"

He stared at the face of his phone. "She says to come home right away." He looked at her. "Something's wrong."

ꕥ ꕥ ꕥ

Jake tried to call Gracie on the way back to the house, but she didn't answer.

"What's happening?" Brooke asked as he drove at breakneck speed.

"I don't know," he told her. "But for some reason, she's no longer answering."

As soon as Jake pulled up to Gracie's house, the neighbor Brooke had met at water aerobics and the three boys ran out the front door and met them outside the truck. "What is it?" Brooke asked. "Where's Ben?"

Jake put his arm around her shoulder and, too frightened to care, she didn't shrug him away. "Gracie drove him to the hospital," the neighbor said. "I don't know what all happened. I wasn't here. She had Alex call me."

"His stomach hurt," Alex said. "And he started throwing up real bad. He was all doubled over, and Mom said he was burning up with a fever."

"Where would they have gone?" Brooke asked.

"The medical center," Jake said.

"Yes," Alex said. "That's where she said she'd take him."

Jake pointed to the boys. "You stay with Mrs. Simpson and be good." He turned to Brooke. "Come on. I'll get you there."

On the way there, Brooke imagined every possible scenario. "What if it's appendicitis?" she asked Jake. "He wasn't very hungry this morning and he said he wasn't feeling well but I checked him for a fever, and he didn't have one."

"We'll know soon enough, Brooke. And Gracie's got him."

"But why isn't she answering?"

He reached for her hand, and she didn't flinch or pull away. She needed whatever strength he could give her, and she'd take it any way she could.

"Let's not try to second-guess everything," he told her. "Let's pray."

"Okay," she whispered and then closed her eyes and listened while Jake led them both in a prayer of safekeeping for her son. When he finished with an "amen," she silently added, *Oh, God, he's so little, so young, and I'm not with him.*

Nineteen

A blast of cool air hit them as soon as they entered the emergency room of the medical center. Brooke folded her arms against it as she stepped up to the front desk. "I'm Ben Haddon's mother," she said to the woman sitting on the other side of the Plexiglas partition. "My son was brought here a little bit ago."

She bounced on the balls of her feet while the woman looked up the information on the laptop in front of her, then asked for ID, which Brooke produced. "Your son is in Room 5." The woman pointed toward a set of double doors. "I'll buzz you in."

Brooke and Jake hurried past several numbered doors, medical equipment, and numerous hospital personnel before Jake pointed to a door left ajar and said, "It's right here."

They rounded into the room to find Gracie sitting beside an empty area where a gurney had been. She stood quickly and said, "Ben mentioned a stomachache on the ride home and then all of a sudden he doubled over. I checked his temp and knew I had to get him here as fast as I could. Then the vomiting started."

Brooke stood slack jawed. "Where's Ben?"

Gracie looked toward the door. "They took him for some tests. Brooke," she said, her voice low and steady. "They're going to need information from you. Insurance and so on. I explained to them that I was watching him and that you were on your way."

Brooke looked up at Jake as if he'd done this kind of thing several times over. "Should I go now? Find someone?"

"No," he said. "Right now, we wait and . . . and we pray." He took her hand in his, then Gracie's. Gracie followed suit by taking Brooke's. "Father," Jake began, "First, we thank You for blessing Brooke with

Ben for over five years. Lord, we know everything is Yours and in Your hands. We're placing our faith and trust in You, that this situation will be controlled only by You. Be with the doctors, the nurses, all the workers here, and with Brooke that she may feel the comfort of Your presence. Be most especially with Ben. Let him feel no fear but only very real knowledge that You are here with him. Your will be done in this and all things. In Jesus' name, amen."

Brooke felt it. The fear, the urge not to say, "Thy will be done," but to beg God to save Ben's life. She tried to move away, but Jake wouldn't let go of her tension-filled hand. "Lord, I have no strength," she finally began. "I know You love him more than I am capable of loving. But I want him with me, and I pray You may see fit to allow that. Thank You for the years of joy I've experienced with Ben. He was my life jacket in my sea of trouble. Lord, help me to be his life jacket now. I pray that Ben's needs will be met by You—and I want his recovery—but, Lord, I'm trying to also want Your will."

She wasn't even sure she could mean it wholeheartedly but knew what she must pray. "Thy . . . will . . . be . . . done," came out in a choked whisper. "I'm trusting You, Lord. Forgive me for thinking of myself. Help me to be what Ben needs at this time."

Brooke began to sob, and feeling her hands relax, Jake released them, then opened his arms. She allowed him to come closer and hold her head against his shoulder. With the strength of his arms around her, she cried. When she felt cried out, she thanked him, then went to a nearby restroom to splash cold water on her face.

When she returned, she found Gracie back in the chair, but Jake was gone. She felt empty without him there. At the same time, she felt that a great calm, rather like a cloud of comfort, had surrounded her, keeping her from fear and wondering and pleading. A blanket of God's presence and love had covered her.

She was about to ask where Jake had gone when a young doctor sporting green scrubs walked in.

"Are you Ben's mother?" he asked, his hands reaching for the ends of a stethoscope slung around his neck. He stood with his feet braced apart, something Brooke had seen Barrett do time and again to relieve the pressure on his legs and back after long days of campaigning.

"I am," she said. "Where's my son?"

He smiled at her, the blue in his eyes warm and encouraging. "I'm Dr. Carpenter," he said. "Our best little patient will be back here soon. Let me go over some things with you. All tests point to appendicitis. Now, there seems to be a slight perforation of the intestines, so we suspect an abscess," the doctor said. "We will monitor him closely for a few hours and give him antibiotic therapy to reduce any infection."

Gracie had come to stand beside her. "What about surgery?" she asked.

"We need to get that infection down before we can consider surgery. We've got him on a pretty powerful IV antibiotic, so it won't be long."

"Suppose it . . . ruptures?" Brooke asked.

Again, he smiled and, again, Brooke felt the peace Jake and she had prayed for. "We are prepared for emergencies, Mrs. Haddon," he replied. He released the ends of the stethoscope and extended his right hand, which she took for a quick shake. "Again, I'm Dr. Carpenter. Just ask for me if you have any concerns. Otherwise, I'll be back later. Your son should be here any moment."

When the doctor left, Brooke let out a sigh of relief. "Thank you, God."

"In all things give thanks," Gracie whispered.

Brooke looked at Gracie more fully then. "Thank you for taking care of my son."

Gracie nodded. "Listen, I'm sorry I couldn't answer the phone earlier. I had my hands full with Ben and then they asked me to turn off my phone when I got in here."

"No, I understand."

Brooke stopped at the squeaking of gurney wheels. She turned to see her sleeping son, an IV tube running into his little arm, being wheeled in by another young man also dressed in scrubs. "Ben," she whispered, but he didn't respond to the sound of her voice, which nearly broke her heart. Gracie's arm came around her and pulled her back so the hospital worker could get the gurney in place.

"He's going to sleep for a while," the man said, then left.

Brooke immediately stepped to the gurney and reached for his little hand, which was warm but not feverishly hot. "They must have given him something for the fever."

Gracie nodded. "Yes, almost the minute we got in here."

Brooke leaned over and whispered words of love—both hers and God's—into his ear. His eyes opened then, and he turned his face toward hers, which brought a smile to her lips. "Hey, sweetheart."

"Mommy," he said, then closed his eyes and returned to dreamland.

Brooke straightened and turned to Gracie. "He's so sick," she said.

"But he's in the right place," Gracie said, then began to cry. "Oh, Brooke, I was so scared. I mean, it's one thing when it's *your* child, but quite another when it's someone else's."

Brooke wrapped her arms around her friend.

"I should be helping you, not the other way around," Gracie said with a short chuckle.

"You are," Brooke said. "But why don't you go home? Your boys need you."

"Jake's coming back in a little while. I'll go then."

Jake. So much had happened since that morning. Jake's confession—as confusing as it was—followed by the hurried trip to Gracie's and then to the hospital. Twice he had prayed with her. Twice. And now, wherever he had gone, he was returning.

Brooke didn't have strength enough to argue. She determined not to think about the fact that Jake had been in prison. No. Not right then. Right then, the only thing she would allow into her mind was Ben. He was *her* responsibility.

Still, when Jake returned a few minutes later bearing cups of steaming hot coffee, she found that his presence helped. She could call her parents and have them fly down, but somehow Jake's optimistic outlook was the comfort she needed. No matter what—confession or no—he was someone she had come to count on during the past months and she would not send him away.

~ ~ ~

Within hours, Ben was admitted into his own room on the pediatric floor and then, shortly after, he was taken into surgery. Brooke and Jake followed behind the gurney until it disappeared behind the double doors of the brightly lit surgical unit.

"I love you, Ben," Brooke called out, hoping he had, somehow, heard her.

Jake pointed to a grouping of chairs in a quiet alcove where a single low-wattage lamp offered scant lighting. "Let's sit down," he suggested.

Brooke sighed. "Jake, if you need to go—"

"No way," he said.

She bit on her lip to keep from crying again.

"I don't want to cause you any distress," he said as they sat side by side. "But I want to be here for Ben *and* for you . . . if you need me." He paused before adding. "No strings attached."

She nodded in understanding.

"By the way," he added. "When I went to get coffee, I called the pastor. He wanted to come down, but I told him I'd keep him apprised."

"Thank you," she said. She hadn't even thought to call the pastor.

"Also, he's got a round-the-clock prayer chain going. Oh, and a friend of mine is going to run over to your house to make sure Taz is okay."

Brooke rested her face in the cups of her hands. "Oh, Jake. You've thought of everything. I didn't even—"

"It's okay," he said. He held out his hand and she placed hers within the warmth and strength of it, then laid her head against his shoulder. The rhythm of his breathing nearly lulled her to sleep until he added, "That's what I'm here for."

~ ~ ~

The doctor burst into the waiting area, all smiles. Both Brooke and Jake breathed sighs of relief when he said that surgery revealed that peritonitis had not developed and that there was no infection. "Little Ben will have three small laparoscopic scars to brag about, but as he grows older, they will grow more and more faint."

Brooke nearly laughed with relief.

"We'll probably release him tomorrow. For now, if you want to go on up to his room, he'll be back as soon as he's out of recovery."

The moment the doctor walked away, Brooke turned to Jake, who held out his hands. She took them and they closed their eyes. "Thank You, God," Jake prayed.

"Thank You," Brooke added.

∽ ∽ ∽

The next morning Jake walked into Ben's room bearing the gift of a little stuffed dog that looked remarkably like Taz.

"Look, Mom," Ben exclaimed as he wrapped his arms around the pup. "But can Taz come see me?"

"No way," Jake said. "That monster would eat all your Jell-O and crackers."

Ben smirked. "I want pizza."

Jake looked at Brooke who sat curled in the recliner she'd slept in the night before. "He's definitely healing," he said.

Brooke laughed. "Definitely."

Jake took Ben's hand in his. "Okay, pal. A few more days and you'll have your pizza. Now you rest, so you can get well and go home. If you're good, I'll smuggle a few boys over to your house to see you."

"Okay," Ben said, then flopped his head over and pretended to go right to sleep.

Jake nodded toward Brooke. "Have they given him his walking papers yet?"

Brooke shook her head. "Not yet, but the nurse said probably by later this afternoon he will be released."

"Sounds good. I've got to hurry on to work," he said. "But call me if you need me."

"I will," she said.

Later, as Ben slept, Brooke took the much-needed time to try to discern her thoughts and feelings. Right before the emergency, Jake had told her the most alarming news. He'd shared his most well-guarded secret with her, and she'd been unable to respond. *Jake was a criminal.*

That may be true, she reckoned. But he said he wasn't guilty of the crime. And Jesus said that a tree is known by its fruit. The Jake she knew—and the fruit he bore—gave no indication at all of criminal behavior. He helped others. He served others. He was caring. He had that whole water-basin attitude.

And what were her fruits?

She raised a brow. She hadn't put God and His will and ways first in her life during her marriage and she was only just learning that now. Maybe she'd been at fault too. She'd never said she didn't want the big house, the fine car, the beautiful clothes, and all the attention. She had wanted them. And was that any different from Jake's wanting something so much he committed a criminal act to get it?

But Jake had said he was *not* guilty.

Had she, with her judgmental attitude, condemned an innocent man?

Brooke's car was still in the parking lot, but with Gracie's help, they made it home a little after five o'clock. Gracie then took her keys and said, "I'll have your car back here shortly."

As Brooke looked out the screen door while cradling a cup of coffee and waiting on her car, Jake drove it into the driveway. He walked up dangling the keys and sporting a sheepish smile. "I talked Gracie into letting me return the car to you," he said as she stepped onto the porch. "How's the little man?"

She opened her palm to receive the key fob. "Sleeping," she said.

"And what about the little man's mama?"

Brooke held up the cup of coffee. "I'm working on cup number two. Can I get you some?"

"No, thank you. Ah,"—he leaned against a column—"can I bring something up for just a sec? I mean, it's not my business, so tell me if I'm out of line . . . I'm sure you have medical insurance on Ben, but—"

"It's not much—"

"I can help," he said, his eyes never leaving hers. "If you'll let me."

She held up her hand to stop him from saying anything more. "I appreciate that, Jake. But I have to try and do this on my own and I've already talked with someone at the hospital. They've promised to help me out." She sighed. "Besides, if I'm going to have faith in God, then I have to depend on Him, not other people."

"But sometimes His way of working is through other people," Jake said.

"I know. My father says, 'Let's see what God allows.' So, that's what I'm going to do. I'm going to see what God allows."

Jake smiled at her. "Well, just so you know, the pastor has already told me that a collection was taken last night. So . . ."

Brooke dipped her chin and slowly shook her head. "That's incredible. That's just . . ." She was at a loss for words.

"That's what church family is for," Jake added.

She looked up and gave him a smile that was easily returned. "Thank you," she said softly.

"That's all you need to say," he told her.

∽ ∽ ∽

The next morning, Gracie came alone, and when Brooke told her about the church's gift, Gracie expressed no surprise. "Our church is a giving church," she said. "They do this kind of thing."

"I'll bet Jake was in on it," Brooke said.

Gracie grinned. "It's all confidential."

"Mmhmm," Brooke said. Gracie's lack of an answer had given her the answer. She smiled. "Well, if you're not going to spill the details, how about some iced tea?" Brooke asked.

"Sounds good."

Once she and Gracie had settled, Brooke said, "Gracie, Jake told me he was in prison."

"I know. He told me that he'd told you. He also said you really didn't have a chance to say anything before I called."

"Well, his news knocked me back a few steps, I can tell you that. I think I went into shock."

"Didn't he tell you he wasn't guilty?"

"Yes," Brooke said. She took a sip of her drink. "I don't even know what Jake's crime was."

"He didn't tell you?"

"We didn't get that far."

"Oh. Oh, I see." She shrugged one shoulder. "Well, I guess he won't mind if I tell you. He was arrested for income tax evasion."

"*What*?" Brooke exclaimed. "My gosh, Gracie, I've been thinking all sorts of things. But not tax evasion."

Gracie laughed. "Yeah, well, wouldn't we *all* like to evade that?"

"Yes," Brooke agreed. "But we don't."

Gracie took several swallows of her tea. "Ask Jake to give you the details," she said.

"Do you think he's ready to tell me everything?"

"I do. And, if it hadn't been for Ben getting sick, I think he would have." She paused for a moment, then added, "But, Brooke, whether you believe him or not . . . that's up to you."

Twenty

On Tuesday morning, Brooke called Jake to see if he could stop by that evening. "Thanks to the church," she said, "we've got plenty of food here. Although, to stick to Ben's diet, it's mostly boiled or broiled."

Jake laughed. "I can live with that if he can."

After dinner, and after she'd gotten Ben to bed, Brooke and Jake went out on the front porch swing, which Brooke had decorated with a red cushion and a couple of black-and-white-checked pillows. The swing squeaked in protest at being disturbed and Brooke looked up. "Are you sure these chains are going to hold?"

"Oh, the chains are good. Just need a little oil," Jake said, looking from the ceiling to her. "But those suspension hooks . . ."

"Don't tease," she said, furrowing her brow to show she meant it.

Jake chuckled lightly before adding, "I can replace them if you'd like."

"Should I?"

"I would."

"All right, then." She smiled, then grew serious as she turned toward him. "Jake, we need to talk about what you said the other day . . . before the call."

Jake nodded before shifting to bring his arm to rest along the back of the swing. "I suppose we do. And, just so you know, I don't blame you for not saying anything after I told you. I blurted out the fact but didn't have the chance to tell you the story behind it. I'd like to tell you now if you want to hear it."

Brooke listened as Jake told her his story. Then, when he was done, he said, "You remember I told you that it might seem cruel or restrictive to keep Taz on a leash while training him?"

Brooke nodded.

"Well, I feel like God had me on a leash in prison, but His instruction was the best for my life. Before that, I was a believer. I never doubted there was a God, and I believed He was the God of the Bible. I never doubted that Jesus was His Son and that He died on the cross for the sins of the world.

"However, it wasn't really personal for me." Jake leaned forward to rest his elbows on his knees, his feet flat against the floorboards. "Oh, I prayed when something went wrong. But it was always a 'gimme' type of prayer. I never had the Spirit of God leading me. I never felt the obligation to tell others that Jesus truly changes a life. That He gives life with all its craziness meaning."

"I get that."

"In prison, I learned I was *not* in control of my life, that I needed to depend solely on the Lord. I was in a situation not of my making, and no one was able to help me," Jake said. "Not family, friends, attorneys—no one. And, you know, no matter what, some people will always believe I'm guilty." He looked at her, waiting, but, as on Sunday, she said nothing. She wanted to hear everything he had to say before she commented further. "I didn't commit that sin, Brooke, but I have committed others, and I needed the blood of Jesus to wash me clean. Those six months in prison became a time when I searched the Word of God and, as the psalm says, made it a lamp unto my feet, a light unto my path."

"Oh, Jake," Brooke said. "Even if you *had* committed that crime, I know the kind of man you are today. I've never known a person who lived his Christianity more devotedly than you."

"Even if?"

She sighed a smile. "You know what I mean."

"Brooke," he said. "I love you. And I know it's kinda soon, but I would like to marry you and take care of you and Ben for the rest of your lives."

When she hesitated, rather than make her too uncomfortable, he added, "And Taz."

She laughed lightly. "Oh, Jake. That's so tempting. But that's the very reason I can't consider anything like that right now. *I* have the money problem thanks to Barrett's spending. *I* have a son to support. I was helpless for far too long after Barrett died, and I need to be able to stand on my own two feet and support my son without having to depend on a man or my parents or"—her eyes scanned the porch—"his parents. I think I owe that to myself and to Ben." Seeing his nod, despite the disappointment in his eyes, she added, "And Taz."

He leaned back as he laughed briefly. "I admire you for that, Brooke. I won't pressure you. But I'll be here when you're ready." His eyes found hers. "May I kiss you . . . if that's not too forward?"

Brooke's heart nearly burst at his gallantry. "You may," she said. And then his lips met hers.

~ ~ ~

Over the course of the next few days, members of the church stopped by to check on Brooke and Ben. Some brought food, while others brought items they thought Ben would enjoy reading or playing with. The visitor who offered the most interesting information, however, was Carleigh who came a week later while Jake was painting the kitchen ceiling after he'd climbed into the attic, found a tiny hole at the very tip of the roof and plugged it.

Carleigh brought a card signed by the children in Ben's Sunday school class. "You're so blessed to have a man like Jake looking after you two," she said when Brooke walked her to the door. "Makes me pine away for my guy. He's on a special ops mission so I don't even know where he is right now."

"Oh," Brooke said as her face heated from her own misinformation. Or, perhaps, misunderstanding. "I didn't realize you had—"

"His name is Jett," Carleigh said, beaming. "He should be coming home soon, God willing. Maybe the four of us can go out when he does?"

Brooke's smile was genuine. "I'd like that."

Yes, she was blessed. Jake stayed true to his word about not pressuring her, but he was there for her and Ben. He fenced in the back yard and built a doghouse, which Ben helped him paint.

Ben learning how to work with his hands delighted Brooke and gave Ben a constructive sense of pride.

"Come look, Mom," Ben called one afternoon when he spied her watching Jake and him out the kitchen window. "Miss Carleigh said Jesus was a cartpender," Ben said, his big eyes shining.

"She's right," Jake said.

"Well, I'm gonna grow up and be a cartpender just like Jake and Jesus."

"That's a very worthy goal," Brooke said, then smiled at Jake's surprised but pleased expression.

In July, Gracie and Brooke enrolled their boys in the K-5 program the church offered and were assured Ben and Aiden could be in the same class.

Many times, during the summer months, Brooke thought how much easier things would be if she married Jake instead of finding a way to support herself and Ben. She had enough money to exist on—if there were no more emergencies—and she qualified for the right kind of student loans so she could begin nursing school. But while Gracie watched Ben so she could go to the university to talk with a student advisor, he told her about a program the local hospital offered. "The hospital covers most of the tuition if the student works at the hospital for a set period of time," the college advisor told her after she'd gone to gather the necessary information. "However, if the student decides *not* to work at the hospital, then the student is obligated to repay the hospital."

With his words, Brooke bit on her lip and fought back tears of relief. Her eyes automatically lifted toward heaven. When she'd arrived at Hilton Head, she'd barely had the faith of half a grain of mustard seed. But she had prayed, God had heard and come through for her.

After checking with the hospital to confirm the possibility, she rushed back to Gracie's to tell her. "Most of the money I had saved was for tuition," she said excitedly. "But I'm not going to have to pay tuition. I can't believe this. I don't have a lot, but I'm better off now, even with having paid off what was left of Ben's hospital bill, than I was when I thought I was going to have to pay tuition."

Gracie just grinned knowingly. "The Lord works in mysterious ways."

"Yes, He does." Brooke glanced at her watch to check the time, then back at Gracie. "Where's Jake? Shouldn't he be home from work by now?"

"Not far from here," Gracie said. "He met this older couple when Ben was in the hospital. They are the grandparents of a little boy who was in for a concussion he got from falling off his bike. He wasn't wearing a helmet. The grandpa had bypass surgery three months before. Jake found out they could use some help, so he's been over there a few times."

"I wonder," Brooke said, "if he could use a partner."

"By all means go ask," she said before giving Brooke directions to the house. "Ben's playing. He's fine to stay here as long as need be."

Brooke stopped by a bakery for sweet rolls, then drove to the house. The woman answered the door. "I understand Jake Randolph is here making repairs," Brooke said.

The woman confirmed and invited her in, then led her to the kitchen, and introduced her to her husband, who was talking to Jake while he worked.

Jake appeared shocked as Brooke gave the rolls to the woman. "I'm from a church up the way," she said. "I heard your husband recently got out of the hospital, and I wondered if there's anything I can do."

"Why, how nice of you," the woman gushed, and Brooke knew she was feeling overwhelmed, the same way Brooke had felt when Gracie had come to her house. "But no, I don't think we need anything. We're doing fine." She laughed and spoke ironically, saying they had trouble keeping up with her husband's medicine. "He has so much to take and forgets it half the time. When I try to help, I have no idea if he took it or not."

Soon Brooke and the woman were sitting at the kitchen table with a legal pad and Sharpie, and Brooke made out a schedule chart for the medication. She made two copies. "Use this until I can get to the drug store to pick up some daily pill boxes for you. That way, you'll know what to take and when to take it."

"I'll see to that. Oh, this is perfect."

As Jake packed up his toolbox, Brooke said her goodbyes, ensuring they left the house together.

Outside, as they walked toward his truck and her car, Jake asked, "What was that all about?"

She lifted her chin saucily. "You're not the only person in the world with a water-basin mentality, Jake Randolph."

He grinned. "You're a girl after my own heart."

"You're absolutely right," she replied with a nudge of her elbow against his arm. Then she laughed, jumped into her car, and took off for Gracie's to retrieve Ben. When they pulled into the driveway, she spotted Jake sitting on the front porch swing.

As soon as she got Ben out of the car, he tore off in the direction of the back yard.

"Hey, buddy," Jake called out. "Where ya going?"

"I gotta go get Taz!"

Brooke stepped onto the front porch and leaned her shoulder against the nearest column.

"What took you so long?"

"I went to Gracie's to get Ben." She gave him her best smile. "Why? Something on your mind?"

He leaned back and propped his ankle on his knee. "I want to know what you meant by that remark?"

"What remark?" she asked, feigning innocence.

"You know."

Brooke stepped over to the swing to sit next to him. "Well," she said, slanting her eyes up at his. "I found out today that I can go to school without having to get another job because the hospital will pay for it. That means, I can be here more for Ben *and* have time to study. So, you see, I don't have to find a man to support me."

Jake stared at her as though he were trying to discern the fullness of what she had said to him. Brooke thought to let him suffer for a minute or so, but then added, "I don't *have* to have a man," she reiterated, "but I *want* one."

The skin around his eyes crinkled as he grinned at her. "Do you now?"

Brooke nodded. "I do." She raised a finger. "But there are certain requirements."

"Like?"

"Well, first of all," she said, pushing the index finger of one hand against the index finger of the other, "he has to have a water-basin mentality."

"Hmmm. Anything else?"

"Yes. He has to be strong, giving, loving, handsome—"

He started to stand. "Then I should leave."

"Oh, no," she said, reaching out to grab his arm. "That man is you, Jake Randolph. You said you loved me. Now, if you've changed your mind . . ."

"No ma'am," he said turning fully toward her and taking her hands in his. "I love you, Brooke. And I would like us to spend the rest of our lives together." Exasperated, he shook his head. "I didn't mean to propose or anything."

Her eyes opened wide, and she drew back playfully. "Then just what *are* you suggesting?"

"Brooke," he said with a chuckle. "You are deliberately putting me on the spot."

"Yes," she said. "I'm afraid I am."

"Let's just be honest," he said.

"I love you, Jake," she blurted before he could say another word.

"And I love you."

"Jake," Brooke said, moving closer to him. "When I came here, I thought it would take years before I could even consider having another man in my life. If then. But you've changed my mind and my life. But I need to know straight up. How would you feel about your wife going to school and working as a nurse?"

"Proud," he said immediately.

"And how do you feel about a house full of children?"

He laughed. "I say we start with four and see how we feel after that."

Brooke laughed too. "Good. Now," she said, kissing his cheek. "We've got that settled."

"Brooke?"

"Yes?"

"Will you marry me?"

"Yes," she whispered. "I will."

"Then come here," he said, pulling her close. "I'm so 'cited about this, I'm going to kiss you right in front of all creation."

Just as their lips met, the screen door slammed and Ben's voice demanded, "Whatcha doing?"

With a great sigh, Jake dropped his hands from around Brooke and scooted over. "Come on over here, son," Jake said. "We all need to have a serious talk."

Ben ran over and plopped on the swing.

"Oh!" Brooke said as a creak and pop followed. All three bounded from the swing seconds before it hit the porch floorboards, the chains following after.

They looked at one another slack-jawed until Ben said, "That was *cool!*"

When Brooke finally stopped laughing, she pointed to Jake, "You're the one in charge of repairs."

"I guess we'll stand for this," Jake said and tested the banister before leaning back against it. He looked at Brooke. "You want to tell him?"

"You can."

"Tell me what?" Ben asked.

Jake squatted down and placed his hands on Ben's shoulders. "Your mother and I want to get married. What do you think about that?"

Ben's eyes grew wide. "You mean, we're going to be a family?"

When Jake nodded, Ben said, "Can I call you 'Daddy'?"

Jake looked up at Brooke whose heart caught in her chest. She nodded.

"If you'd like," Jake said.

"Wow," Ben shouted, "That's even cooler than the swing falling. But I want to show you guys something Taz and I saw." He darted into the front yard and pointed up at the sky. "Over here. Over here."

Brooke and Jake joined Ben to see the faint outline of a rainbow arched across the late evening sky.

"It didn't even rain here," Ben said.

"Not here," Jake said, cupping his hands on Ben's shoulders. "But over that way it may have. But, so you know, that rainbow up there is a promise."

"Of what, Daddy?" Ben asked.

"That even though the rain comes, no matter where it falls, somewhere there's a rainbow."

Brooke slipped her arm around Jake's waist before looking up at him. "I love you," she whispered.

"And I love you," he said, his voice clear and strong.

The End

Book 2

Smoky Mountain Sunrise

One

"My brother's in trouble!"

Rae glanced up, startled by Livi's explosive announcement as the young woman rushed into her office and flung herself into the nearest chair.

With another school year behind, Rae had been cleaning out her desk drawers. Now she paused to study the beautiful brunette who gazed at her with soulful, blue eyes. One could never be sure when Livi Doudet was serious or merely exaggerating. Sometimes, Rae knew, at twenty-one, every moment seemed like a dramatic pause. In fact, Rae reminded herself, sometimes at *thirty-one* the same was true. "Why do you say that?" she asked, now stacking papers into a cardboard box.

"I don't know." Her hesitation confirmed Rae's suspicion that Livi hadn't meant her brother was in *real* trouble.

"Why don't you tell me about it while you help take those books off the shelves. We're not teacher and student now, you know. Just friends."

"Fine friend you are, making me work on a hot day like this." Despite the protest, Livi smiled in her winning way and walked over to the bookshelf, lifting her shoulder-length hair from her neck.

"Hottest May Day ever recorded by the weather bureau in Atlanta," Rae mimicked the noonday weathercaster. "Now, tell me about your brother."

"He's in Florida."

Rae glanced at her. "That's bad?"

"It's *strange*." Livi forgot the books and leaned back against the shelf. "Uncle Lucas and Andy had planned to stay in Switzerland for another week. When I told Uncle Lucas that you had invited me to spend this week with you, he was happy. Now . . ." She shoved her fists into her hips. "Andy has called me from Florida and started asking about *you*."

"Me?" Rae straightened, surprised. She'd never met André—Andy—Doudet. In fact, she only knew what she'd read about him. What she did know was that he and Livi were from a wealthy, close-knit family. "Does he make it a habit to check on all your friends?"

Livi laughed. "Andy wouldn't check on my friends. But it seems he *does* want to check *you* out." She shrugged. The typically mischievous look sparkled in her eyes. "Maybe he's between girls and *maybe* I've been playing—"

"Matchmaker? Oh, Livi," Rae laughed, dismissing the entire idea.

"No, no. Not matchmaker *exactly*. But I do talk about you an awful lot and I guess my big brother has finally—how should I say this—taken the bait."

"Taken the—that's ridiculous, Livi."

"Not for André."

"Let's get these things packed." Rae's tone was no-nonsense now. "The sooner it's done, the sooner we can get to the house."

With that inviting idea, Livi returned to helping with renewed enthusiasm. "At first he asked about you casually. But he got oh-so-interested when I told him how beautiful you are."

"He wouldn't think so if he saw me today," Rae contradicted, touching her hair that curled into tight ringlets when damp. She could feel tiny beads of perspiration on her face.

"He also knows that, even though you're a professor here and I'm a *lowly student*—"

"You should have majored in drama, Liv."

"True," Livi said with a laugh. "Anyway, he's coming here."

"Here? To the university?"

"No, he's going to pick me up at the end of the week at your place. Then we'll drive home to North Carolina together."

"Livi," Rae said with a sense of exasperated affection for this young woman who always twisted things out of proportion. The famous André Doudet was linked with beautiful women from all over the world.

He certainly wouldn't be interested in someone he'd never seen. "That explains it. There's no trouble. It's just brotherly love. You don't spend much time together, so this is just a good chance to catch up with you."

Livi shook her head. "He was more interested in you than in me. And Andy doesn't like to drive. He always flies if possible." She held up a stack of papers. "Are these the exams we took today?"

"Don't you dare touch those!" Rae warned. "I haven't graded them yet, and when it comes to exams, I'm all teacher, and you're still the student. But you don't have to worry about your grades."

"On the written part I do," Livi moaned. "Come to think of it, I don't think I could *ever* be as good as you in the gymnastics routines, either."

"The teacher is supposed to excel," Rae chided gently, accepting the compliment.

"I'll bet when you were my age, you were better than I am *now*," Livi said with admiration.

"Well, yes, but I had the best possible teacher," Rae reminded her and caught her breath. They grew quiet; the only sound was that of books and papers being piled into boxes.

Rae's father, a teacher and gymnastics coach, who had died a few months earlier, had sent several young hopefuls to the Olympics before coming to teach at the university in Atlanta where Rae had served on the faculty for the past three years.

"School's out at last," Livi piped suddenly, lifting her arms into the air and dispelling the reflective mood that had momentarily settled upon them.

Rae smiled, remembering the years she had uttered those words as a student, then as a teacher. But it was different this year. An entire summer without her father held no appeal. It would be lonely. But at least Livi would be with her for this week. A week climaxed by a visit from the nearly famous André Doudet. It wasn't often one had a chance to meet an accomplished athlete such as him.

"Looks like everything's packed," Rae said after taking a quick look around the office.

As they lugged boxes through the gym, Rae's mind replayed the physical education classes she taught there. Her favorite this year had been *gymnastics moderne*, in which she had had an opportunity to exhibit her extraordinary skills along with her instruction.

After driving the few blocks to her home and unloading the boxes, they collapsed into chairs, enjoying the refreshing effect of the air conditioning.

Livi wiggled the toes of one foot propped on a box of books. "You and I are going to have a great week, Rae, seeing everything in Atlanta and doing all there is to do."

Rae laughed. She didn't doubt that. With her own fair hair and green eyes, she knew that she and Livi differed in more than physical appearance. In lifestyles and temperament, too, they were exact opposites. Livi was a fun-loving extrovert with the tendency to laugh at life rather than take it seriously. Yet, Rae knew Livi had depth that rarely surfaced. Rae's faith in God had given her strength to face life with courage after her father's death. But it had been Livi, herself an orphan, who came offering friendship during a difficult time.

~ ~ ~

As promised, the week was filled with fun and laughter, leaving Rae excited about André's arrival, especially with Livi proudly pointing him out in numerous sports magazines. "That's Andy at Uncle Lucas's ski resort in Switzerland." Another pictured the smiling athlete enjoying the slopes of a similar resort in North Carolina. He was on the cover of still another, having won the national tennis competition that year.

The only thing that marred Rae's excitement at the prospect of meeting Livi's brother was the fact that he would take Livi back to North Carolina. Rae would be left to face the reality of her loneliness and the difficult decision about her future.

Rae kept telling herself that Livi was mistaken about her brother's desire to meet her. After all, they were strangers. Nevertheless, on the day of his arrival, she decided to wear one of her prettier summer dresses, something she hadn't done in a while. Not since her last date. Correction, her last *failed* date, which they all seemed to be. Why couldn't she meet a man as rock solid as her father had been? Wasn't that what good Southern girls wanted to find in a man? All the goodness of Daddy?

She tamed her naturally curly hair with a flat iron, then brushed it away from her face on one side, allowing it to fall in a soft wave on the other. The long-on-top, short-in-back style was ideal for one so active and complemented the color her father had often referred to as "spun gold."

When Andy finally arrived, Rae watched from the porch of the modest home she'd shared with her parents and now lived in alone. Livi ran down the front walk to embrace her brother as he exited a low-slung, bright yellow sports car. Towering over his sister, his brown hair gleamed in the sunlight. He was wearing casual slacks and a short-sleeved shirt, but Rae could visualize him in tennis or ski wear, stepping from the pages of sports magazines she and Livi had devoured.

Now this perfect specimen of masculinity walked toward Rae, flashing the dazzling smile that had the power to charm, even from the glossy pages.

Her green eyes met his twinkling brown ones as Livi introduced them. "Okay, brother. Here she is. The one I've been telling you about. Rae Martin."

"Please call me Andy. Most of my friends do," he invited, extending his hand. "And then tell me why your parents named you Ray?"

Rae laughed, having heard that question hundreds of times before. "It's Rae with an *e*," she explained.

"I suspected something like that," Andy teased. "Livi, why haven't you insisted I come here sooner to see you and to meet Rae?"

"How would I know where to find you?" Livi quipped as she turned her face toward his. "Last month it was Paris and Switzerland. Then last week it was Florida. Now, you're *here* in Atlanta." Mischief played in her eyes. "What attracted you to *Hotlanta*, brother dear? Was it the Braves, the Falcons, or the Georgia peaches?"

No doubt Andy's laughter was a polite recognition of his sister's double entendre. Sensing his uneasiness, Rae recalled Livi's premonition that he was in trouble.

"Shall we go inside?" Rae invited, holding open the screen door.

"I made your favorite drink," Livi said as she and Andy followed Rae into the kitchen.

"Sounds like lemonade," he said, smiling down at Livi before pulling out a chair and taking a seat at the small, round table. "It was nice of you to ask Livi to stay with you this week, Rae."

"It was my pleasure," Rae assured him. "Livi and I have become close friends since my father died."

Andy's eyes widened with sudden realization. "Wait. *Rae Martin*. Your father was the gymnastics coach *Raymond* Martin, right? I didn't make the connection when we were introduced."

Anyone seriously involved in sports knew the name and knew it well. In addition to his coaching, Raymond Martin had helped make the gymnastics program at the Atlanta university one of the finest in the nation.

"I'm sorry for your loss," Andy continued softly. "The sports world has lost a great man. Livi and I know about that kind of loss. Our parents were killed when Liv was no more than a baby."

"And you?" Rae asked. "You were just a boy."

"I was barely ten. But there was always Uncle Lucas—Dad's brother—and Gran. Do you have brothers or sisters?"

"No. Both parents were only children, both sets of grandparents are gone. But I try to think not so much of what I've lost, but of what my father has gained. My mother died ten years ago. At least now I have the consolation that they're together again in heaven."

Rae spurned the grief that threatened to overwhelm her. Feeling Andy's intense gaze, she was grateful when Livi brought glasses filled with lemonade.

"Is Uncle Lucas back home?" she asked

Andy shook his head. "He won't be for a couple of days yet. We'll get home before he does." He tasted the frosty beverage and nodded appreciatively. "Say, this lemonade is really good."

"Nothing's too good for my big brother who loves me so much he wants to drive me all the way from Georgia to North Carolina," Livi replied with exaggerated playfulness, cutting her eyes toward Andy.

"Well, there is another reason, Livi. Something I must discuss with you." He seemed uncertain whether to continue as he poked absently at a lemon slice. "As you know I had to make a trip to Florida. That's where I picked up that little gem out there."

Rae assumed he meant the car.

"Okay, what's her name?" Livi asked, amusement coloring the inflection of her voice.

Andy's look of chagrin confirmed his sister's assumption that a female was involved. "We have a long drive ahead of us, Liv. We'll talk about it later." He turned his charming smile in Rae's direction. "Right now, I'd much rather talk about your friend here."

Livi tugged at his shirt sleeve. "You know I have no patience! Besides, Rae doesn't mind. We've shared a lot of personal things."

"I couldn't burden her with this one."

Rae had the distinct feeling he *wanted* to talk about it, which sparked her curiosity. "It wouldn't be a burden," she assured him. "If you want to talk about it, I'm a good listener."

Andy leaned forward with a sigh, propping his elbows on the table.

"There *is* a girl," he admitted. "Celeste imagines herself in love with me. Her parents wrote to Uncle Lucas, mentioning wedding plans. I gotta tell you, Liv, I was completely taken aback when he confronted me with that news. Not once have I ever so much as mentioned 'happily ever after,' so I had to go to Florida to see Celeste. I think I've convinced her to make a clean break, but I don't know."

Livi shrugged. "Oh, Andy, you've been in worse situations. What about—"

"This is different. Uncle Lucas feels I haven't been honest with Celeste. That I haven't made my intentions clear from the beginning.

He doesn't like her parents getting into it, and he even mentioned the possibility of a breach-of-promise suit."

"Can't you explain to your uncle that you made a mistake?" Rae asked. "Tell him Celeste misunderstood your intentions?"

"He doesn't take such things lightly, I'm afraid," Andy assured her. "Sometimes I think he's forty going on eighty."

"Sounds like a happily married man who enjoys matchmaking."

"Oh, no, he's a bachelor. It's just that he strongly believes in being responsible for one's commitments."

"He doesn't like women?"

Ironic laughter shared by the siblings dispelled that notion from Rae's mind.

"He likes women just fine. The problem is"—Andy paused, looking sheepish—"that this is not the first time something like this has happened."

"You *have* left a string of broken hearts around the world," Livi scolded affectionately.

"It hasn't been all one-sided," he protested. "But that's the way Uncle Lucas is beginning to see it. He says there have been too many indications that I'm not being honest in my relationships."

"Why doesn't your uncle let the two of you work out your own problems?"

Andy shook his head. "Celeste's parents involved him when they wrote to him, and he feels responsible since he's the trustee over my inheritance. I'm bound to his decisions until I turn thirty-five." He smiled. "Four more years to go, if I can keep my nose clean."

Rae calculated the math, then said, "Wait a sec. He's forty and you're thirty-two and he's your trustee?"

Andy took a long swallow of lemonade, then nodded. "Initially, Gran was our trustee, but when Uncle Lucas turned thirty, he took over all the financial and legal elements of the family business."

"He's more like a much older big brother," Livi added. "He's Gran's son by her second marriage, see?"

"Also," Andy continued, "it hasn't been easy working things out with Celeste. You know how it is when a woman believes she's in love with a man who stands to inherit a large amount of cash and she *wants* to get married." He air-quoted the last word. "You know, to all that money."

Rae lowered her eyes to her glass. No, she didn't know, although she certainly knew women like that existed. But she couldn't begin to imagine marrying a man for his money. Her parents had shown her what a love-filled marriage was all about; she wouldn't settle for anything less. Not that she'd had a lot of opportunity to date much. At least, not seriously.

"Celeste wanted to bring her parents to our home to meet Lucas," Andy said. "Which would be disastrous. She would take one look at the place and believe herself even more deeply in love. You can't imagine what that girl has cost me in clothes and jewelry." He took a deep breath. "Now we have matching cars."

Noting the shocked expressions on the girls' faces, Andy glanced from one to the other. "Don't give me that look," he said. "At the time I thought I was very much *in like.*"

Livi leaned closer to Rae. "Andy is never in love, but he has been *in like* a few thousand times." Then, to her brother, she added, "Andy, didn't you tell her you were through with her?"

"Yes, but Celeste is not the kind of girl one drops suddenly. You've heard the proverb about a woman's wrath? No, this will have to be done carefully and discreetly."

"Well, if Uncle Lucas plans to invite them to the house, what hope is there?"

Andy traced a pattern on the tabletop as he chewed on his lower lip. "I lied to Uncle Lucas."

"Oh, André," Livi moaned. She reached over to take his hand and his fingers tightened around hers. His expression was more that of a remorseful little boy than a grown man of thirty-two. "What did you tell him?"

"The only thing that would make any difference. I told him I had been wrong about Celeste and was going to Florida to make her understand. Then I said I couldn't marry Celeste because . . ." Andy paused, cleared his throat, then continued in a desolate tone. "Because I had fallen in love with the perfect girl, the kind he always wanted for me. A nice *Christian* girl."

Delight brightened Livi's face. "Oh, Andy, have you?"

"No," he admitted, shaking his head. "I haven't exactly been looking for that kind of girl, I'm afraid."

The three sat in silence, staring at cold lemon slices resting on ice. Rae knew that Livi's older brother had graduated from a university in Switzerland and helped to manage his uncle's ski resort there when he wasn't playing in tennis tournaments. Now she wondered if he had genuinely earned his playboy reputation. She could certainly understand how females would be attracted to him. Physically and materially, he had much to offer. But from this brief encounter, she suspected he lacked the spiritual qualities that would make a long-term relationship possible. He needed guidance but seemed instead to be manipulated by bad choices and what she supposed was a domineering uncle.

Livi's concerned voice broke through the wall of silence. "Did Uncle Lucas believe you when you told him you had fallen in love with a nice Christian girl?"

Had it not been such a serious matter, Rae would have laughed at the scowl on Andy's face as he imitated his uncle in a booming voice. "'Fantastic, André! She must be some girl if you're thinking of settling down. Go to Florida. Clear up this misunderstanding with that other woman and her parents. Then bring your perfect girl home. I want to meet her. Within the week. Otherwise, I'll have to take drastic measures which includes cutting your allowance.'

"You see," Andy said, his voice returning to normal, "both Livi and I come into our inheritances when we turn thirty-five, which, for me, isn't that far off but far enough away if you catch my meaning. Meanwhile, we're given an allowance—albeit a generous one—to live on." He looked helplessly at the two women. "So, then he told me if I didn't bring my fiancée to North Carolina, he was going to do what he should have done in the first place and invite Celeste and her parents to our home." Andy grimaced. "If he finds out I—well, let's just say that I stretched the truth—on top of everything else, I'm doomed. My only chance is to come up with a girl Uncle Lucas would approve of—a nice Christian girl."

"Oh, Andy." Livi sighed in exasperation, but love for her brother glowed in her eyes. "You do manage to get mixed up in some crazy schemes."

For the second time in the conversation, the three found themselves staring at their drinks. Rae traced a design through the moisture collecting on her glass, while the silence grew increasingly uncomfortable. "More lemonade?" she asked in a strained voice. Andy and Livi shook their heads. Rae stood, gathered the glasses, and took them to the sink. Looking out the window at the backyard, she noticed the brilliance of the sunshine bathing the new growth on the leafy trees. Twin maples. After his first heart attack, her father had spent much time under the shade of those trees. *Lord, how I miss him.*

Rae returned to the table, aware that Livi and Andy watched her every move. She sank into the chair and when she looked up, Andy and Livi stared at her with a peculiar gleam in their eyes. Almost simultaneously, they broke into triumphant grins.

"Rae." The confidence in Livi's voice indicated they had found the answer to Andy's dilemma. Despite the physical differences between brother and sister, there was a family resemblance which at the moment was one of sinister determination.

"Oh, *no*," she cried in dismay, their incredible scheme suddenly transparent.

"Oh, come on, Rae," Livi exclaimed. "You could do it. You could do this. And it's not a lie. Andy told Uncle Lucas that he met a nice Christian girl. And he has. *You.*" She turned to address Andy. "Rae and her father headed up the Christian Athletes Club on campus."

"I'm impressed," he said. "As Uncle Lucas would be." He leaned across the table and took Rae's hand in his. His voice was low and persuasive. "Would it be so unthinkable to be *in like* with me for just a little while, Rae?"

Rae pulled her hand from his. "Andy, it wouldn't work."

"I'm not asking you to lie."

"Lying can be by implication. Just tell your uncle how you feel."

"You don't know our uncle," he replied, as if such an admission were out of the question. "You will soon enough, though, and then you'll understand."

Rae could agree with that statement. She *didn't* know their uncle. Livi had made frequent references to him in their late-night talks. She knew he acted as trustee and provider to his wards, but he had remained a distant parent figure in Rae's mind. One she found rather foreboding now that she thought of it.

"I'm sorry, Andy," she said. "I wish I could help. I do. But it just isn't *possible.*"

"Well," he said. "At least I *thought* I had found the solution." Andy sighed away the scheme. "*Do* you have plans for the summer, Rae?"

Rae's thoughts shifted from those regarding Andy's plans, to her own. She hadn't signed the contract to return to her position at the university in the fall. The administration and faculty had been more than understanding and sympathetic throughout her father's illness and death, assuring her that the position would remain open indefinitely. Now, she felt, a complete change was in order. But she hadn't yet decided what that would be, and nothing had popped up over the horizon.

"I'm not sure," she admitted. "I've considered a short vacation. I may even try to find a summer job."

Andy's eyes lit up. "I have the perfect job for you. And for a teacher of gymnastics. As the daughter of Raymond Martin, it would probably seem like a vacation. Our summer camp in North Carolina for young athletes opens up in June. Right now, it's only for boys—something we're planning to change soon—but we have female trainers and counselors for the younger ones."

"That's perfect." Livi's eyes brightened. "You should see Rae when she's teaching. She's *magnifique!* Everyone loves her, but she commands respect too. And she makes us believe in ourselves—that we can do anything we set out to do. She could head up the gymnastics program. She's equally good in swimming and—"

"Wait a minute," Rae protested. "You don't know if your uncle would approve of me as an employee, even for the summer. The job sounds intriguing, but I—well, I'd need to find renters for the house, and—"

"Oh, I get it." A look of resignation settled on Andy's face. "There's a special guy to keep you here."

Rae recognized his ploy, tried to keep the blush from her face, but knew she was unsuccessful. "No, there's no one special." Truth was, she hadn't anyone dated seriously in at least two years and that had ended with her nursing a broken heart. Since then, she'd had a string of "first dates."

A strange silence followed. Then, without taking his eyes from Rae's, Andy addressed Livi. "You know, Livi, I believe Rae *is* the kind of girl Lucas has in mind for me." He smiled. "He thinks my friends are too flashy, too worldly, too caught up in materialism. You're sensible, sweet, and probably the most honest person I've ever met, not to mention the most beautiful."

"Flattery will get you nowhere," Rae muttered.

"I'm not trying to flatter you. I'm even beginning to understand your viewpoint. We aren't exactly infidels, Livi and I, although we probably appear that way to you. I can see that it would be against your principles asking you to pretend something that's not fully there between us." When Rae raised her brow, he added, "Okay, not even slightly there." He leaned forward. "Tell you what, just come with us to North Carolina and consider taking the summer job. And, if you'll do me this *one little thing*, we'll simply say we're getting to know each other for the next few weeks. Perhaps you don't find *that* idea too unpleasant, do you?"

"It's not unpleasant at all," she assured him. "And I'd love the job, but . . ."

"But?"

"Am I supposed to pretend we've been dating? That's not even *remotely* true."

His head tilted. "Can't you pretend a little?"

"No."

"Please, Rae," Livi said, her hands folded in mock prayer.

Rae knew there was no way these two impetuous siblings could understand her reluctance. Sensible people just didn't do things like that.

"All right." Andy slapped his hands against his thighs. "I won't ask you to pretend anything. Fine. Just let me tell Uncle Lucas that Livi introduced us and that I like you a lot and that you aren't quite there yet. That you want to take it slow. We can at least say we're friends and that much is true."

Hardly. How could she say she was friends with someone she'd just met? "As long as I don't have to pretend to be engaged. Or in love." She gasped to realize how close she was to agreeing to Andy's arrangement. Being André Doudet's girl did have its appeal, even to a sensible girl like her. She quickly reminded herself that Andy wasn't taking her seriously, he just needed a girl in a hurry to get him out of a jam. And she could use a summer job. If she could keep that at the forefront of her mind, she could guard against ending the summer in heartache.

Besides, she reckoned, a change of scenery would be good for her and could provide the opportunity for the serious thinking she had to do. Her funds were limited, and she must soon decide what direction her life should take.

Yes, there seemed to be so many reasons why she shouldn't accept his offer. For one, Livi was leaving soon for Paris. For another, this uncle of theirs seemed like someone she wasn't altogether sure she wanted to know. Forty years old and in such strict charge of two young adults? "Your uncle must be—" She stifled the urge to say, "an old tyrant," and substituted, "very strict."

"He's a good man, but he does hold the purse strings."

"And the purse," Livi added, laughing.

Andy grinned. "True."

"But, Andy," Rae persisted, "I might not meet your uncle's requirements. I'm a very ordinary, uninteresting person."

Andy looked amused. "Are you worried about your qualifications for the job or whether or not Uncle Lucas will like you as my girl? Either way, let me reassure you that you're more than qualified for the job *and* you're definitely a nice Christian girl. Exactly the kind of girl he'd want Liv and me to bring home for the summer."

Rae laughed helplessly. "Oh, Andy."

At least the summer promised to be anything but dull.

Two

The low, sleek sports car sped around the mountainsides like a small yellow bird flitting from treetop to treetop before eventually nestling in the heart of the Blue Ridge Mountains.

Around every bend of the Parkway was another scenic delight—deep, emerald valleys; rocky ravines slashed with crystal waterfalls; tangled thickets of flowering shrubs carpeting the forest floor on both sides of the highway. The retreating sun flung visual blockades as subdued peaks of blues and greens were thrust against a graying sky. Wide-open landscapes, endless highways, and skyscrapers had given way to a world of almost primeval splendor. Rae wished the sun would linger so she could drink in the beauty of this paradise.

"It's incredibly beautiful," she whispered reverently.

Andy reached across the front seat of the car and squeezed her hand. "This part of the country compares favorably with any spot in the world," he said. "At times I take it for granted, but you have a way of making me appreciate things, Rae. As if seeing them for the first time." Giving Rae's hand a final squeeze, Andy turned his attention to the serpentine curve ahead.

Rae had not felt comfortable with his one-handed driving yet felt sure her apprehension was due to her own lack of familiarity with the mountains. He maneuvered the car expertly, even in the fast-approaching darkness of night.

Rae turned her face toward the window and concentrated on the fascinating world opening before her. The closer they came to their destination, the more intrigued she became. There was a sweet fragrance she could not identify, and the pungency of pine.

Andy turned off the main road onto a paved, private one. The car began its ascent as it wound higher through trees that joined limbs in a conspiracy against the moonlight.

"It's like a jungle," Rae said in wonder.

"The only place in the world where there is a greater variety of trees is in China," Andy informed her. "Around this next curve you will find our haven from this chaotic world."

After the turn, both sides of the road were flanked by rustic, split-rail fences. Orange trumpets on long, green throats swayed and bent, heralding their coming. Suddenly, like a mirage, a great stone structure appeared. Mellow light gleamed from windows, and floodlights illuminated the landscape. Rather than dominating, the two-story structure blended majestically with its surroundings. Circular wings did not distract but conformed to the natural undulations of the land. Behind the mansion rose an even higher peak, darkened by the night, as if it were some strange sleeping beauty.

Rae could not begin to comprehend what the scenery must look like in bright sunlight; even now shadowed by darkness and lightly bathed with artificial light, the colorful array of springtime was much in evidence. Even her brief glimpse provided the spectacular picture of the fragile among the stately, the delicate amid strength. Dark evergreens, leafy maples, yellow-green poplars, pink and white dogwood blossoms, and bushes laden with purple, red, pink, yellow, and white flowers surrounded them.

At the beginning of a long, sweeping drive was a rustic wooden sign with the words *Mountain Haven* carved into it.

"That's Lucas's name for the house," Livi explained.

Rae had never seen anything like it. The stone mansion with its great expanse of glass windows seemed to draw nature into itself, and at the same time the shingled roof appeared to touch the sky.

Andy didn't turn into the drive bordered by natural rock and lush greenery, which circled in front of the house, but drove onto a secondary gravel drive, around a stone wing, then came to a stop beneath a redwood roof.

As soon as they stepped from the car, Rae was bombarded with a sweet fragrance. "Strawberries," she exclaimed, inhaling deeply.

Livi laughed and pointed to a row of bushes along the stone wall. "We call it 'Carolina Allspice.'"

Rae walked over to them. The blossoms looked like rust-colored wooden flowers. When she touched them, they felt like wood, but when she sniffed, they smelled nothing like wood.

Each taking bags, they climbed the redwood steps alongside the stone wall leading to a high deck at the back of the house.

"It must be something in the air," Rae said. "Tell me flowers don't look like wood, and rocks don't shine."

"Wrong, wrong," Livi corrected. "There's mica in the rock, and when the light strikes just right, it *does* shine. These stones came out of our own area mountains."

Rae stood on the deck for a moment, marveling at the sounds of nature, almost deafening in the absence of car horns, train whistles, and airplane engines.

Once inside, Andy took their luggage upstairs while Rae and Livi whipped up a quick snack, which they ate at the kitchen table. After eating and discussing their next steps to settling in, Livi checked the lounge for mail, leaving Rae and Andy to tidy up.

As they worked, Rae thought of the past two days and Andy's helpfulness with arrangements she'd had to make before leaving Atlanta. Their proximity during the drive had provided an insight into his personality. His interesting conversation had been flavored with humor and intelligence as he related experiences associated with his many travels. She was growing to like this roguish charmer.

It had been a while since Rae had seriously considered settling down to a "forever" with any man. But in the back of her mind was the assumption that the man of her dreams would be both a Christian *and* an athlete. Andy certainly fulfilled one of those requirements. And the other was partly her responsibility in this world to set an example for unbelievers. Yes, with a faith in God to put his priorities in the right order, Andy could become the kind of man a Christian girl could consider seriously.

Their fingers touched as they reached for the same dish. Andy grabbed her hand and lifted it to his lips just as Livi came in from the lounge, carrying a bundle of correspondence.

She held an envelope toward the light. "Who sends letters anymore?"

"Who's it from?" Andy asked, dropping Rae's hand.

"Isobel. Wonder what she has to say."

"Better not snoop in Uncle Lucas's mail, Livi," Andy reprimanded her, and Rae wondered if his irritation was caused by Livi's interruption or by the letter.

"Who is Isobel?" she asked curiously.

"Very likely the future mistress of this house if she has her way," Andy explained. "She's a widow with a young son who very much needs a father. In my humble opinion," he overemphasized, "she sees Uncle Lucas as a game she's willing to cheat to win."

"You think they'll marry?" Livi asked. She didn't appear happy about it.

Andy sighed, as if resigned to the situation. "They've been seeing each other for a while now. Wouldn't be surprised."

Livi nodded in acquiescence, shuffled through the correspondence—mostly to OCCUPANT, she said—then gave Andy his mail, then returned to the lounge with the rest.

"We should say good night, Rae. Tomorrow's a big day."

She knew he was referring to the fact that tomorrow she'd meet Uncle Lucas.

His face grew pensive. "It's not going to be so bad, is it, Rae?"

Although she hadn't yet absorbed her new surroundings, Rae looked forward to working in a mountain setting. And she believed Andy needed her as a buffer against his uncle. But there was something else to consider.

"Much depends on what your uncle thinks of me," she reminded him.

His hand touched her shoulder, and he spoke reassuringly. "He'll like you, Rae. I can't imagine you having too many enemies. But the important thing is that he believes I have special feelings for you."

Rae sighed. "The burden's on you then. I'm only supposed to be thinking over our relationship."

His smile was warm. "I don't think it's going to be at all difficult." He leaned close to whisper. "I suspect we've already convinced my sister."

Rae turned her head in time to see Livi step quickly back inside the lounge doorway. She looked up curiously at Andy who grinned and said, "Good night, Rae. And thanks for everything."

Livi rejoined Rae only after Andy had gone upstairs and closed the door to his bedroom. Approaching Rae, she shook her head. "Andy surprised me tonight," she said. "He's treating you like someone very special."

Rae laughed it away. "Livi, you're imagining things. Your brother's just being polite and charming. It seems to be part of his nature."

"It is. But I know Andy. He doesn't seem to be acting," she said, her lovely eyes aglow. "You and Andy getting together would be awesome."

"Don't be silly, Livi. Andy isn't looking for a girl like me."

"And why not?" Livi asked.

"Different backgrounds. He's rich, I'm poor. He's internationally known, I'm relatively unknown. He's outgoing and I'm more low-key. He's—"

Livi stopped on the stairs, her hands on her hips. "That sounds like you think we're terrible snobs. And I sincerely hope you aren't calling me a snob, because if you are, I'll challenge you to a duel of racquetball."

"You know you always beat me at racquetball."

"That's why I chose it." Livi laughed, and they walked up the stairs arm in arm.

Despite her exhaustion, Rae couldn't sleep.

The cool mountain air, moist and misty, drifted in through the open bedroom window, stirring the curtains. Outside, the shadowy hulk of the mountains spoke of permanence and endurance. She was glad she had come. But there was something mysterious and compelling out there in the night that beckoned to her on air heavily scented with the perfume of a thousand unknown blossoms.

After tossing the coverlet aside, she rose and stepped into her running shoes resting by the bed. Wearing a pair of shorts and tee—her usual nightwear—she looked more ready for a jog than much else.

Quietly she closed the bedroom door. Her shoes made no sound on the carpet in the upstairs hallway. Following the light from the lamp that had been left on, Rae made her way down the stairs, looking up momentarily at the exposed beams of the cathedral ceilings

This was no mountain cabin. She reveled in the aesthetic blend of log and hardwood and beam that carried the hallmark of a sensitive designer, just as the out-of-doors bore its Creator's mark.

Leaving the back door ajar, Rae stepped out into the night. She crossed the redwood deck, walked down the steps to the second deck and on out to a third that was completely surrounded by a veritable jungle.

Inhaling deeply, she savored the wonderful, musty fragrance of earth and trees and wild, growing things. Somewhere a gurgling stream made its noisy way down the mountainside. Insects sounded a symphony, and night birds called to their mates. Everything here was so wild, so untamed, so free, and she responded with a sense of exhilaration she had never felt before.

Lifting her face to the cooling breeze, her eyes were met by the sight of lush foliage, the intertwining branches of the trees so dense that only slivers of moonlight penetrated to splash on her.

She wasn't sure how long she stood there, listening to the night music, absorbing the peace, before she heard footsteps. They were heavy, swift, hesitating only momentarily. She did not turn to look. Andy wouldn't be able to sleep either.

"What's got you up in the middle of the night?" a man's voice said, one clearly not Andy's.

She turned, startled. "You're not Andy."

"No," he said in a surprised voice as she stepped farther into the lighted area of the deck. "And you're not my niece. My apologies if I scared you."

Rae shook her head, unable to look away.

"You're the friend of André's?" he asked, his eyes lingering.

Rae nodded. Was this—could this be *Uncle Lucas*? If so, he was nothing like she had imagined. Somehow, she had pictured a man with a receding hairline and, maybe, a little paunch. There was no way she could call this man "Uncle." Instead, the man reminded Rae of the unknown that had so intrigued her about the night—fascinating, wild, and untamed. His shirt sleeves were rolled up and the neck of his dress shirt was open, as if he had recently discarded a tie.

"Yes," she said finally, "I–I thought you were Andy."

"Forgive me," he breathed, then offered her a small smile. "Again, I didn't mean to frighten you."

Still, his very nearness was disturbing. Something about him was like the unknown wilderness beyond the safety of the railing—compelling, deep, and mysterious, captivating. And something deep within her stirred, reaching upward toward the light and warmth, like some fragile forest flower.

She was aware that she was part of something greater and that things could never be quite the same again.

Sensing her discomfort, he moved away, putting a respectable distance between them.

"Remind me," he said. "My nephew told me your name but I—"

"Ramona," she whispered, looking up into his eyes, amazed to discover that the sensation was the same as when she had first glimpsed the mountains. There was majesty here, power, and unspoken challenge. "I–I mean Rae." She corrected herself, using the familiar nickname with which she had been tagged ever since the day she had begun toddling after her father, imitating everything he did. "Everyone calls me Rae."

"Ramona," he repeated her given name. "I've always been partial to using proper names. Don't ask me why, I have no idea."

She raised her brow. "So, no one calls you Luke?"

He laughed then, the sound of it echoing in her chest. "Never twice, Ramona," he said after sobering.

The sound of hearing her given name again restored her to reality. No one ever used it except her father. Even her mother called her Rae. Just the thought of him brought a tear sliding down her cheek.

"And now I've made you cry?" He reached out, then dropped his hand. "Why?"

Rae didn't know how to tell him that she didn't understand her own behavior, didn't know why her emotions were suddenly as unpredictable and precarious as the mountain roads.

Turning, Rae stepped into the shadows. "It's just that no one ever called me Ramona but my father . . . and he died recently."

"I'm sorry for your loss."

"Thank you."

"I can call you Rae if that's easier for you."

"No," she shook her head, and found that she didn't mind him calling her by her given name at all. Rather than feeling a stab of loss, she sensed a flood of warm memories and turned her face toward him again with a faint smile. He did not smile back but gazed at her in a strange way that she could not fathom.

She narrowed her eyes. Something about this man . . . what was it? "Have we met before?" she asked, then chuckled at her words.

"That's not a very original line," he said, crossing his arms and taking a step back to lean against the railing. "Now," he said, "my turn for questions."

"Questions?"

"For one, wherever did André find you? Tell me what acting school you're from, or how much André paid you for this little job—because I know my nephew well enough to know he'd do something like that—and I'll repay him. Then you can get on with your next paying gig."

The insinuation in Lucas's tone penetrated Rae's consciousness. Was he intimating she was like some of the women in Andy's past? But what else could he think? Still, she had even admitted she thought he was Andy—as if she had been on the deck waiting for him.

"I think I'm getting sleepy now," she said, with little else to say. If she said much more, she could possibly give away the fact that she and Andy had only recently met. "I'll leave you to the night *and* your misconceptions."

Inside, she slammed the door of her bedroom harder than intended, and, without turning on the light, went to the window that overlooked the deck. The dark figure stepped out of the shadows and looked up, as if knowing she'd be there. She moved out of sight with a gasp and sank on the edge of the bed.

After kicking off her shoes in the darkness, Rae climbed beneath the covers. She shivered despite the down coverlet. She could not dismiss the tangled emotions she had felt with that man. No one had ever evoked such feelings in her. In those brief moments, he had stirred something deep within her she felt familiar with but couldn't be certain altogether. In spite of his accusations. She tried to rationalize. Perhaps it was because of the recent loss of her father that she had responded to a man who called her *Ramona*.

She flipped over on her side to face the window and look out past the billowing curtains. The stars were huge, almost as if she could reach out and touch them. Everything here seemed larger than life—the stars, the land, Lucas, and her emotions.

Sleep would not come. Hers had been troubled nights since her father had become ill months before. She had simply accustomed herself to dreamlike snatches of sleep. There would be none tonight, it seemed, but perhaps she could convince her body to relax. *Inhale. Hold for a count of ten. Slowly release the breath, allowing tension to drain away. Inhale . . .* She'd used this technique before gymnastic competition. It had always worked before, but not tonight.

She thought of Andy. He resembled his uncle. Maybe that's why Lucas had seemed so familiar. Even Andy's voice held a quality that might someday mellow into the same resonant tones as his uncle's. But Andy's eyes were not as dark, nor was his hair, nor was his skin. Andy wasn't as tall, or his shoulders as broad, his body as muscular.

"Oh, no," Rae breathed, as if in prayer. She knew—or thought she did—where the confusion lay. Andy was a shadow compared to his uncle. She liked Andy. His masculinity, his charm, and he was certainly good looking. His youthful vulnerability appealed to her, and she looked forward to getting to know him better.

But now she knew that Andy, in comparison with Lucas, was but a facsimile of the kind of man she wanted. The kind she had always gravitated to. Even her boyfriend of two years ago had been nearly ten years older than she. And now, here she was with Andy a hill that could be conquered, but Lucas a mountain too steep to scale.

Rae was instantly aware of a difference in the atmosphere. She pushed the curtains aside expecting to see a spectacular view of mountains and trees and valleys beyond but saw nothing through the dense fog.

She opened her suitcase, pulled out a pair of shorts and a tee, and dressed hurriedly. After brushing her hair, she left the room, retracing her steps from earlier that morning.

The patter of her running shoes stopped abruptly when she neared the back door. He was there, in navy cargo shorts and a white tee, his back turned to her. The mist seemed to swirl about him, threatening to invade the house.

"Don't you ever sleep?" he asked without turning around. She wondered how he knew it was her, but then realized that Andy's footsteps would have been heavier and Livi would have called a cheery greeting and rushed forward to embrace him.

Rae took a deep breath before answering. "I haven't slept much since my father died."

He turned toward her, and in the early light of day his face astonished her. He was as handsome, commanding, and frightening as she had remembered, and she caught her breath as his gaze swept over her. She was accustomed to admiring glances, but this appraisal seemed different, like an evaluation. "You'll find this place to be very conducive to rest." He paused, as if wondering how long she planned to be a house guest. "May I ask, do you have any other family?"

"No. No one. Friends, of course."

"Like André," he said with a half-smile.

"And Livi," she added.

He took a step forward, and Rae abruptly moved back.

"You're afraid of me," he said. "Did I cause that? Or is this, too, an act?"

"I'm not an actress."

"If you belong to André, I shall give you no reason whatsoever to be afraid of me. And if he is serious about you, then I will not attempt to interfere with that. That's how it is."

His words held the ring of truth, and Rae felt a terrible longing that nothing could be done about. Earlier, she had experienced the most unexplainable awakening and he seemed to be saying, "Forget it."

Before she could speak, he asked if she would like coffee.

"I was going to run," she said.

A grin played about his lips. "Again?"

She knew he was making a joke about her having run from him on the deck during the early morning. But she could not help but respond with a smile, seeing warmth now in his eyes.

"You'll need a guide," he said, walking out with her onto the deck where they became enveloped by a velvet fog. She looked down and realized he, too, wore running shoes. Soon they fell into step on a pathway. "The fog is a precarious thing. It may have obscured the entire mountain range for miles, yet we can walk through it for ten feet and find the sun shining through."

Rae's eyes brightened at the prospect. "I've never experienced anything like the feeling the mountains give me," she admitted. "And I've seen so little of them. I can hardly wait to see more."

Maybe it was her lack of sleep, Rae surmised, or maybe it was the mist that rendered the world so dreamlike, so lovely, so different from anything she had ever seen before. The scene was like a lady dressed in all her finery, with the fragrance of perfume to complete the effect.

Just as Lucas had promised, there were spots on the run where the fog had dissipated, and rays of golden sun peeked through leafy branches. A light breeze stirred tender, young leaves. Moisture lay heavy on the pink blossoms of rhododendron, azaleas, and mountain laurel.

Stopping at a stream, they scooped up handfuls of cold, clear liquid and drank, then wiped the drops from their mouths through their laughter. Then Rae followed him to higher ground until, finally, he stopped on a rocky ledge. The fog lay below them, obscuring whatever lay in the valley that stretched on forever before rising to another peak, and yet another.

"Does it never end?" she asked, her hands resting against her hips, her breathing labored.

"It's different each time you see it. Here," he said motioning, "front-row seats."

She climbed down onto the ledge which provided not only a seat but a back on which to lean.

"I'm used to getting up every morning and running," Rae defended her heavy breathing, "but I don't often run up hills and cliffs. I have to admit, this is harder." She gestured toward the valley. "The air here seems thinner too." She pressed against her chest. "Takes my breath away."

"You said you've had no one to lean on since your father died," he said, quietly changing the subject.

Rae bit her lip and frowned thoughtfully. "My father and I were a great comfort to each other after my mother died." She gave him a half smile. "But after my father died, no, there was no one."

Rae looked up then, to find Lucas staring at her in a different way, as though he, too, had experienced the greatest of griefs.

"I know they are in a better world," Rae said, looking out into the distance as if seeing that other world. "But it's still hard to go on without those you love. My father was never the same without my mother and I know I'll never be the same without him. Without both of them."

"Have you shared these feelings with André?"

"Andy?" The truth was that she had not but sharing this could reveal more than Andy would want her to say. Still, she couldn't lie. She wouldn't. "No," she said. "I've kept all of this between God and me." She smiled at him. "And you, now."

"We all need God in our lives," Lucas agreed. "But we also need people we can share the hard times with."

Rae's smile wobbled, she knew, but she gave it her best effort. "Is there ever—can there ever be—another man as good or as wonderful as a girl's daddy?"

"I couldn't answer that," he said with a slight nod. "Perhaps my mother could—she's a wise one—but I wonder . . ."

"What?"

"What about André? Do you see him as one day filling those shoes?"

What about André? Her mind was clouded, and she had to look away from his questioning gaze. Turning her head, she saw the fog hovering over the unseen valley. Though she couldn't see it, she knew the valley was there, just as she knew that somewhere beneath this strange upheaval, this indefinable convolution of Lucas, was Andy. The vague impression began to register that her reason for being here was Andy.

How much could she say without betraying Andy's confidence? Without endangering their tentative friendship? After all, earlier she had begun to entertain the idea of starting something with him. Of opening up her heart and seeing where things led. And what about her relationship with Livi? Summer job possibilities? She would try to be as honest as she could possibly be.

"I haven't known Andy long," she said truthfully. "But I hope to know him better before the summer is over. He offered me a summer job, so I'll be working with him—" She looked at Lucas, remembering suddenly that she was sitting next to the man who would say yay or nay to her employment at the camp. "That is, if you agree." And she hoped he would; she'd already gotten someone to rent the house, furnished, for the next three months. Longer, they'd told her, if the arrangement worked for her.

Lucas's silence and thoughtful expression puzzled her. Perhaps he would question her job qualifications. Instead, his words were tinged with incredulity. "André told me he had met a Christian girl who was special to him . . . I'll be honest; as you've probably figured out, I didn't believe him."

Rae didn't know what to say. To be completely truthful with Lucas would mean she must damage her budding friendship with Andy. She suddenly felt caught in the middle of something, and she had the strange feeling her relationship with Andy was not going to be quite so simple as remaining silent while he pretended that she was prospectively his special girl. But that was something she would have to work out with Andy.

Sighing, Rae leaned her head against the rock. Between her lack of sleep, the thin air, and the run, she had begun to shake a little. She knew extreme fatigue accompanied by quivering, something akin to the sensation of having practiced for too many hours on the athletic equipment.

"How long will the fog linger?" she asked, looking at Lucas.

His dark eyes now seemed to hold a strange resignation as he looked away from her toward the valley below. Rae closed her eyes, listening as he talked in resonant tones that soothed her. He was as much a part of the mountain, she decided, as the rock on which they sat.

"Sometimes it drifts away quickly," he said. "At other times, it clings to the mountainsides well past the morning. Right now, it's rising. Soon it will envelop us. Then when the sun crests that ridge, it will be as if the fog had never existed."

She remained quiet, allowing herself to drink it all in.

"What are you thinking, Ramona?"

The sound of her name touched her deeply. And she found herself pouring out her heartache over the loss of her parents, her indecision, her loneliness. Lucas sat beside her, silent. Right then, he didn't seem to be a stranger at all, but someone she could talk to, someone she had been waiting on and yet had always known, her whole life.

She spoke of her mother and father who had both coached gymnastics and of the young athletes they had championed. She had been born when her mother was in her early forties—the child they thought they could never have. Then her mother had become ill and died when Rae was fifteen—the year she was slated to win at the Olympics. After that, Rae had lost her desire for the Olympic gold. She had gone on to win national awards, was part of her college team, and had stayed on to teach after graduation. Then, several months ago, she told Lucas, her father's stroke had left him physically unable to return to his duties on campus. The doctors' bills, even with insurance, had piled up. The money was gone, and her own future, uncertain.

Rae sensed, rather than saw, the fog when it lifted to surround them. Her eyes were closed now, but she felt the dampness as it enveloped them, then moved away to be replaced by gentle fingers of sunlight. The same happened inside her as the emotion of her losses overwhelmed her, spilled over, then moved away with the mist.

"I doubt I'll return to the university," Rae said, her voice catching in her throat. "Without my father . . ."

"I understand," Lucas said at last, breaking his long silence. "André, Olivia, and I faced such a crisis when their parents died in a plane crash."

"I don't know a lot about it. Livi chooses not to say much."

"They were on their way to visit my sister-in-law's parents." He paused as if trying to grab hold of his emotions. "Their plane went down in the Swiss Alps." He took a breath. "Acceptance didn't come easily, especially for my mother and for Clare's parents who lived—and continue to live—in Paris. Olivia and André came to my parents and me so lost and forlorn, their world in pieces. Then my father died of cancer, leaving just the four of us and, before I could get my bearings, I found myself as the trustee over their portion of the inheritance *and* the head of the company. More than anything, I want to do right by everyone."

Rae watched his face, thinking he was so young to have borne such a responsibility, but marveling that once she had confided to him, he did the same now with her.

Lucas smiled at her. "I may have overindulged Olivia and André at times," he admitted, "but I've done my best. And I'm fortunate to have my mother nearby with her wisdom and faith. Through her I learned that dependence on God you were talking about." His next words were spoken almost reverently, as though he were afraid he'd say too much. "I didn't believe my nephew when he told me about you, Ramona. But he was right. You're exactly the kind of woman I've always wanted . . ." He paused, then added, "for him."

His words were no real comfort to her, she realized miserably. She should be glad that Lucas approved of her . . . for Andy.

Following Lucas's lead, Rae braced her feet against the huge boulder in front of them. Despite herself, she felt herself nodding off to sleep.

She woke in the shadow of the rock and the sun blazed high in the sky. Rae raised her head to find Lucas's head against another rock, leaning to one side, his lips parted in easy breathing, their shoulders near each other's.

As Rae shifted her position, Lucas opened his eyes. Only a second of incomprehension dulled them before he smiled a lazy smile. "Feel better?"

She could only nod.

Lucas stood and stretched. "Want to run back?"

"Lead the way," she answered, eager.

He started slowly, then increased the speed until his long legs were beating the downhill path at a steady, rhythmic tempo. Rae's movements were perfectly synchronized with his. She was so close behind him that when he swept an occasional branch out of the way she was already past it before it could sweep back. Though the temperature had risen with the sun, the trees shaded them as they jogged down the twisting path.

When Lucas's pace slowed, Rae knew they must be nearing the house.

They ran up the steps of the lower deck with Lucas still in the lead. He stopped suddenly, causing Rae to collide with him. Reaching out to break her fall, he encircled her waist, lifted her off her feet for a second or two, then set her down again.

"How was that for a workout?" he asked, breathing hard.

"*Invigorating.*" Rae inhaled deeply. But there was something more. She now knew how much she wanted—no, needed—a pair of strong arms in her life.

They were almost upon the lounging figures on the second deck before she realized there was anyone else in the world.

Three

"Rae, you've met Uncle Lucas." Mischief danced in Livi's dark eyes as she started for him, then stopped. "You're all sweaty."

Lucas leaned over to kiss Livi's cheek, careful not to touch her otherwise, then turned to greet Andy.

"I *thought* you might be out running, Rae," Andy said uncertainly. Looking at Lucas, he added, "I didn't know you were back, Uncle Lucas."

Rae noted tenseness between the two, especially after Andy stepped forward and Lucas's hand extended for a shake.

"Let's go in," Lucas said. "I'm famished. Mind eating in the kitchen?" He didn't wait for an answer. Going inside, he shouted, "Charlotte, where are you?"

When a plump, mature woman appeared, Lucas gave her a big hug. "Now here's a woman for you. Best cook in the world and she doesn't mind my hugs after a run."

"You know that sweet-talk means nothing to me," Charlotte said, but the look on her face denied the words. "Now, if you said 'in all of North Carolina,' I might be inclined to go along with you."

Lucas laughed and took a seat at the oversized farmhouse table. He and Andy sat opposite each other with Rae beside Andy.

"Is that eggs and ham I smell, Charlotte?" Lucas boomed.

"You know it is."

"I'll get the juice," Livi offered and went to the refrigerator while Lucas filled the water glasses from the pitcher on the table.

"You look tired, Rae," observed Livi as she served the orange juice.

Rae laughed. "Really? I haven't felt so rested since . . ." She searched for words and shrugged. "*Ever.*"

"So, when did you meet Uncle Lucas?" Livi cast an inquisitive eye in her friend's direction. "On your way out to run?"

Rae hesitated, but Lucas replied immediately, grinning. "No. I would say about two o'clock this morning."

"What?" Livi asked as Andy blushed and Lucas laughed.

"I got in fairly late," he explained, "and was about to go to bed when I happened to see this young woman standing outside on the deck. For a moment, I thought she was you, Olivia." He offered Rae a smile. "I'm afraid I scared her a bit."

"Coffee, anyone?" Andy asked before Rae could speak. He jumped up, strolled over to a coffee station and returned with a stainless-steel carafe. He poured a cup for Rae. "Sorry," he apologized as some of the coffee spilled over in her saucer.

"It's okay." Rae hoped her expression would convince him he had no cause for concern.

"When do you leave for Paris, Olivia?" Lucas asked as Andy poured coffee into his uncle's cup. This time without sloshing.

"Next week," she said, her eyes lighting up when she looked at her uncle. Their mutual affection was obvious. "Rae and I are going to have a great week before I go and before she settles down to work."

Charlotte appeared then, bearing steaming platters of ham and eggs, hot biscuits, and a large bowl of grits. Before they ate, Lucas asked God's blessing on the food. "I'll be in the laundry room," Charlotte said after everyone echoed their *amen.* "Someone in this house brought home a pile of dirty clothes." Her voice sounded frustrated, but she winked at Andy all the same.

"You know," Lucas said, looking at Rae. "It just dawned on me that I don't know your last name."

"Martin," she answered. "And, before you make the connection, yes. My father was Raymond Martin."

"Of course. The Olympics. Your father is one reason I hoped Olivia would attend the university in Atlanta. Not only did I want her to have the finest academic training available, but the finest physical training. And who better than Ray Martin. *Ramona Martin,*" he said, "in spite of our early-morning meeting and run, we haven't been properly introduced." He reached over to shake her hand. "Hello. I'm Lucas Grant."

Rae reached out, then stopped short. "*Lucas Grant*?" she gasped. She had only heard him referred to as "Uncle Lucas" and assumed he was a Doudet too. But no. Andy and Livi had told her that he was the son of their grandmother's second marriage. "I *knew* you looked familiar, but I thought it was because Andy looks so much like you. You're the Olympic gold medalist." She pointed to him with knowledge. "And you were expected to win again, but you broke your leg on the slopes in Switzerland two weeks before the next games."

She didn't bother to add that, because of the rash of articles and pictures reporting the event, she had also experienced a painful, teenage girl's crush.

Lucas grinned now. "One and the same," he said.

"Why didn't you tell me?"

"It didn't occur to me."

"I *cried* for you," she said. "That was the same year I didn't get to go. Thinking you must feel as disappointed as me, I—I *identified* with you."

"Well, thank you for that." The grin remained on his face. "However, the disappointment was not the heartbreak for me that it was for you. I had already proved what I could do on the slopes. And—I had my 'children.'" He looked fondly from Livi to Andy. Livi beamed, but Andy did not raise his eyes from his plate.

"Children . . ." The tone in Andy's voice chilled Rae.

"A figure of speech, André." Lucas spoke without malice.

"I'm hardly a child now," Andy said.

Lucas looked at his nephew sharply. "Hardly," he said, his voice firm. He drank the last of his coffee, then set the cup on its saucer. "I can see why you said Ramona was special." He smiled at Rae. "You're right. She is."

"You bet," Livi chimed in, her face beaming with pleasure at what she so obviously hoped could and would be.

Rae smiled back, first at Livi, then at Andy, finally at Lucas. "Thank you," she said.

"I'm just relieved," Lucas said with a wink toward Livi, "that you seem to be making better choices these days, André. Makes my job so much easier."

"As I said, I'm no longer a child, Uncle Lucas. There are things I have to decide for myself."

"Oh, I see." Lucas spoke suddenly with the kind of authority that forced eye contact. "So, we're back to that. All right, then. I want the truth. Is Ramona someone you believe you could settle down with?"

Rae held her breath, fearing what was to come. Andy loved and respected his uncle. That much was obvious. She was sure he would have to tell the truth. Rae was only grateful that the question was not directed to her.

Andy did not take his eyes from her when he spoke quietly. "Uncle Lucas, I can honestly say that Rae is different from any girl I've ever known. And, yeah, I think she's pretty special."

Rae swallowed hard. She could scarcely believe the ease with which Andy shadowed the truth. *Different from any girl he'd ever met*? He'd hardly known her a few days.

Lucas cleared his throat. "Well, then. Perhaps I should have tried to get to know Ramona in your presence instead of alone." He turned to Rae. "I hope I haven't offended you in any way?"

"No," she answered. "Not at all." Had Lucas been testing her all along, trying to discover if she was, in fact, Andy's girl? Apparently. The conversation and the connection she'd felt had meant nothing to him. It had only been a test.

Lucas turned with a smile and lifted his eyebrows. "What I can't understand, André, is how you could have allowed her to be missing all morning without tracking her down. I wonder if I'll ever understand you."

Rae recognized what Lucas was doing. He wanted truth from Andy, yet, whether he realized it or not, Lucas had deliberately played with her emotions. And, tired as she was, she wasn't certain she could take much more. "I'm going to ask you," Rae began, her voice low and even, "to stop this. I think we made it clear that Livi introduced us recently and that we are getting to know each other—that we *want* to get to know each other better."

"Have I said anything to the contrary?" Lucas asked.

But Rae was quick to answer. "You insulted me by insinuating that I might possibly be a paid actress."

"Uncle Lucas," Livi breathed out as Andy stood, looking for all the world like he wanted to do battle or as though he were ready to fight some archaic duel.

"Sit down, André," Lucas said, and Andy complied. "Ramona's right. I did ask and you can't blame me. How many times have we gone round and round where your love life is concerned? And, like it or not, condemn me or not, I do find it a bit odd that you, André, were not a little more concerned as to where Ramona was this morning."

"I assumed—"

"Never assume anything where women are concerned."

"This from the great expert on women," Andy said.

Rae stood, no longer hungry. Now Lucas was categorizing women? And he and Andy were fighting like boys? Because of her? "I think I'd like to go upstairs." She placed her napkin firmly next to her plate of nearly untouched food. "If you will excuse me."

"I'm right behind you," Livi said, standing. "Uncle Lucas, *really*. What is this? The 1880s?"

Once Rae made it to her bedroom, Livi right behind her, she fell across the bed, thoroughly humiliated. She did not understand Lucas Grant. Nor herself, for that matter.

"Oh, Livi," she said, her voice muffled in the bedspread, "how awful. What have I done allowing this farce?"

"But it's not, Rae. Is it?" Livi asked, flopping down on the bed beside her. "You and Andy *are* trying to get to know each other better and I'll bet that by summer's end you'll be crazy about each other." She grinned. "I also think it's wonderfully romantic."

Rae turned to face Livi. "What?"

"Don't you see? Uncle Lucas and Andy are practically fighting over you."

Rae sat up. "Are you out of your mind, Livi? They're hardly fighting," she said. "Besides, this whole thing is embarrassing. Out there, up on the mountain, I talked to Lucas about such personal things. Even after he accused me of being an actress."

"He does have a way about him," Livi said with a grin. "Just ask Isobel."

Rae closed her eyes. She'd just as soon not. "And now I've behaved like a—a thirty-one-year-old child."

"How so?"

"By standing up like some *femme fatale* in a 1920s movie and asking to be excused. Talk about being an actress."

Livi giggled, then said, "Well, maybe we both were a little over the top. But you can't leave, Rae, and I can tell that's where your head is going. Andy needs you at the camp, you need a job, and you did agree to help him out." Livi's eyes sparkled. "And who knows? By summer's end you could be my sister-in-law."

She laughed. "Don't hold your breath on that, okay? I mean—"

"Well, there's one thing for certain, Rae," Livi interrupted as though she didn't want to hear another word against her happy-ever-after dream.

"What's that?"

"Uncle Lucas obviously likes you. And he has one weakness . . ."

"Lucas? A weakness? What could that possibly be?"

"My brother and me," she gloated. "He loves us very much. Yes, he's only ten years older than Andy and, yes, sometimes it feels like he watches over us a little too closely. But you have to admit he's done a pretty good job with us."

"Well, at least one of you," Rae teased, which brought laughter from Livi.

"But he has spoiled us too," Livi continued. "Trust me, since Andy is obviously interested in you, Uncle Lucas will first do everything he can to make sure you're not one of those women only interested in Andy's inheritance, and then he'll do everything in his power to nurture your relationship."

"But there *isn't* a relationship, Livi."

Livi's eyes twinkled. "But there could be." She bounded from the bed, then walked to the door, put her hand on the knob, and paused as if debating whether to say what was on her mind. "I can't think of anyone I'd like more for a sister-in-law," she mused and slipped out the door before Rae could think of a suitable retort.

ꕥ ꕥ ꕥ

Livi shook Rae's shoulders and called her name.

"Rae. Wake up. Come on now. You're sure making up for all those months you couldn't sleep. You've slept all day."

It took a while for the words to register. When Rae sat up in bed and looked out the window, she saw the dwindling light of late afternoon. She glanced up at Livi. "I took a shower and laid down and I must have fallen asleep." She blinked. "What time is it?"

"Five-thirty. Dinner's at seven." She planted her hands on her hips. "Hop to it. You've only one hour to get dressed and all."

Pushing the sheet aside, Rae stretched and yawned. "I've slept like a log. Must be the mountain air. But . . ." Her grin was mischievous as she looked in the mirror at the wilted figure and head full of drab ringlets, ". . . it will take more than an hour, I'm afraid."

"I've plugged in your flat iron," Livi said, then left Rae to her privacy.

Less than an hour later, with the flat iron to relax the tight curls, and a vigorous brushing to bring out the highlights, her golden hair was anything but the tangled mess of the earlier morning.

She never completely concealed the sprinkling of freckles across her small, straight nose; she had been told they were quite alluring. Her green dress brought out the color of her eyes, and they were shaded by long, dark lashes. She reached for her glossy lipstick to apply to her full lips. A light blush heightened the color of her cheeks.

She stood to view herself critically in the mirror and wondered what Lucas would think of her now that she looked more like a mature woman who taught at a university. A woman thirty-one years old. She sat again, losing her nerve. Her overdramatic exit from the breakfast table reigned uppermost in her mind, and she was sure he wasn't about to forget that. She could already feel herself cringing.

"What's keeping you, Rae?" Livi asked, knocking on the door, interrupting her friend's reverie. "Don't you know that you don't keep Uncle Lucas waiting?"

Four

Livi's eyes widened when Rae opened the door. "You'll dazzle 'em tonight!"

Surveying the dark-haired girl dressed in scarlet, she shook her head. "Not a chance with you around, Livi."

Livi had been one of the most popular girls on campus, not only because of how cute she was, but because of her effervescent personality. But it was in Rae alone whom she had confided the deeper longings of her heart.

"Well," Livi said, "I will admit I may have a job keeping Brent at a distance."

"Brent?"

"Oh, I've never mentioned him before, but he's joining us for dinner tonight. Brent would make the 'perfect husband,' or so Uncle Lucas insists." She wrinkled her nose. "I can't think about anyone except Pierre anymore. You know that, even if Uncle Lucas doesn't."

Rae nodded, understanding.

"Pierre," Livi exclaimed, hugging her arms to herself. "I'll see him next week. Not a word to anyone, though. If Uncle Lucas knew, he wouldn't let me go to Paris. But what I feel about Pierre . . . oh, how can I describe it? I know," she said, with sudden insight, "I feel like you looked when you and Uncle Lucas came out of the woods, you were . . ." She threw her hands up. "*Radiant.*"

Rae's mouth dropped. "Livi, would you stop it. Besides, we had run down the mountain and . . . oh, come on. We're late."

Livi gave her a brief hug. "I'm so glad you're here, Rae."

Rae wondered how wise it was, her being here. But what else could she do now?

Rae descended the staircase, determined to make the best of the evening. At the landing Livi went to greet Brent, who was talking with Andy in the lounge. Rae knew immediately what Livi had meant about the tall, young man with the handsome face, nice smile, and charming manners. When he looked at Livi, a spark ignited in his eyes. He couldn't conceal his enchantment with the girl in red.

"Now for the blonde bombshell," said Livi under her breath after she had introduced Rae to Brent.

Lucas and the woman Rae assumed to be Isobel stood behind one of the two plush couches facing each other in front of a massive fireplace.

Before the introduction could be made, the woman stepped forward. "You would be one of Olivia's little friends."

Rae cringed inwardly.

Upon closer scrutiny Rae realized the blonde with crystal-blue eyes was not as large or imposing as she had thought at first glance. Still, so much glamour showed in the shimmering white sheath. No doubt those were real diamonds around her neck and at her ear lobes. Her light tan set off a flawless complexion, as did her dazzling white teeth when she smiled. There was no denying she was sophisticated and beautiful and Lucas's age, if not older. So, this voluptuous woman was an example of Lucas's preference in women.

Rae suddenly felt angry—angry with herself for caring what Lucas liked or thought, angry with the woman before her whose eyes did not reflect the warmth of her smile. She seemed to thaw a little, however, when Lucas stepped forward and said, "Ramona is André's friend too. Ramona—Isobel Patrick."

"Well, Ramona. I'm very glad to meet you." Even her voice was well-modulated.

"Rae," she corrected. "Everyone calls me Rae, Mrs. Patrick."

"Oh, you make me feel ancient, calling me Mrs. Patrick. Please call me Isobel."

Rae's gaze swung toward Lucas and found his eyes on her, an amused expression there. Her glance raked his face, taking in the smooth-shaven skin, deeply tanned, the eyes that had seemed so tender earlier. His broad frame was now attired in an obviously expensive, formal suit—so different from the man of the early morning. This man was cool, self-possessed, so in control of his surroundings, the king of the mountain—a perfect escort for the perfect Isobel.

Suddenly Andy was at her side, offering a glass of ginger ale poured over crushed ice.

Gratefully, Rae turned to him, surprised at the affectionate look in his eyes. "You're especially beautiful this evening, Rae," he said softly.

Her smile was one of genuine pleasure. "After this morning, I suppose anything would be an improvement."

"Come on," Andy said, "I want to show you something."

They walked around the great stone fireplace that separated the lounge from the library.

Andy gestured toward the three walls, lined from floor to ceiling with books. "I'm not sure I ever want to read again," he grumbled. "I haven't yet recovered from all the reading we were forced to do in college, but I thought you'd like this a lot."

She laughed with him. "Such torture is not easily forgotten."

He steered her over to a trophy case displaying Lucas's gold medal. Flanking it were other lesser awards, conferred for his superb skiing skills. Some of the trophies were tributes to Andy's expertise in skiing, tennis, and swimming. Listening to Andy now and watching him describe the various meets, Rae realized why women were so attracted to him. He was irresistible when he became animated about the sports he loved, his eyes alight with his intense passion for the game.

"I've got to talk to you, Rae," Andy said abruptly.

"Okay."

"I mean—alone. Where no one can walk in on us. Perhaps we'll have a chance after dinner."

She didn't quite like the idea of that, but she nodded anyway. He placed his arm lightly around her shoulders, and they walked back into the lounge to find Livi and Brent.

When dinner was announced, Rae smiled as they walked into the dining room. Just as she had guessed earlier, the dining room overlooked the decks. Small-paned windows covered almost all the wall facing the back of the house. There were no curtains. None were needed. The effect was a rustic setting, as if the jungle outside were an integral part of the room.

"I must see this," Rae said to Andy, then walked over to the windows.

Shadows stole across the wooden deck as the sun swiftly made its descent behind the mountains. How different the scene appeared each time she looked at it—once in the moonlight, another time in the mist, again in the sunlight, now in the shadows that gave the deep green leaves the appearance of ebony.

Finally, Andy cleared this throat, a discreet indication that she kept the rest waiting. "Oh, I'm so sorry," Rae apologized. "It's just that it's all so fascinating—so very different from Atlanta. I'm afraid I got carried away." She quickly took the seat that Andy held for her.

"I could watch you looking out like that all day," Andy said as he settled himself beside her, "but Charlotte might not like serving a cold dinner."

To Rae's extreme discomfort, she realized that she had been seated to Lucas's right and that Isobel was on his left, directly across the table from her. She suffered a momentary pang before remembering that she was the newcomer, the guest at this affair. Brent and Isobel had obviously dined here many times before.

While the salad was being served, Rae took the opportunity to look about her and was once again reminded of the unique blending of elegance and luxury on the interior with the lush, untamed vegetation beyond. The rectangular room was designed with a brick fireplace at the far end, where two overstuffed armchairs could be drawn up to the fire for conversation or quiet contemplation on a winter evening.

But she would be gone before winter.

They were seated at a long dining table in chairs with high, straight backs, enhancing the aura of formality and precision. Suspended over the table were two magnificent crystal chandeliers and, beneath them, the *pièce de résistance*, bringing life to the otherwise austere surroundings—two huge silver bowls displaying miniature clusters of pink blossoms set against the background of thick, waxy, dark green leaves. They had been gathered, no doubt, from the grounds.

Rae realized she was smiling when Lucas asked, "You recall our brief lesson in mountain flora and fauna from this morning?"

He had pointed out several plants and identified them during the early morning hours.

"Mountain laurel," she replied confidently.

"Rhododendron," he corrected playfully.

"Oh, yes," she finished feebly.

"Don't worry," Andy consoled her. "It takes time to become a mountaineer."

"Oh, darling," Isobel touched Lucas's forearm, apparently bored with the conversation, "before I forget, Kevin made me promise to thank you for the card and lovely game you sent him."

Lucas smiled warmly. "I'm glad he's feeling better."

"He is. Much. He wouldn't miss opening day at camp for anything."

During dinner conversation, Rae learned that Isobel's home was in Raleigh, the state capitol, and that she and her son Kevin, despite a virus that had hung on for several weeks, were visiting Isobel's parents who lived in nearby Asheville.

The conversation turned to Andy's activities of the past year, then to Livi's present interests, which led quite naturally to discussion of Rae's summer employment. This bit of information surprised Isobel.

"Will you be staying here at the house, then, after Olivia leaves for Paris?" Isobel asked her.

Lucas spoke before Rae could answer. "She will stay in one of the cottages at the camp with the other staffers."

"Oh, I see," Isobel said, then smiled sweetly. Rae looked past Brent to Livi, who was making a valiant effort not to laugh. She would have to remember not to glance at Livi too often. No doubt Isobel would be wondering how Andy had become acquainted with an ordinary working girl. The woman's next question proved her correct.

"I'm always interested in romances," Isobel said brightly. "How and when and wherever did you two meet?"

Andy answered immediately, "On one of my stops to see Livi in Atlanta."

"Oh? Love at first sight?"

Rae felt a stab of resentment at Isobel's assumption and her patronizing tone.

"Something like that," Andy replied and returned to his eating, as if the discussion were closed. But where Isobel left off her questioning, Lucas took it up.

"I can't imagine Ramona believing in love at first sight. Perhaps you are speaking for yourself." His tone sounded accusatory, and Rae suspected he had not completely accepted Andy's apparent sincerity.

"I don't think love is necessarily sensible," Rae said defensively, looking directly at Lucas, "or reasonable. It can be quite disconcerting, unpredictable, and unexpected." She instantly wished she'd said nothing. What if they asked which pool she drew her beliefs from? But now she was in the conversation, so she added, "I think the important thing is whether it is treated lightly, as some passing fancy, or treasured for a lifetime."

Lifting her chin, she determined to meet Lucas's sarcasm head-on, but discovered something surprising in his eyes. He looked as if he could not agree more.

Thankfully, Livi started up a conversation about Brent. Now twenty-two, he would receive a master's degree in business in another year, then would go to work in his father's firm.

"Where he will eventually work his way to the top," Livi informed Rae. "It will probably take all of five years."

"Well, I think Dad plans to hold that top position for a while yet," Brent countered. "But it is a real possibility for the future." The way he looked at Livi indicated he would be happy to have the beautiful girl as a part of that future.

But Rae knew it was not Brent who interested Livi. Her heart belonged to Pierre. Livi's thoughts were with him too; she began to speak of Paris, fashions, and trips abroad. Isobel, quite a traveler herself, joined the discussion enthusiastically.

Invariably the conversation drifted back to sports—a subject Rae never tired of.

"Ramona's father was a famous coach," Lucas informed Isobel and Brent.

"That's certainly . . . interesting," Isobel said, laughing lightly. Too lightly, in Rae's opinion.

Rae couldn't resist a retort. "You either eat and breathe sports or you don't. I'd rather swim than . . ." She paused, thinking. "Breathe."

Lucas laughed heartily while Isobel's smile still did not reach her eyes.

"A fish, huh?" Lucas laughed again.

"At least half," she replied, glancing at Livi who winked.

"And I know what the other half is," Lucas said, as all eyes turned to regard him curiously.

Rae drew in her breath and held it for a long moment.

"A gymnast."

Livi nearly hopped in her seat as she began a recitation of Rae's athletic abilities, including her medals and honors.

"I guess I'm just a homebody," Isobel said.

"If telling your staff what to do classifies you as a homebody, I suppose you're right." Lucas chuckled.

"Now, Lucas," Isobel reprimanded, placing a well-manicured hand on his sleeve, "I'm turning into a regular gourmet cook. And I can prove it. One evening soon?"

"I suppose I'll have to take you up on that," he responded.

After dinner Isobel regretfully announced that she soon had to return to her young son. Taking her arm, Lucas led her from the lounge where they had retreated for coffee to show her the gifts he had brought back from Switzerland.

Unsuccessfully stifling a yawn, Livi stretched. "Guess I'm still tired from the long drive from Atlanta."

Taking the hint, Brent stood to leave. "Some of the gang are coming to my place for a luau on Friday. Would the three of you care to drop in—especially since it will be Livi's last night in the States for a while?"

"We'd love to," Livi replied, then rose. "I'll walk you to the car."

As soon as the couple left, Andy moved closer to Rae. Emotionally drained, she leaned her head back against the couch and closed her eyes. At the touch of his hand on hers, she opened her eyes.

"Rae, let's go for a walk. I have some things to say," he said.

But before he could say anything more, Livi and Lucas returned, lounging on the sofa opposite them, and Andy released her hand and reluctantly moved away.

Lucas removed his tie, then unbuttoned his shirt at the neck, as if for the first time since dinner he could truly relax.

"You managed to get rid of Brent in a hurry," he scolded Livi fondly.

"Like you managed to get rid of Isobel?" she asked with a saucy toss of her head.

"It's not the same, and you know it."

"To tell the truth, Uncle Lucas," she pouted, "I could hardly tear myself away from him."

Lucas snorted. "You could barely tolerate him, you mean."

"You know me pretty well, huh?"

"For several years now," he said.

"You've ruined me for all men, Uncle Lucas. Not one of them can measure up to you."

"None?"

"Almost none," she replied, stealing a glance at Rae. They exchanged knowing smiles.

"Anyway," Livi said, looking back at Lucas, "I promised Brent he could come by and take me to church in the morning."

"Be back in time for lunch," Lucas said. "Gran is coming to meet Rae. Would you like to worship with Gran in the morning, André?"

"Sure," he replied, "if Rae wants to. It doesn't matter much to me."

Rae's voice was quiet, but firm. "It matters to me, Andy."

The soft music from the stereo did not fill the uncomfortable silence that followed.

Ever diplomatic, Livi hurriedly changed the subject. "Is extra help coming in next week, Uncle Lucas?"

"Marie will be here on Monday morning." His voice held a note of wry humor. "Don't worry. You won't have to do your own laundry."

"I did plenty of it at school. But that reminds me," she said, jumping up, "I'd better see what I have to wear in the morning."

As soon as Livi left, Andy excused himself too. "I'll be right back," he said to Rae as he walked through the doorway.

"How long have you been here?" Lucas asked when they were alone.

"Almost twenty-four hours," she said and looked down at her hands folded stiffly on her green dress.

His next words echoed her thoughts. "Incredible," he said under his breath. "It seems much longer. I feel I know all there is to know about you."

Five

"You haven't even seen all the house, have you?" Lucas asked, standing.

When Rae admitted she hadn't, he exclaimed, "Ah, let me show you the best part of the living room."

She walked with him from the lounge. He mentioned that his study, bath, and bedroom were behind the closed doors next to the lounge. The foyer and staircase were separated only by space from the living room with its cathedral ceiling. A dim light burned on the wall near the foot of the stairs.

"Over here," Lucas said, without turning on another light. They stood looking out beyond the wide picture window where the mountainsides were dotted with tiny lights. The dark outline of mountain ranges seemed to stretch on forever, eventually fading into the sky.

"Is it so important to you, Ramona?"

"Is what so important?" she asked, studying Lucas's profile as he looked out toward the mountains.

"Attending church tomorrow—and André's lack of interest."

"I believe the most important thing in a person's life is commitment to Jesus Christ as personal Savior," she replied thoughtfully. "Church attendance is just one expression of that commitment. Families should worship together. I can't imagine being married to a man who doesn't share and understand my beliefs."

"Perhaps it's not an insurmountable problem," Lucas replied, and she felt his eyes search her face in the near darkness.

The subject shifted to the magnificent view before them.

"Asheville lies in that direction," Lucas said, pointing. "Not to be compared with Atlanta in size, of course, but it supplies our needs. In front of you is the Swannanoa Valley and, off to your left, is a little town called Black Mountain . . . You're not looking," he said with surprise.

No, she had not looked at anything but his face since he had come to stand beside her. She could think of nothing but how she had felt earlier that morning. Did he think of this too?

"I see only mountain peaks dotted with light. A whole blue ridge of them."

"I've looked at this view so many times," he said, "that I can see it with my eyes closed."

Suddenly brilliant light flooded the room.

"Wondered where you had gone." Andy strode across the floor toward them. His eyes held a strange gleam of triumph. "I just talked to Gran," he said. "She's happy that we'll be going to church with her in the morning. She's eager to meet you, Rae."

"That's wonderful, Andy," Rae said sincerely.

"Now," Andy continued, "let's ride down to the camp. The lake is very romantic in the moonlight. But you'd better get a sweater. It'll be cool by the lake."

They said goodnight to Lucas, and when they neared the staircase, she paused. "Andy," she said, "would you mind very much if we waited until tomorrow?"

At his look of disappointment, she almost changed her mind, but instinct told her she shouldn't. "I haven't unpacked," she continued. "And even though I slept the day away, I'm still pretty tired." Her words did little to lighten Andy's dark mood.

Reaching out, he placed a hand on her shoulder and the warmth she had detected earlier returned to his eyes. "I understand. There's plenty of time for us to see the lake—tomorrow, or even next week." He shrugged. "I should spend this evening with Uncle Lucas, anyway. We have a lot of catching up to do."

Leaning forward, he gave her a sweet kiss, one that, because she was aware that Lucas was probably watching, she didn't return. But it was a nice kiss, and Andy was a nice person.

After a moment, she moved back and smiled up at him. "Sleep well, Andy."

"See you in the morning," he said softly, then turned to rejoin his uncle.

∽ ∽ ∽

Rae was pleasantly surprised on Sunday morning when Lucas appeared at the breakfast table and announced that he would drive them to church. Gran had planned to meet them there.

When they arrived, Gran was waiting for them in the church foyer. Rae was not surprised to find a tall, elegant woman who appeared twenty years younger than her seventy-plus years. Her silvery-white hair was beautifully coifed, and her alert brown eyes were much like Lucas's with the warmth of Andy's. Upon being introduced, Gran had immediately insisted that Rae call her Gran.

There was no time for conversation, but Rae felt comfortable sitting between Andy and Gran during the worship service. After church, Gran got into the Lincoln with them to accompany them to lunch, and on the way back to Lucas's house, she told Rae about the historic sites in the area: The Biltmore House and Gardens, Thomas Wolfe's home, Carl Sandburg's home, Mount Mitchell, and the Blue Ridge Parkway.

"Stop," Rae said with a laugh. "I'm overwhelmed just looking at the mountains. And now you tell me there's *more*."

"Not to mention the camp and the ski resorts," Andy teased.

Then Gran told her about the religious conference centers in the area, as well as several colleges. It all sounded fascinating, and Rae feared she would never be able to visit all those places in a single summer. It would be over all too soon.

During lunch, and afterward when they went into the lounge, Rae learned that Gran was active in church work, served on several civic committees, and was athletic like her children and grandchildren. She had her own exercise room and remained a member of a tennis club. And a live-in staff took care of things during her frequent travels.

"A lady friend travels with her," Lucas explained. "Gran has turned up at many of André's competitions and at mine when I was more actively involved with sports."

"Well, Lucas. We Grants must stay busy. We have a capacity for activity," Gran said. "Too many evenings spent alone can make one old before one's time. But that's enough about us. Let's hear about this fascinating girl." And she turned her full attention to Rae, who already felt a bond of kinship. "I'm so pleased to meet the young lady Livi mentioned in nearly every text. It was a comfort knowing she had a friend she could speak of so highly, and one who wasn't afraid to lecture her when she needed it."

Livi pouted, then smiled at Rae.

"When my granddaughter texted me about you, I thought: *Now there's a girl Livi should bring home for all of us to meet*," Gran continued with a sparkle in her eye as she turned to Andy. "I just hope you have the good sense to take this adorable girl seriously," she said.

Andy perched on the arm of the couch, near Rae. "I told you last night, Gran. Rae means more to me every day, but she—" He looked down at Rae who looked up at him. "She needs time."

Only for a second could Rae then meet the warmth and acceptance in Gran's eyes.

"I thought I detected a more serious note in your voice when you told me about her on the phone last night," Gran said.

Rae tried to smile with the others. Gran would not think well of her when she knew the full truth. Such lying seemed to come so naturally with Andy. But Andy was a desperate man. Now she felt herself being drawn deeper and deeper into his predicament. What had begun as a seemingly innocent suggestion was fast becoming a full-blown deception. What was worse, these people accepted her, liked her, wanted her to be part of their family.

"What is it, Rae?" Gran asked quietly.

"Oh—" Rae said, shaking her head. "My mind flew somewhere else. I'm sorry."

"Ramona isn't as ready as we are to express her feelings, Gran," Lucas explained. "I think we embarrass her by speaking of personal matters."

"We *can* be rather blunt," Gran agreed. Then her eyes twinkled and she laughed until Rae couldn't help but laugh right along with her.

⁂

Monday morning started with Rae and Livi running along the horse trails that wound around the camp area and down beside the lake that Livi said covered six hundred acres. The sun peeked over the mountains that surrounded the camp, reminding Rae again that God's handiwork could not be imitated by man. Gentle rays filtered through the cool morning air, moist with mist. The fragrance of honeysuckle, sweet and clean, delighted the senses as they ran past rustic cabins, soccer fields, tennis courts, and even a miniature golf course. But it was the modern gymnasium that intrigued Rae.

"The outside of the gym is used in teaching the fundamentals of rock climbing," Livi explained, pointing.

They eventually reached a spot high above the camp where they could look down upon a pastoral scene with cattle grazing in the valley beneath, surrounded by sloping hills and mountain peaks, green, purple, and gray with haze at various levels. The evergreens were alive with golden yellow-green fingers at the tips of each limb, stretching toward heaven to catch the sunlight.

⁂

The next few days passed quickly. While Lucas and Andy spent much of their time on the campgrounds, Livi and Rae stayed busy swimming, playing tennis, shopping, and visiting some of the quaint little shops on Cherry Street in Black Mountain.

Suddenly it was Friday and time for Brent's party.

"Since the theme is Hawaiian, we have to dress the part," Livi said, rummaging through her closet from which she brought out a brightly patterned silk dress for Rae and one of blue, green, and orange for herself. They donned fashionable flip-flops before walking downstairs, where Andy waited in khaki pants and an exotic short-sleeved shirt. Rae couldn't help but note how handsome he was, but all thoughts of that vanished the moment Lucas, dressed in a suit, joined them in the foyer.

"Well, don't you all look festive," Lucas said, smiling.

"Join us," Livi invited. "It will be fun."

Lucas laughed. "I'm afraid I have other plans."

"A gourmet dinner?" Livi teased. "In a romantic A-frame?"

Lucas gave her a noncommittal glance before saying, "Don't be out too late. And behave yourselves."

"If *you* will, Uncle Lucas," Livi said mischievously.

He looked at his watch, said a hurried goodbye and strode from the foyer.

Rae stared after him. "What was that about the A-frame?" she asked.

"Isobel's mountain hideaway," Livi replied. "It's an—" She created an air triangle. "A-frame."

Rae frowned. Oh, how the three of them, dressed in their Hawaiian costumes, must have looked to Lucas—like children playing dress-up.

Upon arriving at Brent's, Rae discovered it was anything but a children's party. After winding their way up the mountain, Andy pulled the car to a stop in front of a magnificent, two-story, brick home with huge, white columns.

Walking around to the back patio was like stepping into a Hawaiian travel poster. As soon as they arrived, fresh-flower leis were draped over their heads. A live band strummed instruments in accompaniment to native Hawaiian songs. Long tables had been laden with festive decorations and elaborate foods, centerpieces of pineapple, and every conceivable kind of fruit.

"Brent's mom does have a knack for throwing a party," Livi said brightly.

"It's fabulous," Rae agreed. "I've never seen anything like this."

"We'll have one of our own when I get back from Paris," Livi promised. "Oh, but I mustn't think of Paris. Tomorrow, Rae. Tomorrow I leave."

"Then stop thinking about it, Livi," Rae said. "Here, have a . . . whatever this thing is. What *do* you think it is?"

They laughed and sampled the food. Rae determined to forget everything but the party and for the next few hours did just that, wondering briefly at only one point if Lucas was enjoying his evening with Isobel.

When Andy came up to her and led her away to a secluded part of the patio, she welcomed the retreat from the noisy guests until he pulled her close. "After we take Livi home, let's go somewhere, Rae. We haven't had *any* time alone." A rather desolate look appeared in his usually twinkling brown eyes.

Rae searched his face, and her heart went out to him. How could she say what was on her heart and be tactful? "Why don't you take me back to the house, Andy?" she asked. "Then you can come back to the party and find another girl. Maybe someone who truly deserves you."

"Rae," he whispered miserably. "I don't think you understand me. I don't want to be with just any girl. I want to be with you."

Rae lowered her eyes from his searching gaze.

"Look at me, Rae," he said, and she lifted her eyes to his. "It's not what you think. Nothing . . . you know. I want to talk to you. I want to tell you my dreams and my plans. And I want to hear yours."

Rae's breath caught in her throat as he continued, almost hesitantly. "I've never wanted that before, Rae. There's never been a girl who made me think seriously about my future, and my personal actions, like you do. I'd like to think that if you knew me better, you'd see more than a–a playboy."

"Who am I to judge?" Rae protested. "You haven't always made good decisions—that much is true—but we all make mistakes."

"Not you," Andy replied with conviction. "You're sensible and wise."

This wasn't true and Rae knew it. Almost since arriving, she'd wrestled with a ridiculous girlhood fantasy that had come to life in the person of a man who had listened while she poured out her heart to him on a mountaintop. That was not at all sensible. Or practical. Or wise.

But she was certain it would pass. As she became more accustomed to that mountain of a man, she would be better able to deal with her own emotions. And then there was Andy. He had great potential. His skills were admirable. He wasn't just good looking. He was *extremely* attractive. And she figured that once she settled down to face reality again, she would accept these things about Andy with her heart as well as her head. She just needed a little time. Like, a summer.

"I would like to know you better, Andy," she said. "But for now, I have a job to do. That's why I'm here. I need to take things slowly this summer."

Andy looked up toward the starlit expanse of sky and sighed deeply. When he returned his gaze to Rae, the troubled look had disappeared. "Okay," he said, smiling. "Slow and easy it is."

Thirty minutes passed as they said their goodbyes, with Livi promising everyone that she would text as soon as she arrived in Paris. When they returned to the house and entered the lounge, Livi expressed surprise at finding Lucas watching TV in the dimly lit room. "Uncle Lucas," she said, hurrying over to stand by his chair where his lean frame was stretched out, his feet propped up on an ottoman. "Is everything all right?"

"Of course. Why shouldn't it be?"

"Did you and Isobel have a fight?"

"Isobel and I plan to spend the day together before she returns to Raleigh tomorrow evening. Now, does that sound like we've had a fight?"

"No," she admitted. "But you don't usually sit in the dark, watching TV."

"And you aren't usually home at this hour," he countered, looking from Livi to Andy.

"I'm too excited about Paris to keep my mind on anything else for long," Livi said, adding, "which reminds me, I have to finish packing." After a quick kiss on Lucas's cheek, she left the room.

"Did you enjoy the party?" Lucas asked Rae.

"Very much," she replied and looked at Andy. She wanted to give him an opening to return to the party. "But it *is* early."

"Maybe I'll watch TV with Uncle Lucas," he said.

"Fine," Lucas said. "Care to join us, Ramona?"

"No, thanks," Rae replied. "I promised to help Livi pack."

She started to turn but Andy reached for her arm and gently drew her to him, then placed a light kiss on her lips.

Rae stepped back immediately, expecting Lucas to be watching, but he seemed absorbed in finding a channel on TV. As Andy said goodnight, the tones of a lively commercial rose in the background. But it was Lucas's low-pitched, "Good night, Ramona," that lodged in her consciousness.

Six

Rae greeted Sunday morning with both anticipation and apprehension. She was excited about beginning her job at the camp but wondered if she were equal to the challenge. Livi insisted on rising before daybreak and Gran arrived early; the two were already on their way to the airport and Lucas had left for the campgrounds.

"Our lives won't be the same for the rest of the summer," Andy said when it was time to head down the mountain toward the camp to begin a week of staff training and indoctrination before the campers arrived.

Andy drove down the steep, winding incline which led to the side of the gym and onto the gravel road in the center of camp. A short distance farther, he parked the car, then retrieved her bag from the backseat. They hiked up a winding path leading to a log cottage posted with a crudely carved sign reading *Off Limits*.

"It means what it says too," Andy said. "None of the male staff members and counselors are allowed up here." Rae suspected its authority had been challenged more than once.

A pleasant-looking woman in her mid-forties came out onto the deck as Andy and Rae set the luggage down. "Rae," Andy said, "this is Marge, the director's wife."

"I've heard a lot about you from Lucas and Andy," she said. Marge's rather plain face, surrounded by short, brown curls, came alive when she smiled, and her blue eyes expressed warmth. Rae liked her immediately.

"I'd better get myself down to the dining hall and meet the incoming staff before Uncle Lucas or that husband of yours, Marge, calls for me over the PA system," Andy said, as if reluctant to leave, but he lifted his hand in parting and hurried down the steep path. She watched as he got into the yellow car, turned it around and drove away.

Marge stood beside her and pointed out her house, several yards from *Off Limits*. The rustic mountain home with a shingled roof was situated in the center of camp and almost obscured by lush, green foliage and thick clumps of rhododendron, growing down the banks of a fast-flowing stream. A bridge arched high above the stream, leading to the deck across the front of the house.

"That long, modern building at the far end of the lake is office space on the top floor and the infirmary on the lower floor. The nurses have quarters there during the summer—the female nurses. The male nurses stay in the men's quarters."

"You have both male and female nurses," Rae said, noting the wisdom.

Marge smiled. "Some of the older boys especially are more comfortable with a male nurse," she said with a wink.

"Got it."

Marge opened the screen door, and they stepped into the living room, furnished with no-frills but comfortable furniture. "The fireplace is the only source of heat. Some evenings get a bit nippy, but you won't notice it most of the time. You'll be so tired you'll simply fall into bed and crash."

"That's encouraging," Rae said, pulling her luggage up next to her. "I think."

A doorway to the left led to Rae's bedroom. The furnishings were spartan—two twin beds, a dresser, and a chest of drawers. From the front window, she looked out on the deck, then out toward the view of the lake and mountains beyond.

"You'll share your bedroom with one of the rifle instructors," Marge told her. At Rae's quick glance, Marge added, *"She's* an expert. Has won marksmanship awards for years. And she's only twenty-two. She was with us last year. Of course, we also have a male instructor, but I dare say the older boys prefer Leslie to Jason."

"Naturally," Rae said with a laugh.

The two crafts assistants would room together in one of the other bedrooms, Marge told her, but the crafts director—a male—stayed in the men's cabins. Of course.

"I'll take all of you on a tour this afternoon. Go ahead and get settled. I'll see you in the dining hall at noon."

Leslie, a pretty redhead with freckles cascading down both sides of her nose, arrived shortly after Rae finished unpacking. "So, you're the expert marksman I've heard about?" Rae smiled as they shook hands.

Leslie's grip was firm. "Well, marks*woman.*"

"You go, girl." Rae plopped on the side of her bed. "Do you mind if I hang out while you unpack?"

"Not at all."

While Leslie unloaded her things, the two chatted easily. "Hungry?" Leslie asked with a final close of a drawer.

"A little," Rae admitted.

Leslie pointed toward the door. "Let's go eat."

As they walked toward the dining hall, Leslie spotted a kind-faced young man with a golden complexion and raven-black hair nearing them from another path. "Hey, Atohi," she called out with a wave.

"Leslie."

"Rae," Leslie said, stopping long enough to make an introduction. "This is Atohi and his name means 'woods.' Appropriate, huh?" she asked with a wide smile. "He's the director of crafts."

"What kind of crafts do you teach?" Rae asked as they continued toward the dining hall.

"I'm Cherokee," Atohi answered, his dimples slicing into his cheeks, "so I bring the art of my culture to the boys. We teach painting, basket weaving, and jewelry-making . . . but the finer point is to educate the boys about the Native American people and their culture."

Rae felt herself beaming. She lifted her hand for a "high-five" and Atohi returned it. "I think that's wonderful," she said. They walked down to the dining hall where the kitchen staff had set out long tables in the main part of the building topped with hamburgers with all the trimmings; crisp, raw vegetables; and platters piled high with fresh locally grown fruit.

Carl stood at the head of the line, restraining the hungry staff. When everyone was in line, Lucas went to the microphone and asked that they bow their heads. His prayer was a short, simple one, thanking God for the food, for the staff, and asking His guidance as they prepared to share their lives with boys and young men who would soon join them.

After the "amen," Rae regarded him long and seriously.

Lucas's acknowledgment of God was not just a ritual but seemed to be as much a part of him as breathing. Though much about Lucas was a mystery to Rae, she sensed a deep religious conviction within him. She had felt it when they were on the mountain that first morning together, when he said he wanted a Christian girl for Andy, and when he admitted his own dependence on God.

Considering all the things that appealed to her about Lucas, she realized he had never appealed to her as much as he did at this moment. Regardless of how much money a person had, or how physically attractive, a man was never taller, nor stronger, nor more intriguing, than when he admitted his need for God.

Rae turned and moved with the line to fill her plate. Her sudden elation was replaced by a sinking feeling. Her own faith in God would mean nothing to Lucas without a life to back it up. No matter how able she might prove herself to be on the job, she was sure that, when he learned the *whole* truth, he would not approve of her . . . not even for Andy.

Rae forced her mind from these unhappy thoughts and followed Marge and the others to the screened-in deck overlooking the lake. From this vantage point, they could see a huge, colorful float near the diving station.

Marge explained that it was called the "blob." A camper could crawl out to the edge and sit on it. A counselor or several small campers would then jump off the diving board, land on the air-inflated blob, and the camper would fly up into the air, then come screaming down into the water, arms and legs waving wildly. "They all love it," she said.

After lunch, Lucas welcomed the staff and introduced the husband and wife team of Carl and Marge, praising their efforts in directing the camp operation all year in preparation for these few weeks during the summer.

When Lucas introduced Andy, he stressed his experience and training—leaving no doubt that Andy held his position as assistant camp director, not because he was the nephew of the owner, but because of his own unique qualifications.

"This is a time for self-analysis and recommitment to the boys and young men who are sent here from all over the world to receive the best athletic training available. We're here to give them just that."

Carl asked the staff to stand and introduce themselves, leaving Rae to wonder how she would ever learn all the names. Being able to state her own qualifications for being a part of such a select group gave her a good feeling and pride rose in her voice as she spoke of her father.

After lunch, Marge took Rae and her cabinmates on a tour. She parked the Jeep in front of the long, two-story office building. In the infirmary they met two of the nurses, Marcus and Suze, who assured them that at times those rooms would be filled to capacity. Sometimes, although rarely, a virus ran through the camp. There would be the inevitable scrapes, sprains, and bruises. And, occasionally, young campers would be stricken with homesickness.

Marge took them upstairs to the offices and introduced Ann, the executive secretary and receptionist. Ann opened her mouth in welcome, but before she could get a word out, the urgency of the phone demanded her attention.

"Sorry, guys," she said.

"Now let's get your summer uniforms," Marge said, and they walked down the hallway to the clothing room where each of the girls was issued several sets of forest green shorts and khaki shirts. The shirts displayed the camp's emblem on the left pocket, and the word *staff* embroidered above it. White socks also bore the emblem.

After leaving the office building, Marge drove them along the main road, which led to the front and back entrances of the camp. She pointed toward mountainsides dotted with cabins, each of which would accommodate eight to ten campers, a counselor, a junior counselor, and a counselor-in-training. Nearer the lake were cottages for male staff and directors.

The gym fascinated Rae. Storage space for all kinds of athletic equipment ran the entire length of the huge building. One large room was devoted solely to gymnastic equipment.

"The gym is also used for church services on Sunday morning," Marge explained. "It's the only building large enough to accommodate all the campers at one time, except for the dining hall. Some of the campers are sons of noted Christian athletes, so Lucas often asks the fathers to speak."

Soon Marge led them back toward *Off Limits*.

"You should get to bed early tonight," she suggested, handing each of them a packet. Later, when Rae looked over the papers outlining the schedule during the next week of training and orientation, she had the feeling Marge had given good advice. They would be needing all the rest they could get.

After they turned out their lamps, Rae lay on the cot nearest the front window, where she breathed deeply of the cool, moist night air and snuggled under warm blankets. All was quiet except for the sound of crickets and insects claiming their right to the night, and she could feel herself drifting off to sleep before she had finished her prayers.

Seven

"What was that?" exclaimed Rae, sitting up in bed. Outside her window and permeating her consciousness were the strident notes of a trumpet belting out the tune of "Carolina in the Morning."

With a groan, Leslie turned over. "I'm afraid that's our alarm clock for the entire summer. One of the male staffers gets up every single morning before the roosters even know to crow and blows it into the PA system."

Soon enough, figures clad in green shorts and khaki shirts jogged down the mountainsides toward the dining hall, including Lucas, who—attired in camp uniform like the others—welcomed everyone. After breakfast, Rae sat with the rest of the staff around the tables on the dining hall deck for Lucas's indoctrination, much of which included an explanation of the material in the packet Marge had given her.

"Our most obvious purpose," Lucas said, "is to provide the campers with a fun-filled, enjoyable three weeks. They are divided by age: junior camp—ages seven to eleven—and senior camp—ages twelve to sixteen.

"Normally a camper of thirteen, fourteen, fifteen," he continued, "who has attended camp for several years is ready to be tested for physical endurance." He straightened and smiled. "*Attitude* is a major test. To reach the highest goal, our campers must also be gentle and helpful, as well as brave and strong.

"We will expose each camper to a variety of activities and encourage him to excel in at least one area," Lucas continued. "Staff members must make written reports on each camper under their care. This will demand careful, meticulous evaluation."

Rae grew increasingly apprehensive as she listened to the stringent goals that required professionalism and organization. All other new staff members had submitted an application, with references that had been thoroughly checked. She had not. Her only references had been Andy and Livi. But, like everyone else who'd not been there previously, Rae would have to "try out" for her areas of expertise.

After this briefing, the new staffers were told to get into their swimsuits and meet at the lake in fifteen minutes. Because of the many water sports—swimming, diving, canoeing, sailing, and life-saving—water safety was a must. Rae had always felt comfortable with water sports and was especially skilled in diving.

Lucas and Carl joined the others where testing in all the other disciplines continued through that day and the next, until it was Rae's turn to demonstrate her expertise in gymnastics along with two young men.

"Could the guys go first?" Rae asked Andy.

"Sure," he said, after a moment's hesitation. His smile was warm, but his eyes held a questioning look. Her usual case of crazy jitters struck as always before competition, and she knew she'd grown pale. She must prove to herself, as well as to Lucas who insisted on the best in what he offered young campers, that she was a qualified instructor.

Rae watched from the sidelines as the two young men took their turns. They were good. Excellent, in fact. Her heart hammered, her palms grew moist, and she felt nauseous, despite the fact she had known better than to eat any breakfast.

Rae had spent some time in the gym the night before, practicing a few routines and testing the surface of the tumbling mat. She had decided to perform barefoot. The exact routine was familiar, one that she had used hundreds of times in competition, exhibitions, and classes.

Now her music, as much a part of her equipment as her warm-up suit and leotards, was ready on the sidelines. She joined in the enthusiastic applause for the young men, for it was well deserved. But she had been trained by Raymond Martin, and she was ready to demonstrate what he had taught her.

Were this a match of physical prowess alone, she knew she would fail; the young men had displayed superior strength on the pommel horse and parallel bars. But her *gymnastics moderne* classes and their stringent routines had given her an undeniable edge.

She knew what she must do. She would not give less than her best. She would not simply display the correct movements, the results of many years of discipline and training, but she would give an exhibition. A tribute to her father and his years of tireless effort. She would draw upon the inner strength he always stressed.

And then Andy called her name.

Her father had always said, "When you see nothing but that vault, it's time to go." She stood, forcing the spectators from her mind, telling herself it was not Lucas she must please ultimately, but herself. She welcomed the intense surge of concentration.

Unconsciously she tugged at her leotards, brushed at the hair that was already turning into ringlets, positioned her body, lifted her chin, felt the silence of an audience holding its breath, then stared at the vaulting horse until nothing else occupied her mind.

Her flight began. Rae sprinted for the vault table, and within a few seconds was performing a round-off onto the springboard strategically placed before the vaulting apparatus. This board gave Rae the momentum she needed to perform a back handspring with a full twist onto the table. She then completed the gymnastic move with a flip and a twist, landing the vault with a flourish. The effort, concentration, and years of practice that had gone into the vault, culminated almost as soon as it began.

Rae wiped her hands and her forehead, allowing herself time to catch her breath and decrease the rapid beat of her heart before she moved to the balance beam. In competition, one slip there could cost a medal or a career. While teaching the young campers, she would not have to follow all the rules or perform the more difficult maneuvers. She would be expected only to demonstrate a knowledge of the basic tenets. However, for herself and her father, she intended to perform as if the gold medal were the prize.

She mounted by jumping from the springboard and landing on one foot at the end of the beam, keeping the other foot free at its end, and extending her arms. Her graceful movements incorporated the *moderne* technique. Strength, balance, agility, and personal innovation were evident as she performed her cat leap and turn, arabesque holding position, forward springs, aerial walkover, and, unrelentingly, a standing back somersault. She worked the entire beam, first supporting herself on her hands with one foot touching the beam, then kicked up to a handstand, turned 180 degrees to face the opposite direction, then executed a forward walkover and dismounted to land with her back to the beam.

With this part of the routine successfully completed, Rae couldn't allow the tension and pressure to leave her yet, but she could breathe a little easier. The uneven parallel bars gave her opportunity to exercise creativity in a way the vault and balance beam could not. These required much more rigid, meticulous movements. The asymmetric bars demanded a continuous movement, calling upon strength, agility, flexibility, and stamina developed through a regular program of exercise.

From a running position, Rae jumped from the springboard into the air, executed a 360-degree spin, grasped the low bar, circled over it forward, down and up again, supported herself above the bar, and dropped down. Then, hanging from the low bar with arms straight, she moved her legs forward in a pike position and propelled herself through a 180-degree turn upward to grasp the high bar. She performed the swinging movements, suspension, and passage of her body between the bars with fluid grace. Finally, after circling up through a headstand on the high bar, she swung down, did a backward somersault, and dismounted, facing the bars.

Rae's father always had told her to smile before she began her floorwork. She knew she had not failed her father this day, nor herself. Her broad smile reflected her appreciation of the audience's applause. Her next routine would be for them.

She could not relax completely even though the floorwork was her forte and called for the kind of movements she had taught almost daily at the university for the past three years.

Standing at the edge of the floor mat, she lifted her arm. The music began. For the next minute and a half, her routine displayed the beauty and elegance of the female form as she combined artistic and gymnastic movements in her handsprings, somersaults, handstands, pirouette spins, and jumps.

Rae loved this, for it was the most aesthetically beautiful of the gymnastic events, providing graceful interludes between the tumbling movements. She perfectly performed a roundoff and a double back somersault, landed in a gymnast's graceful stance. After a quick bow, and a lift of her arms, she ran from the floor.

Her radiant face, framed by damp curls, turned toward the audience that had risen to their feet spontaneously, applauding enthusiastically. That tribute was especially appreciated, for many of them were just as capable as she in their own skills.

She looked toward Lucas for approval, but he was talking to Carl and Andy, studying the clipboard in Andy's hand. Her heart sank.

Rae slipped into her warm-ups, then sat on a bench to put on her socks. When she saw a pair of masculine legs in front of her, she looked up.

"Raymond Martin would have been very proud of you today," Lucas said in a voice meant only for her.

Eight

Assignments were given on Wednesday. Rae would instruct gymnastics for the junior camps with the other two young gymnasts teaching the older boys, and she would also take her shifts in watersports.

Rae spent the next several days studying and absorbing camper applications and photos until she felt she knew them well, even before their arrival. For sure, by Saturday evening after the intensive week of training, everyone was ready for a change of pace.

Rae had become so accustomed to seeing the green shorts and khaki shirts that it seemed strange now to be confronted with campers dressed in jeans and western shirts. She had asked Andy to bring her something appropriate for the night's activities from Livi's closet.

Lucas was standing near the door of the gym, greeting many of his guests for the evening, when Rae walked up dressed in a pair of jeans and a plaid shirt.

"You'll be a converted cowgirl before the night's over," Lucas predicted. His friendly manner reminded her of the first morning they had spent together on the mountaintop.

"There's definitely a twang in the air." Rae laughed as she started to walk past him.

Lucas reached out and grabbed her arm, then steered her through the doorway. "The Mountain Creek Boys," he said, gesturing toward the small bluegrass band.

"Oh, look." Rae pointed. "I didn't know Andy could do that." She was intrigued to see Andy clogging with an attractive brunette. There was toe-heel-toe tapping to the hip-slapping music of guitars, and those on the sidelines clapped to the beat, patting their feet, and calling out a few "yee-has."

After the clogging exhibition, a square dance was announced. Andy and the brunette paired off, while others formed a circle.

"Now it's your turn," Lucas said, but Rae shook her head.

"I don't know how," she said regretfully.

Challenge rose in his eyes. "You don't need to know how. Just follow me."

Taking a deep breath, Rae squared her shoulders and walked to the circle with Lucas.

"All join hands," came the call.

Lucas grabbed her left hand and, simultaneously, she felt the right one being grasped. She looked around into the smiling face of one of the directors. Before she could object, the caller sang out, "Circle left," and for the next twenty minutes, she wasn't able to utter a word.

The circling was easy, but the calls confused her: "Texas star . . . Circle four . . . Swing that girl . . . Now your own."

The only thing Rae understood was that when the caller said, "Now your own purty little gal," she was in Lucas's arms, then just as quickly someone else whisked her away.

"Duck for the oyster, dive for the clam!"

After a few more calls, but only briefly, Andy was her partner. "Having fun?" he asked.

She could only nod, fearful that by the time she answered, she would be handed off to another. It didn't take long for her to realize that no matter how confused she became, or how lost, Lucas always found her.

"Promenade around the ring, promenade that purty little thing." Two by two they circled, Lucas's arm around her shoulder, his hand holding her other lifted one.

After the dance, Lucas was introducing Rae to the director of a nearby summer camp when Andy came up to claim her. When the next round began, he asked, "Want to try it?"

"No, I think I've had enough for a while," Rae said, laughing. "Go find yourself a *good* dancer and have some *real* fun."

Andy squeezed her hand and looked down into her eyes. A special gleam was there, and his smile was sweet. "You're one girl in a million." He winked affectionately, then walked away. Andy found his previous dancing partner, and they joined the square dance circle.

Slipping through the doorway of the gym, Rae inhaled deeply of the brisk air. The coolness felt refreshing on her warm skin.

"You're apparently not the jealous type," Lucas said, joining her.

"It wouldn't change anything if I were."

Lucas's face wore a forbidding frown. "No, I suppose not."

"I encouraged Andy to find a good partner," Rae explained. "After all, you danced with me."

"Yes, but I'm family," he countered.

Rae looked away, unsure what to say. How to answer. Maybe a change of subject. "Beautiful, isn't it? The stars are so bright and yet so quiet. So peaceful."

"You should see them reflected on the lake," he said. "And tomorrow, we'll have about that many boys *in* the lake."

Rae laughed. "Noisier than the stars, I expect."

"Ah, quite." He took her elbow. He gestured toward the gym where the bluegrass music continued to swell. "Even noisier than that." They walked down the path, toward the lake.

"I meant to ask you, is Isobel's son still ill?" Rae asked.

"No," Lucas replied, glancing toward her. "He's fine now."

"I'm surprised she isn't here tonight for the festivities."

Lucas grinned. "This kind of primitive exertion doesn't appeal to Isobel."

"Doesn't she like camp life? I mean, if you marry her, wouldn't she help you run all this?"

Lucas's glance made Rae wonder if she had become too personal. He gazed out into the distance before answering.

"Isobel appreciates what the camp does for her son. During the winter, Kevin attends a private school. Here, we give him discipline,

attention, and a sense of belonging. He needs that, and Isobel knows it."
Rae felt her face flush. "Do you think I would marry a woman because she might be an asset in my chosen field?"

"No," she said honestly. "At least, I don't think you would."

"If you must insist upon knowing my deepest secrets, fair maiden," he said as he guided her to a canoe tied up in a stall along the lakeshore, "then I shall whisk you away to yon faraway deserted island."

Laughing, Rae settled into the shaky craft. Lucas was a man of many moods, and this was a side of him she had not seen before. "Yon island" was all of fifty feet from the edge of the lake and not more than that in length, with two solitary trees on it.

"Now," he said, paddling on alternate sides of the canoe, "what were we talking about?"

"Why you never married," Rae said. "Why haven't you?"

Lucas looked surprised, then laughed low. "Ramona Martin, I have the sneaky feeling you're prying."

"Works both ways," Rae said, lifting her chin. "You have asked me all sorts of questions. What's good for the goose and all that."

"Touché," Lucas replied with a laugh.

Rae stared down at her shoes, then glanced up through lowered lashes. Lucas's expression had turned serious. "If I were to guess, I'd say that you're a girl who follows her heart instead of her head."

"You're wrong," she argued. "I'm like my father. I generally think things through before I make a decision."

"Probably," he conceded. "It's just that the things that seem important to you are not the things most women in your position would consider priorities—financial security, social status. No," he spoke with conviction, "I believe you would wonder if you could live with a man for a lifetime, have his children, love him when he's at his worst."

"During my mother's illness, my father and I became extremely close. There is something about the bond of suffering that draws people together. Because of her hospital expenses, we had financial difficulties, but no amount of money could have bought the love we shared. And our faith gave us strength to face her death. Then, when my father became ill, I learned all over again the sufficiency of God's grace. I suppose that's why, although I guess I enjoy material things as much as any woman, I know there are more important things in life."

Lucas was silent, only occasionally stroking the water with the paddle. He took the oar and laid it across the canoe in front of him. "I'm going to tell you something I've never told anyone."

Part of Rae wanted to hear how he felt, what he thought, what was going on inside of him. Another part feared what he might say. Everything was still as she waited. No sound of music. Even the night's noises were being driven into the background by the sound of her own heart beating in her temples. Only the two of them seemed to exist. "All right," she said.

"Ramona, I've been all over the world, skied down just about every well-known slope. But there is a mountain in Switzerland that intrigues me."

Rae looked at him quizzically.

"We're not compatible, that mountain and I," he continued. "She's treacherous, has thrown me many times. But I get up laughing, determined to accept her challenge. When I am skiing down that slope, I feel that I make an important conquest if I reach bottom upright. Frankly, I rather like it when she wins." He looked at her then.

This was what he'd never told anyone? But what did it have to do with—ah. "And that's the kind of woman you want?"

His laugh was light. "I used to think so. I often wondered if there was a woman out there for me who expected more of me than gliding smoothly along the slopes of life. But there always seemed to be a missing ingredient."

"Do you know what was missing?" Rae asked, her voice barely a whisper.

"Of course," he replied immediately, that mocking expression on his face. "I thought I would fall in love. As you seem to have done."

Rae found his sarcastic tone irritating. "I wouldn't marry a man I didn't love," she assured him.

"Ah, love," Lucas said with amusement. "Is love some tangible thing, or some illusory fantasy? Is it not some figment of imagination one finds in a novel? Is it not wiser to be practical, sensible? Chasing love might be like chasing rainbows. Looking for that pot of gold that can never be found."

"You mean you think I should consider how much I might gain financially when I marry?" Rae asked, resenting his cynicism.

"I didn't say that," Lucas replied. "I merely suggested that you consider your options."

In that instant Rae realized that what often seemed like tender moments with Lucas turned out to be another of his attempts to explore her motives regarding Andy. And she had fallen for it every time. "So, you no longer believe in love," she fired back.

Looking at her levelly, he lifted his brow. "I know the mountain exists. Perhaps the woman does too."

Rae shook her head in confusion. She did not understand him. Glancing over at him, she saw he was amused. It was difficult, if not impossible, to know when he was serious and when he was not.

He sighed. "As one grows older, however, the tendency is to be more of a realist, and less a romantic. I think I have concluded that such a woman does not exist. At least, for me. Perhaps I should settle for compatibility."

Rae watched as his jawline tensed. She almost regretted having been engaged in such a conversation, for now he seemed remote and sad.

"But there have been times, Ramona," he said, as if talking to himself, "when I have longed for a woman, not just to fill my arms, but to fill my heart. I think the most irresistible woman in the world would be one—" he spoke hesitantly, almost fearfully—"one who truly loved me."

His rugged profile seemed to be carved from the mountain itself. There was something touching about this man beneath whose steel and fire ran deep reservoirs of tenderness and longing, springing up like some subterranean stream from the heart of the mountain. He was a man who had everything yet longed for something more.

"You have Isobel," Rae said quietly, and his gaze returned to her.

"Of course. And Isobel would fit perfectly with my lifestyle."

"But you said she wouldn't care for camp life."

Now he looked at her as though she had three heads.

"This is only a small part of my life, Ramona," he explained. "The camp is very important to me, but I also have a winter resort in Switzerland. And perhaps you aren't aware of my line of sports equipment. Isobel would be greatly admired in those circles."

"You seem to so enjoy preparing for camp, and the boys, the square dance," Rae said, remembering his vitality, his hearty laughter. He was a part of these mountains, this culture.

"I can live without it," he replied tersely. "All this will be André's someday. You would be an ideal partner to work alongside him. You're good for him, Ramona."

To cover her sudden discomfort, she sought a subject that would take his mind off her relationship with Andy. "It has occurred to me that it seems a shame that only boys will be here to take advantage of the expert skills of your staff. Have you ever considered making the camp co-ed?"

"You must be a mind reader," Lucas replied immediately. "I've even thought of discussing the possibility with you. It would take a very special kind of woman to direct it. With your background, skills, and Christian commitment, Ramona, parents of girls and young women would admire and respect you. They would feel comfortable sending their girls to such a camp."

"I wasn't speaking of myself," Rae protested.

His smile was warm and beautiful. "But I believe you are that very special person who could make it successful." He reached for the oar and began to maneuver the small craft toward the island. "When I started this camp, I only felt qualified to direct boys. But with someone like you and André—"

Rae felt panic rising. Her thoughts were in turmoil. She wanted to blurt out her and Andy's deception, free herself of the weight of guilt before things went any further.

Strange, when she had agreed to accompany Andy to North Carolina, it hadn't seemed so complicated. She had justified his silly scheme in her own mind by telling herself she was helping a young man who had made a foolish mistake. She had even thought she might be a good influence on him. But now it had grown all out of proportion. Telling Lucas the truth about her and Andy—that they were *really* no more than friends nor did she expect they would be—would ease her conscience. She could then obtain Lucas's forgiveness and try to set a better example for the camp.

But the timing was all wrong. Beginning tomorrow, each of them faced tremendous responsibilities. Lucas had emphasized that the campers were their top priority for the summer. Her confession would cause division among Lucas, Andy, and herself. Rae would just have to suffer silently for the sake of all of them.

Rae lifted her hand to her head, then looked for any sign of distraction from her thoughts. "Oh, look," she exclaimed as something broke the surface of the water farther out and she leaned over just as Lucas swung the oar.

"Watch it," he cautioned abruptly, but too late. The canoe tipped, and before she could regain her balance, she plunged headlong into the water.

Lucas released the oar and followed her. For an embarrassing moment, they flailed about, reaching for the paddle.

"Oh, Lucas," Rae sputtered away the lake water. "What an awkward thing for me to do."

"I agree," he said, attempting to right the canoe.

Rae swam around to the other side. "We'll never get back into this thing."

"We'll just have to drag it back to shore. And to think," Lucas said with amusement, "we were almost stranded on a deserted island."

"Almost," Rae repeated, trying to imitate his joking manner, then added incredulously, "Am I doing all the work?"

"It would appear so," he replied. "Why don't you relax and try walking?"

"Walking?" Rae stammered, then realized they had reached shallow water.

They both laughed as they found their footing on the bank. Lucas was then able to flip the canoe, emptying the lake water. After Lucas secured the canoe, he came over to where Rae stood shivering. "Your clothes are at The Haven, aren't they?" he asked.

"Everything except my camp uniforms and what I wore the day I came here, which is dirty."

"Let's jog up there," he suggested. "We can change, then I'd like to discuss those plans with you."

When they neared the gym, Lucas spied a counselor. "Tim," he called, "would you please find Andy and tell him that Rae and I have gone up to The Haven?"

"Sure," Tim replied, a grin spreading across his face at the sight of the soggy couple. "He was inside just a minute ago."

"Let's go," Lucas said to Rae, and they began to jog up the road by the gym, their shoes squishing with every step.

After reaching the house, they sat on the top step of the first deck to remove their shoes and socks. "Sorry I ruined your evening," Rae said apologetically.

"Ruined my evening?" Lucas asked, as if the idea were preposterous.

"You probably weren't ready to come home yet."

"If I hadn't been," he replied, pulling off his socks, "I would have stayed there and drip-dried."

"I'm glad you're not angry," she said.

"I will admit I hadn't planned on taking a—swim—" he said, taking her shoes and his own. He set them side by side at the edge of the deck, with the wet socks on top. Then he came back and pulled her up by her hands. "But the evening was not a total loss," he assured. His voice grew soft.

Rae looked up at him, his dark eyes shadowed as he bent his head toward hers.

"It was fun teaching a city girl how to square dance. And how *not* to rock a boat."

Rae told herself Lucas was just being kind, trying to make light of their misadventure. That perhaps that intense look on his face was her imagination. But the feel of his warm breath against her cheek was all too real. "Fortunate is the man who will have the privilege of teaching you," he added, "everything."

Rae longed to tell him she wished that he might be that man, but his next words seemed to contradict any such possibility. "And I believe he's here now," he said as tires screeched against the gravel on the driveway.

A concerned Andy bounded up the steps. He stopped suddenly, taking in their wet clothing and bare feet.

Lucas laughed as he pointed at Rae. "She dunked me," he said. "Right out of the canoe."

Nine

"Uncle Lucas tells me you have some terrific ideas about implementing a girls camp program," Andy said after Rae entered the lounge, clad now in slacks and a warm sweater, her hair still damp.

"I don't know anything about this kind of thing except what I've learned this week. And that knowledge hasn't been proven yet." She shrugged. "So, I'm not about to tell you how to start and then run a girls athletic camp like the one you already have," she said adamantly.

Andy only smiled at her.

"What?" she asked. "Why are you looking at me like that?"

Andy blinked slowly. "You're beautiful," he said, "even without your hair fixed, and with your nose all shiny."

"Uh-huh." She smiled and sat beside him on the couch. "Flattery will get you nowhere. I'm still not going to put in two cents about how to run a girls athletic camp."

"We don't expect that much, Ramona," Lucas assured her as he entered the room carrying a tray of mugs filled with hot chocolate. "We just want your opinion on a few things. There were times when I had hopes of Olivia's taking an interest in this venture, but I've abandoned that." He set the tray down on the coffee table. "I've been waiting until I felt the time was right. Perhaps, now, it is."

Both she and Andy reached for their mugs as Lucas walked over to a file cabinet near his desk and removed a folder, then returned to the easy chair he had pulled up to the coffee table across from Rae and Andy. He moved the tray aside and unfolded a large piece of paper holding a blueprint.

"This is the area at the back of the camp, beyond Marge's and Carl's house, where cabins could be built. And this mountain here," he said, pointing, "could be leveled and a new gym built there. Do you think the girls gym should be separate from the boys?" he asked Rae.

"I think so," she asserted. "It would be good to have some interaction between the boys and girls—even competition—but their training should be separate. They would want to impress each other with their skills, but I don't think they would be comfortable together while in the learning process."

To prove her point, Rae related some experiences she had had as a child at church camp. "They should be together for meals, though." She smiled, remembering.

"Then I would need to extend the dining hall," Lucas mused, looking at Andy for his opinion.

"There's plenty of room to expand," Andy said. "And even for extending the deck out over the lake. How many girls should be enrolled?"

"What do you think, Ramona?" Lucas asked

"*If*," she began, "if it were my decision, I would limit the number of girls and accept only girls with proven interests in athletics. It's so important to train them properly when they're young. Some of the girls in my classes at the university had learned habits that were almost impossible to overcome and hampered their technique."

"A small group of girls, seriously interested in athletics." Lucas nodded in approval. "That would diminish some of the supervision problems that have concerned me."

Rae nodded in understanding. "Well, there will always be *that,* but I think with the right staff, you can handle natural, raging hormones." She grinned to lessen the insinuation. "I also think this is an obvious next move for the camp."

"If we get the right person to direct it," Lucas said.

Rae scanned the blueprint further, then pointed and said, "Is this what I think it is?"

"If you think it's another Olympic-sized swimming pool for the girls, you're correct," he answered with a smile.

"Oh, to be that young again," Rae exclaimed. "I'd like to be one of those campers myself."

Andy laughed. "I'm sure Uncle Lucas will let you sign up."

"I've kept you two long enough," Lucas said, standing. "You probably want to get back to the square dance."

"Shall we?" Andy asked, eagerness dominating the tone in his voice.

"Fine by me," she said.

"Thanks for your opinions and suggestions," Lucas said. "And André," he continued seriously, "although you have done a good job with the camp in the past, I detect a new sense of direction and a more positive attitude about you this year. I'm confident this will be our finest summer yet."

"Rae has a lot to do with that, Uncle Lucas." Andy smiled down at her. "I'm beginning to understand what you meant when you talked to me about taking life and relationships more seriously. Maybe it just takes that special person to make a guy realize it."

Lucas nodded. "I want you to know something else, André. Whenever you're ready to settle down and take over the running of the camp, I'm ready to begin releasing more responsibilities to you. And Ramona," he continued, looking deep into her eyes, "I consider it a privilege having you on our staff. I can well picture you heading up the girls camp. Think it over."

Lucas's acceptance and approval of her was not only reflected in his words, but in his eyes. How pleased he seemed to be in believing she and Andy might grow closer, perhaps marry.

"Lucas," she began, and his questioning gaze invited her to continue. But Andy's quick intake of breath told her that a confession at this moment would destroy the confidence his uncle had just expressed in them. "Good night," she said.

Andy steered her out the door before she could reconsider.

"How could you possibly put on such a blatant display of hypocrisy, Andy?" she blurted after they settled in the car. "It's bad enough to know we're playing this deceitful game, but you're behaving as if everything is settled between us. Because it's not. It's not settled at all. You've gone too far!"

But Andy, undaunted by her anger, smiled tenderly. "I'll tell you all about that in about three weeks. A date?"

"What does that mean?"

But Andy wasn't bending. "Yes or no? A date?"

"I suppose," Rae answered. She knew she must try to come to terms with her emotional conflict. But she couldn't think about that now, not with three weeks of camping ahead.

~ ~ ~

Sunday morning dawned bright and clear. Although registration was scheduled from one o'clock to five, campers piled from cars, and buses full of noisy boys arrived from the airport before the 11:00 church service scheduled in the gym.

A local pastor spoke on the wonder of the body, the temple of God. He praised Lucas for his ministry to the physical growth of boys and young men and emphasized the even more important need for spiritual growth, which could be accomplished by an acceptance of Jesus Christ as one's personal Savior, then a daily exercise of the Lord's teachings.

After the service, everyone shared in a picnic lunch outdoors, because the dining hall was being used for registration lines.

Later, Rae assisted on the waterfront. Each camper had to be tested to determine if he belonged in a beginner, intermediate, or advanced swim class.

She knew they'd have to give time for lunch to settle before allowing the boys into the water, but by 1:30 she was clad in her swimsuit and visor to keep her nose from turning into a beet in the hot sun. She carried a clipboard with an alphabetical list on which to rate the swimmers.

Time passed quickly and by four over half the expected three hundred campers from all over the country and abroad had completed the test. Rae stretched, feeling the tightness of her muscles from having sat so long observing and evaluating the style, speed, stamina, and confidence of the boys as they swam.

"Take a break, Rae," Tim urged. "You deserve it."

"I do need to stretch my muscles," Rae replied and turned.

A woman's platinum hair caught her attention first. Holding tightly to Lucas's hand was a little boy with hair the same startling shade.

She was so intent on the newcomers that Rae scarcely noticed the camper who walked up to her on the dock. She only vaguely saw what appeared to be a rope around his neck. She opened her mouth to tell him he couldn't go into the water with it when he peered up at her and said, "Will you hold my snake while I swim?" He extended his arm as the slithery creature coiled tightly around it.

Rae shrieked and was forced to exhibit some of her fanciest diving techniques. Realization of what had happened was instantaneous. Everyone laughed as someone reached for her hand to help her back up on the dock where Tim was telling the stricken camper that he couldn't keep the snake. He must either put it back where he found it or take it to the nature center.

Rae's heart went out to the little fellow. Careful not to get too close, she apologized for screaming. "I just didn't expect to meet him," she explained. "It's *really* a very . . . nice . . . snake. I hope I didn't scare him."

"Oh," the camper said with a grin, "he'll be all right. I'll just put him back. You think he'd like that better than the nature center?"

"I think so," Rae replied, and he smiled with relief.

There was no longer any way to avoid the trio waiting at the edge of the dock. Dripping wet, she'd lost her visor, her hair was in tight ringlets, and she could feel the heat in her face.

"I—he had a—" she began but found herself stammering under Lucas's amused expression and the cool, tolerant look on Isobel's placid face.

"We saw," Lucas assured. "Congratulations. You've been fully indoctrinated into camp life." He looked down at the child. "Miss Ramona, I want you to meet Kevin."

Feeling uncomfortable in the presence of the immaculately groomed Isobel, Rae knelt in front of Kevin, who was still clinging to Lucas's hand.

"I've heard a lot about you, Kevin. Are you feeling better?"

"I've heard about you too," he said. Unexpectedly he leaned forward. "I know how you feel," he whispered.

"You don't like snakes either?" she whispered back.

Frowning, he shook his head. "But if you let anybody know, they'll try to scare you all the time. On purpose."

"Then I'd better be brave," she said with wide eyes. "You want to be brave with me?"

He straightened his frail shoulders and nodded.

"Hey," Rae called to the camper, "may I go with you to put the snake back? Kevin's going along to protect me."

"Sure," the young boy replied and walked over to them. "Girls are scared of snakes," he confided in Kevin. "My name's Bobby."

"I'm Kevin."

Isobel's thin smile was Rae's only clue that the woman was pleased with the attention Rae was giving her son, but Lucas winked his approval. She and the two little boys and the snake headed off down the path.

After Kevin and Bobby were tested, Kevin was breathless.

"Can I be in intermediate?" he asked, his eyes large and pleading, his new friend beside him. "Bobby and me can be buddies if we both make it."

There was no doubt that Bobby qualified for the more advanced rank, but Kevin was another matter. Yet Rae felt qualifying for intermediate was important to Kevin. He was a very lovable child, and she doubted that he made friends readily.

"You got very tired, Kevin," she reminded him kindly.

"That's because I've been sick. But I'm okay now. Honest! Ask Tim. I was in beginners last year, and he said I might could move up this year."

Knowing determination could play a major part in one's accomplishments, she relented. "I'll talk to Tim about it, and we'll see."

"All right!" Kevin grinned over at Bobby.

By Tuesday, the camp was settling into the routine it would follow for the next three weeks. Kevin was in Rae's beginner gymnastics class, and just as she had feared, he was not well coordinated and hadn't the strength for many of the routines. However, she suspected he might be good at tumbling, so she encouraged him to try. But what Kevin needed most was a personal touch and, since there were only ten boys in this class, Rae was grateful that she and her assistants could give him the individual attention he craved.

Lucas put in an appearance during her first beginner class.

"There's more to camp life than athletic training. You're doing wonders with Kevin. I appreciate your sensitivity." He looked at his phone with a grimace. "I've got to go. See you around." And he was on his way.

Rae turned her attention to the boy with the mop of pale hair. He was an adorable child, eagerly reaching out for affection. Yes, Kevin needed a father. A father like Lucas, she admitted.

Almost before she knew it, the beginner class was over, and the intermediate had taken its place, demanding more than training in balancing, tumbling, handstands, and cartwheels. Coaching the advanced class required all her discipline skill, for the boys had already learned techniques that needed to be refined. Here, however, they did not utilize music which she had found so valuable in her teaching at the university, for it provided rhythm, an aid in timing.

During the remainder of camp, Rae felt that her head never quite touched the pillow before the now familiar strains of "Carolina in the Morning" called her to a new day. Like a spring, she bolted from under the covers, welcomed during the cool nights, and sat up in bed to read the Bible and meditate. Each day the view out the window was different—sometimes clear, sometimes with a smoky haze encircling or resting upon the lush, green mountain peaks. Inhaling deeply of the fresh morning air, she thanked God for the beauty He had created and for the joy of sharing it with others.

Rae had Sunday off. After attending church services in the gym and eating in the dining hall, she went with Andy and Carl to see what was being done to the mountain behind the boys camp.

Carl pointed to a portion of mountain that had been leveled and cleared for the foundation. "That's where the new gym will be."

"Lucas mentioned naming the gym after your father," Andy told her. "The Raymond Martin Gym."

Rae was speechless. After a few moments she managed to ask, "Lucas would do that? For my father?"

Emotion welled up in her eyes. She was hardly aware of Andy's arm circling her waist and squeezing. Later, they walked over the mountainside, discussed the cabins, the spot for the pool, the plans for the dining hall. What had been only marks on paper one night in Lucas's study were becoming a reality.

She longed to ask Lucas about it, to express her appreciation for his tribute to her father, but there was not the opportunity during the next week, nor the next. Rae was aware, reluctantly, that the first session was rapidly coming to a close.

Suddenly it was Sunday afternoon again, and the first camp session was over. Rae stood in front of the dining hall saying goodbye to the many campers who promised to email her.

When Kevin came by, his handshake was surprisingly firm. Rae felt her eyes misting and there was a catch in her throat when she told him goodbye. In case she wanted to text, he said, he gave her his phone number, then added that he would be staying with his grandparents in Asheville during the following week.

Isobel, too, seemed strangely moved when she came to collect Kevin and his belongings. "Thank you for what you've done for my son," she said, before the icy veil of reserve dropped over her eyes once more. Only once did they brighten as she looked past Rae. "I'll see you tonight, darling," she called in her soft, Southern drawl.

Rae didn't bother to turn. There was only one person to whom Isobel could be speaking.

"Olivia called early this morning," Lucas said to Rae when Isobel and Kevin had left. "It appears there's to be a wedding. I suspected that would happen when she left for Paris."

"She loves Pierre so much." Rae turned then to face Lucas. "I'm happy for her. But I didn't know you knew."

"I make it my business to know everything about my niece and nephew," he retorted. "Olivia's grandparents in Paris are also aware of her actions." His attempt at smiling appeared to be more grimace. "They keep me informed."

Rae detected a certain reticence. "You don't approve?"

"From all I hear, Pierre is a fine man. And you're right. Olivia does love him very much. Incidentally," he said, changing the subject. "You will stay at The Haven this coming week. Most of the staff will be gone until next weekend." His tongue clicked. "Then we begin again."

"Is it all right if I come to The Haven tomorrow?" she asked. "Andy is taking me out tonight, then later I have to finish my reports for Carl. So, I would like to stay at *Off Limits* tonight."

"Fine," he said, then added, "Oh, and my mother will also be coming to The Haven tomorrow to spend the week with us."

Only Charlotte was at The Haven when Rae and Andy arrived there to dress for the evening. After taking a leisurely shower, Rae straightened her hair, then donned an all-white, off-the-shoulder sundress. She fastened pearl earrings at her lobes, then slipped her feet into dressy sandals. Her skin had grown bronze during the past three weeks, and her cheeks glowed naturally. Only a little mascara and lip gloss was needed.

Feeling ready for a night out, she hurried to the lounge, expecting Andy to be waiting. She stopped short. Lucas stood inside the doorway, dressed in evening clothes.

"You look lovely," he said and then, as if to explain his comment, added quickly, "Our costumes are quite different from that of the past few weeks."

But Rae knew that did not explain why she didn't seem able to take her eyes from him. His physical attraction was undeniable, but even more than that were the wonderful inner qualities he had displayed during the past month. She had seen it in all he did—in his express purpose for the camp, his involvement with the staff, his concern for a fatherless boy, his kindness to a fatherless woman.

"Lucas," she said, remembering, "the new gym. Have you honestly considered naming it after my father?"

"I intend to," he replied. "Your father made a significant contribution to the sports world. Through his daughter, that contribution has been extended to my camp. His name will not be forgotten. I'll make certain of that."

"Why?" she whispered. Rae did not mind that his dark eyes probed hers, as if seeking out her innermost thoughts. Her gratitude was something she wanted him to see.

"Why?" he repeated, then she felt some kind of withdrawal in him as his eyes left her face. "I would do anything within reason for my family. And you're likely soon to be a part of it." He glanced over his shoulder to Andy who had just entered the room. "Enjoy your evening."

~ ~ ~

Andy had reserved a table by a window at The Montford Rooftop Bar. Here they could look out above the traffic of Asheville, beyond the city lights, to the dark peaks forming a protective background against the graying sky.

The silence was not uncomfortable as they smiled across the intimate table for two. Rae sensed that this would be a significant evening. The very ambiance of the restaurant suggested it.

After their order was given, Rae looked out where the land touched the sky. "The stars are shining," she said softly. "I sincerely doubt there is a more beautiful place in the world than the Smoky Mountains."

Andy made no comment and Rae turned to look at him. He was twisting his glass thoughtfully.

"There's a little village in Switzerland near Uncle Lucas's ski resort. It's quaint and charming. There's a certain chalet on the side of a mountain where you can look out and see for miles. When the area is covered with snow, there's nothing else like it anywhere."

Rae was surprised at Andy's declaration of love for Switzerland. He seemed to be trying to convince her, pausing only long enough for their food to be set before them, tasting it, and making complimentary remarks.

"There is a sports shop on a main street in town there. It's for sale. A friend and I have talked about buying it and seeing if we can make a go of it."

"I love hearing about your dreams, Andy," she assured him, sharing his excitement. "But, have you told Lucas?"

"That's the only problem," he confessed. "You've seen how Uncle Lucas is so eager to turn the camp over to me. He has trained me, set his hopes on me. I've tried, but I don't seem able to tell him that I would turn down a probable lifetime security with the camp for a shop in Switzerland that might fold at any minute. It doesn't sound very responsible, does it?"

"You've proved you can be responsible. I've seen it this summer. So has Lucas. And I think your plans are commendable. Lucas would understand you wanting to do something on your own. I don't think he wants to force you to run the camp. He's just offering it to you if you do."

"When I go, Rae," he said with determination, "I want to take you with me. As my wife." At her light startle, he added, "Surely you know I've fallen in love with you."

Did she know? There had been indications, but it hadn't registered. They had been so busy during the past weeks. Her gaze slowly turned from Andy's waiting eyes toward the sky, twinkling in its blanket of stars.

It occurred to her that her acceptance would be the perfect solution to almost all her difficulties. Lucas would not have to wait any longer to marry Isobel. Kevin could have his much-needed father. She and Livi could be lifetime friends. Sisters, in fact. And, with everything they had in common, she and Andy could be compatible.

But slowly creeping into those thoughts was something more akin to the dark peaks beyond—so unmovable, mysterious, foreboding.

"I'm not asking for an answer right now," Andy said across the silence. "I'm just asking that you think about it." He looked at his plate. "Hey, this is delicious steak. How's yours?"

"Perfect."

"And the pianist?"

She looked toward the dark corner. "Excellent." Then it dawned on her that Andy was trying to put her at ease, telling her to relax. "It's a wonderful evening, Andy." She smiled with genuine pleasure.

"There can be many more like it, Rae."

Yes, she knew. An exciting, romantic life could exist for the two of them. Here, or in Switzerland. A lifetime of being loved by Andy should be all, and more, that a woman could ask for.

When Andy parked below *Off Limits* later that night, Rae did not protest when he pulled her gently toward him and pressed his lips against hers in a lingering kiss. Wishing with all her heart that she was in love with him, Rae allowed herself to be wanted, to be desired, to be loved, until his mouth became more demanding.

When she gently pushed him away, Andy sighed heavily. "Rae," he said seriously, "there have been many things I've wanted to hang onto rather than settle down. But now, I would give them all up . . . for you. You will think about what I've said, won't you?"

"Yes, Andy. I will," she promised. She would try, with all her might, to think about what Andy had said.

~ ~ ~

Too tired to stay awake, Rae postponed her thinking and her work. She spent the following morning finalizing evaluations and making reports. Later in the afternoon Marge drove her and her few belongings up to The Haven.

Seeing no one about, Rae went upstairs to the room she had occupied a month before where she slipped into shorts, a tee, and sandals, then put away her few personal items. Downstairs in the lounge, she walked over to the window and peered out. A change had come to the air.

The late afternoon sky, heavy with clouds, looked as if it had deliberately waited until after the campers left before spilling its contents. The blue sky became gray, then almost black, as the rain pelted the house and deck with heavy drops. The heavens rolled and rumbled. Bright flashes of light revealed the downpour upon the foliage. Gutters could not hold it all, and water splashed upon the deck. Sheets of lightning lit up the world, while streaks sizzled down the mountainsides. She crossed her arms against it.

"Ramona, are you frightened?"

Rae gasped lightly as she turned, dropping her arms. "Frightened?"

"The electricity is out," he explained. "André is bringing lamps."

Rae shrugged. "I didn't know. I've just been standing here watching the storm roll in."

He came to stand beside her. "They can be ominous in this view."

One moment the lightning bathed his tall, athletic frame in light, its strange reflection in his eyes; the next moment, he was clothed in semi-darkness. The air was so still in the room that she parted her lips for breath and gazed up at the darkened figure, the face turned toward her, the man not touching her, yet seeming to. She was not sure if the vibration she was feeling was from the thunder or from somewhere deep inside.

"I seem to be awakening here in this primitive country, and I don't quite understand it."

Rae was allowed only intermittent glimpses of his inscrutable face, with the lightning gleaming in his eyes, his face shimmering with silver streaks, then fading into the darkness again.

"But you aren't afraid."

"Maybe I *am* afraid," she said, her voice in a whisper.

The world was so strange with the turmoil outside contrasting with the breathless calm inside the room.

"The fear of a storm is a healthy respect," Lucas said. "Even those trees, which have weathered many storms and have grown strong and tall and seem indestructible, can be reduced to shreds in a storm like this. No matter how mature, they are quite defenseless against the forces of nature."

"Defenseless," Rae breathed. A crash broke like a mighty clashing of an orchestra full of cymbals.

In response Rae jumped, grabbed Lucas's arm. She trembled, as vulnerable as the time-worn trees. All sorts of things could happen in a storm like this. All sorts of things, and they were happening—in her mind, in her soul, in her heart.

Ten

"There you are. Are you okay?"

Rae opened her eyes to a yellow glow in the lounge doorway where Andy stood, a lighted oil lamp in his hand. She stood frozen, immobile, conscious only that she and Lucas had been silhouetted against the window. She could not be sure that Lucas had stepped away before Andy appeared.

"Storms in the mountains can be frightening," Lucas said. "Go with André, Ramona. I'll meet you both in the kitchen."

Andy left the lamp on a small table for Lucas. In silence, with Rae's hand on his arm, they walked into the kitchen where another oil lamp burned in the center of the table, and others, casting crazy shadows on the walls, flickered around the room.

Lucas entered behind them, saying, "Gran called. She felt it best not to venture out in the storm."

Andy nodded, but Rae had the distinct feeling his mind was not on what Lucas was saying. While they ate a cold supper of ham, green salad, applesauce, and spice cake, Rae tried to keep her mind on the few comments made between Lucas and Andy about previous storms and the damage they had done.

After they had finished eating, Charlotte came in to clear the table.

Finally, Andy broke the silence. "I'm not sure how to say this," he began, and Rae's heart seemed to stop beating.

"If you have something to say, André," Lucas said quietly, his voice carefully detached, "then out with it. I can't read your mind."

Rae braced herself.

Nervously Andy ran his hand through his thick, brown hair. "I got an email from Celeste today." He raised troubled eyes to his uncle after looking apologetically at Rae. "She knows the camp schedule and that I have this week off. She's coming here."

"I thought that was over and done," Lucas said bitingly, his eyes sparking in disapproval.

"It is as far as I'm concerned," Andy assured him, glancing again at Rae, then adding helplessly, "but she didn't ask. She just announced that she was coming. And"—he cleared his throat—"her flight arrives in the morning. She might be expecting to stay here."

Lucas leaned away from the table. Dark shadows clouded his face. "So what do you do now?"

"I don't know," Andy admitted.

Lucas leaned forward again. His dark eyes flashed in the lamplight. "Perhaps we could allow Celeste to stay awhile, André. Ramona could go to Gran's, or to the cabin, or even stay with Marge and—"

Andy's sudden intake of breath and look of incredulity halted Lucas's words. "Uncle Lucas," he said, "Don't you understand?" His voice rose to a higher pitch. "You can't do that. Rae is the woman I'm going to marry."

Rae felt certain Andy would shrink beneath his uncle's stare. Finally, Lucas rose from the chair. "I'm just trying to determine what you're made of. I thought you might be forgetting what you have in this girl here."

He nodded toward Rae who quickly rose from her chair and walked over to the window above the sink. She could hear Andy's reply. "I have no intention of forgetting, Uncle Lucas."

"*Hello*?" Rae blurted. "You can't discuss me as if—as if—I'm a tossup. Heads, somebody wins. Tails, somebody loses." She grit her teeth against the frustration of the past few weeks. "And I've made up my mind about everything! Andy, I cannot . . ."

Before she could finish her declaration, Andy was on his feet, striding over to her. "I know you're upset, Rae. But let's not discuss it further tonight. You'll see once Celeste gets here that she means nothing to me. There's no one else for me now but you. Don't forget that for a minute."

His eyes pleaded for her to say nothing more.

With a sense of resignation, Rae nodded.

"Please, Rae, please be patient with me," he whispered. "This will soon be over."

Lucas interrupted. "I'm going to check on Gran," he said looking at his phone. "She's not answering my calls or texts."

"Would you like me to go?" Andy offered.

"No. I also need to stop by the camp."

"May I go too?" Rae asked. She wasn't sure why she said it. It just suddenly seemed necessary to get away from Andy. And to escape the unbearable tension in this room.

"In this storm?" Andy asked.

She looked at Lucas for his reaction.

"It seems to have subsided a little," he commented, looking out the window.

"Do you mind if I go?" she asked again in a small voice. "If your mother's not answering, you could need a woman to help . . . in case . . ."

Lucas nodded at her. "There's a raincoat of Olivia's hanging just inside the laundry room," he said and walked across the room, returning with one of the Kate Spade raincoats Livi owned, and Rae had always marveled at. Even in the rain her friend managed to be fashionable.

"Here you go," Lucas said.

Rae slipped her arms into it before they walked toward the doorway.

"We'll be back in a little while," Lucas said. "Gran might return with us so will you make sure her room is ready, please?"

Andy nodded. "Yes, sir," he said, his lips drawn tight.

In the Jeep, Rae felt a strange calm, a lull inside, steeled against the storm raging around them. It had eased some, the rumbling distant, the flashes of lightning less frequent and farther away. The wind wasn't as strong as before.

After Lucas headed down the drive, Rae said, "Do you think it was okay? Leaving Andy alone like that."

"He has a lot of thinking to do."

They remained silent as the Jeep bounced down the gravel road, flanked by swiftly flowing streams, swollen from the downpour. Lucas stopped outside the dining hall, where a faint glow shone from the windows. Inside, staff members were gathered around, playing games, eating, and talking.

Catching sight of the newcomers, Marge called, "Great night for ducks! Why don't you stay? It isn't often we can *really* rough it." Her gesture included the oil lanterns and the flames licking at logs in the fireplace.

Carl walked over and told Lucas that the electric company had found the reason for the power outage and assured him the lines should be back in service within a few hours.

After climbing back into the Jeep and heading toward Gran's, Rae stared at Lucas, who was watching the road, apparently unaware of her fixed gaze.

When he looked in her direction, she shifted her eyes to the wet streets. Although visibility was greatly diminished on the interstate, Rae did not feel frightened, even when the rain picked up again.

As soon as they pulled up in front of Gran's house, she opened the front door wide.

"I thought you'd come by," she called out as they jumped out and dashed toward her. "But I've told you it isn't necessary to keep such an eagle eye on me. I won't break—or melt."

"Mother, why aren't you answering your cell phone?" he asked, his hair now plastered by the rain.

"I forgot to charge it," she said. "And now, with no electricity . . ."

"What am I going to do with you, Mother?"

"Never mind me. Come in before you drown," she invited, opening the door wider.

"We're not staying. Would you like to go back with us? André is preparing your room."

"Not on a night like this," Gran protested. "But maybe Rae would like to stay here for the night instead of enduring this storm by Jeep."

She shook her head quickly but looked away from Gran and out toward the rain. "Thank you, but no," she said. "I like the rain."

"Well, that's good, because it's flattened your hair to your head."

Rae was sure she looked like a drowned rat as she ran her hand over her hair and the trampled curls.

"So you left Andy to prepare my room?" Gran asked.

"Yes," Lucas answered. "And you should know that we're having a guest tomorrow. One of André's former girlfriends is dropping in. So be prepared for anything."

"That doesn't sound sensible to me."

"Nor to me," he replied. "I suppose we'll see you in the morning."

"I'll be there early and by my own power. Now you two take care."

"We will." He kissed her cheek. "Good night."

A steady downpour continued as they headed back up the mountain. Lucas concentrated on the road. "These roads can be tricky," he said.

"If we get stuck, we'll just get out and walk."

"I think you'd like that," he said, glancing over at her, then had to do some fancy maneuvering when the Jeep gave a light fishtail.

"Keep your eyes on the road, please," Rae bantered.

"I'll try," he said, and managed until he pulled the Jeep to a stop.

Once inside the house, Rae peeled the slick raincoat from her shoulders. "It's so quiet. Andy must have gone to bed."

"Charlotte, too, I imagine." He looked down at her. "You're all wet," he said. "There are towels in the linen closet inside the laundry room."

A single oil-burning lamp cast a lonely circle of light on the kitchen table and ceiling. Lucas grabbed it and walked it into the laundry room, placing it on the counter.

"There's a hook inside the door," Lucas said from behind her, opening it. Rae could not see it but reached up.

"Here, let me." His hand touched hers and then he pressed lightly against her. His bulk blocked out the light, thrusting her world into total darkness. Or maybe her eyes were closed. She wasn't sure. She only knew that she had ceased to breathe. There was a suffocation, a wonderful, terrible inability to comprehend any other world outside this vacuum created by Lucas's nearness.

One or both of them—again, she couldn't be sure—moved until his lips—chilled and yet remarkably warm—found hers. Emotion coursed through her body as his hand caressed her neck, his fingers twining around her mass of curls. A new storm now raged, this one inside her, a flood about to break loose. "Ramona, Ramona," he whispered against her ear, her lips. His warm breath was labored against her cheek until he kissed her again.

"Oh, Lucas. I've never felt like this before," Rae whispered against his lips when they finally parted, now standing on tiptoes, never wanting to leave the magic of his arms. Looking up into his face, barely outlined by the dim light, she whispered the truth she had refused to acknowledge. "I care for you so much, Lucas." She wanted him to know the truth. The whole truth. She wasn't *in love* or even *in like* with Andy. Her heart belonged to Lucas alone.

But before she could say she loved him, he stepped back. A pained look crossed over his face, which played out in shadows from the light. "André loves you, Ramona. Olivia and Gran. But . . ." His voice shook as he added, "But I, *we* can't—"

Then he moved her farther away from him. Rae could not even lift her head. She was wrong when she had assumed she could take such a dive and survive. She felt as if she had truly drowned. "I'm wet," she whispered. "And cold. Let me . . . go." She did not think she could ever face him again.

"Ramona," he said. The way he spoke her name sounded so helpless. "Please forgive me. I can't explain it. Can you—will you forgive me?"

She nodded. She understood. She could hardly explain it either. Somewhere in this house was a fine man—Andy—who loved her. Who wanted to marry her. And yet her feelings went toward his uncle, a man who couldn't or shouldn't return those feelings. "Yes," she whispered. Then she reminded herself not to panic. It was like losing a major competition. On second thought, she had not even been in the running. She hadn't stood a chance with Lucas from the very beginning.

Surely, he could not see her tears in the darkness. Please, not that too. Then his arm lay gently across her shoulders, guiding her out. There was nothing to do but fall into step beside him.

At the kitchen table he stopped, took the lamp, and handed it to her. Whatever words he attempted to speak were not forthcoming. He sank into a kitchen chair, leaned forward with his elbows on the table, his face in his hands as Rae quickly left the room.

Eleven

After removing her wet clothing, Rae dried herself and slipped into her usual tee and shorts, then lay in the darkness, listening to the distant mumblings of the abated storm. She would like to drift with those clouds, sail off into the night, disappear somewhere.

The wonder of Lucas's arms around her, the hope that he had begun to care for her as she had begun to care for him shattered when he drew away. He'd regretted his actions and had asked for her forgiveness.

Trying to force the humiliating scene from her mind, her thoughts turned to how far they had all come since that afternoon in her kitchen in Atlanta when it seemed her part in this charade was simply to allow Andy to say he wanted to marry her—ultimately Andy's dilemma. No one else's.

But it wasn't that way at all. This family—what affected one, affected all. The Scripture verse came back to haunt her that what one sows, one surely reaps. Now, the pretense would be extended further. Even to Celeste.

Lucas must have a very low opinion of her, she surmised, throwing herself at him that way in the pantry. He must wonder what kind of girl invited his kisses while supposedly dating another man. The misery increased. When Lucas learned that she and Andy had played such a game with him, his scorn would be unbearable. She was torn between wanting Lucas to know the total truth while another part of her wished he never had to find out.

∽ ∽ ∽

Her muddled mind was invaded by sporadic snatches of sleep, but when nature's limbs stretched toward the gentle rays of morning sun, her own lay listless. While feathery, white clouds skipped gaily along the blue ridges outside her window, her own inner longings were suppressed by a smoky, gray haze.

Tossing the covers aside, she willed her body to move. The back of her neck ached with tension. Perhaps later she would go to the exercise room and work the kinks out. She wished there were such a room for the mind and the soul.

After brushing her teeth and washing her face, she slipped into shorts and a tee. Last night's wet clothing still lay in a heap in the bathtub. There wasn't much she could do with her hair without washing it, so she gave up and let it curl in wayward ringlets.

Hearing voices, she walked to the window, then stepped back and sat on the edge of the bed. On the deck, Lucas and Andy chatted with Gran. A few minutes later, Rae peeked out to see the two men retreating down the steps leaving Gran lounging in a chair.

When she thought it safe, Rae went downstairs. "Good morning," she said.

"It's always so clean and clear after a heavy rain," Gran replied. Rae returned her smile. She walked over to the edge of the deck. The scent of earth and pine perfumed the air.

Charlotte stepped out onto the deck and asked Rae when and where she'd like to eat her breakfast. "Eat out here if you like." Gran pointed to a nearby chair. "And would you bring some coffee for me, Charlotte, please."

Rae was grateful for the suggestion. It would be impossible to choke down a single bite in the kitchen. She sat in a chair by a table.

"I hope you aren't coming down with a cold, Rae, after being out in that downpour."

Rae shook her head. "I don't think so." Her hand went to her hair. "I haven't done anything to myself yet."

"It's charming, dear. No, I just meant that you seem a little tired, that's all." Gran smiled. "This week should be for relaxing. There are still three hectic ones coming up at camp."

Rae thanked Charlotte when she brought her breakfast. It looked good, but she wasn't very hungry. Feeling the need for black coffee, she reached for the cup.

Gran shifted so that she sat closer to the table. "There was quite a discussion going on when I arrived this morning." The older woman sipped her coffee. Rae stirred the scrambled eggs with a fork. Charlotte had prepared them with mushrooms—a gourmet treat. Still, her appetite was not tempted.

"I hope you aren't letting this disturb you too much, Rae."

She looked away from Gran's worried eyes, wishing she could tell her that it was not Celeste's arrival upsetting her. Instead, she forced a bite of food into her mouth.

"But of course, you're upset," Gran added with a sigh. "Everyone in this household is. That's why Lucas has ordered Andy to bring Celeste here."

"Ordered?" Rae gasped, almost choking on the bite of food.

Gran nodded. "He seems greatly perturbed with Andy."

Rae reached for her orange juice. "Can't he just let Andy handle this?" she asked, her voice barely above a whisper.

"That's what Andy asked. He said he was going to tell Celeste that he loves you and put her on the next plane to Florida." At Rae's quick glance, Gran continued. "But Lucas reminded him that he had tried that before. That Andy was supposed to have settled the matter with Celeste over a month ago but hadn't. Since Andy doesn't seem able to handle his life maturely, Lucas is taking matters into his own hands."

Rae was almost afraid to ask. "What is he going to do?"

"Lucas said that Andy is not going to play his games with you," Gran said, looking out where the gentle breeze stirred the leaves of a tree. Then she glanced back at Rae, with a strange light in her eyes. "He's going to demand that Andy make his intentions clear concerning you and Celeste, right in front of everyone."

"Everyone?" Rae questioned, afraid of the answer. Gran's concern was apparent. "Yes. He'd planned to discuss Livi's engagement with the family tonight. And Isobel mentioned that she wanted to discuss Kevin with you since you had spent so much time with him at camp. So . . ."

Rae pushed the plate away and stood. "I can't," she said, shaking her head. "I can't sit at a dinner table across from," she choked back the tears before adding, "everyone. It's just impossible."

"My dear," Gran said in a whisper. "We're all on your side."

Yes, she knew. Lucas had told her how they all cared for her. "I'm sorry," was all she could say before turning from Gran's sympathetic eyes and running across the deck to the safety of her room.

∽ ∽ ∽

The tears had dried on her face when, over an hour later, a knock came to her bedroom door. Andy called her name and pleaded for her to let him in.

"Just a minute," she said, went to the bathroom to douse her face with cold water, then returned to sit on the edge of the bed. "Come in," she called.

"Gran told me how this is upsetting you." Andy said, kneeling on the floor in front of her. Misery was written on his face. "Believe me, Rae. I never intended to hurt you in any way."

"I know. No more than I intended to hurt your family. But they will be when they know what we've done."

"Rae, I know I was wrong. But we don't have to confess our mistakes to my family. You and I can deal with it ourselves, can't we?" A ray of hope sounded in his voice. "You see," he continued, "what started out as a lie has become the truth. I have asked you to marry me. You did say you would think about it. So why do they have to know?"

"Andy," she said quietly, "I hope I will never be able to deceive people and feel good about it or explain it away. Even if they never knew, I would know. I can never have peace of mind, or seek *God's* forgiveness, without telling your family and asking *their* forgiveness."

"I knew you'd say something like that," Andy sighed. "Can you be here tonight when I tell the truth in front of Lucas and Celeste?"

"Truth, Andy? What truth?"

"That I love you and want to marry you."

Her heart went out to him; she knew how it felt to have love rejected. She opened her mouth to protest, but he stood to leave, with a look of determination in the set of his jaw.

"I don't want Celeste here at the house today. I'm going to drive her around the area and convince her that she and I have no future together. And tonight," he promised, "everyone will know for certain where I stand with you."

"Please don't, Andy," she said, but he ignored her plea, leaving her to stare at a closed door.

Her shoulders sank. She'd been brave enough—bold enough—to kiss Lucas in the linen closet. Why couldn't she be brave enough—bold enough—to tell Andy the truth about her feelings concerning him? Or her increasing feelings about his uncle?

Rae stood with a new determination. She had slipped from a balance beam upon occasion, failed to grasp an asymmetric bar, even during competition. But she had forced herself to continue while knowing her final score would be lowered.

She reminded herself that a team member in gymnastics pushes herself, even after an embarrassing fumble, to keep on for the ultimate good of the entire group. That's what she must do tonight. There was the ultimate good of the camp to consider, as well as Andy's feelings.

But there was one thing she could not do—sit at the dinner table and pretend that she was not in love with Lucas Grant.

When Charlotte came to her room to say the family was ready to dine, Rae truthfully replied that she was not feeling well and would not join them for dinner. A short while later, Charlotte returned with a tray, exemplary of her culinary expertise.

Rae forced herself to eat a little, then pushed it aside. She decided not to sit in her bedroom and wait to be summoned and made her way to the living room. She stood watching the sun go down behind distant peaks when voices traveled toward her from the hallway. Turning, she saw a young woman between Isobel and Andy.

Andy must have lost the courage to tell Celeste he didn't love her, Rae surmised. Otherwise, the young woman could not be holding onto his arm like that, while engaging Isobel in such lively conversation. Celeste was not the picture of a girl whose heart had recently been broken.

They walked into the lounge, followed by Lucas and Gran, talking quietly. Gran entered, but Lucas stopped at the doorway.

He glanced toward the staircase, then, as if sensing her presence, turned and looked in her direction. He was silhouetted against the light, and Rae stood in near darkness, yet she felt his eyes on her. How could it be easier to walk a balance beam than to cross that expanse of floor?

Neither spoke as she passed him, and the other voices soon died away.

Andy, looking uncomfortable, walked forward with Celeste, who continued to hold onto his arm possessively. After a quick appraisal, Rae realized the brunette's dark eyes held the expression of a confident woman prepared to do battle with her rival.

If sheer outer beauty of dress, face, and figure enticed a man to fall in love, then Isobel and Celeste were unsurpassed. They had dressed elegantly for dinner in a mountain mansion, and their beauty complemented the attractive men in that room.

In contrast, Rae had chosen an illusion-sleeved, A-lined black dress, enhanced only by birthstone earrings her father had given her the Christmas before he passed. But the young woman's vivacious beauty, nor the trace of hostility in her voice after they were introduced could waiver Rae's resolve in who she was and what she had to do.

"Rae?" Celeste questioned skeptically. "A boy's name?"

Rae's smile was genuine. Celeste couldn't be more than twenty-one and reminded Rae of some college students she had known who were still young enough to believe that verbal combat was the only method of dealing with a rival. "I was named Ramona, for my father, whose name was Raymond," Rae explained. "I like it, but it doesn't compare with yours. Celeste is a beautiful name."

Celeste mumbled a thank you.

Not wanting any undue attention, Rae looked around and found a place to sit between Gran and Isobel. Celeste and Andy sat on a couch opposite theirs, Celeste chatting away to Andy about the good times they had together. Rae was grateful when Isobel mentioned Kevin.

"He was like a different child," Isobel said with genuine pleasure, "when he showed me the certificate he received for tumbling."

"A little encouragement can go a long way in building a child's confidence," Rae replied and suggested some exercises that would increase Kevin's physical strength.

A glance across the way told Rae that Andy was aware that Lucas now stood behind him. He spoke in low tones to Celeste. Just when there seemed to be nothing else for Rae and Isobel to say, Celeste said, "Can't we go somewhere and talk about this, Andy?" a tad louder than Rae knew Andy wished.

One word penetrated the hushed silence that fell upon the group. "Well, André?" Lucas's voice carried all the force of a speeding arrow, heading straight for the bull's-eye.

Andy drew a ragged breath, and Rae knew what courage it must take to stand, to turn, and to surrender to his grim-faced uncle's question.

"Look . . . I told her, Uncle Lucas," Andy said and looked down at Celeste with a shake of his head. "I told Celeste that our relationship is over and—" He looked at Rae. "I told her that I'm *not* in love with her, that I'm hoping to explore my relationship with Rae better." He took a ragged breath. "I don't know what else to do or to say."

Rae quickly looked down, embarrassed, not only for herself, but for the girl. Gran reached over to pat her hand.

"And is that how you feel?" Celeste asked, her eyes shooting darts at Rae.

"I—" Rae began, but then Isobel stood and discreetly cleared her throat.

"Celeste, why don't you come home with me tonight?" she asked as though there were any other choice. She gave a maternal smile. "I'm not altogether sure that tonight is the right time to get into this with André."

Celeste stood, her shoulders back, but her esteem clearly withered. "I'll call you tomorrow, Andy," she said, her voice shaking and barely over a whisper.

She walked swiftly toward the door, followed by Isobel, who—from Rae's point of view—had just proved what an asset she could be to Lucas, in helping to ease a difficult situation. She looked around. "We can find our way out," she said, smiling sweetly at Lucas.

After they left, Rae stood, ready to make her escape. "I think I'll go to my room."

"Not yet, Rae," Andy said with determination, striding over and sitting on the edge of the couch opposite her while Lucas took his place opposite them. "I don't want you carrying this burden any longer." His voice softened. "I only want to make you happy." He looked around at his uncle. "It's time you knew the truth."

"The truth?" Lucas asked, as if that were something all the philosophers in the world had sought, but to no avail.

Andy told the entire story. From beginning to end. He took full blame, explaining that Rae was only the victim of his persuasion. He told of her reluctance to go along with the scheme initially, of her decision to only go along as a possible interest of Andy's, and her need of a job.

"I'm sorry, Uncle Lucas. It seemed the easiest way to get myself out of this situation with Celeste."

Lucas leaned forward with his elbow on his knee and his hand on his forehead, moving his head from side to side as if he could not believe what he was hearing.

Rae couldn't look at Gran, sitting so still beside her. She could not bear to see the hurt and disappointment on that dear face.

"Andy," Rae said after a long pause, "stop blaming yourself. Your family should know that I make my own decisions. And I made a wrong one. I'm sorry too." She shook her head in remorse. Tears stung her eyes. "I'm sorry I allowed you to accept me for something I'm not. I'm so sorry."

"I knew there was something. Call it intuition, call it knowing my nephew better"—he looked at Andy—"than I believe he sometimes knows himself."

"I just need to know what to do from here," Andy said.

"As usual—once again, André, you've made this all about you."

"I apologized!" Andy stormed, now standing.

"And you think that's all there is to it? Confess? Receive instant forgiveness? Never mind what this has cost me . . . Celeste . . . Ramona."

"You?"

"Trust, André. Trust." He stood, turned his face to Rae. "And you? What about the trust I put in you, Miss Martin?"

Although difficult to face his expression of fury, she looked at him resolutely. "I know I have failed each of you. I know you thought I was that fine Christian girl you wanted for Andy. You certainly can't think that of me any longer. It didn't seem so wrong in the beginning. But now . . ." She shook her head. "I'm so ashamed."

Andy halted her words of apology. "Rae," he said. "We aren't going to be spanked like naughty children. We've said we're sorry. There's no longer any pretense."

"That's right, Andy," she replied miserably. "And I can't pretend that I'm going to marry you, not even to spare your feelings. I'm not. You have to understand that. I can't marry you." She hated what she was doing. How could she tell Andy she didn't love him? Humiliate him further? Break his spirit? She could only repeat, "I can . . . not."

"You don't mean that Rae," Andy soothed. "We've come clean, we can start fresh. You'll see. Tomorrow, everything will be different. Let's just drop the subject for now."

"I agree," Lucas said and stood as if the matter were ended. "We will get through the next three weeks of camping. Then Olivia will be here, and we will all sit down and discuss this in a reasonable manner."

Rae stood. She couldn't bear his treating her like a wayward child. "No, Lucas," she said. "I'm not your ward to be told what to say and when to say it. And whether you believe it, I'm not going to discuss this further. In fact, I think it's best I leave tomorrow."

"Oh, dear." Gran sighed, reminding Rae that the woman was still in the room.

"Please, Rae. Please don't," Andy pleaded.

"No, Ramona," Lucas said, his voice strangely calm. "You signed a contract to work at the camp for the full season. It's only half over. The going gets tough, and you want to quit. Answer this question for me—is this Raymond Martin's daughter I'm hearing or is this another act?"

The fight went out of her. She could only stare down at the floor. "He would be as ashamed of me as I am of myself," she replied, her voice in a whisper. "All right. I'll stay. But I can't stay here. I don't belong at The Haven. I'm going to pack my bags now and go down to the campgrounds with the rest of the staff."

"Wait until morning, Rae," Andy suggested.

"No." She shook her head. "I have to go tonight."

Lucas did not protest, and she knew he felt that was best. She was just an employee now, not a prospective member of the family.

Rae turned to Gran. "I'm sorry," she said, choking back her tears, then hurried from the room.

After she packed everything she had brought from Atlanta and set the bags in the hallway, Lucas appeared to drive her to the campgrounds. She wished, somehow, that she could walk the entire way.

On the short Jeep trip to *Off Limits*, Lucas kept his tone to that of an employer talking with his employee. He simply informed her what to expect and what would be expected of her during the week between the camp sessions. After they arrived back at the camp, he parked in front of *Off Limits* and took her bags up. Marge appeared long enough to speak and see Lucas setting the bags inside the screen door.

"Ramona, can I trust you to stay until the end of the camping season?" he asked, and the quietness of his voice surprised her.

She looked up at him, and his seemed to be the only face in the world, the only eyes, as she stared at him and nodded.

"And to think," he said so low she almost didn't hear. "That slope in Switzerland only broke my leg."

He turned and left the deck. Rae looked after him for a long time, wondering why he made such a remark. Had he meant she had done worse? He probably meant she had broken his trust in her. Perhaps his faith in human nature. Those things were more important to him than human limbs and bones.

Twelve

How simple things might have been had she fallen in love with Andy rather than Lucas. But she hadn't. And despite the ache in her heart, and the belief that neither Gran nor Lucas could ever again respect her, she felt a great burden had been lifted now that the truth was known.

Rae was grateful for the stringent demands of the second session's youngsters, who needed and wanted her undivided attention, and left her exhausted at the end of each day. She saw Andy and Lucas only briefly. Andy dropped by during some of the morning junior classes and Lucas, in the afternoon, each of them seeming determined to concentrate only on camp business.

One evening when most of the campers had gone with their counselors to Cherokee to see the play, *Unto These Hills*, she and Andy agreed to a walk by the lake. The sky was star spangled, the evening, mild and clear.

"Would you reconsider our relationship, Rae?" he asked seriously when they came to a stop along the water's edge.

"I'm sorry, Andy, but I can't."

He sighed deeply. "I've been thinking some more about Switzerland."

"You should tell Lucas."

"I can't just yet. I've pulled too many surprises on him recently. But, Rae," he said, taking her hands in his, "I do love you."

"Thank you, Andy," she said softly. She knew it was true, but he probably loved Switzerland more, and for that she was glad.

Lucas did not approach her unless it was a matter of business. Through Carl she learned that he was aware of her renewed interest in the plans for the girls camp and heartily approved.

Time moved swiftly. It seemed she had just watched the sun go down, only to rise to the melodious "Nothing . . ."

Nothing! The word echoed in her mind. *Nothing* from Lucas ever. Not his respect. Nor his admiration. Nor his love.

She went for one last swim the morning the boys and young men left the camp. After leaving the lake, she tied the terry cloth wrap around her, then spotted Lucas sitting in a wrought-iron chair near the dock. She had to pass him to get to the cabin, a realization that gave her pause. What could she say?

He stood when she came near. "Beautiful morning," he said. She stopped, nodded, and looked around as if seeing it for the first time.

"It's over," he said, but she was already aware of that. This was her last day. She could leave anytime. Her paycheck would be ready.

"There's something special about working with young athletes who have such potential for accomplishment," he said.

Rae nodded. Next year someone would be working with the girls in the same capacity. She had offered some valuable suggestions; the program would be good.

"I've loved the work," she said honestly. "It isn't just work, but a sharing of oneself."

"You have a feeling for it," Lucas said, then looked out over the lake and mountainsides. "I expected you and André to be working together this time next year."

"I'm sorry I disappointed you," she said, but avoided his gaze, staring at her bare feet on the wooden boards.

"It seems the other way around," he countered. "I believe we disappointed *you*. We couldn't offer you the things you find important. And you aren't swayed by money or outward appearances."

Not swayed by outward appearances? Not swayed by the personal magnetism of a man whose appearance was superb—breathtaking as a tall pine, glorious as a vivid sunset, calming as a gentle breeze on a misty morning, sweet as a ripple on a lake, fragile as a blossom on a shrub, strong as a mighty oak, all-encompassing as a leafy maple? Not swayed? Of course not. Her rapid heartbeat was a figment of her imagination;

the sudden quickening of her pulse when he came near was a fantasy; the deep longing for his arms about her and his lips on hers was not real at all. It was all a mistake—another mistake.

She could only dip her chin, hoping he would not see what was in her eyes: the truth, the longing, the desperation, the misery. The silence seemed interminable.

"Do you have plans?" he asked.

She shook her head.

"Would you do me a favor?"

"I'll try."

"Go with Gran to pick up Olivia at the airport."

She looked up then. "When?"

"This afternoon."

"Of course. I'd love to," she said, then smiled at the thought. Livi was coming home.

The smile he gave her in return was beautiful and the sunlight gleamed in his dark brown eyes. "At least there's one member of our family who hasn't disappointed you," he said, then added, "yet. She would never understand if you didn't have dinner with us to share her excitement over the engagement. Then we'll talk."

Rae stiffened. What was there to talk about? She had already expressed her caring for him, but either he didn't believe it or disregarded it.

"I have nothing more to say, Lucas, and I just don't feel like socializing."

"Only the family will be there—André, Olivia, Gran, you, and me. As I've explained before, Ramona. All of us . . ."

She couldn't bear to hear him say *that* again. "All right. I'll be there." She turned quickly and walked toward the cabin knowing he would not rest until everyone was completely debilitated with their sense of guilt for having deceived him. She would attempt to bear one more night of humiliation.

On the way to the airport Gran commented on the oppressive heat. "We can expect a few days like this toward the end of summer," Gran explained as if apologizing because it was not another of many perfect days. Rae wore a cool sundress and had slipped her feet into sandals.

A wonderful reunion took place near the carousels of the Asheville airport baggage claim. Livi's face shone almost as brightly as the impressive diamond on her finger. Love certainly agreed with her.

Rae felt that Andy and Lucas were as glad as she that dinner conversation consisted of a full-course meal of Pierre. Tonight, she was here as Livi's friend and only as Livi's friend. At least she didn't have to pretend anything with Andy, who was quieter than usual, but obviously pleased for Livi.

After dinner they settled in the lounge with coffee while Livi discussed her plans. She wanted to return to Paris, marry Pierre right away, and complete her last year of college at the university where he taught. She might even decide to teach there until she and Pierre were ready to have children.

"Let's approach this realistically," Lucas said.

"What does that mean?"

"It means that your life experiences are still . . ." He paused as though searching for the right word. "Limited. You've never worked, Olivia. I never encouraged you as I should have."

"I've settled down for three years with my studies, Uncle Lucas, and I didn't do too badly." She looked at Rae for confirmation and Rae nodded. "Oh, Uncle Lucas! I could live in a tent with Pierre and be utterly content!"

Lucas smiled. "Of course you could. For a month or so."

"Oh, it's going to be fun, Uncle Lucas. He has a nice home near campus. We would be at the same school every day. But," she teased, "if you feel we would be too confined, you could, for a wedding present, give us a little place on the Riviera where we could escape on weekends."

"A little place on the Riviera," he repeated. "Just like that."

"Oh, Uncle Lucas, I'm just teasing," Livi said. "I love him so much. He'll take care of me. He loves me. You know how impulsive I can be. Well, Pierre is the sensible one and has made me see that we must work at a growing relationship. He was afraid I would have my fun with him, then leave and break his heart. He wouldn't let me do that. Don't you know, Uncle Lucas, how hard it is being away from the one you love?"

"Yes, Olivia. And I'm beginning to approve of this Pierre, but I'll reserve judgment until I see for myself. First, we have another matter that must be settled. It seems we have done this young lady a terrible injustice."

Rae put her hand to her throat. What on earth did he mean? She looked at Andy, who had leaned forward, elbows on his knees, and was staring at the floor.

"You mean *me*?" Rae gasped.

"Yes, I mean you," Lucas replied. "This entire summer has been a fiasco of my niece and nephew taking advantage of you."

"Advantage? No one took *advantage* of me," she protested. "I made my own decisions based on what I felt I could and could not say. I had nowhere else to go. Nothing to do. And—and you've all been wonderful to me."

Livi meekly took a seat near Gran, who took her hand and patted it in a consoling gesture.

Lucas looked from one to the other. "You were supposed to be her friend, Olivia. Yet, knowing she had no one and had just lost her father, you did not offer her a home in the name of friendship, but as an accomplice to your brother's scheme."

He looked at Andy. "And you didn't offer this girl the job she needed as a gesture of kindness. You planned to use her for your own benefit." Andy and Livi reddened under Lucas's words. "What kind of friendship is that?"

"You wanted a real relationship, André. But how could she ever trust you to tell the truth? You think a girl wants to marry a man who has lied since the first moment she met him?"

"Please, Lucas," Rae began, but he silenced her with a look.

"You'll have your turn. I'm talking to Olivia and André now."

Rae leaned back against the couch helplessly. Gran gave her a sympathetic look.

Livi's lips trembled. "I'm sorry. It didn't seem so serious. It was just a little game to help Andy out of a spot. Rae needed a job, and I thought—well—that maybe the game would be justified if she and Andy got together. I was thinking of what might result from a summer spent together."

She lifted moist eyes to him. "It did occur to me to ask her here. But I was only going to be here a week before leaving for Paris. I guess my mind was on my trip . . ."

"Even in the midst of her trouble, she didn't hesitate to invite you into her home in Atlanta, did she?"

"You make it sound so reprehensible," Rae protested, unable now to keep quiet.

"It is," Lucas replied.

"And André, did you think of the possibility of Ramona's falling in love with you? She had nothing and no one. You were offering her a world of plenty. Suppose she *had* fallen in love with you, but you couldn't return her love? Would you have given her a car or jewelry like so many of the others, then tell her to run along?" Andy twisted his fingers, popping them as Lucas continued. "She wouldn't have accepted those things, knowing her, and then she would have had nothing."

"You're right, Uncle Lucas," Andy agreed meekly. "I can't blame her for not loving me."

Rae fought the impulse to say she loved Andy, would marry him. Anything to stop this torture.

"All right," Lucas said. "So you two are sorry. And what do we do now? Olivia will go to Paris and marry Pierre. André will gallivant off to Switzerland and find someone else to console him while his heart is mending. But what about Ramona?"

Livi rose and started toward Lucas. "You're going to make it difficult for me to marry Pierre, aren't you? Uncle Lucas, I love him. Don't you understand?" She shook her head, a fearful look rising in her eyes. Her voice became accusatory. "You don't know what it's like to love someone!"

"Don't I? When love—what some people know as love—becomes the only important factor in a relationship, then it is a destructive element. Love can be a selfish thing, when all else is excluded. Real love is something that two must share, must build upon, must cherish. You might be able to survive it, to meet its challenge, if you give it the deference it deserves. But love can be as devastating as it is beautiful. And how do I know these things?" His tone was curt. "I've been around just a few years longer than you—and your uncle isn't immune to Cupid's fiery darts."

Livi muttered a faint, "I'm sorry, Uncle Lucas."

Andy rose from the couch without looking at Lucas and walked over to the fireplace. He stood with his back to them. Gran's eyes were fastened on Lucas. When his eyes met hers, a smile settled about her lips. Lucas shifted uncomfortably and looked away from her.

When his gaze swept her way, Rae could not meet it. With bowed head she stared at the floor. Lucas had been, or was, in love. Perhaps he had discovered that Isobel was like that challenging mountain after all. Maybe that was part of the redeeming and devastating qualities about love; it wasn't particular about whom it attacked.

"What do you think I should do, Ramona?" Lucas asked. "Is there any way we can make it up to you?"

Rae swallowed hard, not sure what to say. "Lucas, I know you feel you have to reprimand them because you're their trustee and older and all that. But they didn't intend any harm. Intentions mean a lot. Livi is my friend, and I've come to appreciate Andy. The job opportunity was a lifesaver. Being here this summer has been"—she looked down at her hands clasped together—"the most wonderful time of my life in many ways. I don't blame Livi and Andy. I'm grateful."

"Well," Gran cut in. "I, for one, am grateful too. I'm grateful Rae came into our lives and I'm grateful my grandson and granddaughter seem to be growing up right before my eyes."

"We're all grateful," Lucas said, his tone now softer. Kinder. "And you're wrong, Olivia. If you want to go to Pierre right now, I'll get online and get you on the next flight over. You can have a new wardrobe. I'll finance the wedding of your dreams.

"And, André, I'm not going to make this difficult for you. In three years, you'll inherit everything your parents left you. In the meantime, if you want to travel all over the world, I'll finance it, and deduct it from your inheritance. I'm not going to tell either of you what to do, so don't look so downcast. You're going to make your own decisions this time. Olivia, send your good friend a postcard from Paris sometime. And, André, call her from Switzerland. Show her how much you care."

Andy turned and faced his uncle then. He looked crushed. "I would marry her if she'd have me. That's how much I care. I'm not the insensitive jerk you make me out to be. Okay, I was wrong. I admit that. But it's not the end of the world and I *do* care for her."

"But marriage is about more than caring, André. Much more."

Thirteen

Lucas leaned forward, his feet wide apart, his hands clasped between his knees. He stared at the floor for a moment, as if uncertain whether to speak. A weariness seemed to settle upon him. "You're right," he said slowly. "It's not the end of the world. Rather, it's the end of something that never really had a chance to begin."

He got up and walked around to the back of the couch, his fingers absently moving along the printed fabric. "I've given this a lot of thought. At first, I decided to remain silent, or perhaps talk to each of you separately. However," he drew in a deep breath, "since your offenses have been brought out and confessions made openly, I feel I should do the same."

"*You*, Uncle Lucas?" Livi asked suddenly, disbelieving.

"I am the worst offender, Olivia," he assured. "I need to apologize and ask forgiveness too. Just as the two of you have done." He looked from Rae, sitting by Gran, over to Andy by the fireplace.

He paced slowly as he talked, glancing occasionally at his audience. "You see, from the first moment I saw Ramona, I had feelings for her. My tactics were not exactly those befitting a gentleman. But I could not believe André had found a girl he wanted to marry, and certainly not the kind I had always wanted for him. It seemed too sudden—too pat. As I said earlier, I was suspicious."

Lucas looked at Rae. She wondered what condemnation might follow now, but she was not prepared for the gentleness in his voice. "And Rae," he began, "when you and I sat on that mountain, with all of nature around us responding to the rise of the sun, something happened inside me. You needed me that morning. It was like a revelation. You know, André," he said, turning his attention toward his nephew, "the kind of girl I always said I wanted for you, was in reality the kind of woman I wanted for myself. It was wrong of me, I confess, but I secretly hoped you were, once again, playing one of your games with me. And the only thing that prevented me telling Ramona was my belief that her heart belonged to you."

Andy paled and could no longer look at his uncle.

"That morning, your inner beauty warmed my heart, Ramona," he said. "And if I hadn't been unsure of the relationship between you and André, I could have begun to love you then."

The sudden elation that had begun to soar in Rae plummeted to the depths. Lucas could have loved her. *But that was in the past. He said it was over, before it had a chance to begin.* She wanted to protest that it was not Andy who occupied her thoughts, who had stolen her heart, but she could not say such a thing in his presence. Perhaps it was too late anyway.

"Bear with me a bit longer," Lucas said. "Now that I have begun, I must say it all. Ramona, when you asked me what kind of woman I wanted to marry, I couldn't be honest. But I want to be honest now. My fulfillment does not come in seeing the Grant label on sports equipment and clothing. Nor does it come from socializing at ski resorts. It comes from sharing myself with growing young men, who demand more of me than I normally would give. It comes from being a part of their spiritual and physical growth. It is my ministry in this life. I've always wanted a woman to share that ministry with me. But I could not say it, because I would have been telling André's girl that she had captured my heart.

"You see, André," he said turning to speak to his nephew who could not meet his eyes, "I would never betray you—even for the best woman I've ever met. So, I did the next best thing. I tried to arrange it so you two could have the life I wanted, eventually working together in the two camps. And Ramona," he said, his voice husky with emotion, "I'm so sorry that I was in a position that allowed you to witness my weakness, rather than my strength."

Rae felt tears scald her cheeks. She could hardly fathom his words. They were so beautiful, yet so terrible. So loving, yet so impossible. Each hope that rose in her was being dashed to pieces. There were so many things she wanted to ask him, but this was not the place, not the time.

"We didn't mean to hurt you, Uncle Lucas," Livi said.

"I know that. I'm not condemning you. I don't expect any of you to be perfect. We all know I'm not. But when we do wrong, we should be big enough to admit it, learn from it, and make it right if we can. And I can't tell you what to do," he said. "You're adults now. You will have to find your own solutions."

Rae sat, unable to lift a hand to wipe the tears from her face.

"Ramona, I can understand if you have lost respect for this family. However, I know how much this summer meant to you. You are the kind of person who needs to give of herself, and those young people needed what you had to give. So, entirely separate from any family involvement, I'm offering you a job with the camp. You would work with Carl in the planning of the girls camp, and if you would, direct it next summer. Otherwise, I will have to abandon the project until a later date. But if you leave, as you have threatened to do, I wouldn't blame you. This family will never harbor any ill will toward you—whatever your decision." Rae looked at him then, but before she could speak, he said, "Now if you will all excuse me, I will be at Isobel's. There are some things I should have said to her a long time ago."

With that, he strode from the room.

Her heart sinking, Rae ran from the room. Just as she reached the deck, his car retreated down the drive. She slumped against the door's frame.

Then Andy stood beside her. "You love him, Rae?" She couldn't answer. "You do," he said incredulously. "You have all along. I can see it now."

"Oh, Andy. I'm sorry. I never intended to hurt you, or anyone else."

"I know," he said, "nor did I. But I've done all sorts of damage with that scheme of mine. I can't blame you for loving Lucas. I'm not half the man he is." He nudged her. "Who knows? Maybe someday I'll deserve a girl like you."

Rae turned to him. "You're wrong, Andy. You are every bit the man he is. And you will find someone who deserves you. What's important now is that you fix this with your uncle. Go. Go after him. Tell him you *don't* love me. How could you have? Tell him that his love and respect mean more—"

"Rae," he said with determination. "I don't ever intend to lie to Uncle Lucas again. I'm sorry. I can tell him how much he means to me, but I can't tell him that I don't have feelings for you."

Andy turned and walked back through the house, leaving Rae staring out across the deck where she had first met Lucas. There had been a chance that he could love her. Now it was gone. And Lucas had turned to Isobel. If he made a commitment to her, he would never back away from it. He was that kind of man.

Rae didn't know where she would go, but she knew she could not be there when Lucas returned to announce his engagement to Isobel. He might even bring her back with him.

Rae returned to her room and was throwing things into her suitcases when Livi came in.

"Oh, Rae," she wailed. "Do you hate me?"

"You know I don't, Livi."

"Then why are you packing? Where are you going?"

Rae shrugged helplessly. "I don't know, but I can't stay here."

She tried to finish packing, but the blur before her eyes prevented her even seeing what she was doing. Sitting on the bed, she let the tears come. Livi was right beside her. "You love Lucas, Rae?"

"Doesn't everybody?" she asked miserably. "What difference does it make? He's gone . . . to Isobel."

"Let me help you pack," Livi said, then added firmly, "We're going to Gran's."

"To Gran's?"

"Yes, we have a lot of thinking to do."

The following day Andy appeared on their doorstep, more exuberant than she had seen him in weeks. "I told Uncle Lucas! Rae," he said as they walked out back on the patio at Gran's house. "I told him about Switzerland. He liked the idea." He laughed with relief. "I—I honestly didn't think he would."

"See, Andy?" Rae smiled, genuinely happy for him. "I know you'll make a success of that little shop."

"Go with me, Rae. We could have a good life together."

Rae shook her head. "You're a fine man, Andy. Like I told you before, you'll find—"

"Don't say that. Don't say 'someone else.' It doesn't help. Maybe I've grown up a little? Maybe I've changed?"

Rae chuckled. "Maybe . . ."

He took a deep breath, then let it go. "All right then. You can't blame a man for trying." He pointed at her and winked. "*But!* If I can't have you, then I hope you and Lucas do get together. And I honestly mean that."

She lowered her eyes. "I'm afraid it's too late for that."

After a long moment, Andy leaned over and kissed her on the cheek. "If you change your mind, let me know."

~ ~ ~

A week passed before Gran, Livi, and Rae felt the time had come to relate their new plans to Lucas. The four of them sat in the padded redwood furniture on Gran's patio.

Tall, frosted glasses of lemonade were a welcome respite from the warmth of August. After raising the back of the chaise, Livi slipped out of her sandals, stretched her legs out and wiggled her red-painted toenails. Rae's and Lucas's glasses sat on a table between their chairs. Rae was grateful she didn't have to face Lucas but could, instead, look out upon the dark green canopy of trees obscuring the view of nearby houses.

"I want to tell you what I've decided, Uncle Lucas," Livi began hesitantly.

Lucas waited.

"I've decided to finish my senior year at the University of Asheville before marrying Pierre. I'm going to move in with Gran while going to school, which will be easier since Rae refuses to move to The Haven, and I need her to help me with my wedding plans."

Rae suddenly realized Lucas might want Isobel to help with the wedding. That would be logical if he were planning his own marriage. "You may have other plans, Lucas," she said. "This is a big event, and I'm sure there's more expert advice available than mine."

"We'll hire all the experts we need," Lucas assured her. "But I'm not making Olivia's decisions any longer. And I can readily understand her wanting a friend to talk things over with."

"I want you to be proud of me, Uncle Lucas," Livi said, as if being released from his dominion was not as appealing as it might once have seemed.

"Your decision to finish school before getting married could not have been an easy one. There are many plans to be made in Paris. So, to show you how proud I am of you, I'm sending the three of you to Paris during Christmas holidays."

Before Rae could protest, Livi shrieked, jumped up, ran to her uncle, and hugged him fiercely.

"Oh, I love you, Uncle Lucas!" and in the next breath added, "I've got to go call Pierre and tell him."

"Then you're not going to Paris, Lucas?" Gran asked.

"No, at least not now," he replied. "I plan to fly to Switzerland and spend Christmas with André."

Gran looked at Livi's sandals, left behind in her haste to call Pierre. "I'd better take Livi her shoes before she wonders where she left them." She went inside the house.

Rae reached for her glass, thinking she might join the women, but Lucas spoke. "Carl tells me you're on the permanent payroll as of Monday."

Rae leaned back, looking out where the sun was retreating. "I have no real ties in Atlanta," she said, beginning to relate her decisions, a result of much thinking and praying during the past week. "The job you offered me is a place where I can share with others the faith and values my father stood for and have become a part of my own sense of purpose and commitment. If you agree, I'll work with Carl, then help direct the girls camp next summer. You have a wonderful ministry, and I'm honored that you want me to be a part of it."

He stood and stepped over in front of her, looking down. "Without you, those dreams of mine could not materialize for next summer." She must have been mistaken in thinking his hands moved forward as if to reach for her, and that his eyes held a kind of excitement, for he straightened, silhouetted against slopes darkened by a dying sun.

"Any ideas you have will be welcomed, Ramona. After you have worked with Carl for a while, we'll discuss the plans and decide exactly what direction to take. And believe me when I say we are fortunate to have you join our staff."

As the days and weeks passed, Rae shared her emails from Andy with Livi and Gran. He was now co-owner of the little shop and apparently loved every minute of it. He said he might go "big time" and expand, possibly handling Lucas's sports equipment and clothing and opening a branch office.

"There isn't much time for girls, Rae," he wrote. "But I manage to see them occasionally. I hope you get all the good things you deserve. Give my love to Liv, Gran, and Uncle Lucas."

She would. But she wished she could give him her own. Since Lucas was away on business most of the time, he made the house and lake available to Gran, Livi, and Rae during fall break.

But even when Lucas was home, Rae never found herself alone with him. Sometimes she wondered if he deliberately avoided her. He seemed to want her to understand that the awakening love he had thought possible had fled and would never surface again.

The day before he was to leave for the North Carolina resort, then Switzerland, dawned bright and clear. He drove the Lincoln up the Parkway with Gran in front, Livi and Rae in back.

"Of all the seasons in the mountains, I do believe fall is the most beautiful," Rae exclaimed when they stopped at Craggy Gardens. The mountainsides were splashed with brilliant reds, golds, oranges, greens, yellows—deep, rich colors that gleamed in the sunlight. "I've never seen such spectacular colors."

Lucas moved closer, pointing out the garden before them. "Magnificent," he said, then their eyes met. "You'll never want to leave the mountains, will you?"

"No," she said. She would like to come to this spot again, and here she would remember the man who might have loved her.

They walked back to the car, and Lucas drove higher and higher, where the balsams were scarce, their limbs growing on only one side of the trunks. Most of the trees were bent, all in the same direction. Others lay on rocky ground.

"The winds," Lucas explained, "are terrific up here in the wintertime. These roads are closed and there's snow on Mount Mitchell most of the season."

Fog, mist, and clouds obscured much of the view from the lookout. Oddly, the memory of Lucas kissing her, both of them drenched, washed over her. Did Lucas remember too?

Rae didn't sleep well that night, thinking about his plan to leave right after breakfast the next morning. She rose early, before breakfast, and ran down the stairs, calling over her shoulder, "I'll eat later." She didn't want Livi to have a chance to ask where she was going or offer to go with her.

Running down the mountain to the lakeshore, she shed her shorts, shirt, running shoes, and the towel she had around her neck. Clad in a bathing suit, she ran around to the deeper part of the lake, jumped in, swam back to the shallow side, then climbed out and lay on her back on the towel, allowing the early morning sunshine to dry her. At first, chill bumps dotted her body, but soon the constant rays of the October sun warmed her skin and she dozed off until she was awakened by the sound of a car coming down the road, gravel crunching beneath the wheels. She didn't move, not even when she heard the footsteps on the wooden planks. She didn't want to say—she couldn't say—goodbye.

Fourteen

Sitting up, she reached for her shirt and slipped her arm through the sleeves. "I'm a mess," she said.

"You're always saying that," Lucas replied, squatting down, resting his forearms on his knees. He looked out, beyond her to the mountainsides on the other side of the lake. "Wait till you see this place in wintertime," he said. "You'll love it when it snows. Be sure to light a fire in the fireplace in the lounge."

She looked up at him. What was he saying to her? Why was he making such small talk when she felt her heart breaking? "All right."

"Any message you'd like me to give to André?"

"Tell him hello, of course. We've been emailing—as friends."

"When we speak, he never fails to ask about you." He took a breath, exhaled. "So what do you think? Will he ever stop loving you?"

"I don't think Andy was ever truly in love with me." She bit back a small smile, remembering their first meeting and Livi's words about her brother. "Maybe in *like*."

"It can be pretty miserable, pining away for a girl who can't be yours."

It could also be miserable, Rae thought, pining for a man in the same way.

"Well," Lucas said standing. "I'll be back."

"Take care," she said as he walked toward his car. He got in, and then, after a wave, drove away.

~ ~ ~

The leaves lost their brilliance and fell to the ground, reflecting the bleakness of Rae's world without Lucas. But the prospect of Paris was exciting, and Livi's exuberance proved contagious.

The trip was far from a sightseeing tour, however. Christmas Day was spent with many guests, including Pierre's family, at Livi's grandparents' fashionable Parisian home. Most of the conversation centered around the wedding. It seemed all of Paris held or attended a party for Livi.

The highlight of the season was a card from Lucas which read:

How do you like Paris?
The snow here is great. See you in a few weeks.
Lucas.

Back in North Carolina ice and sleet marked January and February. Livi's classes were canceled several times, and Rae didn't even attempt to drive to the campgrounds.

Then the rains came, accompanied by swollen streams and flood watches. Livi laughingly called it "liquid sunshine" and marked the days off on the calendar.

Finally, the warm rays of sunshine began to dry the saturated earth, and tiny green shoots made their appearance. Lucas appeared, too, during Livi's spring break from school. He and Carl finalized camp plans to allow Rae time to help plan Livi's farewell party at The Haven.

The April showers ceased long enough for the sun to shine on the day of the party. After a wonderful dinner, someone said, "Tell us about the wedding," which was all Livi needed to fill the next hour with details.

"All of you are invited," she said at last. "It's a huge wedding. Since Pierre teaches at the university, all the faculty and administration are invited, along with students. Grand-mère and Grand-père know everyone in Paris, as do Pierre's family. Uncle Lucas has friends and business acquaintances there, not to mention my own friends."

Lucas held up a restraining hand. "Why don't you just invite the whole world?" he asked, laughing.

"I thought we had!" She laughed and went over to hug him.

"At least it's only once," he said affectionately.

After Livi's friends had gone, Lucas asked, "Why don't you all stay here tonight?"

"I don't have to be asked twice," Gran replied, walking out of the lounge toward the stairway. "Good night, chickens."

"Do you know," Livi said to Rae and Lucas, "that so far I've received five toasters for wedding gifts? I mean, what am I supposed to do with five toasters?" Livi asked, then turned her eyes around at Lucas. "I'll bet you think I don't know what to do with *one*."

"Do you?"

"Of course," she admitted, and grinned. "Rae showed me the week I stayed with her. I also know I have to write some thank-you notes." With that, she began to rummage around in boxes scattered all over the lounge floor until she found the notepapers. Then, with a cheery wave of her hand, she hurried up the stairs.

"Let's have a cup of coffee," Lucas suggested to Rae when the excitement had died down.

Charlotte was leaving the kitchen when they walked in. "There's fresh coffee in the pot," she said and shook her head, a knowing smile on her lips. "Just like this crew to start dirtying dishes after I've cleaned the kitchen."

"We promise to clean up behind ourselves," Rae called after her.

"I'm sure," Charlotte teased in return.

Lucas took two cups from the cupboard and poured while Rae sat at the table. "I'm bushed," she admitted, rubbing the back of her neck.

"I can imagine," Lucas sympathized, bringing the coffee over. "You've had to run after my niece this whole time and I've only had to pay off a few credit card bills, but I'm ready to call it quits for at least another twenty years or so."

Rae could only nod. If he married Isobel and had children of his own, he probably would be ready to give away a daughter at just about that time. Then again, it had been a while since she'd seen Isobel. She started to question Lucas as to how she'd been but decided to stay on safe ground. "It's amazing how much progress has been made on the new camp. The gym is ready, the cabins built, and Carl says the pool will be finished within a month after the rains stop and the crews can resume work."

"And in two short months, your young ladies will be here," he added.

Rae glanced over at him and smiled. "I remember you telling me that about the boys camp. I couldn't have dreamed of the excitement and wonder of being involved in their lives. It's so exciting to see the applications coming in, reading about those fresh-faced young girls with their goals and ambitions. It's also such a tremendous challenge, I sometimes wonder if I can possibly live up to the responsibility."

"I have confidence in you, Ramona. I brought some folders up that I want to look over with you. That is, if you're not too tired."

"Oh, not at all." Rae drained her cup, wondering if she had reacted too enthusiastically. "Talking about something other than the wedding is refreshing."

Lucas pushed his chair away from the table. "I'll meet you in the study in a little while."

Rae went to the room she had occupied when she had first come to The Haven. She turned in front of the mirror as if expecting something to be out of place. It wasn't. Her dress was the color of early spring leaves and suitable for the current in-between weather. She applied a bronzed gloss to her lips and noticed the unnatural brightness of her eyes, and the flush on her cheeks. How ridiculous to have a rapid heartbeat over a business meeting with an employer.

Lucas was in the study when Rae entered. He'd removed his suit coat and tie and rolled up his sleeves as if he were ready to work. "I thought we'd be more comfortable on the couch than sitting at the desk," he said.

Rae sat near him. He had spread several folders out on the coffee table and began their discussion about the staff. Rae recommended counselors, activity directors, skills leaders, and even talked about interviewing secretaries to work only for the girls camp.

"Much of the decision-making is up to you," Lucas reminded her.

"I appreciate your confidence," she said. "But I'm not as experienced as you in this."

"Your sensitivity to the inner needs of the girls with athletic dreams and drive is important," he assured her. "It would be easy to overlook that and focus on what we offer in the way of physical facilities and equipment. Your suggestions of having Marge serve as sort of a mother figure is an excellent one. Each of us needs someone to share our feelings with, don't we?"

Rae nodded, not daring to look at him.

"You can't imagine what this means to me, Ramona, the two of us working together like this. I've always dreamed of . . ."

His words were interrupted by a light tapping on the door. Livi walked in. "I'm going to bed. Night has long passed, so I'll say good morning." She handed them each an envelope, then walked away, yawning.

"Oh, Lucas, look," Rae said with a chuckle. "Thank-you notes."

He smiled down at the loving words Livi had written. "I've trained her well."

"And you approve of her fiancé?"

"I think so. Not the stereotyped teacher at all. He's a sports enthusiast. And Olivia is impressed with his mind—and his heart. He helps many of his students, I understand." He turned a little to face Rae. "As you know, he's several years older than Olivia. She needs someone like that, I think. All those years I felt they needed me," Lucas smiled reflectively, "I think I needed them just as much."

"We all need people," she said and realized she needed to break away from staring at his face so intently. But, just as suddenly, she knew she had to *know* where things stood with him. With Isobel. "Um—how is—how is Kevin these days?"

"Kevin?" Lucas seemed genuinely surprised. "I suppose he's doing well."

He supposed? "Aren't you going to marry Isobel, Lucas?"

Surprise flooded his face and his eyes opened wide. "Marry Iso—what gave you that idea?"

"Well, you said you had to get things settled. I assumed . . ."

"I meant I had to be honest with her and let her know there's no chance of that. I never said there was."

Livi's thank-you note bent under the pressure of her fingers, so she laid it on the coffee table.

Lucas straightened. "Why do you ask? Really?"

Rae wanted to smile but didn't. Everything seemed to hinge on this moment. Her answer. "You mean, *no lie*?"

"Not even a little white one."

She took a deep breath, then plunged. "Because of the way I feel about you."

"The way you feel about me?"

"I thought my feelings were pretty clear. That night, in the linen closet—"

"And I thought I was pretty clear."

Her heart sunk. "Afterward, yes."

"No. Later, when I admitted my love for you. You said nothing."

"When?"

"The night I admitted to the family how I felt about you from the moment I saw you," he said, looking at her as though she'd just crawled from under a rock.

"But Lucas," she said, fully facing him. "You said it as if that was something in the past. That you *might* have loved me, but that it never had a chance."

He shook his head. "Ramona, I thought you knew what I meant. I couldn't be so—so *blunt* in front of André. He was hurting. But I tried to make myself clear, so that you would understand."

"Lucas," she breathed out his name. "A person doesn't assume a thing like that. It has to be said. Not to mention that the night I tried to tell you how I felt, you stopped me."

He halted, his face registering calculations and memories. "You mean, when you said you cared?"

She nodded.

"I thought you were going to tell me that you had feelings for André. I stopped you because I couldn't stand to hear it." He chuckled before adding, "Ramona?"

"Yes?"

"Could we start over?"

"No," she said, her desire for him greater than her fear of his knowing her heart. "I can only continue. I started loving you long ago. I love you still—now and always."

Lucas took her face in his hands. "Just so there is no further misunderstanding, Ramona, let me say, here and now, that I love you too." He smiled. "And I want to marry you. Right away."

"Oh, Lucas," she cried, her heart overflowing. "But when will I ever find time? The camp? The girls?"

"You'll make time." His laughter exploded from deep within. "Even if I have to fire you! And I'm not waiting twenty years. But I suppose you want a big wedding like Olivia."

Rae shook her head, beautifully aware that he still held it in his hands. "A small one. Maybe in Gran's church. Nothing fancy, just family." His fingers caressed the sides of her face. "Then a small reception with a few of your friends and those I've come to know from camp."

"Sounds perfect," Lucas said. He grinned. "How long have you had this planned?"

"Well," she said, "I've never thought of the wedding before, but I have dreamed of spending my life with you. That's the important part."

He kissed the tip of her nose before he released her. "We should be married before we go to Paris for Olivia's wedding," he said. "We can have a short honeymoon there before coming back for the camping season." He gave her a sorrowful look. "We won't have much time for just the two of us for a while."

She sighed. "We'll have a lifetime."

"Yes," he sighed in return, "a lifetime."

"Lucas," she said quietly. "Why don't you stop looking at me and keeping me at arm's length and take me in your arms. That's where I belong. That's where I want to be."

"I've spent almost a year trying *not* to do that, thinking you didn't feel for me what I . . . Oh, enough of looking back. Let's only look ahead from now on. Sound like a plan?"

"Sounds like a plan."

He slipped her hand into his, then stood and gently pulled her to her feet. "Come on," he said, and led her through the house and out onto the deck and down to the third one, where they had met that first morning.

They stood looking out upon the dark green foliage and upward toward the smoky gray haze lingering along the peaks, visible evidence that the moisture had risen from the forest floor.

"This setting will always be a reminder to me," she said, "of all the misunderstandings and heartaches."

"Yes, Ramona, but beyond that darkness is the beginning of a whole new day."

One arm went around her shoulder, and he held her closely as he pointed with the other hand. "Look. You can see it. There in the gap between those peaks."

Rae could see the faint fingers of dawn just beginning to reach into the shadowed coves and hollows.

"It's like us, Lucas," Rae whispered. "Like all human beings. The sun doesn't move—it's the earth that turns away, causing the night. God doesn't move—we look away from Him, bringing darkness into our own lives."

Lucas nodded his agreement. "And like our love. It didn't disappear. It was there, waiting for us until we could recognize it and express it in the right way and at the right time."

For long moments they watched the glow spread along the ridges, dispelling the last shadows, touching the haze, turning it to gold.

Lucas drew Rae closer into his arms until she was forced to tilt her head back, searching. His dark eyes mirrored the majesty of the awakening mountains and her heart swelled. "Ramona," he said. "I love you."

His lips met hers, tender at first, then deepening. Before them, the sun rose higher into the vaulted sky. But neither turned to watch, allowing only the warmth of its gentle caress to grow around them.

The End

If you enjoyed this book, will you consider sharing the message with others?

Let us know your thoughts. You can let the author know by visiting or sharing a photo of the cover on our social media pages or leaving a review at a retailer's site. All of it helps us get the message out!

Email: info@ironstreammedia.com

 @ironstreammedia

---

Brookstone Publishing Group, Iron Stream, Iron Stream Fiction, Iron Stream Harambee, Iron Stream Kids, and Life Bible Study are imprints of Iron Stream Media, which derives its name from Proverbs 27:17, "As iron sharpens iron, so one person sharpens another." This sharpening describes the process of discipleship, one to another. With this in mind, Iron Stream Media provides a variety of solutions for churches, ministry leaders, and nonprofits ranging from in-depth Bible study curriculum and Christian book publishing to custom publishing and consultative services.

For more information on ISM and its imprints, please visit IronStreamMedia.com